Advance praise for *Azimuth Point*

"At last...a novel that fully exposes the politics and manipulations that occur among hospital board members. Azimuth Point accomplishes that feat brilliantly, offering a wonderfully entertaining unmasking of characters that live in an elite, oceanside community. The humor, the love story, and the intrigue...I can't recall having a better time reading a novel." Jane Altman

PUBLISHER'S INFORMATION

CARROLL KENYON BOOKS

http://www.CarrollKenyon.com
email: carroll@carrollkenyon.com

Paperback and eBook design and distribution by the eBook Bakery

Cover design: Holley Flagg http://www.holleyflagg.com

ISBN 978-1-938517-12-9

AZIMUTH POINT

Book I

A novel by Carroll Kenyon

The azimuth is the angle between the north point and perpendicular projection of a star on to the horizon.

TABLE OF CONTENTS

ACKNOWLEDGEMENTS

With great appreciation to the South County Writers Group: Myrina Cardella-Marengi, Agnes Doody, Enid Flaherty, I Michael Grossman, Tracy Hart, Ginny Leaper, Camilla Lee, Richard Parker and Jeannie Serpa for their corrections and encouragement. Also thank you to Alice Boss-Altman, my neighbor Marshall Lawson, Glennie Kalen, Izzy Goff, Liz Cochran and Christina Clifford for reading the first attempts and offering helpful suggestions. Special thanks to I Michael Grossman of the eBook Bakery for his design and production of Azimuth Point, Tracy Hart for editing, and Holley Flagg for her beautiful watercolor map of Azimuth Point. This endeavor started when my childhood friend Chris Ogden, a noted author, said as we were sitting at the beach a few years ago, *"You should write a book."* Thank you, Chris for helping me believe I could. Thank you to my son Tidge Holmberg for building the websites and helping with my upcoming second book.

DEDICATION

For my husband Tom, without whom
this book would not be titled
Azimuth Point.

Trustees of East Meridian Hospital

PROLOGUE

In the summer of 1856, twenty-eight-year-old Aaron
Peabody Canton walked up from the sweltering village of East Meridian and stood on top of a barren hill.
Aaron, no stranger to the art of a deal, had become very
wealthy building mills - and wealthier building retail stores
his workers had to patronize. Looking out at Narragansett
Sound to the sea he ran his hand through tousled black hair,
grinned and laughed out loud. Sweeping his right arm wide
he swirled around and shouted into the wind, "This will be
mine!" And soon it was.

The hill and surrounding acres were bought from a desti-
tute family grateful to be rid of it. The path was widened into
a road named Canton Avenue. The mansion built was brick in
the Georgian style, three stories high, with thirty-eight rooms
and four porches. He named this manor house Canton Hill.

Aaron married well, though not a girl who would have
summered at Azimuth Point. They produced a large family
and he added another wing to the original house in the 1860s.

But as sometimes happens, the descendants of strong, vibrant men turn out to be shallow and self-indulgent. By the late 1920s the Canton wealth had been squandered. With the advent of central heating and electricity, the hill was now a prime real estate location offering ocean views and summer breezes. Not having any particular skills or capabilities, the heirs sold off much of the surrounding acreage to support their moneyed lifestyle of big cars, big parties, big trips to Europe and the requisite mistresses they felt they so rightly deserved. Eventually the last of the line, Aaron Peabody Canton IV, died in the mansion on the hill, alone, alcoholic and broke.

The once imposing mansion on Canton Hill lay cold, decaying and empty for years. Local children spent happy hours sledding down the snow-covered hill in winter, and on hot summer days families picnicked on the rocks, cautioning offspring not to go near the edge.

Year-round lovers took advantage of garden sheds and small barns on the property, and on Halloween, teenagers doubled-dared each other to go into the Canton mansion through a broken window. Years later some of the same people dreaded going into the building again, but for different reasons.

In squalls and sometimes hurricanes, groups of people climbed out on the rocks to look at huge waves churned up by the storm. Once in a while one slipped on the wet surface and slid into the ocean. After being repeatedly dashed against rocks in front of the horrified gathering, they were swept away forever into the swirling sea.

It was after one of these storms and the death of a child from Azimuth Point, that the mansion was given another purpose. During a September hurricane, three-year-old Emily Wells developed a high fever and was in severe pain. Her distraught parents summoned the family chauffeur to drive them to the hospital in Providence. The equally distraught chauffeur tried in vain to find a road out of Azimuth Point to the north, not under water. He finally raced to Kingston Station hoping to find a train to take the child not north but south to Westerly Hospital; due to the storm, trains were not running.

Emily's appendix burst. Clutching her beloved stuffed Peter Rabbit she died in her mother's arms. Mary and Alliston Wells were devastated over the death of their child.

In their grief they sought solace in the realization that they could found a hospital in East Meridian that could save other children from untimely death. They raised money among their Azimuth Point friends and relatives and bought the mansion on the hill.

These Azimuth Point families were the original trustees. The families have continued to serve the hospital, as well as themselves and sometimes the community of East Meridian, for over seventy years.

JANUARY 2000

R obb Wells put the pen down and rubbed his hands
over his eyes. He was not looking forward to the late
afternoon meeting at East Meridian Hospital. In retro-
spect he didn't know why he had agreed to pick up his father-
in-law, John Lansdowe. They disliked each other. Shaking
his head Robb pondered the absurdity of the situation. As
the closest relative of the long-gone little Emily, he had been
asked to represent the Wells family on the hospital board.
He never should have become involved. The board was a
travesty. His marriage wasn't much better. Robb and his wife
Helene, John's daughter, had absolutely nothing in common
except a long-ago rebound wedding and a thirteen-year-old
child, Miranda. What Robb was looking forward to, was seeing Diana Manning at the meeting. Reluctantly he left to pick
up John Lansdowe.

****

Sadie Brockwell sat in the library of her Azimuth Point

home, basking in the warmth of the fireplace. It felt good on her arthritic bones. Graves, her driver, would arrive shortly to take her to the hospital meeting. She didn't want to go out into the cold, but was concerned about the direction, or lack of direction, the board was taking in defining the future of East Meridian Hospital. Looking up at the portrait of her late husband, her face softened. She remembered fifty years ago when Edward Brockwell had fallen for New York showgirl Salome Starr, née Sadie Nork, formally of Fish Bait, Idaho. She was twenty-three, blonde and enchanting, and Edward, at fifty-two, fell in love for the first and last time. He had been dead now for ten years and how she missed him. Sadie's housekeeper Louisa came in to say Graves had arrived. She helped Sadie bundle up. Sadie took her walking stick and ventured out into the chilly afternoon, shoulders hunched against the wind coming off the ocean, to the warmth of the car.

****

Sarah James told her babysitter what to feed her children for dinner, to make sure they did their homework, and to not let them watch TV. She ignored the distinct possibility the kids and sitter would watch TV and eat the junk food she was sure the teenager had stashed in her backpack. She wished she had never said she would give Anna Morgan a ride to the trustees meeting. Sarah struggled to get her coat on, juggling car keys with one hand and meeting paraphernalia with the other. The papers fell on the floor. Exasperated, she jammed her hands into her coat sleeves, bent down, swept up the papers, and stomped out the door.

****

Dr. Diana Manning was exhausted from a day of difficult surgeries. The only reason she looked forward to the hospital meeting was that as soon as it was over she would be in bed with Robb Wells. Childhood sweethearts, they had a heart-wrenching breakup, married other people, had children, and

6

had pushed away any fleeting thoughts of each other over the years. They met again in the boardroom of East Meridian Hospital after she was widowed, her husband having died in a plane crash leaving her with twin babies. Robb was still married. For a year they ignored the age-old attraction to each other, until a hospital convention in Palm Beach. She sighed; hiding the relationship was nerve-wracking. Robb wanted to get a divorce, but couldn't seem to figure out how to tell Helene. And Diana wasn't sure she could deal, right now, with all the commotion it would cause her family.

****

Brax Montgomery gazed grimly at the landscape from the back seat of his chauffeur-driven limousine as he calculated how fast he could get through this tiresome hospital meeting. Even as chairman of the board he had to put up with a bunch of meddling nincompoops determined to stifle his plans for the hospital building. He smiled, thinking he *would* get it done. With strategically placed allies all would be successful.

****

Robb's hands clenched the steering wheel of his Jaguar XKE in frustration as he drove up the winding driveway to the front entrance of East Meridian Hospital. The conversation with his father-in-law was not going well.

"John, I am serious. Look at us for God's sake; we have no integrity as a board."

"What do you mean?"

"Look at the nominating committee; Whip is a wimp."

"Always has been."

"Brax made him the chairman. And then he put that female barracuda on the board."

"Who's that?"

"Kimberly MacComber."

"Well, what about her?"

"She's a very clever woman. She knows Brax has the hots

7

for her and that's how she got on the board. I would bet my board seat he's not getting any either."

"Really? Hmmm. Anyway, what's the problem?"

"He put her on that committee and the executive committee as well."

"So what, Robb? She's just the secretary, signs the minutes. She does what she's told."

Robb parked the car and turned to his equally annoyed passenger. "John, I'm beginning to think you're having martinis for breakfast."

"All right, what am I missing here? She works for New England Coast Bank. She's on two committees and she sits near Brax at the meetings swinging those great legs until he almost drools. I wish she were swinging those legs at me."

"Kimberly would never do what she was told unless something was in it for her."

"Robb, if I've been downing gin with my cereal, then you've been reading too much George Will. It's a hospital board, not the bank or corporation board. Let young O'Connell run the place. That's why we hired him. Best thing a board member can do is stay out of the way. What do we know about running hospitals anyway?"

"It's a business, like any other, and I don't like what is happening."

John signaled the end of the conversation by getting out of the car.

Yanking the keys out of the ignition, Robb slammed the car door and followed his father-in-law across the parking lot into the hospital. Entering the dreary institutional beige-on-beige conference room, Robb watched Whip Witherspoon nervously smoothing his hair and pulling at his collar as Kimberly MacComber engaged him in conversation. Shaking his head in disgust Robb turned and saw Sadie Brockwell. In her late seventies she was still a handsome woman. Dressed in a timeless white Chanel suit, trim legs crossed at the ankles, her hazel eyes swept the room, landing on Robb. She gave him a wink and beckoned him.

As Robb walked over he remembered his mother, who was

fond of Sadie, talking about the summer Edward introduced Sadie to a scandalized Azimuth Point. The men were secretly envious of Edward and quite taken with Sadie. The ladies with raised eyebrows were not. That fall, much to her surprise, the Point's shock and Edward's delight, Sadie became pregnant. The next summer, on a very hot Fourth of July, Sadie was swimming in front of her house and went into labor. After a wild ride through streets thronged with holiday visitors, they wheeled into the back parking lot of East Meridian Hospital and screeched to a stop. Sadie lurched out of the car and Edward half carried her to the back door. It was locked. In those days one had to ring the bell to gain entrance to the emergency room. While Edward banged on the door, Edward Albert Brockwell III almost came into the world on the porch.

A year after the arrival, the Brockwells, along with young Edward III, gathered at a ceremony to break ground for the new Brockwell Emergency Room wing of East Meridian Hospital. Edward wanted to make sure that no one else had to bang on the back door or ring the bell repeatedly to gain entrance. Upon his death he left an endowment to the hospital for the emergency room and put Sadie in charge of it, giving her a place on the board for as long as she wished. Sadie smiled as Robb came toward her. Seating himself next to her, he grinned and leaned over to kiss her cheek.

"How is the most beautiful woman in the room doing today?"

"Very well, thank you."

She leaned near Robb. "Would you join me for lunch next Thursday? I am not happy with some things going on here," she whispered. "At my house, 12:30. I will have Louisa make your favorite lobster salad."

"Well, Sadie my dear, you're looking well. Will you be leaving for Palm Beach soon?"

Startled, Robb looked up, wondering how long his father-in-law had been standing there.

Sadie raised her eyes to John, "Why, John, fancy meeting you here. Did they cancel the bridge game at the Agawam this afternoon?"

"Sadie, you know I have this hospital's best interests at heart and would be here if I had to drive through a blizzard."

Robb looked at her quizzically. He had always known that John and Sadie had little use for each other, but never knew why.

Dr. Jim Simpson joined Robb and Sadie. Good friends for a long time, he and Sadie had commiserated over the years about the hospital and their families as well as happenings on Azimuth Point. It was his father who had delivered her baby that hot summer day.

"Robb, nice to see you."

"You too, Jim. Those twin grandsons of yours are impressive athletes. Are you and Letty going to Sydney to cheer them on?"

"With bells on. We're even taking Letty's mother. Sadie, how is the most beautiful lady in the room?"

"Twice in one afternoon! You gentlemen are certainly good for my ego. Jim dear, please sit here and tell me all about the boys and the plans for the trip," she said. Robb stood up, silently mouthing "Thursday" to Sadie as she gave him a slight nod.

Robb turned and noticed Anna Morgan coming through the door deep in conversation, out of the side of her mouth, with Sarah James. It was very distracting to sit next to Anna at a meeting as she constantly whispered sneery little comments, then wiped her nose and stuffed the hankie up her sweater sleeve after every utterance. She was one of those women of indeterminate age, average height, with tightly curled gray hair and old-fashioned, plastic-rimmed glasses.

Looking at her, Robb thought, nobody would have guessed that for years Anna had been the mistress of Jeremiah Foster, the head of the local bank. Anna must have singled out Jeremiah as a good candidate for what she had in mind. Marriage was obviously not where she was heading; Jeremiah was already married to Hannah Sheldon, daughter of Middleton Sheldon, owner of the bank. Anna's goal was a position of importance with power and more money. She ingratiated herself to Jeremiah in every little way and soon became his assistant in the mortgage department. Robb couldn't suppress a grin wondering if Anna had shown Jeremiah positions other than those available at the bank.

The arrangement lasted years. Jeremiah followed his father-in-law as president of the bank and promoted Anna to head of the mortgage department. A year later, as chairman of the hospital, he put her on the board. She seems intelligent, but she's so pedantic, Rob thought. We probably shouldn't ignore her take on situations; that certainly works in Brax and John's favor.

Rob learned, what became common knowledge, about Anna a number of years ago when Jeremiah died. Not in Anna's embrace, but on the toilet reading a Playboy magazine. Hannah got rid of the magazine before she called 911. What Hannah could not get rid of was the will. Jeremiah left his wife and children well compensated, but Anna as well. Jeremiah's lawyer delicately revealed that she was the recipient of a fine house on Canton Avenue and the directorship and income from a small trust, which would revert to the hospital upon her death. Hannah fainted. Later she and the children sued and lost. Anna kept everything left to her, retired from the bank with a nice pension, and much to the hospital board's dismay, decided to remain one of its members. Although a very bright woman, her attitude made others avoid her.

Robb watched Sarah, after possibly an interminable ride with Anna, listening with a pained expression. Sarah obviously was not in agreement, and started to answer Anna. Uh oh, he thought, not a good idea. Anna drew herself up, clicked her teeth together and hissed out a fetid breath of displeasure in Sarah's face.

"Whew, we've all been there," Robb mumbled.

"Reduced to talking to yourself, huh?" Hunt inquired amiably as he walked by and gave Robb a thump on the back. Breaking into a wide, rubbery smile, he honked out a laugh. With a backward wave he ambled, loose-limbed, toward the conference table and sat down.

Hunter Latimer had grown up with Robb. Their families had known each other for generations. During summers on the point they graduated from sand pails and swimming meets to cut-throat tennis tournaments, racing at the yacht club, and adolescent fumbling and bumbling with girls at the beach club's Friday night junior dances. Then came college, sailing, sex, and drinking. Now they were married and at times a bit surprised to look around and realize they had become their parents.

Hunt's freckled, doltish, lanky appearance was misleading. Within that unimposing frame was an exceptional mind. He was sharp, more than doubling the fortune he had been born into before he turned twenty-five. He was a natural for a position on the board as his Latimer relatives had been founders of the hospital. Robb followed Hunt and slid into the chair next to him.

"Brax is up to something," Robb declared.

"Anything more than usual?"

"I really think so. You realize he put Kimberly on the nominating committee. And he made Whip chairman, but we know who will be running it now."

Hunt drummed his fingers on the table. "Yeah, Kimberly. What do you think he's up to? And ... why? Also these monthly financial reports of Lansdowe's don't make any sense."

"I know. They're given to us in a different form every month. Sadie's worried too. She wants to have lunch with me on Thursday. We need to talk about this. Let's have lunch early next week. How about Monday at the Hale Club; is 12:30 okay?"

"The Hale Club. Now I'll really get to take the pulse of Rhode Island."

"I'll get a private room so we can discuss this without being overheard," said Robb, ignoring Hunt's reference to the stately, former men-only club.

"Speaking of a private room, did you hear what happened at that bastion of East Side blue bloods last week?" asked Hunt. Robb shook his head no.

"Well that stuffy old fart, the president, what's his name ... Bhirghess, hired a group to give this lecture on life in medieval times. Nothing like a little Chaucer to liven things up;

that *Book of a Duchess* can be a killer. Get this: the lecturers turned out to be strippers."

Robb stared at Hunt in disbelief. "The Hale Club? Strippers?"

"Yah, almost too good to be true. After a booze-soaked dinner, the strippers arrived dressed in full medieval costumes, with two young men playing the flute and zither. Well, play they did. The strippers disrobed after a few pages of Chaucer and the flutist started prancing. Then some of the more inebriated gentlemen, and I use that word loosely...."

"Inebriated?"

"No, gentlemen; some of them joined the entertainment, whirling around the half-naked women. The zither must have whipped them all into a frenzy. At the height of this merriment a couple of the old geezers passed out. The rest of the group fell over the ones on the floor, tables tipped over and general pandemonium ensued. The rescue squad took half of them to the emergency room. To keep the whole mess quiet, the statement to the press said the group suffered food poisoning. I guess the club and the hospital figured that was more dignified than what really happened."

"You must be kidding. How did you find out?"

"Uncle Jesse was there."

"What happened to him?"

"By the time the rescue squad arrived he was driving down Benefit Street. Anyway I'll be there on Monday."

Robb looked around the table and made eye contact with Chairman of the Board Braxton Montgomery, who gave Robb a cursory nod. Their dislike for each other was mutual.

Robb wondered how he got where he was today. Okay, women might say Brax was of average height, dark and handsome, with cunning china-blue eyes, a firm jaw and sensual mouth. But his stance was always tense, his dealings Machiavellian. True, he's always impeccably dressed. It looks like donning custom-made French-cuffed shirts gives him pleasure. Robb was pretty sure being in control gave him pleasure. His cosmetic surgeon taking ten years off his appearance probably gave him pleasure too. He liked power and loved to deal. Any deal would do, as long as he made it happen ... his way. Brax also loved the chase. And the best chase of all was after attractive, strong, young women. Robb bet the woman he was after right now was Kimberly MacComber.

Robb saw Brax flick a glance toward dark haired Kimberly, clad in a black dress, her arms folded in front of her, one hip resting against the conference table, giving Whip Witherspoon the benefit of her charms. Whip, head of the nominating committee, could hardly concentrate as he gazed at her cleavage. Knocking his Brooks Brothers bow tie askew, he took out his monogrammed handkerchief and mopped his brow. Nodding rapidly, he agreed with everything Kimberly said.

Robb watched Kimberly move her size-six self in a demure and very seductive manner while she talked earnestly with Whip. Good ole Whip, Robb thought, is getting in such a state he might have to boff that skinny stick of a Boston Brahmin wife of his tonight.

Brax swirled around and slammed his board paper on the conference table. The people nearest to him stopped whatever they were doing and looked at him. Brax, never one to be at a loss for words, cleared his throat and grinning, announced, "Now that I have your attention, shall we be seated?"

Robb got up and went to the buffet table next to Diana, without acknowledging her. She held a plate of fruit, bottled water and a glass of ice, and had also watched Kimberly, although through narrowed eyes. Robb reached for some bottled water and listened as Diana leaned toward her childhood friend, Rose Ellen Brown, known as Sweets. Diana murmured, "Kimberly MacComber is unbelievable. She has Whip in a state of total disarray. Quite the creamy performance, don't you think?"

Just then Whip rushed to the buffet table and rapidly piled ice in a glass.

"Hi, Whip," greeted Diana cordially. "You a little warm?"

"Huh? Yes, no, no, not at all. I'm just a bit dry and wanted some ice water before the meeting begins. These rooms get so overheated in the winter," he declared, waving the ice tongs and rattling the ice cubes around the glass.

Diana and Sweets stared at him. He over poured his glass with water and dashed to his seat spraying droplets on everything in his way. Robb smiled at Whip's antics, and then slowly followed Diana and Sweets to the conference table.

Brax sat down and cleared his throat, "Shall we begin, ladies and gentlemen?"

Robb studied the trustees gathered at the conference table as the minutes were approved. The CEO, Liam O'Connell, was staring off into space with a concerned look on his face. Liam had been hired a year ago from a hospital in New York City. Robb looked with approval at Diana Manning's willowy body perched in her chair. She was intently drawing doodles on her copy of the president's report.

Next to Diana was Sweets, whose fluffy reddish-blonde head was bent over papers Hunt had handed her. Sweets's family was a big contributor to the hospital and also from Azimuth Point, but why she was on the board was a mystery to Robb. Probably she was the only one in the family who had shown any interest. Her two older brothers were always off in deepest Africa shooting things, her father was a drunk and her mother died years ago. Diana's mother had figuratively adopted Sweets when the girls were teenagers.

Robb's attention returned to the meeting as Liam ended with a request that the board form a nominating committee to formulate a strategic plan, possibly starting out with these topics: Community, Quality, Physicians, Feasibility/Operational Integrity and Informational Systems.

Robb leaned forward and addressed Liam. "That's a wonderful idea. We should get right on this, especially informational technology. Most businesses spend about nine percent of their gross expense budgets on informational systems. I think we only spend two percent. Look at the growth of the Internet and related technologies. We are at the dawn of the digital age. The implications are staggering."

Brax glanced at John Lansdowe with a raised eyebrow, folded his hands and sat back in his chair.

Liam turned to Robb and said excitedly. "Robb, you're right. We have a fantastic opportunity here. The way hospitals do business is going to change radically. Informational accessibility and portability will become great levelers for health care organizations. We could gain new sources of revenue by offering online shopping for pharmaceuticals and services. Think of web-based purchasing, clinical quality support, and web storage of patient medical information including digitized images. The technology is available now."

"All that sounds very dangerous, to me," said Whip. "Why, we won't even let anybody e-mail our hospital web page because it might allow someone to enter the hospital computers." At this everyone switched his or her attention from Liam and Robb to Whip.

"Whip," Robb asked incredulously, "Don't you realize the web page server has never been connected to the hospital? It's just a page created by that fly-by-night marketing firm who offered to put it on the web if their name was on the design." Robb added silently, "you pompous ass."

John drummed his fingers on the table quietly and narrowed his eyes. "While I enjoy entertaining thoughts about this hospital's future, I do believe you two talked us all into enough expensive technology with your dire predictions of that Y2K nonsense, which as we all know, turned out to be a very costly non-event fiasco."

"The reason it was a non-event was because of our preparation."

Brax sat forward and said smoothly, "I'm sure it was, Robb. We'll think about everything you've mentioned and, Liam, the board will look at anything you wish to write up about this strategic plan. John, shall we get on with the financials and Whip's report and then we can all get out of here and go home?" Brax looked smugly satisfied that he and Lansdowe had aborted the technology talk.

Liam and Robb, thoroughly dismissed, sat in their chairs, steaming. It was all Robb could do to not storm out of the conference room, but he would not give Brax the satisfaction. He sat there gritting his teeth, listening to John's tedious financial review, which the board didn't want to admit they didn't understand. Furiously, he wondered whether he would even bother speaking to his father-in-law on the ride home.

****

Diana snuggled next to Robb's warm comfortable body, wiggling her toes under the down comforter. She listened to the hiss of sleet against the windows and the rhythmic bleat of the foghorn off Newport ledge warning ships to beware the hidden rocky shore in the storm. She kissed his tousled brown hair lightly as his head lay on her shoulder. His long muscular torso relaxed in sleep, one arm thrown over her naked body, his hand resting on her hip.

The cabin, a few miles south of the hospital, in the Matunuck area of Rhode Island, had been in Robb's family for five generations. Over the years it was haphazardly fixed up only when something literally fell apart. Rob had inherited it from his grandfather. And he loved it.

We've come a long way, you and I, she thought, closing her eyes, remembering their childhood at Azimuth Point. They had lost touch during the summers of their early teen years; he had gone to the Midwest and she to Europe.

They met again at Azimuth Point Yacht Club in the summer of '80. He was getting his J29 ready to go out for a sail and she walked down the dock. Glancing at her, he smiled, then his light blue eyes widened in recognition, "Is that you, Diana?"

She nodded. They just stood looking at each other, the instant attraction between them so strong neither one could speak.

"Come sailing with me."

She put her hand out and he helped her into the boat. They sailed over to Newport and back again until sunset, talking and grinning with delight. When he opened the door of his old BMW to drive her home, he kissed her ever so gently. She put her arms around his neck, crushing her full, young breasts against his chest. He drew back and said in a ragged breath, "Do you want to go sailing tomorrow?"

They went sailing, swimming, and dancing. They were

17

drunk with love and sex. Each day began with the exhilarating thrill of being with each other and the anticipation of touching each other's sensuous bodies. They met in the late afternoons in the empty chauffeur's apartment over his grandmother's garage.

The week after Labor Day they lay on the bed naked, damp bodies entwined. Dust particles shimmered in wisps of late afternoon sun shining through grimy windows, open to distant sounds of sea gulls and rolling surf. He caressed her firm breasts and tight nipples with his tongue while running his hands in circles on her tan stomach. Later they put on swimsuits and ran down to the ocean playing like children.

That September afternoon, Murielle Wells, Robb's grandmother, enjoying a martini on her veranda, watched Robb and Diana frolic in the surf off to the left of her house. After putting two and two together she made a visit to what she had thought was the unused garage apartment.

She decided, knowing that Robb and Diana were returning to school the next day, to take care of the situation without bringing any undue attention to it. The apartment would not be empty next season. Ever since he was a child Robb had visited Granny Murielle as soon as he arrived at Azimuth Point for the summer. She would casually mention to him that she had rented the garage apartment to a nice couple from New York, Mimi and Steve Holley; they had wanted to rent it for years. This would give Murielle a reason to fix it up.

The following summer could not come soon enough for Robb and Diana. At school they telephoned and arranged to meet at the garage apartment the very afternoon they arrived at Azimuth Point.

It was unfortunate that Robb did not visit his grandmother immediately; instead he raced to the garage apartment to be there first, to surprise Diana. When he got there he noticed that the windows were already open in the apartment. She got here first! So intense was his rock-hard desire, all sane thought and observation left him. Otherwise he might have noticed that not only were the windows open, but the trim been freshly painted and tubs of geraniums stood on the landings leading up to the apartment. He started to unbutton his shirt taking the stairs two at a time.

Robb burst through the entrance to the apartment throwing his shirt on the floor, one hand on his belt buckle as he ran toward the figure that leapt out of the shadowy bathroom door stark naked.

Steve Holley and Diana arrived in the driveway of the garage apartment at the same moment, he in his car and she from the beach. They stood speechless listening to the commotion coming from the apartment.

"Who the hell are you?" Mimi screamed, waving her arms around as if a robe or some covering would appear out of mid-air.

"I'm Robb Wells," he stammered as he staggered backwards grabbing his shirt off the floor and reaching behind him trying to find the door handle.

"Christ Almighty, your grandmother didn't say you came along with the deal! Haven't you ever heard of knocking?" she hissed sarcastically through clenched teeth.

Steve and Diana looked blankly at each other and then turned to look up at the half-naked figure stumbling backwards out the door of the apartment.

Robb, beet red and clutching his shirt, belt and unzipped pants, clambered down the stairs saying, "OhmyGod, I am so sorry. I didn't know that Grandmother had rented the apartment."

He grabbed Diana by the hand and dragged her toward the beach and up into the dunes. The Holleys figured out the situation and had a good laugh; in fact they even had a little fun with it.

The next night when Robb and his parents arrived at Murielle Wells' obligatory once-a-week "cocktails with Granny," Robb and the Holleys met again. Murielle grandly introduced the Holleys to her family, stating that it was time that tired old garage apartment was spruced up and put to good use, and by such nice people.

Robb, with a stricken look on his face, glanced at his grandmother, wondering just how much she knew about what use the apartment had been put to the previous summer.

Then Mimi Holley, with a devilish look on her face, took Robb's hand. "I would have known you anywhere," she purred.

Robb murmured without thinking, "Me too," blushed to his hairline, and hoped that the floor would swallow him up.

Mimi smiled wickedly. "You have the same beautiful blue eyes as your grandmother."

Diana, coming out of her reverie, laughed out loud.

"What's so funny?" Robb asked groggily with one eye opened to look at her.

"I was just thinking of us all those years ago," she whispered, hugging him.

"Were we that funny?"

"Some of the things that happened were. Remember the day you surprised a very naked Mimi Holley?"

"Oh, God," he groaned, "I don't want to remember that...."

Diana heard the foghorn bleat again in the distance. "You know, I will always think of us when I hear a foghorn," she whispered.

"Ummm ... me too," he mumbled.

Diana let her mind return to her daydream. That fall she had returned to Miss Porters for her senior year and Robb went off to Brown University. The next year Diana followed Robb to Brown. She was in a dorm. Robb had an apartment on Power Street. One beautiful crisp fall day, late in the afternoon, Robb took Diana to his apartment. They had some Moët, and undressed each other against the College Hill sunset. Slowly they made love.

Later they fed each other cider and doughnuts, licking sugar off still-tanned warm skin, laughing, loving, and vowed never to be apart. The college years went by very fast and they enjoyed every minute. Until one day, when Diana ran over to Robb's apartment to tell him her secret. She had been accepted into the Harvard Medical Program. He, equally excited, greeted her with a small box containing an engagement ring and his plan for them to get married now and join the Peace Corps after she graduated.

What followed was their first and last bitter argument. If

they had been older and less impassioned they might have worked it out. Instead, they parted in harsh anger and brutal pain. To his family's wonder she did not attend his graduation, and to her family's amazement she told them not to speak of him again.

That summer Robb married a childhood friend, Helene Lansdowe, and they went to Guatemala with the Peace Corps. The day Robb got married, Diana went to Robb's grandmother's garage apartment on Azimuth Point and sat on the steps for a long time, her heart so sore she could hardly breathe.

Then ten years later they met in the boardroom of the East Meridian Hospital. A year later they both attended a Hospital Trustees Conference at The Breakers in Palm Beach. The afternoon the conference was over, they found themselves alone in the elevator. Robb asked Diana to join him for a drink. That turned into dinner and a walk on the beach. When they returned to the boardwalk Diana noticed she had stepped in some tar. Robb found paper toweling and solvent in a box on the deck and started to clean the tar off her feet when something splashed on his face. He looked up and his heart constricted. Diana's eyes were brimming with tears. She reached down, gently taking his face in her hands. With tears rolling down her face she whispered, "That foolish fight so long ago, we were so young and so stubborn."

Reaching up he put his arms around her; they sat in silence as deep as their emotions. After a while he stood up and led her past the swimming pools to the little-used elevator near the ballrooms. They went to his oceanfront room on the third floor.

The evening breeze was cool, and Diana started to shiver. Robb wrapped her in one of The Breakers' terrycloth robes. Sitting with one foot tucked under her she told him about her life those past years: the birth of the twins, her career in New York; her husband Bart's death in a plane crash and her decision to return to Rhode Island, to give her five- year-old twins a country lifestyle. She started to cry again when she told him about sitting on the steps of the garage apartment the day he got married.

He told her about his marriage. Helene seemed to drift through the Peace Corp experience without feeling any of the excitement and adventure he encountered. They never had any disagreements. Once back in Rhode Island she settled into married life and ran their Providence and Azimuth Point homes perfectly. She dutifully provided Robb with a child, a girl named Miranda, and lay quietly in the night as he tried for a boy who never arrived.

Diana shook herself out of musing and nudged Robb awake.

"Wake up, you slug," she said.

"No."

"I have to leave; I have a patient I need to check on and get home for the twins. Lisle's parents are here from Austria and taking her to New York. I'm without a governess for the weekend."

"You can't leave. It's very dangerous out there; just listen to that storm."

"We drove here through that storm; in fact, it was worse a few hours ago."

"Hmmm. Well, we have to finish what we came here for," he murmured, nuzzling her neck and running his hands lightly over her body.

Diana responded to his touch, relaxed a little bit and whispered in his ear, "We did finish a couple of hours ago and I would like to again, but I can't. I have to get home."

"You've got Mildred."

"I didn't plan this too well; I don't have a housekeeper either. Mildred went to Foxwoods with a friend early this morning and they're staying overnight and going to the Wayne Newton concert.

"Wayne Newton? Wayne Newton?" he hooted and started singing *Dankeschön* in a falsetto voice.

"Robb, don't be such a snob," she laughed. "Mildred loves him. Last year on her vacation she took a bus trip with her lady friends to Las Vegas to do the strip and see Wayne Newton every night."

"Now there is a trip I wouldn't want to miss."

"Oh, for heavens' sake, grumpy, I'm sorry I woke you up. Go back to sleep. I just wanted to tell you I was leaving."

"The reason I'm grumpy is because I can't stay here. I was called this afternoon on my way down here, to attend a meeting tonight with a group who wants to rethink the Providence Plaza project. They remembered my proposal two years ago and want to look at it again, tonight of all nights, in this weather. I think it's in my office at home, and if not I'll have to pick it up downtown on my way to the meeting."

"The storm really isn't as bad as it was when we arrived."

"Let's take a shower together."

"I'll take a shower now ... alone."

"Humph, you're no fun...."

Shaking her head she reached over and started tickling him until he gasped for mercy.

"Stop, stop, you know I can't stand that."

"Say uncle."

"Uncle, uncle, ohmyGod, just stop."

Diana jumped out of the bed, threw the comforter on top of Robb and ran into the shower. When she finished she dressed quickly, and briskly walked into the living room to get her coat and leave. She found Robb stark naked waiting for her at the door holding her coat. "You look very dear standing there in your altogether, holding my winter coat."

"Perhaps it will entice you to stay a little longer," he leered at her.

"Oh, Rob, you are too much." Then casting her eyes downward she inquired, "Chilly?"

"Actually I'm freezing. Give me a kiss. I'll call you after the meeting."

Diana dashed through the sleet to her Lexus sports wagon, grateful once again for having splurged on the car. Of course, she thought, so much easier for a doctor to drive in inclement weather, not to thunder down a sloppy slushy dirt road to a cabin in the woods to get naked and have wild sex ... yeah sure.

****

Helene Wells had always been interested in the theater as well as art; with Miranda at boarding school she decided to attend courses at The Providence School of Design. One of the courses she signed up for was stage design. Selina Pitt, of New York and Hollywood fame, was spending a year in Providence working on sets for two plays at The Repertory Theater and had been talked into giving a course for one semester.

Selina was very exciting. Tall and wiry, she looked at the world with snapping black eyes. Her skin, which had been dewy olive when she was young, had thickened with age, scotch and sun. Her blunt cut shoulder-length black hair, kept glossy at great expense by Manuel at Elizabeth Arden, swirled as she flung her head dramatically to make points during her lectures.

Smiling wickedly while running her tongue over her perfectly capped white teeth, she would then purse her dark sensual lips, run her hands through her mane of hair, fix her mesmerizing eyes on someone in the class and intone huskily, "You do understand, don't you?"

Always conscious of Helene, Selina would stride up and down the room with vigor. With her thin, taut form clad in velvet or leather pants and expensive silk wrap blouses she would expound on what did or did not work in set design. Putting one hand in her pants' pocket and bending her shoulder forward showing the cleft of her breasts she would raise her other arm and point at someone in the next row and bark out a question.

Helene Lansdowe Wells did not know what to make of Selina Pitt. But Selina Pitt knew exactly what she wanted to make of Helene Wells.

Helene and Robb held season tickets to the Repertory Theater. Robb was surprised at Helene's intense concentration at the performances. But knowing she was taking courses and having heard her mention Selina, he did not think too much about it and actually was glad she had finally found something that interested her.

In late fall Selina invited Helene, along with a few other students, to visit the sets at the theater and to tea at her rented

Benefit Street apartment. By winter, Helene was comfortable among the actors and artists who made up Selina's world. She only went to Selina's apartment for dinner when she knew Robb would be staying at his little house in Matunuck. It never occurred to her to wonder why Robb was spending so much time there.

Eventually Selina asked Helene to dinner alone. Her apartment was warm and inviting, dimly lit by flickering candles, with new age music quietly playing in the background. They hugged when Helene came through the door. "Helene my dear, your shoulders are so tight. Have you had a busy day? Here let me rub some of that tension away."

Helene trembled at Selina's touch. "I ... I brought you some wine. I think it is the kind you like."

"Of course I will like it. I would like anything you give me." Selina ended the massage with one hand lightly grazing Helene's breast as she turned to take Helene into the living room. "Come, come let's enjoy these marvelous hors-oeuvres."

Helene sank into the sofa and took a gulp of wine. Selina fed her exotic food and looked deeply into her eyes, hanging on to everything Helene said. Still denying anything was out of the ordinary, Helene stumbled home from dinner with her head in a fog and her emotions in overdrive. These private tête-à-têtes increased. Helene longed for Selina's invitations, yet ignored the possibility this might be more than friendship.

Helene felt happy when Selina asked if she'd like to accompany her to a theater matinee in Boston, but on the way home a full-fledged snowstorm was in progress. Helene drove, as Selina, being a New Yorker, did not have a car. Helene grew pale and was a nervous wreck. Selina, seeing that Helene was upset, suggested that Helene drive right to her house on Cooke Street and Selina would get a cab to her apartment. Upon entering the garage Helene slumped over the wheel and started to shake.

"Helene, you poor thing."

"I was so scared. I've never driven in weather like that. I thought I was going to kill us both," she shuddered, tears running down her face.

Selina got out of the car, ran around to the driver's side, opened the door and helped Helene out of the car, and walked her into the kitchen. Taking Helene's shivering thin form in her arms, she hugged her warmly and wiped the tears from her face. Backing off, she took Helene's freezing cold hands in her own and looking at her, realized this was no longer just a conquest. Closing her eyes she once again took Helene in her arms and softly caressed her hair.

"There, there, it's okay. I'm so sorry I didn't know you were so frightened. You drove very well and the roads were terrible. I should have offered to drive."

"You ... you can drive? I thought New Yorkers didn't have cars."

"I don't have a car. But I can drive. Although probably not as well as you did in all that sleet and ice."

Helene looked up at Selina with watery eyes and started to sob.

"Helene, you poor girl, we have to warm you up and get you to bed. This has been exhausting. You go up and take a hot shower and I'll make you some tea." Selina turned Helene around and gave her a gentle push on her rump heading her toward the back stairs.

"I'll find my way around this kitchen and be up in a few minutes," she told her. Selina made tea, and added a healthy slug of brandy she found on the bar in the den.

Helene was still in the shower when Selina entered the master bedroom. It's always the master bedroom, she thought. Well, I guess mistress bedroom doesn't fit either. She glanced around the room noticing a few family pictures on tables and bureaus. Interesting: Robb and Helene looked straight at the camera in every picture and barely smiled. If the child was in the photo, one parent or the other would have an arm around her. Selina saw the girl grow up through the photos. Pretty child too, she noticed. Well, at least she was grinning or laughing at her parents or the camera. Whatever was, or was not, going on in this marriage did not seem to outwardly affect their daughter.

This room is so plain, thought Selina. I don't feel any aura at all. She went into the bathroom, and putting the tea down on the shelf, grabbed a big fluffy towel and knocked on the shower door.

"You had better come out of there before you turn into a prune," she shouted above the torrent of water. Helene shut off the water and stepped out, rosy from the hot water, into the steam-filled room. Selina took a deep breath staring at the rivulets of water sliding down Helene's slim, firm body. Helene's nipples hardened; she started to shiver. The strong sexual emotions coursing through her body urged Selina to reach out to touch Helene intimately. Then she noticed dark circles under Helene's eyes and fatigue on her pale face, and instead wrapped Helene in the warm towel.

"Where is your bathrobe?"

"Over there in the closet."

"Dry off. I'll get it for you and then turn down the bed."

Selina helped Helene put on the bathrobe, took her into the bedroom and sat her on the bed. Selina handed her the tea, which she quickly drained. Helene let Selina swing her legs up on the bed and laid back in a daze, half-asleep from the brandy and the exhausting day. Selina reached over to pull the covers up over Helene, and was ready to quietly leave. Helene shifted her position and the bathrobe fell slightly apart. Her body was still pink from the hot shower, her nipples tight from the chill of the room. Selina looked down at her; months of wanting this woman formed a churning sexual need, which was hard to ignore. She ached to caress Helene's innocent body, to show her how it felt to truly be loved.

Helene opened her eyes and looked up. Selina returned her gaze. Helene reached down to pull the sheet up, touching herself by accident. She was so aroused she gasped at the sensation and then flushed in embarrassment. Selina quickly took off her clothes and slipped into the bed. Helene stiffened but did not say anything. Responding to Selina's touch, Helene found at last what had been missing from her life. Slowly Selina showed Helene how to return her love.

Satiated, Helene slept soundly, her naked body wrapped in Selina's arms. Selina's mind was racing. What have I done?

This is just a game I play, fooling with people. I don't want to care about this woman.

At that moment Robb drove in the driveway and noticed tire tracks from Helene's car in the melting sleet. She must have had quite a ride from Boston, he thought. I can't imagine why she went. He let himself in the back door and went down the hall to the den, expecting to find Helene watching some boring thing on PBS and drinking one of her endless cups of tea. The lights were on but the room was empty. He noticed that a bottle of brandy had been taken out of the liquor cabinet and left on the bar. My, my, I never thought of Helene as a closet drinker, and brandy of all things!

He rummaged through the closet where he kept his old projects and finally found what he was looking for to present at tonight's meeting. He started back down the hall to leave and then thought he had better check on Helene and tell her he was going to a meeting downtown and would be home this evening, not staying in Matunuck.

He put his paper work on a hall table, and went up the thickly carpeted front stairs. As he walked down the hall toward the light spilling out from the open master bedroom door he sensed something strange. Shaking his head and brushing the premonition off, attributing it to the weariness of a long day not yet over, he stopped and stood looking into the room.

The weirdest things go through your mind when faced with a discovery like this, he realized. His whole married life appeared before his eyes. This only happens if you're drowning, he thought, gaping at his wife of sixteen years sound asleep and naked in the arms of a woman. The woman moved her arm over Helene in protective defiance, at the same time staring at Robb in fear.

Not a word was spoken, but two relationships changed immeasurably, forever. Selina silently pleaded with Robb for compassion and Robb's eyes filled with tears as the shock of the situation sunk in. All those years Helene had closed herself up. She had been miserable and did not know why. He felt shame at the offhand way he treated her during their marriage, because he never loved her. Robb felt dizzy. He took a deep breath and looked at the woman again. Recognizing Selina, Helene's activities of the past months made sense.

He put his hands in front of him as if to wave away the whole scene. And then looking up at Selina's apprehensive face, he rested his finger on his lips, then turned and walked quietly down the stairs. Picking up his drawings he left the house in shock.

Selina lay back on the pillow, closed her eyes and let out the breath she had been holding in a deep ragged sigh. Helene let out a little snore and snuggled closer to Selina. Selina was amazed and mystified at Robb's reaction. Is this man so controlled he could walk away, not yell or at least say something? No, more likely this revelation, while shocking from the look on his face, was going to be useful to him. Thoughts about problems that could come out of this situation, as well as wondering whether Robb might return, plagued Selina's fitful, sleepless night.

****

"Diana."

"Hi, Mom, are you keeping warm this miserable night?"

Diana rested the phone between her head and shoulder as she struggled out of her coat, hung it up and leafed through the mail on the hall table. Inky Dinky Doo, wiggling and wagging his tail, was offering her one of his treasures in his soft Lab mouth. The twins ran toward their mother yelling, her pager was going off and her cell phone was ringing. Someone was at the front door and now the dog was barking.

"Can we go, can we go?" they chorused.

"It sounds like a madhouse; what's going on over there? I tried to get you at the hospital and on your pager, but no one could find you. You must have a lot of patients."

"Er ... well, I do, and I just walked in the house. I'm kind of up to my ears here."

"That's why I'm calling. We want to take the children to Vermont skiing for the weekend."

"Now ... tonight? Mom, please wait a minute, just let me

29

answer the cell phone and check the pager." Diana put the phone down on the table. Marianne immediately picked it up to talk to her grandmother, and then Jamie pulled the phone toward his ear and started to talk too.

"Grammy, we're all packed. When are you picking us up? Can I sit in the front seat? How much snow is there? Do you have Cheerios for breakfast?"

Diana looked at the children in exasperation as she answered her cell phone.

"Dr. Manning."

"Diana, I have to talk to you." Recognizing Robb's voice, Diana thought, good Lord, this is all I need.

"Um, yes Doctor, I understand. Could I call you back in a few minutes?"

"I have to see you!"

Realizing that Robb wasn't even listening to her, she motioned to Lisle, who was coming into the family room with her parents who must have been at the front door, to deal with the twins who were now wrestling to gain control of the phone. Diana moved away into the dining room and asked Robb quietly, "What on earth is wrong?"

"You won't believe what just happened."

"I really can't talk right now, can't you call later?"

"Yes, yes, but I have to see you."

"Okay fine, but call me back later. Are you all right?"

"I'm not sure; this is unbelievable. Bye."

Diana looked at the cell phone with a puzzled expression. She returned to the family room where Lisle was on the phone with her mother and Lisle's parents were entertaining the twins. Lisle nodded that everything was arranged and gave the phone to Diana.

"Mom, sorry about the commotion. Now what about skiing? I can't believe you want to drive up to Vermont tonight."

"We don't. I mean we won't. Now you have me not knowing if I am coming or going. You make life so confusing, my dear."

Diana sighed, thinking, you have no idea just how confusing my life is these days, Mother. Choosing to ignore her mother's reference to her penchant for doing six things at once, Diana said quietly, "Please explain what you want to do."

"It's quite simple really. Your father and I want to take the children to Vermont for a long weekend. And...."

"Lisle won't be able to go with you to help out. She's going to New York with her parents. In fact they just arrived."

"Diana, will you stop interrupting me? I know Lisle won't be there and that Mildred has gone to Foxwoods. I'll never understand why anyone would want to go to there. Anyway, you are so busy at the hospital I just wanted to help out and before you interrupt again I have a surprise for you, and they will help me with the children."

"Mom, lots of people go to Foxwoods; Mildred *loves* it. Just because it does not appeal to you doesn't mean ... they ... who are they?"

"Mac is here," intoned Mrs. Manning, ignoring Diana's sharp retort about Foxwoods. "In fact he's been trying to find you at the hospital. He asked Keighley to come to Vermont with us." She lowered her voice, "I think they're getting serious; isn't that wonderful?" Raising her voice again, she continued, "They've offered to take complete charge of the twins for the whole time!"

"Mac is there! Put him on the phone." The twins were dancing around, tugging at her skirt whispering, "Can we go? Can we go? We're all packed. Lisle did it for us earlier."

Diana waited for her brother to come on the phone, waved hello at Lisle's parents and looked questionably at Lisle, who shook her head, "yes," she had packed for the children.

"You are one hard broad to find. Are you off in the woods having a wild affair with some hot shot?"

"Don't be ridiculous," she answered weakly.

Diana and her brother, growing up, and over the years, had sometimes been able to know what the other one was doing or thinking. But this time she felt Mac was trying to be funny. Their mother was of the old school and would not be happy with Diana's soirees into the woods of Matunuck with a married man. And Mac wouldn't say anything in front of their mother if he thought she really was having an affair.

31

"Hey, I can't wait to see you. We're coming over right now to get those two monsters and visit for a while. Here, Mom wants to talk to you."

"Diana, we aren't leaving for Vermont until tomorrow, but Mac and Keighley will bring the children back here to spend the night so we can get an early start. I know you're on call, and now you don't have to worry about anything. Although I don't know why you do this to yourself ... why you don't let one of the men doctors be on call in this weather ... I wish...."

"Goodnight, Mom, and thanks," declared Diana, cutting her mother's diatribe short. "The twins are very excited about Vermont. I'll visit with Mac and Keighley for a bit and then send them all back to you."

****

Diana flopped down on the sofa exhaling a huge sigh and massaged her temples and the back of her neck. The arrival of her brother and Keighley, and the ensuing pandemonium as he chased the six-year-old twins around the house; saying hello and goodbye to Lisle's parents; getting everyone straightened out with the right suitcases, skis, skates, helmets and parkas; plus the long day left her drained.

Inky came over looking at her with sorrowful brown eyes; he slowly slid himself up on the sofa next to her. Pretending not to notice he was in a place off limits, Diana rubbed his soft black ears, assuring him she was not going to leave him too. She put her feet up on the footstool with the Chinese design cover she had stitched while waiting for the arrival of the twins. Her ob-gyn had advised her to cancel all patients much earlier than planned because her pregnancy turned out to be difficult. She went into labor twice, much too early to deliver two healthy babies, and she was relegated to resting until they were born. She never would have finished the colorful needlepoint masterpiece otherwise.

Diana yawned and looked around the big, comfortable room full of books and family pictures and listened to the waves breaking on the Azimuth Point beach in front of her house. If I had the energy and wasn't on call, she thought, I'd make a fire and enjoy a glass of wine. She started to doze, and her cell phone rang.

"Dr. Manning."

"Diana, I have to see you."

"Robb, what on earth happened? Did your project get accepted?'

"Yes, but that's not what I have to talk to you about. Diana, what are you doing right now?"

"I'm sitting on the sofa with the dog, pretending he's really on the floor and that I have a glass of wine and a seven-course meal in front of me."

"Can you come down to the cabin?"

"Robb, I am too tired to even move at the moment, plus I'm on call. You come here and bring food, any kind of food except liverwurst."

"Liverwurst?"

"Yes, I'm sure that hell must be a place where all there is to eat is liverwurst, the mosquitoes never leave you alone, and you feel eternally guilty because on occasion your mother is nice to you."

"Well, I feel that way about broccoli."

"How do you feel about mosquitoes?"

"I hate mosquitoes. Diana, are you all right?"

"I'm fine, exhausted and hungry. Please come here with edible gifts."

"Er, what shall we tell your assembled household? That I'm from Pest Control and need to do night spraying?"

"No, I'm going to tell them that I ordered from Zabar's and you are the delivery boy, and after driving all the way from New York you have to spend the night ... in my room."

"Do you think they will buy that?"

"Actually my household has disassembled for the weekend. Mildred, as you know, is filling in for you at Foxwoods; Lisle is visiting with her parents, and my parents have taken the twins to Vermont. Or rather my brother and Keighley are in charge of the twins moment to moment, and my parents will oversee the whole thing from their martinis at the ski house until Monday."

"Great! What do you want to eat?"

"Robb, I don't care. Anything hot. We don't have to worry about the gatehouse. No one is on at night in the winter and you have your card to open the gate, don't you?"

"Yes, I'll be there in half an hour."

The dog put his head in Diana's lap. She patted his head absently and thought about herself and Robb. The situation was awful. She hated the lying and sneaking around. It was not the way she wanted to live. She hated the word *affair*. But what could they do? Until Robb came to grips with what he had to do, they were at a standstill. Sometimes she wondered if they both would be better off going their separate ways, again.

Soon after, she heard Robb softly toot the horn in the driveway. Rousing herself she hit the button for the automatic garage door and he drove in. Diana met him at the door and took the bags of food from him. "What a day. I'm glad you're here, for lots of reasons. One being I'm very hungry!"

Robb made a fire while Diana put the hot, thick vegetable soup in bowls and arranged sandwiches on plates. Inky did not lie down next to the warm fire until he was quite sure Robb was an okay guest who wasn't going to hurt Diana. Robb poured wine for himself, sat down and looked at Diana. "You're not going to believe this. I'm still having trouble with it."

"You look like you have seen a ghost. What happened?"

"I went home to get the proposal I needed for the meeting and I figured I'd better tell Helene I was going out to a meeting and would be back later. She wasn't downstairs so I went up to the bedroom. I sensed or had some kind of premonition outside the door. I looked in the room and there was Helene in bed with a woman."

Diana's eyes widened, her hands flew to her mouth. "What?"

"Never in my life did I think I would see that. I stared and then waved my hand, like I wanted to make it go away."

"Who was the woman? What did Helene say? What did

you say?"

"It was Selina, the one whose class Helene had been taking. Helene didn't say anything because she was asleep. Selina looked apprehensive and didn't say a word. I didn't say anything either; I walked away and called you from my car."

"Robb, I'm in shock. It's so hard to believe; and Helene was asleep, so she doesn't even know you know."

"Not unless Selina tells her when she wakes up. I feel so guilty because all I can think is how this makes it so much easier for you and me. I still can't believe what I saw. And what do we tell Miranda?"

"Actually, Robb, you shouldn't tell anybody anything. The whole thing rests with Helene and Selina at the moment. You don't want to be the one who throws the doo-doo into the fan. I can imagine the righteous indignation of slimy, old Lansdowe when he learns about his daughter. He'll blame it on you. He is a master of that."

"You're probably right. We'll wait and see what happens. I don't know what, if anything, Helene will say when I see her. Why do you call John slimy? Not that I'm too crazy about him.

"When we were kids, twelve, thirteen or so, not really old enough to tell an adult to fuck off, if you get the picture, John would watch us in the pool at the club. And not like the proud father watches his kids swim. In fact, I don't remember seeing Helene around. He would stare at us. The only one who didn't mind was Sweets. The rest of us would get out of the pool and go to the beach. She stayed and swam around. I guess she liked the attention. He gave me the creeps, and still does. He is a mean bastard. He tried something on a cousin of mine years ago; Natalie kneed him in the nuts and threatened to tell her parents, his wife and the police. She was a girl ahead of the times."

"My God, do you think John molested Helene as a child?"

"I hope not. That is a terrible thought. I'm not sure, but I don't think that would turn her into a lesbian."

"She never refused to have sex, but she wasn't ... umm

35

... well ... she didn't react. And she never initiated lovemaking. I figured she was too shy and ... well hadn't been brought up in a loving home."

"Perhaps she never thought of herself as a lesbian. Poor Helene, it is going to be hard for her if she wants to be with Selina. Coming out of the comfortable cocoon—and I'm not being snide, referring to coming out of the closet. I'll bet Helene didn't know she was *in* the closet. It seems like her life with you hasn't been happy or unhappy, just safe. This could be traumatic for her. Unless it's not her first affair with a woman...."

"I highly doubt that; I mean, I think this probably happened because of that class she took and the instructor turning out to be gay. What should I do? I'm at a loss. I know but she doesn't know I know. What should I do?"

"Well, as I said before, at the moment nothing. Let's take it easy and try to think this thing out. In fact I'm so exhausted I have to get some sleep; and I don't have the energy to get my clothes off."

"Want me to take your clothes off?" Robb leered at her, moving closer and starting to unbutton her blouse.

"Yes, that would be fine, but I would love you more if you walked the dog."

"Oh, it's come to that, has it?"

"Actually, I don't think he would go with you. So I will walk the dog."

"It's miserable out there. The mist turned to rain and the fog is thick."

"You are a wimp. Take the dog."

"He won't go with me; you said so yourself."

"Okay, you win; I'll let the dog out by himself for a few minutes. He hates the rain anyway, and we'll all go to bed."

"A Labrador that hates to get wet?"

"Yes."

"What's this we *all* will go to bed?"

"Say goodnight, Robb."

"Goodnight."

****

"Robb dear, come in. You are so nice to come out to Azimuth Point to have lunch with an old lady. Would you like a bit of sherry or a real drink on this chilly winter day? I told Louisa to serve our lobster salad on trays in the library by the fire. It's so much warmer than the dining room."

Robb kissed Sadie on the cheek, offered her his arm, and walked with her toward the wood-paneled library. "I love having lunch with you. You are not an old lady. And you are far more fun and much more interesting than three-fourths of my friends. Sherry sounds great."

"This was Edward's favorite room. I haven't changed a thing since he died," Sadie said wistfully.

For a moment Robb was afraid Sadie was going to cry. But she patted Robb's hand then gestured toward the bar as she seated herself in one of the armchairs warmed by the crackling fire.

"Be a love and pour us both some sherry. Let's talk about that dreadful Brax Montgomery. He seems determined to reach the highest level of mediocrity possible in governing the hospital. His officious behavior toward you and Liam at the meeting was unpardonable. I didn't say anything because I wanted to watch the reaction of the others, to see who else would tip his hand, so to speak. It is John, you know. Whatever Brax is up to, John is in it with him."

"John? Really?"

"Yes. You and Liam were so worked up you didn't notice the interaction between the two of them. Brax steers the meetings in the direction he prefers—which seems to be no direction at all these days. What do you think is going on, Robb?"

"Well, we both know Brax leads the meetings around in circles; we listen to endless committee reports, ridiculous because all we need from the committees are their recommendations for the board to act one way or another. But Brax, or John, always suggests we table any decision until the next meeting. The question is: why this lack of direction?"

"Perhaps we should be looking in the direction of the,

shall we say, less than demure Miss MacComber ... Her performances with Whip are worthy of an Oscar. She manages to mix the allure of a porn queen with the fervor of Mother Teresa and packages it in an Armani business suit—sans panties, I'm sure."

Robb threw back his head in laughter, spilling sherry in his lap.

"I know I'm being nasty. As my grandmother always said, if you don't have anything nice to say, come sit by me." Sadie grinned, handing him her cocktail napkin to help mop up. "Do you want more sherry? We're having a Montrachet with lunch. Perhaps you would rather have some of that?"

"I'll wait for the wine with lunch. Seriously, why do you think Kimberly's involved?"

"Brax is on the board of New England Coast Bank. That is how he met Kimberly. She is, as you may have noticed, always in his line of vision. My guess is that she finagled a situation to get Brax in on some kind of a deal."

"And it has something to do with the hospital?"

"It must; why else would Brax go to all this trouble maneuvering everybody and everything. Just for the fun of it? As that young man said in that movie, 'Show me the money!'" smiled Sadie.

Hearing the library door open and the rattle of the tea trolley, she exclaimed, "Oh, Louisa, just in time. We are both hungry and so looking forward to your special lobster salad."

Robb stood up and gave Louisa a hug. "Hi, Louisa, you're looking wonderful." Taking the wine out of the ice bucket to uncork it, he noticed it was Puligny Montrachet '97. Smiling, he thought, '97 was a good year, not only for wine but also because that was the year Diana came back to Rhode Island. Out loud he said, "Sadie, this is a wonderful wine. Once again you have outdone yourself."

Louisa placed the trays on folding tables in front of the fireplace next to Sadie and Robb's chairs. As Robb poured the wine he noticed the small baskets of steaming hot cornbread.

"Louisa, you made cornbread, my favorite. I haven't had real cornbread in years."

Feasting on a delicious lunch, they discussed the hospital. Over coffee and Louisa's chocolate mousse cake Robb told Sadie about the luncheon he had set up at the Hale Club with Hunt and his intention to ask Jim to join them. "Perhaps you would also like to come, Sadie? We could use your expertise and perceptiveness."

"The Hale Club!" Sadie exclaimed, shaking with laughter. "Did you hear what happened last week at the so-called Chaucer reading?"

Robb opened his mouth, about to relate that he must have been the only person who had not heard about it. That both Hunt and Diana had told him the story. Diana gleefully had shared it at breakfast when he had spent the night. He caught himself just in time. That would give an interesting turn to the conversation, letting Sadie know he even talked to Diana, never mind was sleeping with her. Instead, he smiled foolishly at Sadie, "You heard what happened?"

"Yes, you'd be amazed at what an old lady is told, and I love it all," she chuckled. "Who told you?"

"Hunt told me at the hospital meeting."

"Thank you for the invitation. I will regret, even though I am now allowed, I understand, to enter the front door these days without being reminded, by some pompous old fart lolling on a leather sofa sucking on a gin, of the sacrosanct rules pertaining to the presence of the fairer sex in those hallowed halls. Usually the same old fart who, the night before at some party, had tried to 'take advantage of me,' as we used to say, breathing whiskey-soaked fumes as he leered at my bosom and insisted on a walk in the garden. A heel on the instep worked quite well."

"Sadie, you should write a book."

"Perhaps I will, but it would be best to publish after I am gone. Robb, keep me posted on the outcome of your luncheon meeting. Perhaps we can all get together here before I go to Palm Beach in February. I don't want whatever is going on to gallop to fruition behind our backs over the winter. It would be just like Brax to reschedule meetings when he knows any of us 'problem people' will be away."

"You're right, Sadie, I'm so glad we got together on this and I'll call you after lunch at the Hale Club to report. Thank you for a delightful visit and thank Louisa. No, never mind, I'll go thank Louisa myself on my way out."

"Robb, you're a love; come give me a kiss. I won't walk out with you into that chilly hall if you don't mind. It's so warm here by the fire I'll sit and read my book and with my prerogative as an old lady perhaps take a snooze."

****

"Hello," a voice said licentiously. "I wanted to call at our usual time."

Kimberly MacComber frowned, tapping her manicured red nails on the highly polished desktop. "Brax, I didn't know we had a usual time," she said sweetly. Rolling her eyes, she listened to Brax speak in what he assumed was a sensual, intimate manner, droning on about thinking of her and bragging about the big business deals he was going to close throughout the day. Give me the strength to put up with this salacious, aging bastard for a few more months, Kimberly thought, as Brax continued being his own best audience.

"This Friday is going to be a bit slow for me; I could fly up early and meet you at the Biltmore for lunch. We keep a suite there and...."

Kimberly sat up straight. Thinking fast, she realized this could be the perfect opportunity to talk to Brax about the RT1 property. "Brax, that sounds wonderful. Let me call you back after I check on the time of a meeting I have to attend," and she hung up.

Hurriedly Kimberly dialed the phone, smiling to herself that it was going to take some maneuvering to keep Brax's fly zipped. He was probably writhing in anticipation of his planned seduction.

"Mr. Tedisco's office."

"Kimberly MacComber to speak to Mr. Tedisco please."

"Mr. Tedisco is in a meeting at the moment. What is this in reference to? Do you wish to leave a message?"

"No. I wish to talk to him right now."

"I'm afraid that is not possible. Mr. Tedisco left strict orders he was not to be interrupted. Who shall I say called?"

Kimberly's upper lip curled as she narrowed her eyes, thinking: you fat-assed bitch.

"Listen, Marie, trot your twat into Louis's meeting and give him a note saying I am on the phone and need him now! One more smart mouth outta you and it's back to the Hill filling sausage casings! Capisce?"

The phone went dead. Kimberly didn't know whether Marie hung up on her or had gone to get Louis.

"Kim, what's the matter?" an irritated Louis exclaimed when he came on the line. "It better be important. I left the head of the largest drugstore chain in the Northeast cooling his heels in my office to take this call."

"It is. And it will help rope in your drugstore mogul. Brax Montgomery wants me to have lunch with him in his suite in the Biltmore this Friday. I want you to come."

"Kimberly, I have a feeling that Montgomery is looking to have you for dessert and would not welcome me for coffee."

"Let me take care of that. Will you keep the time open?"

"Sure, but do you really think we can buy that property? It's in a trust or something and Brax's wife is the trustee, I think."

"I tell you this will work. And your pharmacy czar will jump at that location. Just don't tell him exactly where it is until we know where we are going on this. Hey, have I failed you yet?"

"In business, no," Louis said matter-of-factly.

Kimberly chose to ignore his comment and continued on. "I'll call you back and leave a message about the time and suite number."

"From the look on Marie's face you better e-mail me. What did you say to her, anyway?"

"I just reminded her where we all came from."

"Wonderful. That should make the rest of my week a lot of laughs."

Kimberly smirked with delight, thinking how furious Marie must be, as she hung up from Louis and quickly called Brax in New York.

"Brax, Friday will be great. I think I'll be able to have Louis Tedisco join us for lunch. He could be a great help when it comes to the legislature. I'm not saying we should talk about PuisSantMeritor or your plans for the hospital right away. But he is very eager to get something going in the southern part of the state."

Kimberly took a deep breath, very much aware that Brax had not uttered a word. Realizing that she had to keep Brax's monumental ego intact, she hurried on knowing he would annihilate the family dog if it would seal a deal.

"And the best part is...." she paused for effect, "he has lots of money. Perhaps a good idea would be to suggest to him a million for the hospital. Which, of course, would guarantee him a seat on the board. Then you can work the plans you have for the future. We need board members on our side and Louis will be perfect." More silence. She pushed on. "You have amazing finesse when it comes to maneuvering people. It's a win-win situation!"

Brax replied in a deadly calm voice, "Kimberly, from now on, make sure you know exactly what flag you're waving when you say you're going to join the parade. I will expect you and your cohort on Friday at 12:30, suite 1147." And he hung up the phone.

FEBRUARY

Sarah James leaned over the kitchen sink, her nose almost touching the frosty window; she looked anxiously down the snow-swirled lane for her children's school bus. This storm was much worse than predicted, a perfect excuse not to go to that damned hospital board meeting, along with other reasons.

Reliving last night's discussion with her husband Bill brought tears to her dark-lashed blue eyes. She angrily wiped them away, determined not to go to the meeting looking as if she had been crying. It's bad enough those people are much older, wealthier and intimidating. Now I have to go along with everything I feel is wrong or Bill will lose his job.

One hot tear slipped down her cheek; she sighed and her lower lip quivered. She had been so excited two years ago when the call came from Mr. Lansdowe asking her to be on the hospital board. He told her the younger people of the town needed a voice and she would be the perfect spokesperson for the mothers and children who used hospital services. In fact, she had been secretly amused that Bill was a bit jealous when she had been asked instead of him. She was more assertive than Bill, and Mr. Lansdowe knew she worked on many community projects and the Democratic town committee. Even though Mr. Lansdowe and the board are probably Republicans he must appreciate my youthful exuberance and outlook, she had thought with smug naïveté.

After a year of being used to raise funds, run events and cajole friends into helping—friends she was told would be considered for membership on the board—she realized it was a farce. Yesterday Bill was called into Mr. Lansdowe's office and told, in his sinister manner, that Sarah had to vote with him for the good of the hospital. He actually said anyone as young and inexperienced as Sarah would naturally welcome the wisdom of the older generation. Surely Bill could realize how important these decisions are to everyone involved and he'd mention this to Sarah before tomorrow's meeting, wouldn't he?

Good of the hospital, my ass. One opposing vote and I wipe out my family's livelihood. Bill is not a courageous man. He doesn't want to set the world on fire. His idea of the good life is three meals a day, a job that does not cause him angst, and, oh yes, sex and racquetball on Saturday—these days more racquetball than sex. He was thrilled when asked to join the winter racquetball league at the Azimuth Point Country Club. "This means we will be asked to join as regular members," he had told her excitedly.

She burst his balloon with a sharp retort, spitting out what a fool he was to entertain that thought. "The only reason you're there is the club takes in winter memberships for a few acceptable locals and the only reason you're acceptable is that you work for John Lansdowe!" Closing her eyes she remembered the wounded expression in his large brown eyes. She had grown up here and knew, only too well, those people on the Point and the unwritten rules. Another tear slid down her face as she recalled barking at him, "You didn't grow up here. You don't get it. They are just using you to get money in the off-season. "

44

Abruptly, devastating depression swept over her. Memories, hidden deep inside, surfaced. She felt the heat of the afternoon summer sun, heard the ocean in the distance, her stomach hurt; she wrapped her arms around her middle. She could feel his warm, muscular, suntanned skin as he held her close, kissing her feverishly as he ripped off her clothes. This boy from Azimuth Point she loved so desperately.

She gripped the edge of the counter remembering the searing agony she felt as he rammed his swollen shaft into her. Then the raw thrusting as he fulfilled his desire. Spent, he fell on her heavily and then casually rolled off. Sarah, lying there taut, in pain, her thighs wet with virgin blood, watched him calmly sit up and light a cigarette.

Reaching under the bed for the towel he put there earlier, he wiped himself off, jumped up and started looking for his clothes. Studiously avoiding her gaze, he dressed. Then, while opening the door of his family's guesthouse, he paused and turned back to look at her almost as if recalling admonitions from past deportment classes. He smiled his engaging smile and said, "That was fun. Uh, I have a tennis date. I'll give you a call." He never called. She had lain there gulping for air, tears coursing down her face.

Shaking she remembered her mother pointing her finger and warning her, "Just keep in mind, young lady, don't have anything to do with the likes of those boys from the Point unless you go through the front door and their parents ask you to stay for dinner."

Part of Sarah's anger at Bill was really shame and rage from her past. Her mother's words haunted her still. She rested her head against the cold windowpane and closed her eyes, determined not to cry.

The mudroom door flew open; two little rosy-cheeked blonde girls raced into the kitchen amid a blast of wind and cold. Dressed in pink and lavender parkas, they danced around the marble-top island chirping away as they dropped school backpacks on the floor and struggled out of snow-covered clothing. Sarah opened her eyes and whirled around, wondering how she had not heard the school bus.

45

"Wow, Mom, what a snowstorm!"

"Is this a blizzard, Mom?"

"Can we go sledding?"

"I'm hungry."

"Help us build a snowman, please?"

"The driving is very dangerous. Mr. Nevins almost slid us into a snow bank," said Leighanna, the older of the two girls, in an unconscious but perfect imitation of her Grandmother James.

Good Lord, the girls are spending too much time with Bill's mother, thought Sarah. Then it dawned on her what Leighanna had said. "What do you mean, Mr. Nevins almost drove you into a snow bank? Didn't you come home on the bus?"

"Nope, Mr. Nevins drove us. And he picked up Nana before he came to get us at school. And she's going to stay with us while you go to the meeting," finished Leighanna knowingly.

"That's right, dear, you do have the most wonderful husband," gushed Sarah's mother-in-law as she strode into the kitchen, picking up the girl's coats and backpacks from the floor. "Bill cancelled the sitter so she wouldn't have to drive in this weather, and he arranged for Mr. Nevins to pick me and the girls up and to drive you to the meeting."

Disappearing back into the mudroom after wiping an invisible smudge off the doorjamb, Irene James' forceful voice, with its usual chiding edge, floated back as she hung up the girls' jackets and started to empty the backpacks.

"He is such a considerate husband and father, isn't he, dear?"

"Nice beyond belief," growled Sarah, glaring at the mudroom door in fury. Clenching her fists, she thought, that bastard Bill. He wanted to make sure I voted with Lansdowe. And that woman is unbelievable. In less than a minute she has managed to convey that my girls are messy, the house is dirty, that their backpacks haven't been cleaned in two years and that her son is the product of the second coming.

Maybe I should tell her he hasn't been able to come at all lately, she thought nastily. That would make her purse those

46

rubbery lips over her yellow buckteeth. Then the thought of the expression on Irene's face if she told her that darling Bill couldn't seem to get it up these days seemed so hilarious, Sarah laughed out loud.

"What's so funny, Mommy?" asked Lauren, looking up at her mother, puzzled. Sarah stooped down and gave her youngest daughter a big hug, kissing her forehead and rumpling her soft blonde curls.

"Mommy is just happy that you and Leighanna will have Nana here to stay with you while I go to the meeting," Sarah gushed back with a grimacing smile aimed at her mother- inlaw peeking around the mudroom door.

Sarah stood up and gathered together her papers for the meeting while telling Irene that there was a casserole, salad and French bread for dinner in the fridge with ice cream for dessert. She thought that Irene would be far happier if nothing was made for dinner. Then she could charge out into the storm, slay a stag, dress the kill and cook it over a bonfire of six trees she managed to rip out of the earth with her bare hands, anything for her boy Bill.

Smiling, Sarah thought, I am losing it. I had better get going and face the music. Kissing her girls goodbye she trudged out into the storm. She climbed into Mr. Nevins's snug SUV and thanked him for waiting for her. She settled into the warm seat and gazed out on the snowy landscape, dreading what lay ahead.

****

Anna Morgan was heading toward her front door to check how much snow had fallen and if she needed boots to go to the hospital board meeting, when the doorbell rang. Opening the door she was confronted by the red-cheeked, bundled-up, smiling face of her mailman, Spider Smith. Spider, whose real name was Horace, had earned the nickname as a toddler due to his fascination with bugs.

The nickname stood him in good stead at East Meridian High School where his long- armed prowess on the basketball court was second only to his mastery after the games. Many a night a cheerleader's voice could be heard chanting Spiiiider! Spiiiider! Oh, SPIDER! from his Nash Rambler parked beside the moonlit lake at Old Mountain Field.

Spider, a cheery, uncomplicated and extraordinarily lucky soul, did not impregnate any of the cheerleaders until the summer after graduation. Whereupon he settled down, went to work for the East Meridian Post Office, fathered five children and delivered the mail with the same good nature as when he put the ball in the proverbial home court.

"Hi ya, Anna! Colder than a witch's tit out heah. Thought I'd put ya mail in the front hall for ya. Rung the bell so's I wouldn't surprise ya, in case you was entatainen' George Clooney. Heh, heh, betcha woulda liked that, almost as good as workin' at the bank," he bellowed along with a sly wink. He was, of course, referring to the scandal about Anna and Jeremiah.

"Good afternoon, Horace. Thank you ever so much for thinking of my welfare," replied Anna in a voice equal to the temperature of the day as she grabbed the mail and shut the door in his face.

Anna looked through the mail, separating bills from letters then throwing the ads and the chances to win million dollar prizes in the hall wastebasket, when the phone rang.

"Dr. Lombardi's office for Miss Morgan."

"This is Anna Morgan."

"Could you hold for a minute please? The doctor is just finishing with a patient and would like to talk to you."

"Yes, I'll wait," sighed Anna in exasperation. What does he want me to plead for at this board meeting? Remembering the conversation after her annual examination two weeks ago, she thought she made it clear that any application for new equipment needed at the hospital had to go through the Committee on Medical Affairs.

"Anna, may I stop by late this afternoon?"

"Listen, Hank," interrupted Anna," I already told you there is nothing I can do about that equipment you want for the hospital. You really must go through channels, and I need to leave now or I will be late for the board meeting."

"Anna, this is not about the hospital. This is about you. I really would like to...."

"Hank, tell me on the phone."

"Are you sure? I'd rather...."

"Hank, just spit it out."

"Your mammogram has shown something and I am scheduling you for a biopsy. We can do it here at East Meridian with a fine-needle aspiration or a core-needle biopsy. How is next Monday at 9:30? Now, I don't want you to get too upset, we really don't know what we are dealing with until after the biopsy."

Anna started to shake. As the phone slipped down off its perch between her shoulder and ear she grabbed it. Pressing the receiver to her ear she asked in a faltering voice, "Hank, how serious is this? Why did I have to wait two weeks to be told about this?" As the words left her mouth Anna looked down at the unopened letter in her hand from Diagnostic Imaging.

"Anna," Hank Lombardi said gently, "this was one of the situations I've been trying to discuss with the board and the hospital. This shouldn't happen to you or to anyone, for that matter. But East Meridian is way behind the times when it comes to women's breast health. We should be reading mammograms right after they are done and talking with the patient immediately, if there is a problem. But at this point that is neither here nor there. I will let you know the results. And, Anna, can't I stop in later to check on you?"

"Thank you, Hank, no. No, I'm fine. You don't have to come by." Anna felt faint as she hung up the phone. She sank slowly into a small chair next to the telephone table. She thought, aimlessly, this chair seat is the last piece of needlepoint my mother worked on before she died. In all her life Anna had never felt such a wave of despair descend upon her being. Anna's mother had died of breast cancer when Anna and her sister were teenagers. And when her sister died of breast cancer in her forties, Anna had worried endlessly that she might be next. But nothing had happened; she scheduled regular mammograms each year and eventually forgot to worry. Now, to find out that she might, in her sixties, have breast cancer was more than just a shock: it was horrifying.

She sat trembling with her shoulders hunched up in the drafty hall, the letter unfolded in her lap. Clutching the sides of the chair, her thumbs touched the familiar mosaic pattern her mother always used for backgrounds. Anna had trouble breathing. Her years-long clandestine affair with Jeremiah precluded any close friendships. Her cousin Maude hadn't spoken to her since the scandal after Jeremiah's death. If Hank had not thought to call her, a matter-of-fact letter from some typist in Diagnostic Imaging would have notified her. This isn't right, she thought, shaking her head as she read the letter. Overwhelmed, she stood up, got her winter coat, put it on and went out the front door. She did not put on her hat, boots or gloves. Sliding into the front seat of her car she started the engine and was jolted out of her daze when her bare hands gripped the freezing-cold steering wheel. Pulling the sleeves of her coat down over her cold fingers she backed out of the driveway and drove down the street to the hospital meeting.

****

Louis Tedisco tipped back his slate gray leather chair, as he gazed out floor-to-ceiling windows in his spacious office suite atop the new twenty-floor Tedisco Building. Below him, downtown Providence twinkled in the gathering dusk. Snow had been falling for over an hour and the city looked like a fairyland. My city, he thought, his handsome face breaking into a grin. I've worked hard to get here and here feels really good.

Resting his elbows on the arms of the chair, he made a tent of his fingers, unconsciously tapping one side of his nose as he reflected on his life. His new Benefit Street home flashed into his mind as he watched the cars creep down snow-slicked Angell Street and skid to a stop at the Thomas Street light. He loved his restored Greek Revival house as much as his wife Vi hated it. Opening the front door and experiencing the building's gracious warmth gave him a sense of satisfaction. He had hired a well-known East Side decorator. He and his wife didn't move in until the whole place was completely furnished, an arrangement that did not sit too well with Vi.

She complained loudly that the bare wood floors were cold and looked funny with those Asian rugs on them. She wanted wall-to-wall carpeting. Vi found the décor much too plain and yearned for the flocked velvet wallpaper and mirrors of her childhood. Secretly she was ashamed to have her friends visit because it looked as if Louis didn't have enough money to decorate the house in the elegant style someone in Louis's position deserved.

Viola Vincente Tedisco had not wanted to move from Fruit Hill. She despised the large drafty house and the East Side, and longed for their large, warm, friendly Italian families back in North Providence. Louis knew that Vi lived for Sunday dinners at Louis's Nonna's house. With at least twenty relatives from both families vying for center stage and joking with each other unmercifully, it was a hard place to get a swelled head. He also knew Vi went back to Fruit Hill to visit her mother much more than she let on.

Louis took a deep breath and frowned. He hoped Vi would get pregnant soon. That would help her loneliness and their marriage. He wanted his sons to go to Moses Brown and his daughters to Wheeler. He knew in his heart his children would always be more comfortable than their mother with this life, but he chose not to dwell on that.

"Penny for your thoughts?"

Louis whirled the chair around in startled surprise. His heart quickened as he looked at Kimberly. She was stunning. Her cheeks were pink from the cold air and her saucy brown eyes sparkled with merriment as she grinned at him. A white fur hat accentuated shiny dark curls and matched the fur collar on her white wool coat.

"You look like an ice princess."

She threw back her head and laughed. "That's the first time you ever called me that." She reached up caressing the white fur collar showing off her deep-red manicured nails and smiled seductively at Louis as she sat on the edge of his desk.

"Wanna test the ice?"

"Perhaps Cherry Ames would be more appropriate," he mused.

"Cherry Ames? Who is Cherry Ames?" she asked, looking puzzled, not liking the turn the conversation was taking.

"I was just talking to my parents, telling them about my being asked to go on the board of the hospital. Pops got all sentimental and puffed up at the same time. Then he zeroed right in on what for him will always be the heart of the matter: do they need a buildin' or sumpim? Mom was ecstatic and told me how as a little girl the Cherry Ames books were her favorite stories and that she wanted to be a nurse for the longest time until her Papa put a stop to that. Then from out of the kitchen I hear my Nonna Tedisco, no fool, bellow out, "Bambino sciocco, voi avete pagati QUANTI per guesto posto?"

Kimberly looked quizzical. Louis shook with laughter, gasping out, "There's my Nonna, almost ninety, and she still comes over to my parents' house each week to make the gravy for my father because that Irish girl he married, forty-five years ago mind you, still hasn't learned to do it right."

Now Louis was howling with laughter.

"Well, what's so funny? You know I can't speak Italian."

"It's not that what she said is so funny it's how she said it."

"Well *what* did she say?"

"She said: how much did they hit you up for? Only in her Toscano dialect it was a bit more colorful. It loses something in the translation. "

"Knowing your Nonna it was probably more along the lines of, 'Louie, my Niño, don't let the bastards get in your pockets'." Kimberly uttered this in a perfect imitation of Nonna's broken English. "The bitch...."

"Why, Kimberly, you can speak Italian!" Louis said in mock amazement and he laughed even louder. "Actually Nonna always spoke highly of you, too, when you lived next door, back in the old neighborhood," he grinned.

"Yeah right, anyway I didn't come here to talk about your

Nonna."

"Why did you come here, as a matter of fact?"

Kimberly slid off the desk quickly, scooted around to Louis's chair and landed in his lap. Louis inhaled her familiar perfume, willing himself not to react to her. She kissed him lightly on the nose, grinning delightedly like a child with a wonderful surprise.

"I have a car and driver downstairs to take us to your first hospital meeting. The weather's getting worse and this way we won't have to worry about driving and we can talk about the project."

Louis moved Kimberly off his lap as he stood up. His hands rested lightly on her shoulders and she reached under his jacket, her fingers touching his hips. They looked at each other. Kimberly's soft red lips parted slightly. Louis could not help being drawn to her. She slightly increased the pressure of her fingertips on his hips, staring at him, not saying a word. He bent down and kissed her gently. Feeling her tongue caress his he pulled her toward him. As their bodies touched his erection was instantaneous. When she moved against his hardness a turbulent passion roared over both of them. Her hand pressed against his pulsating shaft slowly, remembering how to arouse him. He wrenched away, turning toward the windows, taking ragged breaths.

"No, no, Kim, no. I have Vi now. It's over between us. You didn't want me, remember?" he raged savagely, struggling to get a hold of his emotions. Not hearing anything behind him he turned around. Kimberly had fled. He fell into the chair and put his head in his hands.

****

"Letty Hon, I'll be home later than I thought. I forgot there's a hospital board meeting at 5."

"Jim, being a doctor's wife, I know you'll always be getting home late," she answered good-naturedly.

"I know, but I promised to take you out for dinner 'cause you are such a good kid and you've been feeding those grandsons of ours for two weeks while their parents are enjoying themselves in the Bahamas. But now I think we should postpone it. This storm is getting worse and I would rather spend the night in front of the fire with you and the kids and a scotch. Do you want me to pick up something for dinner?"

"No, don't bother; I'll get some steaks out of the freezer. And don't worry, you won't have to grill them outside!" Letty answered with a laugh.

"Okay, I shouldn't be too late. There doesn't look like anything exciting on the agenda."

****

"Dr. Manning, Dr. Harrison is on the phone for you."

Diana looked up from her paperwork in annoyance, trying to recall Dr. Harrison.

"Hello."

"Hi, it's me."

"Robb, you dimwit, why are you calling me here?"

"Because you didn't answer your cell phone. Seriously, Diana, the weather is terrible. I don't think we should plan to meet at the cabin after the board meeting. Much as I want to, we might get snowed in and that would not be the best thing for either of us at the moment. Needless to say I couldn't talk this over with you at the meeting."

"You're right about all of the above. I've been so busy I didn't realize it was snowing." Diana looked out her office window. "Wow, it's really coming down. I lose track of the outside world in here. Good thinking, I'll miss you too, but we had better not chance it. I'll call Mildred to make sure the twins are home and tell her I won't be very late tonight. This meeting doesn't sound very exciting. It will probably be over soon. I can't even believe Brax will deign to grace us with his presence on a snowy February day. He's probably screwing some secretary in the Caribbean. Don't forget to go to great lengths to ignore me in the meeting. Love you!"

"Love you too. Hey, maybe we can meet in an empty room. Will you be wearing any underwear? Will you be sober? I hope not; it's always better when you're drunk and half naked. Easy access and all that...."

"There are no empty rooms this time of year; it's flu season. Goodbye, Robb"

****

When her driver Al swung into the hospital parking lot the car started to fishtail on frozen slush. Kimberly lurched forward sending her trustee packet careening over the floor.

"Shit."

"Sorry, Miss MacComber, I didn't realize the driveway was so slippery. Jeez, ya'd think a hospital would put some salt on the road."

"That's how they get more customers, by letting them crash into each other right by the front door."

"Really?"

"No, Al. *Not* really," she snapped, rolling her eyes.

Kimberly did not want to think about the scene in Louis's office. She put it completely out of her mind. But God forbid anyone should get in her way for the next few hours.

"Oh, I get it."

"Just park this thing."

"How about next to that limo from New York? Maybe dat guy would like a coffee. Can we use the cafeteria?"

"Yeah, sure, whatever. I'll call you on the cell phone when the meeting is over. No, wait a minute. I don't have any boots on and the snow is getting deep. Let me off by the front door."

Al headed back to the entrance, stopped and jumped out to open the car door for Kim. She finished stuffing the papers back into her briefcase and checked her makeup in a mirror. He reached for the briefcase and at the same time helped her out of the car. Got a great pair of legs, that one, he thought. A looker too, but what a bitch; I wonder if she's hot stuff? He mused on, lost in fascinating fantasies of whipped cream, bare flesh and black lace underwear. Kimberly wrenched her briefcase out of his hand, bringing him back to reality. She

55

glared at him, and his face reddened. He turned and stumbled into the front seat, then drove off in the softly falling snow. She whirled around and marched into the hospital in a controlled fury, the words "lecherous, low-minded creep" running through her mind.

****

Brax noticed Kimberly come through the conference room door. What a bewitching sight: her striking dark good looks against her white outfit. Louis arrived right after Kimberly; he headed over to Brax, who kept an eye on Kimberly. She went right to the conference table and sat down and took out her board papers, ignoring everyone. Well, something obviously did not go her way today. Good, he smiled. That conniving teasing bitch needs a taste of her own medicine. He still smarted from what she pulled last month when she invited Louis to what he had intended to be a private luncheon. What was more exasperating, she set up the whole deal at that luncheon. She is smart and doesn't give up until she gets what she wants. I'm not going to give up either, he pledged to himself, watching her look up to talk to Whip Witherspoon.

Whip, as usual when anywhere near Kimberly, turned brick red. She slowly stood up, listening to his explanation of what had taken place at the nominating committee meeting she missed. Leaning back against the edge of the table, she seriously pondered his whispered dialogue. She leaned forward, smiling seductively. Her perfumed breasts filled the scooped neckline of her form-fitting, red wool dress. Running her tongue around her shiny moist lips, ostensibly deep in thought, she answered Whip, nodding in absolute agreement. Flicking her eyes glancing at Brax and Louis, she almost laughed out loud at the expressions of carnal desire on both their faces. Immediately she put her hand on Whip's arm assuring, him of something and he staggered away, pulling at his collar. Kimberly sat down with a smile on her face. She was in control again.

****

Louis, trying to regain his composure, turned to Brax, "Have you read *The Social Transformation of American Medicine* by Paul Starr?"

"Er, um ... no, can't say that I have."

"It gives a definitive history of the medical profession in America. It's heavy but very readable after you get by the first chapter. In fact I would hope that all your trustees have had it recommended to them. It got a Pulitzer in the eighties."

Brax narrowed his eyes with concern. It had never occurred to him that Louis would have any real interest in hospitals. Better stop this in its tracks, he thought. He cleared his throat and said, "Let's sit down. We had better get this thing going before the storm turns into a blizzard and I can't get back to New York."

******

"This is turning into quite a storm," said Robb, sliding into the seat beside Hunt.

"Who is that guy? He looks familiar. "

"What guy?" mumbled Hunt as he thumbed through his board packet.

"The one with Brax."

Hunt looked at Brax and the stranger. "I dunno, no, wait a minute. Isn't that Louis Tedisco? His father is in the sand and gravel business. Louis ... hmm ... hasn't he been involved with the revitalization of downtown and the Providence Plaza project?"

"Good Lord, you're right. That's why he looked so familiar to me," said Robb in recognition. "He was at the meeting I had with the Plaza project group last month. He didn't say much that night and I don't remember being introduced."

"That's his stock in trade. He never says much, but he sure pulls a lot of strings behind the scenes. You must have noticed his new building downtown. I know it caused some controversy, but I think it's handsome. Of course some architects, who did not get the contract to design said building, might not agree," continued Hunt, looking up at the ceiling.

"For your information, I, too, think it is an interesting design and most importantly a good fit downtown. But seriously, what is he doing here, with Brax?" asked Robb looking at the two men suspiciously.

"I don't know. "Perhaps now we'll find out what we were trying to figure out at lunch last month."

"I can't believe Brax is here, can you? I thought for sure he would be entertaining some babe in the warm sun," murmured Robb. "I wonder if his presence has anything to do with his new friend?" He steeled himself not to look at Diana who had made the comment earlier.

****

Sarah James sat dejectedly in her seat. She kept rolling a pen around in her fingers, absentmindedly staring at the table. The nominating committee meeting had been a joke. Whip put the résumé of Louis Tedisco on the table at each committee member's place. After a glowing report about him presented by Brax and John, the committee voted unanimously for him to become a trustee of East Meridian Hospital. The vote was taken without any discussion and no one even looked at each other. Sarah felt sick to her stomach. She wished with all her heart she could get up and walk out of the conference room and never have anything to do with these people again.

Sarah felt the chair next to her being pulled out. She looked around, groaning inwardly as Anna Morgan seated herself quietly in the chair. Sarah stole a look at Anna. She sat in the chair, wearing her coat, clutching her purse and board packet in her lap. Sarah was mystified. Anna looked very pale. Her fingers were white, almost blue, as if she had not worn gloves in this terrible weather. That's odd, thought Sarah. Usually Anna had enough gear for any type of inclemency short of a monsoon. In fact, Anna was the only woman Sarah had ever seen wearing rubber things over her shoes. Looking down,

Sarah noticed that Anna's shoes were wet and dripping on the rug.

Jim Simpson seated himself next to Anna and, when he didn't hear her usual onset of complaints, took a good look at her. He too realized she seemed frozen in her seat.

"Anna, would you like a cup of tea?" he asked, looking at her with concern. Getting no answer from Anna, he glanced over at Sarah who opened her hands, palms up in bewilderment.

"Anna, are you all right?"

"What? Oh yes, yes, I'm fine," she murmured absently.

"Let me get you a cup of hot tea," Jim offered again.

Sarah pushed back her chair and jumped up saying, "No, no, let me get it." Coming back she put the cup of tea with lemon and extra sugar in front of Anna. Jim had just helped Anna take off her coat and was draping it around her shoulders.

"Let's get this meeting going before we are all snowed in here for the night, okay?" Brax said heartily. "First, I take great pleasure in introducing our new board member, Louis Tedisco. Could we all go around the table and introduce ourselves.

In the absolute silence that followed, the members of the nominating committee either looked at the table or at anything other than their fellow board members. The rest of the board stared in stunned silence at Brax and Louis. Kimberly, rarely at a loss for words, introduced herself, grinning broadly at Louis then turned to Jim Simpson, indicating his introduction would be next. Sweets glanced at Diana, who looked surprised, then at John who smiled back at her. The introductions continued around the table in voices that ranged from quiet introspection to astonishment. Brax, sensing discord about to erupt, immediately called the meeting to order.

"Do I have a motion to accept the minutes of the January 17, 2000, East Meridian Hospital Board meeting? No changes? Good. Jim, will you give the medical staff report? I think we should move right along because of the storm and get us all out of here fast."

You oily bastard, thought Sarah, you want to get us out of

here and fast, before someone starts a commotion. The board-room was deathly quiet as Jim Simpson gave his report. Before anyone could say a word, Brax asked John for the treasurer's report. Louis Tedisco wondered if the other board members understood what Lansdowe was reporting.

As John finished, Sarah James started to collect her papers. Brax seemed to notice and spoke up hurriedly that the development report would be mailed out to save time and that he had an important announcement. Sarah opened her mouth to say something, then shrugged her shoulders and flounced back in her chair.

Robb and Hunt pushed back their chairs and wearily gazed at Brax. What now, they were wondering. Robb fleetingly locked eyes with Diana, a fact that did not go unnoticed by Sweets. Anna had not moved or drunk her tea. Jim was frowning. Whip busied himself with the papers in front of him and Kimberly looked smug. Liam was furious that he had not been told about this new trustee, and he wanted to get to his president's report. He had important issues to bring to the board and for once he wanted them dealt with, snow or no snow.

"I have some news," Brax exclaimed, delightedly rubbing his hands together. Everybody's attention was riveted on Brax; this exuberant manner was so totally out of character.

"Our new trustee, Louis, has most generously donated a million dollars to East Meridian Hospital," he gushed.

"Well," whispered Robb to Hunt, "at least we're getting a good price for these seats."

The board members smiled warily at each other when Brax spoke up with, in his estimation, the best news of all.

"The money will be used to build an atrium at the entrance of the hospital. The Tedisco Pavilion. It will have a three-story waterfall and indoor garden. The top two levels will be for sunrooms and...."

"Are you crazy?" exploded Robb, sitting up in his chair and slamming his fist on the conference table.

Louis looked surprised at Robb's outrage.

"An atrium?" echoed Liam in disbelief.

The voices in the conference room reverberated with uncertainty; some board members unsure they had heard correctly, when Liam's pager sounded. He went over to the house phone, his face tense with anger. Receiver in hand, he paled in response to what he was hearing, and issued orders in a quiet grim voice. Just as the voices in the boardroom were reaching a crescendo, Diana's and Jim's pagers resounded in a cacophony of beeps. The doctors got up from the table, looking at Liam, wondering what had happened.

"There has been a serious accident. All doctors in the house are to come to the ER."

Diana, Jim and Liam hurriedly left the room. Snow pelted the windows of the silent overheated boardroom.

John cleared his throat. "Ahem...Well, on behalf of the board I would like to thank Louis for his most generous gift. And I make a motion we accept. Do I have a second?"

"Yes, yes, I second that," said Brax hastily.

"All in favor say aye."

A murmur of "Ayes" followed.

"Nay," blurted out Robb and Hunt together.

"The ayes have it," smiled Brax to no one in particular. "I suggest in light of this interruption and the storm, we concur that we have no more business to attend at this time and the meeting is adjourned." He stood up, gathered his papers and walked out of the room with John and a very mystified Louis.

Sarah watched the rest of the board slowly push back their chairs, gather papers and brief cases, struggle with coats, scarves and gloves, and leave. Except Robb and Hunt, who slumped in their chairs. Amid muffled goodbyes, the metallic click of an outside door was heard. As usual, too intimidated to speak, she followed her fellow board members who had ventured into the storm.

****

The atmosphere in the ER crackled with apprehension. A nurse at the front desk was in phone communication with the police and 911 medics; other nurses and doctors waited by the doors, tensing as they heard the loud blast of sirens indicating rescue wagons at the emergency entrance.

The wagons backed up to the ER and the staff burst into action as the automatic doors slid open spilling forth stretcher after stretcher of injured young people. Some were moaning, covered with blood, others yelling and thrashing around in pain, and a few lay still, unconscious of the turmoil going on around them. Snow-covered paramedics and police barked out the injuries as they raced gurneys through the doors.

"Head injury, unconscious tachy at one-ten, BP is one-thirty over ninety. No response with Narcan or dextrose."

"Broken leg, crushed sternum."

"Boy about eighteen, unconscious since we picked him up."

"Gash near spleen, lost a lot of blood."

Again and again the doors hissed open to the freezing cold wind and swirling snow, admitting more and more injured to the crowded ER.

The waiting room began filling with young people injured but able to walk, their faces pinched in pain and white with shock. Some sobbed in agony, cradling broken arms and wrists, while others held bandages to bloody injuries pleading with the triage nurse to help them or their friends.

"Jim, Jim!"

"Letty, what are you doing here?"

"I heard on TV there had been a terrible accident and all nurses were asked to report to the hospital," her face crumpled and her eyes filled with tears. "Jim," she whispered her shoulders sagging, "our grandchildren were on those buses; remember their parents didn't want us to let them to drive in the snow. Are they here?"

" Dear God, I don't know, I just got...."

"Dr. Simpson, please come into trauma 3, we need help," pleaded a nurse as she rushed by.

"I'll be there in a minute. Have either of my grandsons come in?"

"I don't know."

"Diana, have you seen my grandsons?" Jim uttered in a

panic as Diana sped by Jim and Letty on her way down the hall struggling to put on some yellow paper scrubs.

"No, Jim, I haven't. Oh, no. Were they on those buses?"

"Dr. Simpson, please come to Trauma 3," urged another nurse to Jim and Letty.

"I will, I will. I want to check to see if my grandsons are here in the ER."

"That's why they want you in Trauma 3 ... your grandsons were just brought in there."

"Both of them?" whispered Letty, grasping Jim's arm as they hurried after the nurse down the hall.

A disheveled teenage boy paced the doorway of the room. "Grandpa, Grandma, thank God you're here," cried Jim and Letty's handsome grandson Josh. "It's Chip; he won't wake up."

Letty went over to Josh and put her arms around her grandchild; his lanky six-foot frame shook with sobs.

"Josh, are you all right? Are you hurt?" asked Letty.

"No, Gram, I'm okay, b ... b ... but Chip?"

"Josh, what happened?" asked Jim looking at Chip's chart.

"We won the game. And we were singing school songs and laughing, and you know Chip, he and Marylou were standing in the aisle leading the singing. He was lifting her up as she cheered. The bus wasn't going fast because of the snow. The windows were all steamed up and we were making a lot of noise, when all of a sudden something slammed into the side of the bus and we started to skid. Chip pushed Marylou into a seat and fell on the floor. Then the bus in back of us smashed into our bus. We all landed on top of each other and Chip was on the bottom. We were wedged in; lots of kids got hurt. It was dark and I couldn't get to him. I kept calling but he didn't answer. Oh, Grandma," sobbed the distraught teenager.

"Jim, I came as fast as I could through this snow. The patient is your grandson?"

Letty held Josh tighter as Jim turned toward the man approaching the bed.

"Joe, thank God you were able to get through. Jim's face revealed the concern he felt about Chip's condition as he looked at his old friend Joe Bettencourt. "Joe, I...."

"Has he had a CAT scan?"

"I don't know. I just got here, but I don't think so."

"Okay. I want to get him on a respirator and start medication to control any cerebral edema. Then we'll get him up to the ICU. Please hand me the chart, thanks."

As Chip was being hooked up to an IV and a respirator, Josh looked wildly at his grandfather. " Grandpa, is he worse? Why is all that stuff on him? Oh, God, is he dying?"

"Now Josh, it's all right. All this is to help him and to monitor and control his breathing, blood pressure and other vital functions," replied Joe Bettencourt soothingly. "We'll be taking him up to the ICU in a few minutes. You and your grandmother can go up and stay with him.

****

Diana, her body sagging with exhaustion, came out of the operating room; a bright light hit her face. She glanced toward the window and realized it was the sunrise. She leaned on the windowsill and looked out over the newly fallen snow to the cliff and the sparkling ocean below. With such a beautiful morning the horror of last night almost seemed hard to believe.

A helicopter took off from the hospital helipad to her right and flew across the snow- covered lawn out over the ocean, then turned left toward Boston. That must be Jim's grandson on the way to the Trauma Center at Mass General. There's nothing more we can do for him here. She watched the helicopter fly into the rising sun and her eyes filled with tears.

MARCH

"Diana, I just talked with Sadie."

"How is she?"

"Huh, oh, fine, but she doesn't know what Brax is up to with Tedisco any more than we do."

"Speaking of Tedisco, it's been almost two weeks since the meeting. Have you gotten a letter releasing you from the Providence Plaza project?"

"No, and to tell you the truth, I'm amazed. I thought for sure that would be on my desk in twenty-four hours. What's the scuttlebutt around the hospital?"

"Hmmm. Well, rumors are running wild. Usually I ignore them but it has been hard these last weeks. With all the turmoil the night of the school bus accident it didn't take ten minutes for gossip about the atrium vote to hit the ER right after the trustees meeting ended."

"I'm not surprised."

"And everyone's upset about the atrium. Union talk has started up again. Liam is walking around with a face like a thundercloud. The doctors are bitching the money should be used within the hospital. God knows we need it. Then of course they start arguing about whose area needs the money more. Getting a group of doctors to agree on anything is about as easy as herding cats. "

65

Robb laughed. "Well, I can understand their frustration. At least you're dealing with talented people who want to do good things. Try dealing with the legislature. It takes forever to figure out who is behind the scene pulling the strings. Come to think of it, that's pretty much what we are faced with right here as trustees, isn't it? God, *now* I'm frustrated. Speaking of frustrated . . ."

"Nice segue."

"How do you know what I am going to say?"

"Let's just say I feel your pain."

"Actually I had feeling something else in mind...."

"Oh ... well what do you suggest?"

"Meet me at the cabin for supper, Diana. This month has flown by and we haven't seen each other. I'll get some steaks and stuff and ... please don't tell me you're scheduled to take out somebody's gallbladder ... we have lots of wine ... in fact I even have Moët." He rushed on, mentally making a note to pick up a bottle of Moët in case he didn't have any at the cabin. "I know that Mildred is taking the twins to McDonalds and then the movies tonight, so what do you think? Okay? Okay?"

"Robb, you sound like one of the twins," she laughed. "And how in the world do you know about Mildred taking them out this evening?"

"There are times when it really is better to be lucky than good."

"Well, short of hanging around the schoolyard or my kitchen, how did you manage to find out?"

"I was in Brooks getting my allergy prescription filled, as sneezing season is around the bend, and Lisle was there with the twins. They were teasing Lisle about her big date tonight and going on and on about plans with Mildred. I felt a bit funny eavesdropping but they were cute, so excited about going to McDonalds and the movie afterward. They also cautioned each other, very seriously, not to tell their grandmother because she hates McDonalds and they didn't want to upset her. They are nice kids, Diana; you've done a good job with them."

"Thanks, Robb, that means a lot. I love them with all my heart," she said softly. Then clearing her throat she went on,

"I've already taken out as many gallbladders as I can manage today, so I would love to come for dinner. And I'll do my best to get somebody to cover for me so I can drink some of that Moët you are going to pick up."

"How did you know I wasn't sure I had any Moët?"

"I could tell by your voice. It's a mother thing; you know, when the little darlings say they thought they would give the dog a bath, that they probably just finished painting him along with the Easter eggs."

"Ah, I see."

"I'll be there as soon as I can, with bells on!"

"And you can count on the fact that I'll get those bells, as well as anything else, off as fast as I can."

"Bye."

****

"Hello, Anna; it's Hank."

"Hello, Hank; I'm not so sure I like the sound of your voice."

"You're right. I'm not happy about the results of your biopsy."

"It's cancer, isn't it?" she said briskly.

"Yes, and I think we...."

"There is nothing to think about, Hank. I want a mastectomy as soon as possible. Can you arrange it for next week? I don't have to go to Providence, do I?"

"Anna, I think it would be best if you come to the office and we talk about this and figure out what treatment is right for you."

"I don't need all that folderol; get rid of it so I can get on with my life."

"Anna, we don't recommend such drastic and disfiguring surgery anymore, only as a last resort. We've reached a far better understanding of breast cancer and our approaches to treating it have changed."

"Hank, is there more to this ... has it spread?"

"Ummm, well, we're not sure. And that's why I want you

to come in and discuss this. How about this afternoon around 4:30?"

"I'm busy ... I can't ... I have to go somewhere ... ," Anna rushed on, then sighed. "All right, I'll come to the office."

"Good, there are many more options now, Anna, not like years ago."

"You mean when my mother and sister died," she cried harshly.

"Oh, Anna, I...."

"It's all right, Hank. Thank you for being so kind. I can handle this. I'll see you later."

Anna hung up the phone, wrapped her arms around her thin frame, and wept.

****

Brax Montgomery took a deep breath, inhaling soft Caribbean air. Life was good. He looked out over the beautiful turquoise sea. The Resort on St. Croix had been a perfect hideaway. Taking Lisabet to his cottage at Lyford Cay would have been dicey. Somebody would see them and surely tell his wife Bitsy. This way was a lot safer.

The last five days had been spent indulging in great food, good wine and very inventive sex. He closed his eyes remembering the wonderful things Lisabet did with him and to him every night.

Scrape ...

Brax's eyes snapped open at the sound of a chair being pulled along the flagstone terrace next door and the sound of voices. He turned and came face to face with John Lansdowe.

****

"Sarah, Sarah, my gosh, is that you?"

Sarah O'Brien James looked toward a vaguely familiar voice. After a brisk walk on the beach she had stopped at the Azimuth Point Coffee Bean to indulge in a mocha latte. The weather being comfortable for March, she had taken her drink outside and was leaning against the terrace railing enjoying the sun and watching the waves break on the sand. She looked at the man standing a few feet away; her eyes grew wide and her face lost all its color. The mug slipped from her hands, and crashed on the wooden deck breaking into a hundred pieces, and spilled brown liquid on both of them.

"My God, Sarah, I didn't mean to frighten you. You're shaking. Here, sit down. I'll get someone to clean this up." He helped her into a chair and rushed inside.

"Are you all right, miss?" inquired the waitress as she bustled through the door, mop and bucket in hand. "You're not cut, are you? Mr. van Dorn is getting you another latte and I'll get this cleaned up in a jiffy."

The van Dorns always get people to clean up messes, Sarah thought dourly as she tried to get her raging emotions and shaking body under control.

David van Dorn backed out of the café's doors holding two steaming lattes. He turned and came toward Sarah and the waitress, who finished wiping up the spilled coffee.

He's even better looking now than he was as a teenager, thought Sarah watching him approach the table. He was frowning and concerned as he sat down opposite her. Reaching over he put down a napkin and placed her coffee mug on top of it.

"I hope it's the kind you like. I'm sorry, I didn't think to ask what kind of latte you wanted," he said with his beguiling smile.

Sarah's heart hurt when he smiled at her and she wrapped shaking hands around the hot mug. She could not trust herself to speak. Looking out at the ocean she wondered what to do. Part of her wanted to run away and the other part kept her glued to the chair. She glanced back as the waitress' voice broke into her thoughts.

"Is everything okay, Mr. van Dorn? Do you need anything else?"

"No, no, thank you for your help. I'll bring the mugs in when we're finished," he said, smiling up at her.

"Oh, no, don't worry about the mugs. I'll take care of them

after you leave. Enjoy this lovely day," she said brightly. Then beaming, she left. Looking back she gave him a big grin.

If I had done this by myself nobody would be rushing out to help me clean up or offering to come get my used dirty mug, Sarah thought mulishly. But if you are a van Dorn of Azimuth Point the world is at your feet. She narrowed her eyes, looking at his handsome face, willing herself to continue to hate him.

Looking down at her hands he noticed the rings on her finger, "You're married?"

"Yes."

"I was...." He hesitated, shook his head as if to clear away a memory. She wanted to reach out and caress the soft curls at the nape of his neck. She jammed her hands in her lap.

"I'm glad I ran into you," he continued. "Well, I surely didn't mean to scare you to death," he grinned, "but I did want to get in touch with you. I didn't know if you still lived here but...."

"What do you want?" she demanded harshly.

Startled, he hesitated. Then, searching her face, he looked anguished. Quietly he said, "I didn't want to just blurt this out, but ... I wanted to ask your forgiveness. I did a terrible thing to you. I hurt you. I...."

Sarah clutched the table glaring at him, her face distorted with loathing. "I'll never forgive you," she growled. Slowly she rose, never taking her eyes off him, and in a whisper she said, "You ripped my heart out, you took my virginity and sauntered away to play tennis. I wanted to die. And a part of me did die. You killed it. I will never ever forgive you."

David turned white and his face became haggard. He opened his mouth but no words came out.

"Never come near me again, do you understand?" she snarled. "I hate you!"

Rising, she backed up, turning over the chair, and ran off the deck into the parking lot to her SUV. Ripping open the door she slammed into the seat, starting the engine in a fury. Speeding away down the road, the tears started. She pulled off into a shopping center, stopped the car and cried big gulping sobs. The torment came pouring out. He had apologized, only years too late.

****

Louis Tedisco felt great. What a night! He was the guest of honor at a fancy dinner at The Westin Hotel and received an award by the Preservation Society for restoration work his company had done in downtown Providence. He had made it. Life is good, he thought toweling off after a warm, relaxing shower. It was a long way from Fruit Hill. Walking nude into the bedroom he slid between the sheets of his king-size bed. The full moon shone through the windows. He turned toward his wife, moonlight illuminating soft curly blonde hair draped over her naked shoulders. He traced the curve of her hip with his fingertips and slipped his hands under the peach satin nightgown. He ran his hands over her hips and gently pulled her toward him.

"No."

"No?"

"No. Louie, I don't wanna do it. I feel achy."

"Achy?"

"My boobs hurt."

"I've got something that hurts too."

"Louie, it's no good."

"Vi, believe me, it really is good," murmured Louis as he kissing his wife's neck and rubbing his hands over her body.

"No, Louie, it's not good," whined Vi. "I feel very achy and I had a horrible time tonight. You made me wear that awful dress. I looked terrible."

"I thought you looked really nice," uttered Louis in confusion, drawing back and looking at her. 'The color was perfect on you, and that new necklace I gave you was just right. You fit in just as if...."

Vi sat up in a whirl, her hands on her hips. Breasts heaving, she let loose. "Yah, Louie, just as if I belonged there ... right?" she snapped. "My feelings exactly. When are you goin' to realize that I don't belong there, and I don't wanna belong there!!!! Those dried- up, snobby women bore me to death.

71

There they are in their pink—and—green outfits for summa', or their dreary skirts, low heels and tweed jackets for winter. I've nevah seen people who can utter whole sentences without unclenching their teeth. 'Dahling, how divine to see you; it's been ages. Did you stay in Palm Beach for the season or did you do the islands for a bit?'" mimicked Vi.

Louis was amazed. "I didn't know you could talk like that, you sound just like them!"

"You'd like that wouldn' ya, Louie?"

"Well, ummm ... you think you could do it all the time?" he inquired seriously, unaware of what he was letting himself in for.

"Do you want me to do it just when we are out with those snotty people you're breaking your ass to impress?" she enunciated sweetly. "Or how about when we have sex? Should I lie there quietly and say, you may do it now, my dearest, and when you are finished you can thank me, say you're sorry and it won't happen again soon. And I could speak like that at your mother's so the whole family would be impressed. Your Nonna would be really pleased, don'tcha think?" Vi spit out, sarcastically reverting back to her regular speech pattern.

"Er, um, well, I'm not sure...." He waffled, realizing he was in deep trouble. He had never seen Vi act like this or even answer him back. She always agreed with whatever he wanted even when he knew she wasn't too crazy about the idea. And she never just lay there during sex. He was alarmed, not knowing where this was heading.

"I'm so sick and tired of wearing those awful clothes and sitting quietly with all those snobs; they're makin' fun of us, ya know ... They talk in the ladies room ... about us and how much money you've made ... and they think we have connections ... and they don't mean Narragansett Electric. I hate my life," she bawled hysterically, tears coursing down her face. "I wanna go home."

Louis sat up and reached for her. "Vi, Vi, you are home. Please stop crying."

"This isn't my home. This is you tryin' to be like them ... you and that nasty decorator. Well, you're not like them and I don't wanna be like them," she yelled.

"Vi, please, I've never seen you like this, please Honey...."

"Don't 'please Honey' me and don't call me Vi any more," she sobbed.

"V ... uh, Sweetheart, what should I call you," queried Louis in worried confusion.

"Don't call me anything and leave me alone," she shrieked, shoving him away. She flung herself down on the bed and wept.

Louis lay back down and pulled the covers up over himself and Vi, or whatever she wanted to call herself now. He felt shaken and astonished by what had just taken place. He had always tried to be a good husband. He certainly gave her everything money could buy; she had a much easier life than either of their mothers ever had. What in the world is wrong with her? Ignoring the niggling thought in the back of his mind that he alone decided how to run their lives without even consulting her, he self-righteously became angry.

What a bitch ... all he wanted was a little nookie. Nookie my ass, he thought, rolling over and punching the pillow into a ball. The size of that new Mercedes I just bought her, I ought to have a good roaring fuck! I don't ask her to do much around here. I buy her nice clothes and expensive jewelry. We go to all the right restaurants and the theater. Christ, I spend thousands on fur coats and look where it gets me ... women.

He closed his eyes and tried to fall asleep, but he was too keyed up. His mind drifted. He thought about the restoration project, which made him think of Robb Wells, the architect. The guy had done a wonderful job on the preliminary sketches and had great ideas for downtown Providence. But Robb sure was furious about the atrium at the hospital, he and that other guy. What was the problem? He had called Brax the next day and offered to try to make amends even though he wasn't sure why. Wasn't the atrium what the hospital needed in order to start the modernization, before starting the rest of the remodeling project, which had to be approved by the state? That's what Brax and Kimberly had advised him to do. But Brax had brushed him off, telling him not to worry about it; that Robb and Hunt always had a hair up their ass about something. Louis grinned. Those two guys are probably pissed off that their precious white-bread hospital's front door will sport my very ethnic name. When you think of it, The Tedisco Pavilion in big shiny letters for everybody to see as they drive by would definitely stick in their craw. He smiled and drifted off to sleep.

The next morning he woke up early and sensed that Vi was not next to him, nor could he hear her moving around in the bathroom. Well, wherever she is I hope she has calmed down, he thought. He walked into the bathroom, rubbing the sleep out of his eyes. His mouth dropped open when he looked at the huge mirror over the two sinks. Vi had scrawled in red lipstick. "I've gone home."

****

Helene, nervously clutching flowers, rode up in the elevator to Selina's apartment. These last few months had been the happiest of her life. Occasionally she felt overwhelmed by the enormity of the predicament her change in lifestyle would cause if it became known. But most of the time she put it out of her mind. She was living in another world. It was easy to carry on this secret life, because she had led such a quiet existence all these years; nobody missed her. Robb was busy with work and rarely home. Miranda had not been home since Christmas, and would not be back until summer because she was spending her spring vacation at her roommate's in Palm Beach. Helene didn't have any close friends, and her mother was occupied running charity events, garden clubs and numerous other activities. Careening from one mind-numbing event to another and lunching with somebody terribly important each day left Neena Lansdowe no time to spare for Helene. Helene suspected her mother found her boring.

Her father was a shadowy figure in her life. He rarely entered her thoughts. She could tell her parents' marriage was in name only; for the most part they ignored each other. When she was younger and her mother was drinking it had been

74

different. She remembered standing on the upstairs landing listening to terrible fights between them. They always ended with her mother taunting her father that it was her money that made them rich, not anything he did and he would not even have a job if it hadn't been for her father's company. She called him names and laughed at him. Helene would run and hide.

But she didn't want to think about the past. Walking down the hall she came to the apartment and pressed the buzzer. Quivering with excitement, she could hear Selina's high heels tapping on the marble floor as she hurried along the entrance hall. Flinging open the door Selina enveloped Helene in a big hug. Pressing against Selina's taut breasts and inhaling her exotic perfume, Helene blushed at her thoughts.

"You brought flowers! How nice. You know how much I love flowers. Here, take your coat off and come in and have a glass of wine."

Helene leaned against the counter-top staring ardently as Selina got a vase for the flowers and plunked them in, added water, and gave them a twist. They looked perfect.

"You make that look so easy. I could try to arrange them for two days and they would never look that nice."

Selina, her back to Helene, gave a pleased laugh. She reached for the ice bucket holding the chilled wine, picked up two wineglasses with her other hand and turned around. She recognized the look on Helene's face immediately, and had a quick battle with herself whether or not to give in to the urge to put the wine down and take Helene right into the bedroom. She opted to go into the living room and do what she had to do. She smiled weakly at Helene and walked briskly into the other room. She poured the wine and handed a glass to Helene. Selina had always responded to Helene when Helene indicated she was aroused. Helene still could not bring herself to ask for sex, but her body language made it so obvious that there was no mistaking her need.

Helene felt confused and uneasy by Selina's brusque behavior.

"Helene dear, come sit down," murmured Selina sitting on the sofa and patting the place next to her. Helene sat down.

Selina took the wineglass out of Helene's hand and put it on the table. Then she took Helene's hands in her own.

"Soon I will be going to New York."

"So..? You go to New York often. Just last week you flew there twice. I took you to the airport. And I picked you up." Helene struggled defiantly to not understand what Selina was telling her.

"Helene, you know what I mean; we have talked of it before," Selina said.

"No," whispered Helene looking down. Selina reached over and raised Helene's chin. Helene looked up chin trembling and her eyes filled with tears.

"Yes, my dear, you knew I was just here until spring. My job will be finished at the theater as well as my lecture series. New York is my home. You know I can't stay here. My life is in New York. I love New York. But I want to...."

"But I love you," blurted out Helene, tears streaming down her face. "Please don't leave, not now. Please just stay for the summer."

"Helene, I can't stay for the summer." Selina gently wiped Helene's tears with her handkerchief. "I love you too. I know I never told you that, because quite honestly, I thought we could have an affair and I could walk away and never look back. But I care for you too much. Helene, my darling Helene, come with me to New York!" she exclaimed excitedly. "We'll be able to live our lives out in the open, no more pretending that we are not lovers. I have so many wonderful places to show you and things I want you to see. We'll be so happy!"

Helene stared at her, dumbfounded. Selina put an arm around Helene, caressing her hair, whispering all they would do in New York. Helene ached for Selina to continue to seduce her, but her mind was in turmoil. For the first time she faced the stark realization of what she had been doing and whom she had been doing it with. And everybody would know. Her body went rigid and she sat up abruptly.

"My family, I can't leave my family. My daughter will be horrified! What would people say?" she cried. "Oh, God, my parents, my parents will be furious."

Selina looked at her in amazement. Helene not only hid their relationship from the world, she also refused to acknowledge it to herself. Selina thought, in many ways Helene's never grown up. This is why it is so easy for her to live in her own world, and that is also one of her endearing qualities, her naïveté. I have rushed her; I must slow down and give her time to decide which she wants.

"Robb will be so upset," moaned Helene, hunched over on the sofa clasping and unclasping her hands.

Well now, that's interesting, thought Selina. Why hadn't Robb confronted Helene about finding her in bed with Selina that snowy night? He has found love in other places. Is he just waiting Helene out? Is he a bastard, like most men, or is he unsure what to do? They both love the child. Oh Lord, the child! I hadn't even thought about the problems that will incur. What am I getting myself into? Maybe I should end this right here and now and save myself a lot of trouble. Or tell her to grow up and make a decision. She looked at Helene, distraught and trembling next to her, and Selina's heart softened. Selina truly loved this kind, gentle woman and wanted her in her life forever. I must help her with this, not give her ultimatums and threats.

"Helene, dearest, I have been so brash. Instead of talking this over with you I threw it in your face without giving you time to think, or consider this possibility. I never even asked you to live with me. Please forgive me. Let's talk this over and see what is best for both of us."

Helene looking up at Selina and smiling through her tears whispered, "You have made me so happy. When I found out you liked just me for who I am, I was so thrilled. Nobody has before."

Selina thought her heart would break. And she felt guilty because she, like everyone else in Helene's life, had charged ahead making all the decisions.

Helene looked troubled again. "I guess I thought we would always be friends, forever. I didn't want to think about you leaving Providence. And I never had any ideas of me leaving Providence, changing my whole life, leaving my family. How would I tell Robb?" she lamented, her voice rising. "What would I say? How can I tell him what we ... um ... that I ... it's not normal ... I mean, oh Lord, I don't know what I mean," she finished lamely, looking at Selina in distress.

"Eventually you will have to," Selina began harshly, about to snap at Helene that she would have to admit to herself and the world that she was gay. And not to expect cheers from those nearest and dearest, either. But she held back in time, realizing that terrifying Helene was not going to help. "Um, eventually we'll straighten this out. There's no need to rush into any decisions right now."

"But you are leaving."

"Yes, but not for a while. In fact you should come down to visit. That way you can get used to New York; and judge for yourself if it is for you."

"I guess you're right," murmured Helene doubtfully. "I think I'd best go home," she sighed. "I ... I have to go home."

Selina's first instinct was to protest and keep Helene in the apartment and try to convince her to take the big step and start a new life. But she took a slow deep breath; Helene had to come to grips with this herself, and she must wait.

"Of course, I understand," Selina said softly as she stood up, taking Helene's hands and pulling her up from the sofa. She wrapped her arms around Helene's slender form and held her close.

"It will be all right; everything will work itself out. Wait and see. Thank you for the lovely flowers. I'll call you tomorrow; there is a little party ... theater people ... you might like to go." She kissed Helene and walked her to the door.

****

Sarah James braced herself as she entered the hospital conference room for the March trustees meeting. She didn't want to see these people, never mind talk to them. She went to the refreshment table and started lackadaisically plopping ice into a glass for water while deciding if a few chocolate-chip cookies would brighten her mood.

Out of the corner of her eye she noticed Diana and Sweets come into the room. They are such good friends, she thought. I envy them. Strange how they're so different: Diana is tall, blonde, slender, but she looks strong, like a thoroughbred filly; and Sweets is small, almost like a teenager. I wonder if she is a lesbian ... ha ... I don't think so. Things like that don't happen on Azimuth Point. They have that Azimuth Point confidence too. Look at them laughing and talking; they command the space they are in; they don't hide in a side pocket like I do. Closing her eyes she almost said aloud, why must it always get back to Azimuth Point? She turned slightly away from them as they approached the table.

"Diana, you'll never guess who I saw on the beach yesterday ... walking a funny little dog!"

"Well, if it was a really funny little dog it must have been David."

"My God, you're right. I didn't get to talk to him because he went up the path to his house but he did wave. David van Dorn walking a dog ... was he going to grill it for dinner? What's he doing here anyway? Doesn't he have a wife richer than God in D.C.?" In hushed tones, but audible to Sarah, Sweets added, "What do you bet he's doing some broad under the dustsheets in the ole manor house, while the wifey-poo is home organizing some charity ball ... Gawd, what a great ass he had ... and the front part wasn't bad either."

"Sweets, my dear, are you going down memory lane? You sound like you might have taken part in that large stiff, movable feast when we were young and horny."

"It was wishful thinking. But I did some heavy looking. He was very busy. Unfortunately he never seemed interested in me. What about you?"

"Well, let's just say when we were very young we practiced a bit."

Sarah listened, slowly piling cookies on her plate, digesting the revelation that Diana and David ... practiced?

"You and David?" Sweets inquired incredulously. "Wow, that one got by me ... and I thought we told each other everything ... well, maybe not everything."

"You are so right," Diana said with a wicked smile. "In fact, I taught him how to French kiss, among a few other things."

"Then you are responsible for putting him on the road to damnation," Sweets nodded knowingly.

"Yep, he was one horny teenager and I was the older woman in his life for a week or two, and let's leave it at that. We did become good friends though, and still are. I've kept in touch with him over the years."

"Well, why is he here in March? Is he, as usual, up to no good?"

"Seriously, it is really tragic. His wife, Fiona, a nice girl, yes, a nice *rich* girl had been visiting her sister in Maryland and David insisted she come back into the city immediately to attend some fancy shindig he felt was important to his career. He was upset Fiona had stayed so long with her sister, so she took a short cut through a bad section of D.C. to get home fast. Her car was held up at a stoplight and she was stabbed and left on the street. She was six months pregnant. By the time David got to the hospital they had delivered the baby by caesarean and she was on life support. She had a massive hemorrhage and died in David's arms and the baby died later that night. David lost his wife and baby son and can't forgive himself. He had a breakdown and came up here to get his life back together."

"My God, I had no idea, how terrible," exclaimed Sweets. "What can we do?"

"Nothing. He doesn't want to see anybody, or talk to anybody. Mildred brings him over meals three or four times a week. In fact she's teaching him how to cook. And he went to the shelter to get that funny dog, Cynthia Verdell."

"He's learning to cook? You have to be kidding ... Cynthia Verdell, what kind of dog is that?"

"It's not a kind of dog. It's the name of the dog."

"What?"

"You know, after the dog Jack Nicholson shoved down the garbage chute in *As Good As It Gets*. Anyway David asked for one that really needed a home and they showed him this sad-looking thing and he said okay. He wanted to name the dog

Verdell and the shelter people told him it was a female, so he named it Cynthia Verdell."

"Oh ... I'm having trouble with all this."

"It does seem crazy; certainly not the David we knew. But he is a changed person. And he takes the dog everywhere. Needless to say the dog adores him," she continued looking down at the assorted trays of drinks, cookies and fruit. "We had better get something and sit down. I'll tell you more later."

Sarah stood motionless, her thoughts a jumble. She cringed at the remembrance of how she had yelled at David a few days ago. She was shocked at what she had just heard. Her heart was pounding ... he had apologized ... he wanted to find her. She felt weak and had trouble breathing. She wanted to bolt out of the room and go to him. She felt someone staring at her and looked across the table to see Hunt watching her quizzically. She looked down at the pile of cookies on her plate, looked back up at Hunt blankly, put the plate on the buffet, and walked like a zombie to sit down. Hunt shook his head, and got a cup of coffee to keep himself awake.

Brax walked determinedly into the conference room and took the chair next to Liam. He pulled folders out of his briefcase. Liam's secretary gave him some papers to sign; he nodded curtly and signed the documents in a flourish with his Mont Blanc pen.

Robb, sitting with Hunt, watched Brax. That bastard pisses me off, he thought. He's convinced that everything he does is so damn important, or at least he wants the world to think it is. He looked over at Diana across from him. Diana returned his look blandly, not acknowledging his presence. He looked down at her fingers and noticed she was doing a rather suggestive movement with her pen and fingers. Robb swallowed a laugh, which came out as a snort. Diana looked innocently around the room and turned to talk to Louis, who had seated himself at the end of the table opposite Brax. Robb gave up trying to talk to anybody and looked over his board packet.

Kimberly, having arrived late, was pleased to find the one available seat next to Louis. She slid quietly into the chair, pushing it slightly back from the table in order to cross her legs. She pretended to study her board packet.

Louis was looking at his board materials but his mind was miles away, mulling over the last two weeks since Vi had gone home to her parents. He fully expected her to be back at their house when he returned that first evening. But she was not there.

He called her parents and got Vi's mother, Aggie. Her voice was very concerned, almost apologetic. She said Vi was in her room and refused to talk to anyone. She kept asking Louis what happened. Louis had hedged on the answer, not wishing to share all that had taken place with his mother-in-law. He said they had had a slight misunderstanding and he would call in the morning and come over to get Vi.

When he called, after rearranging two early meetings, Aggie's voice had a different tone. No, he didn't need to come over; Vi was going to stay with her parents for a while, good-bye.

Repeated calls brought more frosty replies and Louis had not called back in a week. He brooded over this turn of events, as they were not in his plans. Vi's little tantrum was becoming a big inconvenience to his home life and social life. Louis clasped his hands in front of his handsome troubled face. As he looked down he caught sight of a good looking and familiar pair of legs. He looked at Kim and nodded hello, wondering how much she knew about Vi and her return to Fruit Hill.

"Louis, how nice to see you. For once we come to one of these meetings without needing a snow plow," she dimpled innocently.

Louis, in a foul mood because of Vi, snapped, "To bring you up to speed, I have been to one meeting in the snow and this one, which is not in the snow."

Kimberly, knowing full well the reason for his bad temper, kept the conversation light as she swung her arched foot back and forth invitingly.

"Louis, I need your expertise on a big decision I need to make fast."

Louis looked wary and puzzled. "What and why?"

"I've put a hold payment on a wonderful carriage house

on Manning Street and I have twenty four hours to make up my mind before it goes on the open market. You have more knowledge than anyone I know about real estate in Rhode Island. Would you please come and look at it and tell me what you think? I don't want to make a mistake. I've always longed to live on the East Side and this seems perfect."

Louis cocked an eyebrow skeptically and answered nastily, "Not the Highlands in East Greenwich? I seem to remember you couldn't move Mr. MacComber into that suburb fast enough."

Kimberly smiled at Louis, swallowing the sharp retorts on the tip of her tongue. "I made a mistake marrying Willis. I also realized that the suburbs are not for me. You know we divorced. The house has been sold. I'm moving back to Providence and would appreciate your help and advice," she said softly, looking at him wistfully.

Louis took a deep breath and felt some of the past two weeks' tension drain away.

"Oh, okay, Kim, let's look at it after the meeting."

"Thank you. I really appreciate your taking the time." She squeezed his arm and turned again to study her board packet.

Louis gazed at her in suspicious amazement. What's she up to? Kim is never nice and quiet. She needs my advice, yeah right ... Since we've been kids she's been telling me how to run my life and trying to manage everything ... her way ... now she needs my advice. I should be on my guard but I'm almost too tired to care, not that I'll let her know that.

Brax looked up from his letter signing and locked eyes with John. They stared at each other. They had not talked since the surprise encounter in St Croix. Nor had they talked in St. Croix. Brax had recognized the woman John was with, a wealthy widow from New York. If the woman recognized Brax she did not acknowledge it; she kept talking to John in a low voice about the lovely view and seated herself with her back to Brax on the other terrace. Brax dashed into his room, phoned for a car and hustled Lisabet away from the hotel. He convinced her that a tour of the island and lunch in Christiansted was a wonderful way to wind up the trip before getting on the plane that afternoon. This surprised and pleased Lisabet; she had been trying to get him to do this the whole week.

Brax smirked and laughed silently. John smiled conspiratorially and gave a wave of his hand, the good old boy network. Brax said, "Shall we start this meeting? Do I have a motion to approve the minutes of the February meeting? Any discussion?"

"Approve."

"Second."

Robb looked around the room noticing some people were seated in different places than usual. John always sat where he could be in eye contact with Brax. But Louis had moved over to the opposite side of the table, away from the door. And Kimberly had perched herself next to Louis. That's interesting. Is she trying him on for size too? Anna looked pale and worried; Sarah was almost sulking; and Whip, as usual, looked like he had a poker up his ass. Robb turned his attention to Liam giving his president's report.

Diana's thoughts drifted. She tried to concentrate on the meeting but her discussion with Sweets about David van Dorn brought back memories of the summer she and Robb broke up and he married Helene.

She had known David all her life. He was a good-looking kid with quite a reputation with the girls, and she liked him. He was a sailing buddy of her brother Mac and their families had known each other for generations on Azimuth Point.

One night that summer Diana was sitting on the yacht club porch in the dark, a little tight from too many gin-and-tonics, when David sauntered by and stopped in front of her chair. He smiled down at her in the bright moonlight and asked, "What's this beautiful girl doing alone on Saturday night?" She hooked her bare toe under the cuff of his Patagonia shorts and drew him toward her, saying, with a beguiling smile and soft hiccup, "Well, I'm not alone now."

He sat down and she swung tanned bare legs onto his lap. He absently played with her toes as he nursed his drink and looked at the moonlight rippling on the ocean. Loud conversation intermingled with spurts of raucous laughter could be heard from the far end of the porch. The bar was full of sun-burned, soused, sailors, pungent with salt and sweat, exuber-antly extolling the day's successes and failures.

Diana said she was going to get another drink. David, real-izing she didn't need another drink, asked her to wait awhile 'til he finished his and he would get them both another drink. She agreed and in a few minutes she had passed out and was lightly snoring. David put his drink down, picked up Diana in his arms and quietly carried her off to his car. He took her home to *The Haven*, knowing it would not be a problem get-ting into her house undetected; her parents were with his par-ents on the New York Yacht Club cruise in Maine.

Diana woke up the next morning with a splitting head-ache, happy to be alone in the house and to not be volun-teering at the hospital. The realization that David took her home, undressed her and put her to bed made her smile. She stretched naked in the bed and laughed out loud. The noise hurt her head so much she decided that maybe a Corona and lime might be just the thing for breakfast.

Lying nude on the bed in the streaming morning sun and listening to gulls and the waves on the beach awakened a yearning for release from the tension she had been holding tight inside since walking away from Robb. She ignored the nagging feeling within all day. Later, lying on the sand in the hot sun she became aroused, and dashed into the ocean. Re-turning home that afternoon she took a cold shower and sat on the porch drinking wine as darkness descended.

She slowly rocked in the old green wooden cane-backed chair, watching shadows lengthen on the gray porch floor. Back and forth, back and forth, pouring yet another glass of wine. Ultimately darkness wrapped silently around her. She stood up, left the refuge of her porch and walked down the road to David's family's guesthouse.

He opened the door, held his hand out to her and slowly drew her into the moonlit living room. The sex was raw and quick and on the floor, and then again awhile later on his bed. In the beginning, she was the aggressor; she initiated what-ever, whenever and however it was to be done and her release was carnal. But by the time summer drew to a close the lust had evolved into a soothing intimacy that helped heal the terrible wound in her heart. And David had mastered a skill few men ever felt essential; he learned how to bring a woman to ecstasy. They parted with hugs that fall, sharing a summer secret and great fondness for each other that had grown into a strong friendship over the years.

This would be hard to explain to Robb, she thought, not that I would ever think of sharing that part of my past with him. And blabbing to Sweets was not the smartest thing I've ever done. She will be on me like a burr to find out how much really happened, not that I will tell ...

"Dr. Manning, the medical staff report?"

"Huh?" uttered Diana coming out of her reverie.

"Welcome back, Diana."

"I beg your pardon, Braxton, as far as I know I have been sitting right here since the beginning of the meeting," Diana answered sweetly, then continued, "I will give the medical staff report in Dr. Simpson's absence in a moment. What I was thinking about was the funeral we all, or at least some of us, will attend on Thursday and wondering what we, as a board, should or could do in Chip's name for the Simpson family? Needless to say, many of us here in the community, and those who took care of Chip the night of the accident, are devastated by his death and want to do something. I'm not sure what would be appropriate. Maybe it's too soon, but I strongly feel the board should do something," she finished magnanimously.

Brax, slightly taken aback at Diana's quick retort, remained quiet as the rest of the board, except Louis, discussed what should be done in Chip Simpson's memory. Even Kimberly joined in, saying that in a case like this, with the death of the grandson of one of East Meridian's favorite doctors, as well as doing something for all the other youngsters still recovering from the accident, the bank would probably want to be involved.

Robb had a hard time keeping his face straight as the meeting careened out of Brax's control. The board, glad to be talking about anything other than the atrium hot potato, started throwing out all sorts of ideas.

Good save, Diana, Robb thought. From the look on her face Chip Simpson was the last thing she was musing about; nevertheless she sure threw Brax a curve ball with that judicious answer. Brax was getting angry with the amount of time being taken up with the Simpson discussion, but was at a loss as to how to end it.

John cleared his throat very loudly, proclaiming that Diana had indeed brought the board something to think about. And perhaps she could talk with the Simpson family after the funeral and get their feeling as well as ideas as to what would be an appropriate memorial for Chip. In the meantime, considering the many things on the agenda, could she please give the medical report?

Diana smiled nicely at John, "Of course."

Robb gave Diana a barely perceivable wink and looked down at the medical staff report in front of him. Suddenly he was exhausted with it all: the guilt of knowing Helene's secret and wondering what to do about it, wanting to be with Diana, the stress of sneaking around and the damn atrium. If he started more commotion about it, would Louis Tedisco take the Providence Project away from his firm? Why did he even care what happened to this hospital? For once he ignored his dead ancestor, little Emily Wells, whispering in his ear that it was up to him to continue the family tradition of governing this hospital. He couldn't stand being in the room one minute longer or he would explode. He gathered up his papers and briefcase and quietly left the room.

Hunt looked at him quizzically and Diana thoughtfully watched him leave.

Brax, watching Robb's early departure, could hardly contain his delight. He wondered if John had somehow gotten to that prick of a son-in-law and shut him up. He watched Hunt, hoping that he would leave with Robb and they'd both resign. That would be the last he'd have to hear from those two, championing the rights of the townspeople and what is best for the hospital. If I worried about the people in the town and what they think, nothing would get done; I know what's best for this town *and* best for this hospital.

****

"Mommy...."

"What, Pumpkin?" Diana asked distractedly.

"Marianne put a big snake in my car box."

"A snake!" Diana whirled around to look at her son. Jamie's little chin was quivering and his eyes were filled with tears. She sat down on a kitchen chair and took him in her arms.

"A real snake?"

"Yes, and now I can't play with my cars ever again," he sobbed into her neck. "Marianne said if I ever opened the box again it would get me."

"Are you sure it's a real snake?"

"I told you it's a real snake," he bellowed.

"Yes, yes," she soothed him, "it isn't that I don't believe you. I'm just trying to figure out what to do. I'm not too fond of snakes."

"You have to get rid of the snake and wash all my cars," he whined. "I hate snakes, they're scary."

"Precisely why your sister did that I'm sure," Diana murmured to herself. "All right, come on; I'll find something to put the snake in and we'll go get it out of your NASCAR box."

"It's really big, Mommy. You betta get a suitcase or some-thin'."

"Jamie, you have been in Rhode Island too long," laughed Diana. "The words are pronounced *better* and *something*. A suitcase? Why would I need a suitcase?"

"I told you it's a BIG snake; why don't you believe me?" he cried in frustration, stamping his feet.

"Now, Jamie, we don't need any temper tantrums. I'll get the snake out of your box and we will wash all your cars. This should do it...." she mused, pulling a large T.J.MAXX shopping bag out of Mildred's cache of used paper goods.

"Mommy, that's not big enough. And ya need a top!" he shrilled.

"Jamie," Diana answered sternly, "I've had enough of this!" Then more softly, "I know you don't like snakes. You can stay down here and I'll go up and get rid of the snake. Go into the living room and sit on the sofa with Inky and look at one of your books. I'll be back in a minute.

Nothing like a day in the lives of twins, and one twin when I find her will get a talking to from me...." she muttered darkly, marching up the stairs to her son's room. Walking briskly into the bedroom she headed for the large toy box that housed all of Jamie's beloved cars and trucks and lifted open the top. Looking into the box she saw an enormous snake.

Diana screamed, which seemed to disturb the snake because it raised his head to look at her. Diana slammed down the top and ran out of the room, closing the door behind her with a bang. Leaning against the doorjamb, shaking and breathing heavily, she tried to figure out what to do. She remembered reading that snakes could squeeze out of small places, and was terrified that at this moment it was trying to get out of the box and then would slip under the door. Not that there was much she could do about it but at least she would know where it was, or where it was heading. She looked up and saw Jamie and the dog peeking at her from the top of the stairs.

"Jamie, you're right. That is a very big snake. Please go down and bring up mommy's cell phone," she quavered, trying not to scare the pale little boy any more than he already was. Jamie and the dog returned with the phone and gave it to Diana.

"Jamie, dear, I want you to go downstairs and wait by the door. When David or a policeman comes you can open the door and let them in. Then tell them where I am, okay? Honey, everything will be fine. You go downstairs and wait for them."

Diana frantically punched in David's phone number, praying he was home. He answered and said he would be right there. Then Diana called the police. She had almost as much trouble convincing them, as Jamie did her—that it was a very big snake and no, it did not belong to them.

David arrived and took the stairs two at a time. "Are you okay? You look like you've seen a ghost."

"A large snake is much more terrifying than anyone I can think of visiting from the other side."

"How big is this snake?"

"Humm, same question I asked Jamie and the police asked me. Believe me, it is a big snake, like one of those things we used to see on the National Geographic TV shows."

"How did it get in the house?"

"Jamie said that Marianne put it there."

"Well, the plot thickens, but if the snake is as big as you say, where would she get it and how could she manage to get it into the house?"

"My questions exactly. The child has always been inventive; she and her friend Calvin are always up to no good, but this takes the cake."

"Are you feeling better? You're not so white."

"Yes, well, help is on the way...."

"MOMMMY!!! MOMMMY! Grammie is here. Can I let her in?"

"Oh, dear God in Heaven. Just what I need, my mother...." and Diana dissolved in weak laughter.

"You're right, this should be interesting," David said.

"Yes, Jamie, let Grammie in, and tell her I will be right there, okay?"

At that very moment, loud sirens could be heard approaching the house. Diana and David crossed the hall to look out the window. They watched in horror as three police cars, the rescue truck and two fire engines raced up the circular drive spraying gravel all over the lawn, and screeched to a halt in front of the house. All sorts of uniformed men and women leapt out of the vehicles, armed with riot gear, nets, stun guns, poles, and fire hoses and dashed onto the porch followed by medics with stretchers. From below Diana heard Jamie call out, "MOMMY, I think Grammie's dead."

Robb and Diana were lying in bed in the cabin the next afternoon, he roaring with laughter and she pelting him with handfuls of M&M's. Choking he chortled, "You must be making this up...."

"I am not!"

"Well, I don't remember seeing anything in the paper this morning about your mother's demise, so I gather reports of her death were greatly exaggerated."

"She just fainted."

"I see...."

"You might see, but at the time it was impossible to figure out what the hell was going on! David and I ran down the stairs and it was bedlam. Jamie was crying, my mother was sprawled on the floor with two medics working on her and the dog was barking his head off. The officer in charge kept asking me where the perp was and outside the police were cordoning off the house, not letting Mildred or Lisle inside. Mildred was about to hit the officer over the head with her purse and Lisle was mumbling and drooling and looked like she had a stroke."

"Okay. I'll bite. Why weren't Mildred and Lisle in the house and why did Lisle look like she was a victim of a stroke?"

"Mildred had been at Stop and Shop marketing and Lisle had been at the dentist."

"Ah yes, novocaine. It will do it every time. I know I'm going to hate myself for asking, but what happened next?"

"I showed the police the box where the snake was or at least where I thought it still was, the medics revived my Mother, who then of course was furious when she came to, and David went to look for Marianne and Calvin. I convinced the police that Mildred and Lisle were part of the household and they were allowed into the house. The two of them and my mother only added to the confusion as I tried to explain to all of them what had happened. They eventually calmed down and the hunt was on for more snakes. I don't know why, but for some reason the house was searched for more snakes. Then the police wrapped a net and straps around the toy chest and carted it off to the police station. The other officers were still milling around when they got a call that a family named Willowby had just reported that a visiting snake, and a prize snake at that, was missing."

"Willowby? Simon and Claudia here on the Point?"

"I also began to see the light. I just couldn't figure out how they had done it. To make a long story endless, Calvin's uncle, Peter Willowby, and a friend on his way up from New York came to visit and have lunch with Calvin's parents. The friend was a snakeologist who was going to deliver a bunch of snakes to the zoo in Providence."

"A snakeologist?"

"Whatever they're called ... anyway, Marianne and Calvin were in the yard when he arrived. The visitor was delighted the kids were so interested and showed them all the snakes, including one that was very tired and almost comatose because it had just eaten some ghastly rat or something. The kids thanked him and went off on their bikes.

While riding around the Point they hatched this plot to scare the pants off Jamie. So they came back, opened the unlocked car and got the cage with the almost-comatose snake, snuck it up the backstairs of our house and dumped it out of its cage and into the toy box. Then they got Jamie and told him there was a surprise in the car box. Well, it was a surprise all right. They went off down the stairs screaming with laughter, and sped away on their bikes and Jamie came to get me."

"Why is it you have all the fun? You dash around in a white coat carving up people's insides, play hide and seek with a large snake in your very own house and have disaster teams gather at the drop of a hat. Speaking of that, why did all those police, fire and rescue crews arrive for one snake?"

"I asked the same thing. The officer said they rarely get calls from the Point and since this one was in the middle of the day and everybody was in the station houses it was decided to have a practice run and send the whole kit and caboodle. Claudia Willowby was thrilled to see them, too."

"So the outcome was?"

"Marianne and Calvin are grounded. The snake was caged and delivered to the zoo. The kids have to write an essay about the terrible thing they did and go to the police and fire stations, read the essays and apologize for all the trouble they caused. Jamie doesn't want the snaky box back in the house, so Marianne and Calvin have to earn money to buy new cars and a new box. We even had to move Jamie into another bedroom because he was having nightmares. Yes, I do lead an exciting life," Diana agreed, stretching her arms out in front of her. Then looking at her hands, she sighed, "I wish I could have long fingernails with sexy red polish."

"Like Kimberly's?"

"On second thought, maybe the well-scrubbed, blunt cut is better for me. Did you see her putting the move on that Tedisco guy at the meeting? She got him to agree to do something with her. I was sitting close enough to get that much out of their conversation."

"I noticed you obscenely gesturing with your pen, and at the same time eavesdropping on another conversation."

"I wasn't eavesdropping, I was observing my fellow mankind. Robb, why did you walk out of the meeting?"

Robb sighed. "I got overwhelmed by it all: us, Helene, the hospital politics. And as I listened to the useless reports, I got more and more fed up and was ready to explode, so I left."

"Do you want to talk about it now?" she asked softly.

"Nope, not now."

During Diana's snake story and their subsequent conversation Robb had rescued the M&M's she had thrown at him and had been dropping them in strategic places on her lithesome form. Running his fingers gently over her soft skin around all the M&Ms, he whispered, "I just want to make your life even more exciting."

"Oh, yeah? How will you do that?"

Kissing her belly Robb murmured, "By eating some chocolate."

APRIL

Kimberly MacComber paused in front of the open French doors to admire the view and congratulate herself on finding this wonderful carriage house on Providence's East Side. Spring had come early to the city. The ivy-covered walled-in garden was a profusion of narcissi, violets, daffodils, jonquils and tulips savoring the late afternoon sun. The two flowering white dogwood trees with myrtle at their base provided dappled shade on either side of a softly bubbling fountain. She did a little dance and whirled around with the joy of it all. Louis was on his way over for dinner, again.

They never talked about Vi or why he was seeing Kimberly almost every other night. She purposely didn't pressure him into talking about the situation and did her utmost to offer a quiet retreat, candlelit, catered dinners and lively conversation. Kim realized this was probably her last chance to get Louis back where she wanted him—offering marriage.

She had been stupid to let him go in the first place, but she was young, and yearned for another existence. Louis had been her boyfriend for years. Their first sex was with each other and it had been good and hot from the beginning. While they were having sex in every car or empty closet they could find, their respective mothers, pretending to ignore the obvious sexual vibes, prayed nightly to the Virgin Mary that Kimberly would not get pregnant.

Kimberly, not wanting to get pregnant either, put her faith not in prayer but in the local office of Planned Parenthood. She was on the pill. She enjoyed the sex immensely and was in love with Louis. But ten years ago the last thing she wanted was to be married to an Italian with a huge meddling family and required attendance at endless pasta dinners. She wanted out of the neighborhood and that life.

So she married a young man she met at the bank named Willis MacComber. Kimberly's parents, Peg and Jack Keegan, were mystified by Kimberly's choice for a husband and in awe of the MacCombers. The MacCombers were horrified by Kimberly and ignored the Keegans. Willis's mother, a lady of strict Episcopalian upbringing, immediately took over the nightly praying that Kimberly would not get pregnant. With exceedingly well-bred smiles they bided their time, keeping Kimberly out of their lives with surgical precision.

Various members of the clan MacComber lunched with Willis at their clubs two or three times a week, always politely inquiring after Kimberly. The week before Thanksgiving, Christmas or Easter, flowers and presents would be delivered to the young MacComber's home with notes wishing them a happy holiday and to be sure to give their best to the Keegans when they joined them for their family dinner.

Willis, completely clueless about almost everything, especially his family's behavior toward Kimberly, was surprised when Kimberly told him she wanted a divorce. Kimberly realized she was never going to be accepted by the MacCombers, and after two years she was bored to death with Willis. Willis's father immediately hired the best divorce lawyer in Providence and with the understanding that Kimberly must never darken their door again, she was given a nice settlement and the house in East Greenwich.

Within six months Willis was engaged to the childhood friend that his mother had picked out for him, and Kimberly was climbing the corporate ladder at the bank.

In her wildest dreams Kimberly had never thought Louis would become so successful and rich. Now she wanted him back and Vi was playing right into her hands. If she pulled this off, Louis's family would be so furious that they would not want to have anything to do with her, which would be just fine.

She had played it cool and concerned these past weeks. She offered air kisses when he arrived and a sisterly hug when he left. But this morning she stopped taking her birth control pills. Nothing would reel him in faster than a bambino. Sooner or later he would make a move, maybe tonight. The moon was full and Louis had not had any sex in weeks.

****

Anna arrived at the hospital's outpatient surgery department surprised not to find Hank Lombardi there. He promised to help her in Admissions because she already paid to stay in the hospital for two days. Anna left the waiting room and walked out into the hall looking both ways, but there was no sight of Hank. Walking back into the room she heard her name being called.

"Mrs. Morgan, Mrs. Morgan?"

Anna called out, "I'm right here."

"Okay, come with me."

"It's Miss Morgan, not Mrs."

"Er, um, yes," the nurse grunted indifferently glancing at the papers on her clipboard.

"Miss Morgan," she continued, "whoever has come with you will take your clothes with them and they can bring them back when we give them a call from the recovery room as to when they can come pick you up. And...."

"And I think it would be expedient for you to read the in-

formation in front of you before giving me your bored reper-
toire," Anna replied tartly.

"What?"

"And is that the 'editorial we' you are referring to?"

"Huh?"

"You said 'we.' I must presume to assume you will not be
with me in the recovery room?"

"Ah, yes, I mean no, I won't be with you in the recovery
room."

"That's a definite relief," Anna replied, looking down her
nose at the tired and by now angry nurse. "Now will you please
pay attention to what is written down on the papers in front of
you or get me someone more educated than yourself."

"MISS MORGAN, for your information, I will be more
than happy to find someone more educated than myself!" The
nurse stomped out.

Anna folded her hands in her lap, her eyes filled with
tears. She was distressed. She had not meant to act like that.
She felt afraid and alone. There was nobody with her to take
her clothes and then come back to take her home and help
her recover. That's why she had asked Hank to make arrangements for her to have the lumpectomy at East Meridian even
though he had advised her to have the procedure in Providence. She wanted to stay in the hospital for two nights, even
though she had to pay for it herself. In two days she would be
strong enough to walk to her car and drive herself down Canton Avenue to her house. All that nurse had to do was take a
minute to read what was right in front of her.

Lizzie Perrini was mad, tired and fed up. She stalked into
the team leader's office and stood with her hands on her ample hips and growled, "There is an old bitch named Morgan
out there that somebody else had better deal with, because
I've had it!"

"What's wrong?"

"What's wrong? What's wrong? You've got me working
another shift; I've been up all night; I'm dead on my feet and
that old bag is uppity because I'm not educated enough! Why
can't this hospital hire enough staff? We're all so overworked

that everybody will leave or die of exhaustion."

Mary Patterson knew a meltdown when she saw one. "Lizzie, sit down here for awhile and take a break. I'll go talk to the patient. And you are right, the nurses are overworked. I really appreciate you working a double shift and I am so sorry I have to ask you to do it."

"Bullshit, Mary, we both know if I refuse to work this shift I'll get fired by Mona O'Shay, the Head Nurse from Hell. The only reason I'm staying here is I want to work in town near my kids. I could get a job in a minute in one of the out-of-town hospitals like almost half the staff has done already. But ... oh ... damn. I'm too tired to care at this point. But let me tell you, the idea of a union is looking better and better."

"Oh, Lizzie, that's not going to solve anything."

"What else can we do? Nobody will listen. Liam keeps saying we have to cut expenses. He has fired fifteen good administrative people, nurses are leaving left and right and he's building an atrium!"

"He doesn't want to; the board does."

"That bitch O'Shay is as popular as a skunk at a garden party. Why did Liam hire her? And he keeps giving her more and more power. And you know as well as I do, if you say one word against her or don't agree with her you are in serious trouble."

"I know," Mary sighed. "We are all caught in the middle. She keeps us away from the floors with her endless meetings. By the end of the day everything is in an uproar and the next shift inherits the mess. But, you know," she replied thoughtfully, "many of us are not so sure Mona is taking orders from Liam. She charges ahead not letting him know what she is doing, almost as if there is someone else directing traffic. In any case, nobody wants to talk to Liam."

"God, I just want to go home and go to bed. I don't know what aches more, my feet or my head," Lizzie moaned. "How do they expect us to take care of very sick people when we can't even think straight?"

"Lizzie, sit here for a few minutes. I'll talk to your patient and calm her down," Mary said, getting out of her chair and straightening her white uniform coat. A coat Mona O'Shay had decided all team leaders should wear. Actually, Mary thought, it was a nice touch and made them look professional. Mary stopped outside the treatment bay. She knew Anna Morgan was a trustee and she would probably have lots of complaints. Taking a deep breath she pulled back the curtain. The room was empty. The patient had left.

****

Anna slowly climbed the three stairs up her porch and unlocked the back door. Walking into the kitchen she sat down at the small table in the bay window overlooking her backyard. The house was cold. Anna had turned down the furnace because she thought she would be in the hospital for two days. Putting her purse on the table in front of her she gazed out the window. The sunny garden, ablaze with yellow daffodils planted lovingly by the previous owner, was a stark contrast to the chill of the kitchen.

Anna was numb. Her mind was blank. In the distance she heard the phone ring and ignored it. She just sat. Later on the phone rang again, startling her. She looked up at the clock on the wall and was surprised to see she had been sitting for over two hours. And she still had her coat on. Her stomach growled and she remembered she had not eaten anything since last evening. I should make some tea and a sandwich, she thought. But she did not move. She sat at her breakfast table overlooking the spring garden.

She heard a noise on the porch and looked over at the door just as Hank Lombardi knocked on the window. Anna, surprised to see him, got up and opened the door.

"Hank, I … I…."

"Anna, I'm so sorry … ," he started.

"No, no, I'm sorry; I must have caused you a lot of trouble. But nobody knew that I wasn't an outpatient and the atmosphere was so tense and the nurses looked so tired. Is there something wrong at the hospital?"

"Yes, there is lots wrong at the hospital. I've been trying

to tell you that for a year. And no, you didn't cause me any trouble. Someone else is causing all the trouble and I have a suspicion who it is, but we won't go into that right now. That's not why I'm here."

"Why are you here?"

"First of all I brought us some lunch," he smiled, holding up a large paper bag. "As I remember, you like tea with lemon. And you sure need something hot. It's warmer outside than in here."

"I turned down the furnace because ... I ... I," Anna said, her voice faltering.

"Anna, go turn up the furnace, hang up your coat, get a sweater and come back and eat some lunch. I have a plan you might be interested in!"

Relief washed over her as she rose to put her coat in the closet and fetch a sweater. Hank cared about her well-being. It had been a long time since anybody had given her a thought.

****

Helene looked out the window of the train as it raced through Connecticut toward New York. The countryside was lush with the soft greens of spring. The redbuds and dogwoods were in full bloom and the azaleas were a riot of whites, pinks, lavenders and reds. Crocuses and daffodils filled gardens with white, purple and yellow color. Helene felt like the spring she was looking at, blossoming and born again. She also felt trepidation. This was a big step toward a decision she was going to have to make, one way or the other. Not that anyone in my family notices anything that I do anyway, she mused. Robb drove her to the station and wished her a good time on her shopping trip, as if she zipped off to New York shopping all the time. He never even asked where she was staying. She hadn't spoken to her parents in a month and Miranda called from school last week begging permission to spend the summer in France with her roommate's family. Of course Robb said it was a wonderful opportunity and gave her permission, without talking it over with Helene.

As the train approached the outskirts of the city Helene felt a thrill of anticipation. Selina promised to meet Helene at the station and whisk her off to a wonderful bistro for a long, wine-soaked lunch. And later that evening there was a supper party at Selina's apartment, with people that Helene met when they visited Selina in Providence. In all my life nobody has ever wanted to whisk me anywhere for lunch or anywhere else, she thought. I went to Guatemala with Robb because we had just been married. Robb never asked me if I wanted to go there and I sure wasn't whisked. It was more like dragged. But I never said I didn't want to go either. The train pulled into Penn Station and Helene's heart swelled with joy when she spotted Selina waving at her from the platform

****

Brax Montgomery rang the doorbell of what he always thought of, as his penthouse on Central Park West, except it was really Bitsy's. The lovely old fourteen-room apartment had been in Bitsy's family for years. Bitsy inherited it when her parents had died over twenty years ago. Pompously he awaited the door to be opened by Rollins the butler. Bitsy, an only child, and her parents were on a whirlwind tour through Europe celebrating Bitsy's graduation from collage when a tour bus smashed into their chauffeur-driven Mercedes on the winding road leading into Monaco. Bitsy's parents and the chauffeur were killed in the crash and Bitsy spent two months in Princess Grace Hospital. Heartbroken at losing her parents, her recovery was slow.

After returning to New York she was overwhelmed by the decisions to be made, and at a complete loss as how to manage the tremendous fortune left to her by her parents' unfortunate and early demise. Braxton Montgomery, a vice president in Bitsy's father's firm, was only too happy to help.

Older than Bitsy by twelve years, he knew an opportunity like this would never pass his way again. Within six months they were engaged and that summer married at Bitsy's family home, Beachbound, on Azimuth Point. Brax spent the summer in New York, ecstatic with the clout he could wield with Bitsy's money. To Brax's relief Bitsy spent the summer on Azimuth Point reveling in her new marriage and, to her delight, immediate pregnancy.

"Good evening, Rollins."

"Good evening to you, sir. I trust you had a nice day?"

"Yes. Yes. Busy as usual. Where is Mrs. Montgomery?"

Rollins, momentarily taken aback by the question because he, as well as his employer, paid scant attention to Bitsy and had to think where was Mrs. Montgomery. Being a well-trained servant he did not register surprise and quickly answered, "In her sitting room, sir."

Brax handed his coat to the butler and headed toward the stairs without further comment. Rollins wondered, walking to the closet to hang up the coat, if the ensuing conversation would result in Bitsy again taking her meals on a tray in her darkened bedroom for the next week.

Striding into the sitting room he sneered, "Eleanor!" Brax kicked the door shut behind him, his shoe making a black mark on the eggshell colored paint. Bitsy looked up from the book she was reading. She felt a flicker of fear at his appearance and his use of her real name. She raised her left hand to her neck, fingering the knotted strands of her grandmother's priceless pearls. Her large engagement ring caught a shaft of the waning afternoon sun, casting a blinding ray on Brax's face. He flung his hand forward against the light and stepped further into the room. She sat motionless, her large blue eyes following him quietly as he advanced toward her. Her thin blue-veined hands rested on the necklace as she raised her pale face to look at him towering over her.

"Get me the deed to the land on Route 1," he demanded.

Confused, she tried to think what he meant. " Route 1? I...." her mind raced. What was he talking about? She looked down at the book in her lap as if the answer could be found there, her soft blonde curls touched with gray falling over her face.

"Oh, for Christ's sakes, that stupid place you yap about all the time, riding horses ... in the morning sun and the evening with your beloved parents."

"Oh, Auntie Edith's land," she exclaimed excitedly, her face suffused with color. "I didn't realize what you meant." Forgetting that he not only didn't care about her memories, in fact he hated her memories, she continued reminiscing happily. "Mama and I had such lovely rides on that beautiful land early in the morning. The sun would be just rising Mama would hug me and we would be off racing to...."

"Yeah, no doubt you and Mama would win all the blue ribbons at the Dublin Horse Show. Now get me the deed. I haven't got all night to listen to your drivel."

"Auntie Edith's land was left to Ben and I'm the trustee until he is twenty one...." she said seriously, her voice trailing away.

"Yes, I know you're the trustee, and for the life of me I can't imagine why she put you in charge. Anyway, for the last time go get me the deed. That land could play a very important part in a business deal I'm working on."

"That land is for Ben. Auntie Edith wanted him to have it and he wants to put it in the Land Trust; you know that."

He yanked her out of the chaise lounge. Her book fell on the floor and her foot caught the leg of the side table, tipping it over and sending a vase of flowers and her cup of tea smashing to the floor. "Look at the mess you've made. I've had enough of this," he growled, shaking her. Too late she realized her mistake. She should have listened and done what he wanted. Brax twisted her wrists painfully. "Why must you always make me mad? Can't you once, just once behave and do the right thing? No. You force me to become angry. Now let's try this again and see if you are not so retarded that you can't understand. GET ME THE DEED!!! Somebody has to make the money around here."

Does that mean he has spent all mine, she thought dully, tears coursing down her face. I must put myself mentally in another place...and then do what he wants so he won't go after Ben, she agonized. "The deed is in Rhode Island ... in ... in ... I think Uncle Rutherford has ... all the paper work," she gasped. "I can go up and get it this weekend, or tomorrow ...

tomorrow … if you want… I can go tomorrow."

"That's better," Brax said throwing her on the chaise lounge. "Really, Bitsy, I wish we could live a sane life and you wouldn't cause such foolish commotions," he said, wiping his hands and walking out of the room, quietly closing the door behind him.

Rollins hung up the house phone and said, shrugging to his wife, "Mrs. Montgomery called. She won't be coming down for dinner and doesn't want a tray either."

****

"Aggie."

"Yeah, Louie."

"How is Vi?"

"Good."

"Put her on…."

"She's not here."

"Oh, where is she?"

"At work."

"Work? She's working? Where?"

"At the restaurant."

"She's at the restaurant? Working!" He almost hollered in disbelief.

"So what's the matta with that? The wife of the rich and snooty Louis Tedisco, lately of the East Side, shouldn't lower herself to work in her own father's restaurant on the hill?" Aggie said.

"No, no, I didn't mean that, Aggie. I'm just surprised. I mean, I thought she didn't feel well and…." His voice trailed off, but he did mean that and the image of his wife leading people to their tables was more than he wanted to contemplate. Or worse, maybe she is waiting tables, serving food to his business friends. Vi sure is putting it to me, he thought.

"Aggie, I wanted Vi to know that I'm going to Europe on business for a couple of weeks and if she needed me to call the office. They will know how to find me."

"Europe huh, some family business?"

"No, Aggie, I don't have any business with the family. I've managed to avoid that, at least so far," he retorted sarcastically.

"When are ya leavin'?"

He glanced down at his daybook. "I'm taking a flight out of Green to New York right after the hospital meeting on the 21st. Then I'm on a night flight on Lufthansa to Frankfurt."

"You building a hospital?"

"No, I'm a trustee. It's a trustees meeting."

"Well la-de-da. Do ya think they know your wife works in a restaurant?"

Louis chose to ignore that barb. "Aggie, please give the message to Vi, okay?"

"Yeah."

****

Anna Morgan sealed the envelope containing her letter of resignation from the Board of Trustees of East Meridian Hospital with a sigh of relief. She was fed up with the commotion about the atrium and knew she would need time to heal. Sitting back in her chair she glanced at the pile of luggage and boxes next to the front door, wondering how she had found the energy to pack it all. The last two weeks had been exhausting. The lumpectomy would be done in Providence. Anna would stay in Hank's friend Amelia's apartment at Iris House on the East Side for six months. Amelia was a widow spending time in California with her children to see if she wanted to move there, and she needed someone to look after her cat and plants.

Hank also arranged for a nurse to bring Anna to the apartment after her operation and take care of her. Bless his heart, she thought. She felt such overwhelming gratitude her eyes filled with tears and she fumbled through her purse to find a handkerchief to blow her nose.

The doorbell rang. Anna got up to let in Mike, the young man Hank lined up to help her close up the house, drive her to Iris House and help her move in. Mike would check on her house a few times a week and bring Anna down to get her car as soon as she was able to drive. Anna set the new alarm system. Mike helped her into the limousine and suddenly she didn't feel so terrified by her cancer and the operation. As Hank says, I don't have to decide anything right now. Just one thing at a time; get myself healthy, then come back, or stay at Iris House and put my house up for sale. I've always liked those little old houses in Azimuth Point Village. I can afford one of those. Summer will be nice there, near the beach. Maybe I will even go somewhere warm in the winter, she thought with a thrill.

Mike backed out of Anna's driveway and drove up Canton Avenue past the hospital toward the highway to Providence, and Anna didn't even look back. She sat smiling, thinking about her many options. Clutching her handbag in her lap, she thought, what an old lady thing to do. I don't need to clutch at anything anymore. She put her bag down on the floor of the car and took a deep breath, threw back her head and laughed. I feel like Martin Luther King, free at last. Free at last!

****

Diana checked her watch for the fifth time and looked out the window of the tiny plane taking her to North Eleuthera Airport. When she left Providence for her medical convention in Miami, the last thing she had planned on was going to the Bahamas. But Robb called her the night before she was to come home, saying she must meet him in Harbour Island. "Where's that?" she asked, "and why should I meet you there?"

"It's paradise, a paradise for us. A friend of mine in Providence has a wonderful house on the island and we can have it for five days."

After telephone calls back and forth from Florida and Rhode Island, the matter was settled. Mildred and Diana's parents assured her a vacation in the Bahamas would be great for her and not to worry; the twins would either be in school or under the watchful eye of Lisle or Mildred, and the grandparents would check on them at least twice a day. Diana said a small prayer that Marianne would not pull another snake stunt. The plane banked for the landing and she saw Robb waving at her from the ground.

Lightly suntanned from the two days spent on the island, Robb hurried toward Diana and hugged her with such enthusiasm he lifted her off the sandy soil.

"Yikes, I can't breathe," she laughed. "You look wonderful and you smell like salt and the ocean."

"That's because I got out of the ocean, threw some clothes on and raced over here to get you. Are you trying to tell me I need a shower?"

"No, more like I want to go in the ocean and we can both smell like sea and salt."

"Sounds good to me. We can have a swim in the most beautiful turquoise water you have ever seen, shower, down a couple of rum cocktails and then you are in for a real treat," Robb told her as he grabbed her bag and headed toward a rusty island cab.

"I can just imagine what the real treat is," she giggled, climbing into the hot dusty car.

"Not what you think, my dirty-minded beauty," he leered. "After the sun goes down we will be off in my trusty golf cart to Ma Ruby's for her famous Cheeseburger in Paradise."

Diana looked at Robb skeptically, "Will Jimmy Buffet be there too?"

"No, he no be on island right now," joined in the cabdriver. "Maybe later this week he come on boat, I hear."

Diana looked at Robb in amazement. The cab slammed to a stop in a whirl of dust a few inches from the edge of the harbor. Robb opened the door, jumped out and reached back to help Diana out of the cab. Robb paid the cab driver; Diana looked around at the activity on the tiny dock.

Water taxies jockeyed around, competing for the first available space to off-load their passengers from Harbour Island headed for the airport, and pick up those just arriving to ferry them over to the island. Everything from lawnmowers to cartons of beets, cabbage, carrots, eggplant and tomatoes grown on Eleuthera along with cans of motor oil and big plastic bags of toilet paper were loaded on the little boats along with visitors.

The ride across the water to Harbour Island took five minutes and the same beehive of activity greeted them upon landing. One difference was a much grander town dock and well-kept air-conditioned vans waiting to take tourists to hotels and permanent island residents to their homes.

Robb helped Diana out of the water-taxi, shouldered her bag and steered her toward Reggie's Island Taxi. Diana, pink from the exertion, heat and excitement, settled herself with relief on the back seat of the cool van. She looked around with interest as the van sped off the dock and turned left, traveling out of the small village past slips full of boats at Valentine's Marina. The homes on the harbor were imposing and freshly painted. Gleaming white houses sported colorful island trims, and pale yellow, vibrant salmon and occasional cerulean houses were outlined in white. Masses of dazzling red, pink and orange bougainvillea spilled over walls surrounding these homes, and multi-colored hibiscus peeked around the entrances.

The van turned left to go across the island and smaller houses came into view. These had faded pink or blue paint with chips flaking off here and there. Each sported a small vegetable garden, a goat or two, wandering chickens and a huge TV satellite dish, indicating the economy of the island improved over the years since the rich and famous started to call it their own.

Diana, wide-eyed, glancing from side to side, realized they were driving on the left. "Robb, he's driving on the wrong side," she whispered.

"No, that's how they drive here," he whispered back.

"But this is an American car, the wheel is on the left."

"Most all of them are. Sure makes things more interesting, doesn't it? Wait until you start driving the golf cart!"

"I'll let that wait a day or so."

Diana fell against Robb as Reggie swerved the van to the right and headed down the beach road to the southern end of the island. Robb squeezed her tight and kissed the top of her nose.

Reggie looked in the mirror and smiled. Mr. Larry told him Robb would be using the big villa for a few days but he never mentioned a lady coming to visit. Well, he thought, not the first time this happened in paradise. Reggie slowed down and turned right at the Sea Haven sign, and slowly drove up the gently winding drive that led to the manor house.

Catching a glimpse of two smaller houses through the palm trees, Diana noticed a sign reading "Cirrus" and another reading "Crumpet," and asked, "Whose houses are those?"

"They're the guesthouses for Sea Haven. Larry and Lila are coming down next week with a group of friends for a house party and the overflow will stay in the little houses. But lucky us, we have the big house all to ourselves and it is beautiful. Wait 'til you see the view of the beach and ocean. The last two days I've been in a state of stupor or maybe in a stupor of a state. Anyway, I've spent hours looking and listening to the ocean and my bones are spaghetti. It's so different than the ocean at home, much more restful and peaceful."

"Well, believe me, I can use a bit of that after the winter I've had, or perhaps I should say we have had. And oh, yes ... NOOOO ... talking about the hospital! We're going to miss the April meeting and I don't care," Diana said seriously, shaking her finger at Robb.

"That's okay with me, lady. What hospital? I don't know no hospital," he laughed and fell back against the seat as the van came to stop in front of the house. Diana got out of the van and looked at the imposing salmon-and-white two-story villa in wonder. "This is the most beautiful house I've ever seen."

Reggie agreed. "Mr. Larry wanted the best and that's what he got, even if it did take a couple of years to build and two more to get it right. It's one of the nicest houses on Harbour Island. Well, you folks have a nice evening'. I'll be back in the mornin' with Clara and TeeTee round 9 o'clock. Clara, she bring some fresh eggs for your breakfast. "Bye, now." Reggie got back into the van and waved.

"Clara? TeeTee? Somebody's going to make our breakfast? Which one does what? What kind of a name is TeeTee?"

"Clara does the cooking; TeeTee does the cleaning. And I

haven't a clue about her name. Ask her if you dare."

"What do you mean, if I dare?"

"You will get a twenty-minute explanation, none of which you will understand."

"Oh."

Diana threw her arms around Robb and kissed him gleefully. "This is so-o-o-o wonderful; thank you, thank you for arranging it. What a magnificent surprise. And this house, it's right out of Architectural Digest! I don't know what I want to do first, look around the house or dash into the ocean. I feel like I'm in the middle of a fabulous dream."

"You can do it all," Robb smiled, glad to see her so happy. "Let's go in the house and you can look around on the way to the master bedroom. It's on the first floor with an unbelievable view of the beach and ocean, and we have our own private pool." They had reached the wide, welcoming veranda and Robb put down her suitcase and unlocked the front door. Diana walked inside and gazed down the spacious hall to the glass doors and windows framing the gleaming white terrace and pool beyond. The pool seemed to hang in midair over the turquoise sea. She stood mesmerized. "What's holding it up in the air like that?" she uttered.

"It's an illusion. Listen and you can hear the waterfall at the edge of the pool down to the next level. Come on, I'll show you."

Diana followed him outside to the terrace shaking her head. "This is so exquisite, and there's another pool for the master bedroom?"

"Ah, yes, my lovely," he murmured taking her in his arms and nuzzling her neck. "And you are in charge of deciding what we shall do first. Your wish is my command."

"I would love to go in that beautiful water out there ... and then ... perhaps ... umm ... a treat?"

"You want something in paradise? A cheeseburger perhaps?" he asked in mock amazement.

"Well, I wasn't exactly thinking of the Jimmy Buffet kind, if you get what I mean," she said, as breathy as Marilyn Monroe, looking at him seductively.

He drew her into him, kissing her deeply.

****

Shaking, Bitsy held the phone in both hands. She must not break down while talking to Uncle Rutherford. Reflecting on her marriage, tears rolled down her face. She remembered how her life started to sink into a swamp of misery when she and her housekeeper, Agnes, who had been with Bitsy since she was born, returned to the apartment in the city after Labor Day. They found a butler named Rollins; a cook named Nora, married to Rollins; and two maids who came in daily. Brax had told Bitsy that a staff was really needed for their life together. He was quite pleased with them and knew she would be too.

Agnes stayed until the baby, a beautiful boy who looked like Bitsy, was born. He was named Benjamin after Bitsy's father. The day the English nanny arrived, Agnes asked Bitsy if she could please return to Azimuth Point. Bitsy was delighted with her new baby, but bewildered at the loss of control she was beginning to have over her life. She knew Agnes did not like Brax or the new household arrangements but she was not sure how to deal with the situation.

With a sad heart she bid Agnes goodbye with promises to visit during the spring, and assurances they would move to Azimuth Point for the whole summer on Memorial Day weekend. Bitsy rationalized that it would all work out after she got used to the baby and her new life.

Over the years it did work itself out, but not the way Bitsy ever imagined. Agnes saw the handwriting on the wall and when Bitsy and Benjamin came to Azimuth Point, Agnes strove to give them the kind of life Bitsy's parents would have wanted for her. To Agnes and Bitsy's relief, Brax rarely joined his family at Azimuth Point. He had announced with resounding authority that all of Bitsy's friends in New York and Azimuth Point were vacuous and their clubs and lives bourgeois. In actuality he probably recognized early on that Bitsy's friends, far wealthier and more sophisticated than he, did not like him.

Agnes encouraged Bitsy to see her friends during the summer months, a fact they never mentioned to Brax. Agnes also encouraged Bitsy to send Benjamin to boarding school much earlier than Bitsy wanted because they both knew the little boy was better off away from his vicious, controlling father.

Young Ben was now a junior at Harvard, Bitsy's father's alma mater, and rarely home. Bitsy adapted herself to an insular life to keep the peace and her sanity. She kept out of Brax's way in the apartment, gave up her volunteer work, lunched quietly with a few old friends in New York and lived for the summer at Azimuth Point. She knew Brax had many other women, which was a great relief; it kept him out of the house and away from her.

Then to her dismay, Brax started coming to the Point on weekends, bringing business friends from New York. He took great pleasure entertaining them at the golf and beach clubs he previously abhorred, a detail that seemed to have slipped his mind.

Through Bitsy's family's contacts he also joined the Hale Club in Providence. After two years he became the chairman of the Board of Trustees of East Meridian Hospital, a board he forced Bitsy to resign from years ago as he considered her work there meaningless.

Bitsy at times had massive panic attacks that left her wracked, soaking wet and helpless. She was terrified to admit this to anyone. Bitsy, the girl who had everything, was now a woman who lived a life of quiet desperation. She took a deep breath and called her uncle.

"Bitsy, my dear. It is so good to hear your voice. How are you?"

"I'm ... uh ... fine, Uncle Rutherford."

"How is New York this lovely spring day? And how is my favorite grandnephew doing at Harvard? We are so proud of him, your aunt and I. I suppose he'll be coming home for spring break soon."

"Uh, well he might visit one of his roommates for this vacation. We haven't really worked that all out...." Bitsy's voice trailed off.

"These youngsters, always off on a junket somewhere or another. I hope we'll see him this summer though."

"Yes, yes, he'll be at Azimuth Point ... I just don't know when. Er, um, Uncle Rutherford, speaking of Ben, that's why I'm calling."

"There's nothing wrong with Ben, is there?" he inquired.

"No, ah no, of course not. It's ... um ... this is kind of about Ben. Actually it's about the land that Auntie Edith left Ben. I ... I need a favor from you."

"Of course, my dear, anything."

"If Brax calls you and asks about the deed to that land would you please say you are looking it up for me and can't put your hands on it right now but will have it for me shortly?" she said in a rush.

Rutherford knowing that Bitsy knew full well that the paperwork was in a file right in Rutherford's law office, was silent for a moment. Then he went on, guardedly,

"Of course, Bitsy, it would take me a while to put my hands on that anyway. I could call Brax and tell him we are getting right on it, but it might take a while, if you like."

"Thank you so much," Bitsy sighed in relief. "I'll be up in a few weeks to ... um, talk to you about this...." she finished with a catch in her voice.

"Bitsy, um ... why don't you come up this weekend and stay with us? We could go out to dinner and to the theater. You know how much your Aunt Kitty loves to have you visit."

"Oh, no, I couldn't possibly come up right now ... I ... I have so much to do here. But I will come up in a few weeks," Bitsy wavered, her eyes filling up at the thought of her aunt and uncle seeing the bruises on her wrists.

Sensing the distress in her voice, Rutherford didn't want to upset her more. "Of course, my dear, you come visit as soon as possible and I'll give Brax a call tomorrow."

"Thank you, Uncle Ruffy, thank you. Goodbye," and Bitsy hung up.

Rutherford shook his head looking at the phone and slowly put it down. He was very concerned. Bitsy didn't sound right at all. She sounded sad and defeated. And she had not used her childhood nickname for him in years. Maybe Kitty was right; she had told him repeatedly over the last few years that something was wrong in that marriage, but he had brushed it off. He never wanted to believe anything could be wrong. Decidedly, he was not fond of Brax, but Bitsy seemed so happy in the beginning and she adored her son. Something *is* wrong and what is this business with Ben's inheritance all about and Bitsy pretending not to know where the deed is and wanting me to stall about it? I'd better get to the bottom of this and also talk to Kitty. I'll need her advice. Damn it all, I hate it when she is right.

****

Sarah James shoved her SUV in park and laid her head on the wheel, in agony. What am I doing? I should leave right now and go to the hospital trustees meeting. But she didn't want to go to the meeting. In fact she *never* wanted to go to another board meeting. What she wanted to do was see David. More than anything in the world she wanted to see David. The thought of seeing David had taken over her life since she had heard Diana and Sweets talking about him at the March trustees meeting.

For a month she had been going through the motions of her life feeling like a bystander, observing rather than taking part. She found herself standing in an aisle at Stop and Shop with an empty cart, staring into space thinking about David. At home the children vied for her attention, jumping up and down in frustration and shrilling at her, "Mommmeee, you're not listening to us!" She lay awake at night in their king-size bed positioning herself as far away from Bill as possible, her body taut, thinking about David. For the last month she had been barely able to function, she was so consumed with David.

She looked around the Azimuth Public Beach parking lot. It was a warm April day and many people walked the beach, enjoying the late afternoon waning sun. It would not be unusual for her to walk the beach either, she reasoned. It was also low tide. She craned her neck to see way down to the left where the Azimuth Point rocks jutted out, and calculated she had close to two hours before the incoming tide would make it too dangerous to come back around the rocky natural barrier that separated the families of Azimuth Point from the rest of the world.

I want to say I'm sorry that I yelled at him and I accept his apology. That won't take too long. His house is near the entrance to the Point. I won't have to walk far and I can be back long before high tide. You could call him, a voice said in the back of her head. Well, no I couldn't, she told the voice, because the number is unlisted. They all have unlisted numbers ... those snobs!

Sarah opened the door of her SUV. Putting on dark glasses and wrapping a scarf around her shiny blonde hair she locked the car with a flip and set off down the beach. She walked briskly on the hard-packed sand, then slowed down dawdling, to let a group of people with dogs and children get ahead of her and reach the rocks before she did, she guessed they would turn around and be on their way back, not watching when she slipped around the rocks onto the private Azimuth Point enclave.

She stopped and looked back at the group of people now chasing their children and dogs back towards the public beach. She waited for a wave to go out and then ducked under the overhang and hurried across the wet sand around the barrier rocks to Azimuth Point.

It hasn't changed much, she thought, looking down the row of imposing weathered shingled homes, some behind sand dunes, others with vast green lawns gently sloping down to stone walls or rose hip hedges bordering the sandy beach. On the horizon, just before the shoreline curved to the right, she could make out the Azimuth Point Beach Club. Looking at the panorama, a myriad of emotions ran through her. She took a deep breath and continued.

Sarah easily found the sandy path between the rocks to the road that separated the ocean front houses from the inland and riverfront houses. Pausing at the head of the path she looked up and down; no one was in sight. She hurried across to the small house on the other side of the road, unlatched the white gate and walked up the flagstone path to the van Dorn guesthouse. Standing on the porch in front of the door Sarah hesitated. She reached out, touching the "Sea Bass House" inscribed on the plaque below the salt-pitted brass knocker. She raised the knocker and rapped on the door. A dog started barking and someone walked toward the door. Her heart was in her throat.

The door opened and David looked at her quizzically. "Yes, may I help you?"

Sarah took off her sunglasses and stammered, "I ... I ... just wanted to...."

"Sarah! Sarah! For God's sake I didn't recognize you. I thought a movie star had arrived on my doorstep," he laughed. "Come in. Come in." He opened the door wide and the little dog started barking louder and dancing around their feet in a frenzy.

"Cynthia, stop that! She isn't used to company," he explained.

Sarah looked down at the dog and then at David. She hadn't the faintest idea what to say. David bent down and picked up the nervous dog and spoke soothingly to it. "Now, Cynthia, that's no way to greet a guest. I guess you and I have been alone too long out here."

Putting the dog down he reached out to Sarah. "Here, let me take your coat. Would you like some tea? I have actually taken to drinking tea this time of the afternoon. A bit too early to start on the booze," he laughed. "I don't have any latte, not that I would know how to make it anyway."

He took her coat, hung it on a hook in the hall and showed her into the living room. It was not as she remembered. The room seemed bigger and very welcoming. The sofas and chairs were covered in cheerful bright chintz. A fire was crackling in the fireplace. Piles of books and newspapers surrounded the chair in which David had obviously been sitting. An old blue sweater that Sarah remembered David wearing years ago was on top of a pillow in a small basket next to the chair. The dog scurried to the basket and nestled into the sweater, curling up on the pillow, staring warily at Sarah.

"Make yourself comfortable. I'll go get the tea, be right back," he called over his shoulder walking toward the kitchen.

Sarah sat on the sofa opposite David's chair and the dog. She felt decidedly odd, as if she had dropped into the middle of a scene in a foreign film. Noticing the flowers in a vase on the table, she reached out to touch them to see if they were real. The dog growled at her. She flinched, and hastily pulled back her hand.

Looking around the room she noticed two card or game tables, surrounded by brightly painted mismatched wooden chairs, at the far end of the room, in front of a wall of bookcases. In the middle of the bookcase wall was a cozy upholstered window seat filled with large pillows. What a wonderful place to spend a stormy afternoon reading, she thought.

The window overlooked a large expanse of dreary winter lawn, ending at a garden of brown stalks and frost-dried puffs of dried flowers in front of the tall hedge that separated the guesthouse from the main house, where David's parents lived.

David entered the room carrying a silver tray laden with a steaming teapot, a silver sugar bowl and creamer, a dish of sliced lemons and a plate piled high with small cakes and cookies. The dog immediately sat up and eyed the tray in drooling anticipation.

Sarah moved some books to make space on the coffee table for the tray. "David, this is lovely ... I ... um." Again she was at a loss for words. The last thing she expected to happen was to be sitting in David's house while he served her tea.

"The tea service is beautiful."

"It was my grandmother's," David said as he sat down to pour the tea into mugs. "She'll be rolling in her grave as I pour tea into these mugs instead of using the delicate flowered china she always used," he laughed. "But the mugs are so much more convenient. Do you like cream or lemon?"

"Lemon and sugar please."

He poured tea into the two mugs, added sugar and slices of lemon, and handed one to her. "Here, have some of these pastries. I bought them at the fantastic new French bakery that just opened in the village. Actually, I got them mainly for the dog. She has a terrible sweet tooth."

As if on cue Cynthia started to wiggle and dance around in the basket. David broke off pieces of a sugar cookie and fed them to her. Wiping his hands on a napkin, he offered the plate to Sarah. She looked them over and chose a dark chocolate square piled high with mocha frosting. Might as well break all the self-imposed rules, she thought.

"Aha! I didn't know you were a fellow chocoholic," he exclaimed.

Sarah smiled. "No, I guess you wouldn't. I don't remember ever going to tea with you when we were young," she answered tartly.

David, quiet for a moment, looked at the floor. "No, I guess we didn't."

Sarah ashamed, remembering she was here to make amends, reached for her tea. Taking a sip she marveled, "This is absolutely delicious. What kind of tea is it? I have never tasted anything like it."

"Thank my grandmother again. It was her favorite: lapsang souchong. Whenever I drink it I think of her."

"It smells almost like perfume; but it tastes wonderful, in fact, just inhaling it is amazing," she said, taking a deep breath. "This room is lovely, so warm and inviting. I um ... I don't remember it being like this ... before," she finished lamely.

"It wasn't. For almost forty years it looked like it did when my grandmother moved in as a bride. My mother never changed a thing. Not being one for style or décor, she couldn't have cared less. The only thing she has any interest in is sailing or skiing. She's never happier than when on the foredeck of a sailboat. When I think of my mother I see a wiry woman in a white sleeveless blouse and baggy shorts, pulling in lines and yelling orders to my father as they round a mark in one important race or another. To this day she gets deeply tanned. Her only concession to the sun is a floppy hat smashed on her head and dark glasses perched on her zinc-covered nose. If she isn't sailing she's tearing down some snow-covered mountain that sane people half her age wouldn't think of trying."

"She sounds like quite a woman," Sarah concurred.

"She is," David agreed. "I think her children have definitely been a disappointment to her as far as sports go. But my sister's two boys, to our great relief, seem to be showing great promise as future sailors. Anyway, the guesthouse stayed the same all the summers we were here. Mom had something fixed if it fell apart, and if the furniture needed recovering she had it done the same as before. Which, of course pleased Granny immensely, and when Granny died we moved to the big house. Mom never changed anything there either. Walk in there today and it's as if you walked back into 1920."

Sarah glanced around the lovely room and then looked at David questioningly.

He looked distressed. "Fiona did all this," he murmured softly. "She never saw how it all looked finished ... she died before ... it was." His eyes filled with tears.

Sarah's hands flew to her face. "Oh, David, please, I'm so sorry. I didn't mean to upset you. I just meant that the house looks so lovely ... and...." She started to cry. "Please forgive ... me ... I wanted ... to apologize," she sobbed. "For ... yelling at you at the ... the coffee place." Tears coursed down her face as she reached for her purse to get a Kleenex. "I didn't mean to hurt you."

David got up from the sofa. Taking a monogrammed handkerchief out of his back pocket, he crossed over to sit beside Sarah. He took her in his arms and wiped the tears from her face. The dog sat up in the basket, nervously eyeing them both.

"Sarah, Sarah," he said softly. "It's all right. I've done some very hurtful things to a lot of people, including you. I deserved to be yelled at."

"I shouldn't have come here," she moaned. "I should have gone to the damned trustees meeting."

"A trustees meeting...what are you a trustee of?"

"The hospital."

"That's wonderful," he exclaimed.

"No, it isn't; it is terrible."

119

"Oh."

"I hate them and what I'm forced to go along with," she said vehemently.

"Wow, let's have some more tea and tell me what they are making you do," David said with genuine interest, dabbing at the remaining tears on her face.

"I'm on the nominating committee, and they are selling board seats!"

"Well that's not all that unusual, especially when a hospital needs money. Lots of times a hospital will have a large board of rich people and then an executive committee that works closely with the CEO and they run the show."

"Shows how naïve I am, doesn't it? I was so proud when I was asked to be on that board, and you just confirmed my worst thoughts. Get the young, dumb townie on the board and then run roughshod over her."

"I think you're probably being a little hard on yourself. You are young, but you're not dumb. Can't you just vote against the people they put up if you feel so strongly about them?"

"No."

"Why not?"

"Because my husband will lose his job."

"Yikes, the proverbial plot thickens. Are you serious?" Sarah looked at David, her blue eyes tearing up again and nodded yes. "Who is the head of the nominating committee?"

"Whip Witherspoon."

"Whip Witherspoon! You have to be kidding; I can't imagine him being the head of anything. Your husband works for Whip Witherspoon?" David asked incredulously.

"Good Lord, no. It's worse; he works for John Lansdowe. And John Lansdowe and Brax Montgomery, I have come to realize, run the show."

"My God, John Lansdowe and Brax Montgomery. There's an unsavory twosome if I've ever heard of one. I'm amazed that the two of them have any interest in this local hospital. Who are they selling board seats to and why? I can't see any of these old East Meridian Yankees shelling out any money to get on the board of the local hospital. And the Azimuth Point

120

people are a given. They get on anyway," he mused.

"I might be just a townie, but now I know how that works," she grinned at him.

"But you're right. The old East Meridian Yankees aren't shelling out and Louis Tedisco is. He is a Providence developer, and a new board member; he gave a million dollars to build an atrium, of all things."

"An atrium?"

"Yep, don't think the crap didn't hit the fan when that was announced. Half of the board, the CEO and the doctors are furious."

"That does sound odd ... an atrium...." David refilled Sarah's mug and handed it to her.

"Tell me more about this ... who is on the board with you?" Sarah took the tea and settled into the sofa next to David and related what had transpired at the meetings over the last three months. The dog, still eyeing them warily, settled back down into the basket.

David listened intently until she finished. "Wow! All sorts of intrigue going on, but I feel like I'm missing something. Like why use all this money to build an atrium when there are so many other things that must be needed. Is the endowment very large?"

"We don't have an endowment."

"I thought Edward Brockwell left money for an endowment for the hospital."

"He did, but it's only for the emergency room that he built years ago after his son was born. And right now Mrs. Brockwell is in charge of the trust and it doesn't revert to the hospital until her death. I get the feeling that she keeps a pretty tight fist on the money and she decides how it's spent for the emergency room. I also have the distinct feeling that she does not like either John or Brax."

"Probably with good reason," laughed David. "You know, Sadie was a pistol years ago, absolutely beautiful, devoted to Edward and he to her. She never paid any attention to the ladies of the Point, a fact that drove them crazy."

"What does your mother think of her?"

"My mother thinks Sadie is great, but my mother didn't pay much attention to the ladies of the Point either."

"I'll bet it was easier for your mother to do, and get away with, than Sadie," Sarah retorted quickly.

David pondered this for a minute. "You're very right, Sarah. You are very right," he said softly, looking at her with empathy.

Sarah was taken aback at David's insight; she never thought he would ever understand. Her heart melted and she was lost again. With her whole being she wanted to reach out and touch him, take him in her arms, kiss him deeply, do anything he wanted, all the things she wanted. She could hardly breathe. She turned away, digging her fingernails into her wrists in a panic, trying to get control of herself. Looking out the window at the darkness she exclaimed wildly, "Oh no! What time is it?"

"About 7:30," David responded, looking at his watch. "Why?"

"Oh, no, the tide, it must be in by now. I'll never get back!"

"What's the matter? So what if the tide is high, back where?"

"I came up the beach. Like I use...." Sarah fell silent thinking, like I used to do. They looked at each other and David reached out and touched her check. She swallowed hard.

Then he took her hands and stood up pulling her with him. "Well, that's not a problem," he said lightly. "I'll drive you back to your car."

"Thank you. I'd best get home ... it's late and ... and ... um ... I'll get my coat," she said softly, still holding his hands.

David started to pull away, then tightening his hold on her hands, he said, "Thank you for coming to visit me. I have so enjoyed talking with you. Please keep me posted about what happens on your board."

Sarah smiled nervously. "Okay and ... um, I've enjoyed it too. The tea was wonderful."

They walked into the hall and David took their coats off the hooks. He helped her into hers, closing it around her shoulders, and then opened the door and casually asked, "Do you walk the beach often?"

"Ah, yeah; I come down a few times a week. Usually in the morning, it's great exercise."

"Yes, it is," he agreed seriously.

As they walked out the door the dog scooted out with them.

****

Brax Montgomery looked out over the boardroom, in an ill humor. Where is John? I can get up here from New York and the locals don't even show up, he fumed. Then he smiled. John would not be amused to be called a local. Liam's secretary entered the room and walked toward Brax with a pile of papers in her arms.

"Good afternoon, Mr. Montgomery. We have a few no-shows this afternoon, and I have Miss Morgan's resignation letter."

"Who's not coming?" he inquired sharply.

"Mr. Wells' secretary just called and said Mr. Wells would not be attending the meeting. Dr. Manning is at a conference in Miami. Mrs. Brockwell is still in Palm Beach for the winter and of course Miss Morgan will not be here."

Brax, ignoring the secretary, contemplated the board members as they took seats at the conference table. What a relief, he thought, to not have that sanctimonious bastard, Wells, here. Maybe John convinced him never to show up again. And I won't miss that old harridan Morgan. Good riddance. The way it's shaping up I'll have seven members for applying to the town for the building permit and three against and who knows how that Sweets will vote, not that it matters. Good! He grinned. Brax gazed around the table and wondered, where is that young, blonde looker John told me would vote however he voted? Well, it doesn't matter; she's probably home making a tuna casserole to take to the church supper. He glanced up as John Lansdowe entered the room, nodded at him, and cleared his throat.

"Shall we begin this meeting, ladies and gentlemen?" inquired Brax. "Do I have a motion to accept the minutes of the

March meeting?"

"So moved."

"Second."

"Thank you. Liam, the president's report?" he inquired smiling. Liam, with a look of barely hidden contempt, put on his reading glasses and proceeded with a shortened version of his previously submitted written report which everybody should have read, but probably didn't.

Liam finished abruptly. Pushing his glasses up on his head he sat back in his chair. He was becoming increasingly infuriated every day with the heavy-handed way Brax was treating everyone who opposed the atrium.

Brax smiled at Liam and thanked him for a fine report and for doing such a magnificent job of running the operation. Liam sat tensely looking out the windows at the far end of the boardroom. He did not trust himself to say another word.

"Dr. Simpson, would you give the medical staff report?" Brax asked with feigned interest.

Jim Simpson looked at the board members gathered at the table with a strange expression, then looked down at his paperwork and started talking quietly.

Brax settled back, elbows resting on the arms of the chair, his fingers laced lazily together as he continued perusing the room. His gaze shifted to Kim dressed in a stunning peach silk suit buttoned just low enough to show off the swell of her breasts.

She stared boldly right back at him with a wicked half smile. He realized with a start that she had been watching him. She raised her chin, tilting her head slightly, raised an eyebrow and looked at him with amusement. That damnable woman looks downright sensuous; in fact she looks as if she just left someone's bed. Her hair was slightly tousled and her skin luminous. She continued gazing at Brax with a sly smile then she parted her moist plump lips and ran her tongue around her white teeth. Brax could feel the start of an erection and was furious. Kimberly dropped her eyes and demurely started going through her board packet. Brax shifted in his chair and looked down at the papers in front of him as if checking the agenda, and when he was under control he put his head up and glared at John Lansdowe straight across from him. Lansdowe stared back quizzically. Brax shook his head and shrugged with a smile. Kimberly put her hand in front of her bowed head to hide her smirk.

Jim Simpson, with a kind smile at Sweets on his right, said, "That's it for the report."

Brax gathered his notes, ready to start in on the permit proposal, when Jim continued.

"Before we get on to the next thing on the agenda, I want to thank everyone on the board for their kindness during our time of terrible sorrow, and their unbelievable thoughtfulness as well as generosity in starting and funding the James Simpson III College Trust Fund. I know Rose Ellen and Diana have worked very hard on this project. I thank them both, also Miss MacComber for her help setting up the Trust Fund with her bank. The outpouring of the community, financially and emotionally, has been so appreciated by my family. In that vein, I hope you all will understand and accept my resignation from the board."

Surprised eyes were on Jim as he put his head down for a moment to gather himself. "Chip's death has been such a heart-wrenching experience for all of us that we decided a sabbatical would be in order. We hope that giving to others perhaps will help us heal as a family. We're all going to Africa for a year. I'll be working as a doctor and Chip's parents will be teaching. Josh can't, at this time, even contemplate going to the Olympics and will put that on hold for a few years. We had thought about boarding school but he wants to be with us. He will attend the local school. So I thank you for the opportunity to have served on the board of this wonderful hospital. I wish you all the best of luck, and now," he stood up, "I bid you adieu."

Jim gave a slight wave of his hand turned and slowly walked out of the room. The former Young Turk every doctor aspired to be, had become a stooped, broken, old man. They watched him go in shock and then pandemonium broke out.

"My Lord, I don't believe it!"

"What will he do about his practice?"

"Did you know anything about this?"

"Is he having some kind of a breakdown?"

"Can he afford something like this?"

"How do you think Letty feels about this?"

"Letty will go anywhere Jim wants to go," announced Sweets in a loud voice.

Everyone turned to look at her. "No, I didn't know they were planning to do this even though I have worked closely with the family since Chip's death. But I can tell you how deeply devastated the entire family has been over this tragedy. In a way I'm not surprised they are leaving," she ended. She also knew how devastated Jim was about this whole atrium business and that he didn't have the heart to fight it out, knowing he probably would not be on the winning side.

Sweets wasn't sure how she felt about the atrium controversy. She knew in no uncertain terms how Diana felt, as well as those on the other side. When she tried to convince Diana to be more reasonable, a bitter argument ensued. Now they didn't mention it when they were together. It was hard to get Diana to change her mind about anything. She didn't understand how an atrium could hurt the hospital as long as part of the money was used for an endowment. Why can't both sides come to some kind of agreement?

Brax sat, without taking part in the conversation. This turn of events was too good to be true. He knew that Simpson, an old fart everybody seemed to revere as second only to Jesus, would be a problem once he came out of his fog from the death of that kid. And now he was walking away from the table. Brax felt so elated he could barely keep still. He threw John a knowing glance. Lansdowe nodded with a slight sly smile. The opposition was dropping like flies.

Brax said, "I have some other sad news along that line that I must share with the board. This morning we received a resignation from Anna Morgan. She has ... um, not been well and is in Providence for surgery. She wishes us well with all future endeavors. I will pass her letter around."

The board members looked astounded, except for John

Lansdowe who looked thrilled. None of them, except Louis, being new, could imagine Anna Morgan leaving the board willingly.

Brax hurried to get the permit discussion on the floor. "Well, these members will be sorely missed. The nominating committee will have to meet soon and think about new members for this board."

At this Whip looked exceedingly nervous and pulled at his collar. Kimberly looked intrigued and John frowned at Brax. What is Brax doing? John thought. We don't want any more board members. Then, looking at Brax closely, John realized it was a ruse. Brax had no intention of putting new members on the board.

"Now," Brax continued, "Before John gets to the financials, I would like to share with you what the building committee has recommended we should include in an application to the town for a permit to build this wonderful new atrium that will bring so much pleasure to the patients of East Meridian Hospital."

Liam swung his head around to look at Brax in disbelief. What building committee? When and where did this take place? Hunt also snapped out of his reverie, thinking the same thing.

"And just who is on this building committee?" inquired Hunt with great interest.

"Louis, John, Rose Ellen, myself and an architect from town, Donald Sewell. He will be very helpful to us in many ways, one of which is that his brother is on the town council," Brax explained, smiling blandly.

"I'll bet he will be," intoned Hunt with disgust.

"Yes," nodded Brax in agreement, ignoring Hunt's implication. "Now, may I have a vote on the building committee's recommendation that we apply for a permit to build the atrium?"

John, Sweets, Louis, Whip and Kim voted yes. John, looking around the room, realized for the first time that Sarah was not at the meeting. Good thing I didn't need her vote, he thought.

"I vote no. With all due respect gentlemen," Hunt nodded in Louis's direction, "this atrium, as my rich old Uncle Henry used to say, is BALDERDASH!"

Louis stared at Hunt with amusement. Yankees really are not happy about the Tedisco Pavilion one single bit, he thought, making a note to increase the size of the sign.

"Well, thank you for your opinion but the aye's have it. John, Liam and I will attend the next meeting this up-coming Monday I believe, and present our plan to the town council," Brax continued unruffled.

Liam glared at Brax. He did not want to attend any town meeting and talk in favor of this ridiculous atrium. Angrily he blurted out, "Excuse me, I don't believe I was consulted about attending a town meeting on Monday night."

Brax looked down at the table then slowly raised his eyes and turned toward Liam. Not a word was spoken among the other board members. They just stared at Brax, mesmerized. He began to speak quietly, enunciating each word. "Why, Liam, perhaps it slipped your mind. I mentioned the meeting right before we talked about renewing your contract for 2001, remember?" he inquired with malice. The threat hung in the air between the two men.

Liam blanched, gripping the edge of the conference table with both hands. He grit his teeth and a flush spread across his cheekbones. Humiliated, he uttered, "Yes."

"Thank you so much. I was sure it would come to mind," Brax said with a knowing smile. "Now then, as I mentioned, John, Liam and I will be attending the town meeting on Monday next and we will report back to the board the outcome at the May meeting. So, John, would you be so kind as to present the financials?" Brax sat back in his chair with a nod towards John.

John Lansdowe, not missing a beat, proceeded to present the financials in yet another format. The endless pages of numbers and confusing explanations ended with John complementing a very sullen Liam for a job well done, keeping the hospital in excellent financial order.

Louis looked at his watch and realized the trustees meeting was running longer than he had expected. He interrupted with an engaging smile and excused himself, saying he had a business meeting in Europe the next day, and had to leave now in order to catch his flights. He stood up, briefcase in hand, and left the room, willing himself not to glance at Kimberly. He emerged from the hospital; his driver jumped out of the black Mercedes and ran around the car to open the back passenger door.

"The airport, Mr. Tedisco?"

"Yes, George, sorry I'm running a little late."

"That's okay; I'll get you there in time."

Settled in the back seat, Louis thought, this affair with Kimberly is taking over my life. He closed his eyes, rested his head against the back of the seat, and wondered what to do. Out of nowhere, the memories of long ago surfaced. He smiled, recalling their furtive teenage sex: raging hormones and fear of discovery had precluded any foreplay. Climaxing intensely in cars, abandoned sheds, cold deserted beaches and even up against trees in their own dark back yards, they quickly satisfied their lust.

Now, as mature lovers, they had entered a new realm of discovery. He recalled that very afternoon the soft light playing over Kimberly's bare form as she moved on peach silk sheets. Her breasts swollen with desire, her nipples dark and erect, she threw back her head, closing her eyes to savor the moment. Her body gleamed with wanton need. He shifted in the seat, feeling the searing heat again. He had run his hands through her damp curls, down her back, caressing her firm bottom as she moved sensuously against him. She raised her head, her lips open and moist, "Now, please now," she whispered urgently. She slowly lowered herself and then had stopped moving, resting her hands on his chest. "OhmyGod, now, now I can't wait," she had screamed, rocking toward an explosive climax.

Louis felt himself getting hard and tore his thoughts back to the present. Opening his eyes and pulling at his collar he reached over and opened the window for a blast of cold fresh air to cool off his thoughts. Right then he made up his mind to call Kimberly as soon as he got to New York and ask her to join him in Europe ... Italy would be good. Someplace nobody would know them. Taormina would be perfect, he thought. Perfect.

"Everything okay, Mr. Tedisco?"

"Huh, what?"

"Is there a problem, Mr. Tedisco?" questioned the driver again.

"Um, no, George, why?" answered Louis, worrying for a fleeting moment that George had read his mind.

"The window, you opened the window. You want me to lower the temperature?"

"No, George I ... um ... well, I'm going to be flying all night; I thought I would like some fresh air." Louis said lamely. What I really need, he thought, is a bucket of cold water thrown on me.

****

Liam sat at his desk looking out the windows over the expanse of lawn and down to the surf breaking on the rocks below. One of the things that convinced him to take this job was the view from this office. He didn't want to head such a small hospital, but in his haste to get away from New York and his divorce, this job seemed like an answer to a dream. Now the dream had turned into a nightmare. He was seething about this evening's trustees meeting. Brax was definitely running the show and treating Liam like an errant child.

Equally disturbing, getting the hospital management under control was evading him, and he couldn't exactly tell how or why. At meetings, department heads would chirp answers at him but not really say anything, nor would they look him in the eye. And those interminable meetings! He had never worked in a hospital that had as many meetings as East Meridian. But the head of nursing, Mona O'Shay, insisted meetings were necessary; she said the staff was lax and needed constant reinforcement.

Liam felt something was wrong but Mona kept assuring

him that everything was fine and not to worry. The staff had to learn to accept modern procedures. And now this damned atrium. What foolishness! This hospital needs so many other things and we are squandering that money on a glass front hall, with a waterfall, of all things. It's absurd!!

Liam reached for his address book and opened to the number of the headhunter firm that brought him to East Meridian. He stared at the number for a while then looked out the windows again, watching shadows creep across the lawn as the sun began to sink below the horizon. He closed the address book thinking tomorrow is another day. I don't want to make any rash decisions; after all, I haven't been here very long. I love the area and the sailing, maybe I'm just going to have to be more understanding of small-town attitudes and learn how to deal with overbearing trustees.

He sighed out loud, thinking, everything is slipping out of my grasp and I don't know what to do about the situation. He toyed with the idea of meeting privately with Brax and John and dismissed that with a shake of his head. No, the people to have lunch with are Robb and Hunt. I should also meet with Jim Simpson before he leaves and Diana Manning when she returns. Neither one of them seems happy with this atrium either.

Darkness fell and he didn't bother turning on the office lights. He sat for a few minutes longer, listening to the piercing wail of a siren as an ambulance neared the hospital. Dejected, he stood up, and walked out of his office.

****

Diana put on the coral earrings and necklace Robb bought her earlier today at the gift shop on King Street. She twirled around in front of the mirror, her white strapless dress floating around her in filmy swirls. The last few days had been heaven. Her lithe body was tanned, her green eyes sparkled and her blonde hair shone with highlights from the sun and sea.

"You look beautiful."

"Oh!" Diana gasped, turning toward Robb, who was leaning against the bedroom doorjamb. "I didn't know you were there. This has been the most wonderful vacation. The beach, the ocean, the food and this wonderful house and you, wonderful you! I want to stay here forever. We will be beach bums sucking up rum and sun until we turn into wrinkled sots."

"That's an idea," nodded Robb, crossing the room and taking Diana in his arms. "Let's buy a house tomorrow and stay in paradise."

"You almost sound serious," laughed Diana.

"I am kind of serious," he said, looking at her intently.

"It is very tempting, but we have a few other things to get straightened out at home first: your divorce and you getting to know my children." Diana said, lightly kissed him. "So tonight let's just have fun! Take me, my knight in shining armor, off on your speedy golf cart to Pink Sands for a wine-soaked night of dancing and love. And, oh yes, let's not forget dinner!" She put her arms around him and kissed him again. Stepping back she smiled. "Robb, I love you with all my heart. We will work this out; it will take awhile, but you'll see." She twirled away leaving a faint aroma of Cinnabar as she danced across the room.

Robb watched, thrilled to see her so happy and carefree. Diana picked up her white beaded evening purse and wrapped her coral pashmina around her shoulders as she spun around again to face Robb. She gave him a wide grin.

He did his best Fred Astaire imitation across the floor, took her arm, and they danced out of the room laughing with delight.

MAY

"Braxton, Rutherford here. I'm calling about Aunt Edith's Trust for young Ben. Lovely property that, I remember riding around those beautiful fields and woods as a kid, my favorite horse in Aunt Edith's stable was Midnight. He was tricky to handle, that one; threw me off a few times, I'll tell you. And Aunt Edith, what a great old gal she was, she could ride anything and she did!"

Braxton gritted his teeth, listening to Rutherford wax poetic about that fallow stretch of grass and stonewalls on Route1 that would be perfect for developing. Dealing with this old fart and the rest of the bird-and-bunny club was getting to be a pain in the ass.

"Yes, Rutherford, I'm sure it was thrilling," interrupted Brax scathingly.

Good, thought Rutherford, I've got his dander up. "Yes, well, Braxton, as I was saying, I've called a meeting with the partners to look into the instrument. I'm not sure there's much possibility of Bitsy being allowed to do anything with that land except what Aunt Edith wanted done with it. Also the other trustee, the bank, would have to be brought in for any discussion of a change. So I will get right on it and get back to you as soon as possible. Do give my love to Bitsy," Rutherford barked into the phone and abruptly hung up.

Brax seethed with fury. "That fucking pompous snob. How dare he treat me like that!" he snarled, slamming the phone down on the desk. "Miss Bunsen," he bellowed into the intercom, "get my wife on the phone."

"Your wife is in Palm Beach, Mr. Montgomery. You had me purchase the tickets. I don't know where she is staying."

Belatedly Brax remembered that Sadie Brockwell had invited Bitsy to Palm Beach for ten days. He didn't give a damn if she went or not and told her so, but he was surprised Bitsy agreed to go. Sadie intimidated Brax. She came up the same road of hard knocks that Brax had traversed and she saw through him the first time she met him, and he knew it. So he couldn't call Bitsy at Sadie's and give her hell, which made him even madder.

"Miss Bunsen, call the club and have the pro set up a squash game in an hour," Brax snarled into the intercom.

"Yes, Mr. Montgomery."

"And reserve a table for me for a late lunch."

"Certainly, Mr. Montgomery."

Brax stood up and stormed out of the office. As he passed Miss Bunsen she helped him into his raincoat and handed him an umbrella. "It's raining; you're going to need these." Brax snatched the umbrella and strode angrily down the hall.

Miss Bunsen watched him go, shaking her head. I'm glad he is not staying around here, she thought and hurried to make the reservations. She was also glad she didn't have to call that number for one of those girls and pretend not to know what was going on in that office.

****

Mona O'Shay looked up from her desk when John Lansdowe cleared his throat. She smiled cagily, tapping her pen against the desktop.

"Nurse Mona, may I come in?"

"You always do, Mr. Lansdowe. One way or the other…"

John Lansdowe shut the door and locked it with a click. He looked at Mona O' Shay and his erection became harder. Mona stood up and adjusted her starched nurses cap. Her white uniform crackled as she smoothed her hands over her full-busted body. She walked around the desk and slowly reached up under her dress to pull down her white silk panties. They dropped to the floor. She stepped out of them and kicked them off to the side with her white high-heeled shoes. John walked toward her and then stopped abruptly, putting his hand on the chair in front of her desk.

She lowered her eyes demurely. Quickly she flicked a look at John checking to see how evident his erection was; pretty good tonight, she noticed with relief. She unbuttoned the skirt of her uniform letting him gaze at her white lace garter belt and stockings. She backed into the desk and slid up on top crossing her slim legs.

"Is there something you wish to discuss about my performance at the hospital, Mr. Lansdowe?"

"Actually yes, Nurse Mona, there has been a definite problem with trustee approval."

"Really?" replied Mona, crossing and uncrossing her legs and unbuttoning the top buttons of her prim and proper uniform from years past. Her breasts bulged invitingly out of the lace bra beneath the starched outfit.

"Yes, definitely."

"I want to do anything I can to help with trustee satisfaction. Would you like to come closer and show me how we can correct this unhappy situation?"

"Yes, yes, there is so much I want to do to help with the situation," John moaned almost in pain.

"Oh, Mr. Lansdowe, I'm alone here and I need so much help and guidance," Mona whispered, running her high-heeled foot sensuously up and down John's groin.

"Oh, yes, yes, I can certainly help you too," he wheezed.

"I'm so glad," she moaned, breathing heavily. He gasped, wavering, then reached out to grab her breasts. She grabbed his hands kissing them passionately and fastened them firmly to the rim of the desk. She ran her hands up and down his clothed erection. He whimpered.

"That information system Liam wants the board to vote on, we really don't need it. Can you make sure that the board understands what a waste of money it is for a small hospital like ours?" she murmured, unzipping his pants and caressing his member.

"Yes, yes, whatever you need, it's yours," he wheezed.

"You will make it happen at this month's meeting?" she crooned, rubbing him with all her might.

"Yes, yes, whatever you want," he moaned, knees shaking.

She moved toward him, putting her legs around his body, pulling him into her until he shuddered and fell back into the chair behind him. She slid off the desk, dropping a damp towel in his lap. While he recovered, she walked around the room talking as if nothing undue had happened. She reiterated all the things she wanted to take place at the hospital, and when she turned to look at him, her uniform was in place and he was completely dressed.

"Miss O'Shay, I will make sure all of this will be taken care of," he assured her as he unlocked the door and left the office.

"Thank you, Mr. Lansdowe. I'm sure you will."

Mona sat down at her desk. Then she opened her desk drawer and took out a perfume bottle, raised it to her mouth and took a gulp of Jack Daniels. This is almost too easy, she mused. She took off her old uniform, quite pleased it still fit and smashed it into a bag to take home to wash and starch again. Donning her business suit she closed her office and left, looking forward to a couple of stiff drinks, a warm bath, release with her faithful vibrator and her continued power at the hospital.

****

Helene was glowing. She loved New York and Selina and Selina's way of life. By the last day of her visit, Helene knew she had to find some way to extricate herself from her life. I've not had a life, she thought, only a day-to-day existence, never acknowledging how unhappy or lost I've felt for years. Sure was easier that way, she smiled. Real living means making big decisions, scary decisions and hurting people. But I can't go on just existing anymore.

****

Selina Pitt reached for the phone on her desk; she didn't pick it up. She sighed, looking down but not focusing on the paperwork in front of her. She hadn't heard from Helene since her New York visit two weeks ago. Selina did everything possible to make the visit magic; she wanted Helene to love the city. They had dinners with fascinating actors, musicians and artists. They went to all the new plays on and off Broadway, browsed through museums and galleries, sat in the sun in Central Park and enjoyed lunches in out-of-the-way places every day. Selina watched Helene become more beautiful and at the same time more unsettled with each passing day. She hugged Selina goodbye at the train station and said she would call when she got all this straightened out in her mind.

That was two weeks ago, Selina thought again. Should I call? No, I don't want to hassle her into a decision she is not ready to make. This could go on for weeks, even months, Selina thought angrily. Why is this simple decision so hard for her to make? Ah, Selina's other voice said, you didn't have a husband or a child or parents to consider when you decided that you loved Helene. And remember how difficult it was for you to admit to yourself you wanted to make a commitment; Selina sighed again and took her hand away from the phone. She wouldn't call.

****

His tanned, muscular body glistening from a shower, Louis paused in front of the open doors that led to the terrace off his Villa Belvedere suite. Wrapping a towel around his trim waist he walked out to look at the turquoise sea below. The early morning sun felt warm and soothing on his body. Re-

137

flecting on the past week, he shook his head in wonder. What he anticipated as an insignificant occasion of sun, sex and spaghetti in Taormina turned into an amazing renewal of Louis as a person.

Kimberly made him laugh more than he had in years. Every day was a sensual adventure. Lathering his body with suntan oil or licking her fingers after slurping a melting gelato, trailing her nails down his back intoning some sexual innuendo that left him limp with laughter and with a hard erection. Reclining together on the striped, oversized loungers on the beach, she made up horrendously funny stories about the people around them. In the small restaurants dotting the rugged hillside town of Taormina, they devoured, with shameless gusto, wonderful meals of fish and vegetables, melt-in-your-mouth tomatoes, creamy mozzarella, just-picked-basil and crusty bread, grilled meats and plates of fresh pasta. After each lunch they retired to their *matrimoniale*, the Italian word for double bed. Kimberly loved the name and she would repeat it often as they made passionate love, high on the wine, food and atmosphere.

Louis shook his head. Damn, he was falling in love with Kimberly. They were a perfect fit; they had known each other for years, shared a lot of history and now they wanted the same things. They both liked living on the East Side of Providence. Something Vi never did, he mused. Well, Vi left him; she is out of the picture. When I get home I will tell my lawyers to start divorce proceedings.

For a brief moment he felt guilty because he never should have married Vi. He never loved her. Kim married that toad Willis and Vi was there and Louis wanted a family. Funny, one reason Louis had married Vi was for her looks. Being blonde and blue eyed and he figured their children might look less Italian. Kimberly, even though Irish, looks more Italian than the Italians here in Taormina. The stupid things you do with your life, he thought. He would still like a family. He wondered how Kimberly felt about having a baby.

Well, only one way to find out: ask her. He would tell her tonight at dinner that he planned to divorce Vi. He stretched and the towel fell on the terrace.

"My, my, are you letting everyone know what endears you to me?" inquired Kimberly from the doorway with a smile on her face.

Louis turned at the sound of Kim's voice and looked at her hair, tousled from sleep and her voluptuous tanned body clad in a diaphanous white nightgown. He immediately got an erection.

"I love it when you're glad to see me," she purred.

He strode across the terrace, picked her up and carried her to the bed.

****

"Bitsy, these ten days have flown by! It has been such fun having you here. I'm sorry you are leaving," exclaimed Sadie hugging, Bitsy goodbye.

"I'm sorry I'm leaving, too," Bitsy said wistfully.

"Next time you must stay at least a couple of weeks. Are you sure you don't want me to go to the airport with you?"

"No, no, Sadie; I know this is your bridge day. Graves will get me there in fine style, and help with the luggage."

Sadie looked at Bitsy; she was tan and didn't look as tired as when she arrived, but something was very wrong. She is in despair and it's that terrible man she's married to, Sadie thought. I must say something. I think he is hurting her physically as well as emotionally.

"Bitsy, dear," Sadie said softly, taking Bitsy's hands in her own. "I want you to know that I'm here for you at any time of the day or night. I don't want to interfere with your life or your privacy but I can't help but feel that something is not right with you. Is there anything I can do to help?"

Bitsy looked at Sadie, her eyes wide and shining with unshed tears. She started to open her mouth but a terrifying wave of fear almost made her faint. Bitsy looked down, putting her hands at her sides and said in a low voice, "Thank you, Sadie, I'll be fine."

A noise at the living room door made them both turn; it

was Louisa, who wanted to give Bitsy a hug goodbye.

"Miss Bitsy, I hope you visit us more often next winter. Graves has gone up for your luggage and will be bringing the car around in a minute."

"Thank you, Louisa. I adored your wonderful meals. One more week here and I'd look like the fat lady in the circus," Bitsy laughed.

They walked toward the front door as the chauffeur drove up the gravel driveway. The two women kissed Bitsy and wished her a safe trip home. Bitsy hugged them again and got into the car. She waved to the two women on the steps until the car turned left at the gates and was out of sight.

"Fat lady in the circus, my foot," harrumphed Louisa. "That girl is a skinny wreck. What can we do?"

"I don't know, Louisa. I thought I could get her to start talking while she was here. Every time I tried she seemed terrified and changed the subject. I'll just keep trying. Perhaps in June when we get back to the Point I will make more progress."

Sadie, shading her eyes from the hot noonday sun, sighed; she and Louisa turned and walked up the steps and into the comfortable cool interior of her Florida home.

****

"Sarah. Hey, Sarah!"

Sarah James trembled. David was calling her name. She intentionally had not come to the beach at the same time every day. Why, she was not sure. Was she avoiding meeting David or making sure she did see him? At this point it was irrelevant because he was behind her. She closed her eyes, trying to calm down and then turned around smiling.

"Hello, David," she called out, and had a sudden urge to laugh, thinking I sound like Audrey Hepburn in *Sabrina*. Well, I guess that's not too far off the mark. My father isn't the chauffeur but I'm in love with the son of the wealthy family. Good Lord, I've admitted it!

David hurried to Sarah, the dog trotting along with him.

Catching up to her, he hesitated, trying to decide whether or not to kiss her on the cheek, when the dog started to growl. She knew an adversary when she saw one.

"It's a beautiful day, isn't it?" he exclaimed, picking up the dog. "Cynthia, what is the matter with you?" The dog licked his face excitedly.

"Yuck!" He screwed his face up in mock distaste. Putting the dog down he searched in his pockets for a handkerchief. "I'd best wash this adoration off and settle for a salt face."

All three walked to the water. David dashed toward an out-going wave to dampen his handkerchief. Sarah stood at the water's edge eyeing the dog warily.

David walked back mopping his face, azure blue eyes alight with amusement. Her knees felt weak. His longish blonde curls lifted in the slight sea breeze. He stopped in front of her. They were almost the same height. She touched the sun-bleached hair on his muscled, tan arms. He put his hand under her chin, raising her face up and the dog bit her ankle.

"Yowch," Sarah bellowed, jumping around on one foot rubbing her ankle.

"Cynthia, you bad dog!" David retorted sharply, grabbing the dog and putting a leash on her. "Sarah, are you all right? Here, let me look. Did she break the skin? I don't know what got into her..."

Sarah, still rubbing her ankle, had a few thoughts about what got into the dog but decided to keep them to herself. "No, I don't think the skin is broken, her teeth are sharp and it startled me. I'm not hurt, just surprised."

"I'm so sorry. Let's go up to one of those benches and sit down so I can look at your foot."

"It's okay, I'm fine...I don't...."

"Well let's sit up there anyway and I'll check to make sure it's all right. I have a first aid kit in the car if you need antiseptic and a band aid."

They walked up the beach to the boardwalk and sat on the benches overlooking the ocean. The dog jumped up on the bench and sat right next to David. David reached down and picked up Sarah's foot and put it in his lap.

"Gosh, there are teeth marks! You are a nasty dog, Cynthia," he admonished, shaking his finger at the dog. Cynthia hung her head and whimpered.

"You are not getting any sympathy out of me," David said to the dog. "Sarah, I feel terrible about this. I think I should put some antiseptic on the teeth marks. I'll go to the car and get the first aid kit."

Sarah, horrified at the thought of being left with the dog, looked wide-eyed at David and blabbed, "Oh, no ... I mean fine...uh...no, it's okay...um, I..."

"Listen, I'll put the dog in the car, get the kit, fix your foot and go over there to that latte place and get us some, okay?" he questioned, waiting for her approval.

She nodded, relieved that the dog was not going to be left with her. David scooped up the unsuspecting dog and hustled off toward the car. Sarah looked around realizing somebody she knew could walk by at any moment. Reaching into her bag she quickly donned her dark glasses and put on a wide-brimmed panama hat, tucking her blonde hair up into it. Well, at least I have an explanation, she reasoned. This man's dog nipped me and he was concerned that I was hurt. And it turned out I knew him from years ago. Nothing unseemly here ...

David appeared at her side holding the first aid kit and two mocha lattes in a cardboard holder. "Would you hold these while I look at your foot?"

Sarah took the lattes as David sat down. Placing the first aid kit on the bench next to him, he opened it, reached for her foot and put it in his lap. A shiver went coursing throughout her whole body when he touched her. He gently spread antiseptic cream on the tooth marks and covered the spot with a large band-aid. He looked over at Sarah to see if he had done a good job; then he looked puzzled.

"Are you expecting the media?"

"Huh?"

"The hat and the shades. You look like a celebrity hiding from the press," he grinned.

"Oh, no," she laughed weakly. "I don't like to get a lot of sun ... wrinkles, you know."

142

"Well, you seem to be doing a good job," he intoned seriously, peering over her face.

"I don't see one, or even the beginning of one. You should see my mother though. She looks like a map of the moon."

Sarah looked at him in surprise, not knowing what to say.

David laughed. "I'm not telling tales out of school. My mother says she earned every one of them. My sister, on the other hand, takes as much care as you do to keep out of the sun. My mother is always teasing Bradley about being so pale."

"Why was your sister named Bradley?"

"Her name is Mary Bradley after our grandmother. Gram was pleased that she was named after her but didn't want big Mary and little Mary. Molly didn't seem to fit so we started calling her Bradley the baby, and it stuck."

Sarah smiled to herself. These Point people had last names for first names, while her friends were named for soap opera stars.

"Do your mother and sister get along well?"

"Well enough. Bradley doesn't have much of a sense of humor and takes herself rather seriously, while mother is a hoot. She does and says what is on her mind, which used to upset Bradley, but not anymore."

"You sound like you are all very close," Sarah said wistfully, thinking of her own dour parents and bitch of a mother-in-law.

David hesitated and looked out over the ocean. "When I was little I liked my governess better. She indulged my every whim, so of course I adored her and she didn't smoke so she smelled a lot better than my mother, who reeked of cigarettes and was forever telling me to behave. My parents were always off sailing or partying and Bradley was too young to be of any interest to me, and truly, I didn't have much interest in any of them. Then I went away to boarding school and was hell-bent on having a good time."

Sarah shuddered, remembering what a good time he had had with her years ago, but kept silent as David continued.

"But when...when...Fiona and the baby died, my parents were on the next plane. They stayed with me, arranged the funeral with Fiona's parents and got me through that terrible week. Then I...I fell apart...well, to be honest, I had a nervous breakdown. They took me home to Providence, gave up all their beloved sailing in the Bahamas last winter and took care of me. I was a mess. Two months ago I knew I was better, but I couldn't go back to Washington yet. So I told my parents I thought I would be all right at Azimuth Point. It has been a good healer through the years. They settled me in here and then went to the Bahamas to salvage some sailing time. We call each other every other day or so ... I ... I never knew what wonderful parents I had until this happened."

Sarah looked over at David and saw tears in his eyes. She reached down and took his hand in hers, softly caressing his fingers as they both stared out at the gently rolling sea.

****

John Lansdowe stared at the letter from Vista Construction and chuckled to himself. Well, well, well, Vista Construction wants to bid on the East Meridian Hospital project. Of course Vista should bid on the project, and it will win the bid. As head of The building committee I'll make sure of that. And no one else on the committee will have the slightest idea that Vista Construction's parent company is PalynnDrome Associates. Nor will anyone else on the board, except Braxton, know that Louis Tedisco is the largest silent partner in PalynnDrome Associates, a holding company with many subsidiaries. John, with a sly smile, tucked the letter into the folder he was taking to the hospital building committee meeting that afternoon, with a flourish. Then he reached for the phone to call Brax.

****

Brax Montgomery, after yet another nonproductive car phone conversation with Bitsy's lawyers about selling the Route 1 property, stalked into the East Meridian Hospital board meeting. He grimaced; his bad temper darkened as he looked at Robb and Hunt already seated at the conference table with their backs to him. Those sanctimonious bastards, he thought. Stomping to the head of the table, he abandoned his briefcase with a thud, grabbed the notes Liam's secretary held out to him and sat down. The rest of the board members milled around getting drinks, fruit and cookies. An occasional spurt of laughter could be heard as the various groups talked animatedly with each other. None of them seemed to be in a hurry to get down to business, Brax thought angrily, his nasty mood deepening.

The conference room windows were open to the late afternoon warm, spring air. Birds could be heard chirping in the budded magnolia trees in the courtyard below. Brax, reading his board notes, had to strive to contain himself not to order someone to shut those damn windows and turn on the air conditioning, or better yet shoot the birds. Looking up in exasperation, he leaped up from the table in a fury, his face purple. "Bring this meeting to order," he bellowed.

Robb and Hunt looked as astounded as the rest of the board members at Brax's outburst, which of course infuriated Brax even more. The members of the board slowly took places at the conference table in relative silence and glanced warily at Brax.

Brax, turning his anger on Liam, snarled at him to give the president's report. Liam raised an eyebrow and contemplated Brax. He slowly organized his papers, smiled at the gathering and proceeded to give his report. John Lansdowe gazed at Brax with concern. Brax ignored him and stared at the papers in front of him, seething.

Kimberly, sumptuous and radiant in a subtle yellow V-neck cashmere sweater and matching skirt, twirled her chair slightly back and forth. Louis, seated next to her, had trouble keeping his mind on the report in front of him as Kimberly's bare toes caressed his calf and behind his knee.

Liam finished his report with a request from the medical staff that a doctor be put on the board to replace Jim Simpson, and he produced a list of names the medical staff recommended.

Brax barked at Liam. "The medical staff does not recommend anything to this board! The nominating committee does the recommending around here, that's what they're there for. Furthermore, we don't need any more doctors on this board. The only reason that Simpson was on the board was because he was an asshole buddy of the last chairman."

The board members looked at Brax in shocked silence. Sarah James was furious and opened her mouth about to speak out in a reckless manner when John Lansdowe glared at her, clearing his throat loudly. Sarah, remembering her husband's job was at stake, shut her mouth and her eyes filled with tears.

"Braxton, I feel you must have had a distressing ride up here from New York," John said. "Perhaps the nominating committee should address the idea of putting another doctor on the board to replace Jim." John ended, staring narrowly at Brax.

Brax took a deep breath, his face first red and then pale, as he got himself under control. "Yes, John, you're right; it was a tedious drive. I agree that the nominating committee should look into which doctor *they* think will be acceptable to put on this board," he finished.

Liam's face flushed with anger at Brax's condemnation of his request and he started drumming his fingers on the table. Silence resounded loudly in the boardroom.

"Ah, yes." John Lansdowe smiled derisively. Robb and Diana both started to speak when John hurriedly picked up his finance report and began to read it to the board. Diana glared at him and thought, where is Sadie when we need her?

Robb and Hunt looked disgusted; Sarah James looked ill. Whip looked out the window, and Louis looked at Kimberly imploringly. She stopped rubbing her toes up and down his leg. Slipping her foot back into her shoe she moved forward in her chair, putting her hands in front of her mouth to hide her smile and leaned her elbows on the table. Tossing her yellow, red and beige silk Hermés scarf over her shoulder, she sat back in her chair, moved slightly away from the table, and crossed her fetching legs, arching her four-inch high-heel clad feet in a suggestive manner. With an innocent smile she folded her arms under her breasts, which pulled the soft cashmere sweater tightly across her well-endowed Mediterranean-tanned cleavage and stared at the wall over Brax's head, seemingly unaware of the stir she was causing.

Diana watched the entire performance in disgust. Whip, Robb, Hunt and Liam gazed at Kimberly with overt interest. Louis tried desperately to ignore her and the stirring she was causing within him. John finished his report and looked up quickly, taking in Kimberly's posture, and issued a smothered snort of laughter. Brax glared at John. Thinking that John was finding him the source of amusement, Brax, by now in an exceedingly vile mood, launched into a diatribe about the East Meridian Town Council's decision to issue a permit for the construction of the Tedisco Pavilion. The board members, astounded that the permitting had come through so fast, looked at each other and then at Brax in disbelief. Liam shook his head in despair and looked at Robb.

Robb, pounding his fist on the conference table, yelled, "The board has to vote on this. We didn't vote on going to the town council for a permit to build this horror."

Louis looked at Robb, surprised at his violent outburst and the fact that he called the atrium a horror.

Brax, with a malicious smirk, turned to Robb, "Well, Robb, my boy, perhaps you should have attended last month's board meeting instead of joy-riding all over the Bahamas. And if you had taken the time to read your board notes you would have seen that the board did vote for Liam, John and me to go to the Town Council Meeting and apply for the permits. And furthermore, the town will entertain no more other changes for the hospital."

Robb, speechless, paled visibly, wondering how Brax knew he was in the Bahamas, and if anyone else knew he had been there. And with Diana.

"What have you done?" shrilled Diana. "This hospital needs to grow and expand its facilities for the future. The master plan was for two new OR's, Diagnostic Imaging, and changing the overcrowded patient rooms into private rooms—

all the things that the Planning Committee decided on were submitted to the town a few years ago," Diana sputtered in frustration. "I won't stand for this! We have to take another vote!"

"Well, Missy, you'd best take a look at the changes okayed by the By-Laws Committee last month. This vote is final."

"What By-Laws Committee? What changes? Missy ... Missy!" Diana shouted in a rage. "It's Doctor Manning. Don't you ever call me Missy."

"Certainly, *Doctor Manning*, the By-Laws Committee was formed last month, headed by *Miss MacComber*, and the changes were voted on last month. The building committee, headed by *Mr. Lansdowe*, voted this afternoon to award the bid to Vista Construction Company. It's a done deal. This meeting has ended." Brax stood up, snatched his briefcase and walked out of the room.

Pandemonium broke out as Diana, Robb and Hunt started to talk at once; the rest of the board sat and watched with varying expressions of dismay.

Once again, John Lansdowe wrestled for control of the group and tried to calm everyone down. "Ladies and gentlemen, I think Brax has been a bit hasty, and anyone can have a bad day. Now, the town will not entertain any more changes to the exterior of the hospital but we can still look into making the changes within the building for the new operating rooms and other things," he murmured soothingly.

"What are you talking about?" retorted Diana scathingly. "There isn't room in this building for those improvements, and you know that!"

"Dr. Manning, I do not know that. What I do know is that we have hired a consulting firm to look into exactly how we can make use of the existing building in the future."

"Who hired a consultant?" inquired Hunt sarcastically. "Was that also a board decision?"

"No, as a matter of fact," continued John smoothly, "it was the building committee's decision."

"Oh, great," Robb intoned with disgust. "And who are these consultants?"

"They're called Future Concepts and they are out of Alabama." John smiled, as if he had just buttoned down I. M. Pei for the project.

"Alabama..." roared Robb, too mad to even recall why the firm and the location seemed vaguely familiar. "What the hell do we need with a firm in Alabama, when there are so many good firms, knowledgeable in hospital renovations, right here in New England?"

John stood up from his chair and closed his Mark Cross briefcase. It locked with the expensive silence of a Lamborghini door shutting. Smiling condescendingly at Robb, John uttered with exaggerated patience. "Perhaps we all need to calm down a bit. Feelings are running high and we all know this matter can be settled in due time. In fact, I failed to mention in my report that Louis has designated another million to be donated to the hospital. We ought to thank him for his generosity, and perhaps ask his forgiveness for, in my opinion, the extreme rudeness shown to Mr. Tedisco by some members of this board. I have a car waiting. Good evening, ladies and gentleman." John smiled derisively and walked out of the room.

JUNE

Robb got out of his car and paused to smell the salt air and listen to the waves rolling in on the beach before going into his house. As a child he loved coming to Azimuth Point for the summer. He would tumble out of the car and race across the long green lawn to the beach, yelling with delight, his governess in hot pursuit. She always scooped him up halfway down the lawn and took him, yowling with dismay, back to the house to change into play clothes and shoes. When he got older he pleaded with the strict Miss Ebehauer to let him travel to Azimuth Point already in play clothes, so he could run around the yard and down to the ocean as soon as he arrived. The answer was always no, that was not done; he must leave town dressed correctly, and change after they arrived in the country. He smiled about all those 'not done' things the governesses had forced upon him as a child. He made sure, when Miranda was little, that they both ran right to the ocean as soon as they got out of the car. In his adolescent years coming to Azimuth Point meant release from the confinement of boarding school and, most of all, seeing Diana again.

With a sigh, thinking of Diana, he shook his head and gripped the suitcases tightly as he continued across the driveway and up the wide veranda steps. Soon he was going to have to talk with Helene.

****

"Dr. Manning."

"Hi, Diana, I'll be over in a few minutes to take you to lunch. Do you want to try that place full of ferns, in the village? I'm sick of the same winter menu at the country club and the beach club isn't open yet."

"Well, okay, Sweets, but I can't be gone too long. In fact I don't feel very well; all I want is some soup. I want to get back early to go for a blood test. I think I might have Lyme Disease."

"Do you have a tick bite?"

"Not that I can see, but those ticks are very small; it's the big-bullet thing that doesn't show up for a while you have to look for."

"Wow, is that official doctor talk?"

"Sweets, I'm not in the best of moods and I feel lousy. Let's forget lunch. I'll get something in the hospital cafeteria."

"Ah, yes, you're sure to get a culinary delight in that greasy spoon."

Diana gagged inwardly, thinking of the steam table smell of the cafeteria. "Maybe you're right. I'll meet you at the fern place in the village. Give me an hour, though. I'll get the blood test first, so I don't have to come back to the hospital. And I'm not in the office this afternoon anyway, because I'm going to Marianne's recital."

"Marianne's recital? I didn't know she was musical."

"She's not." Diana smothered a laugh.

"I know I'll hate myself for asking, but why is she having

a recital?"

"Well, you know Marianne, she insisted she wanted to play an instrument once she realized all the attention Jamie was getting with his piano playing."

"That figures. What instrument did she settle on?"

"The tuba..."

****

Sarah saw David in the distance walking toward her, without the dog. She hugged her coat around her, not for warmth, as the day was warm, but in anticipation. She had been walking the beach with David at least three times a week during May. And now in June the beach would soon be crowded, and summer people would return to the Point. She knew they could not keep meeting like this because someone would see them. Not the Point people, she thought sourly, because they wouldn't have any idea who she was; but once somebody from East Meridian saw her with a strange man, or worse, someone from Azimuth Point whom they recognized; the shit would hit the fan.

Gossip would start, though all they did was walk the beach. But she knew in her heart that was not all they, or at least she, had done. She lusted after David. All she could think of was David.

At home she performed what was expected of her in a detached manner, as if she was on the outside looking in, or watching an endless television show. Her daughters, sensing that they didn't have their mother's complete attention, were becoming behavior problems. Leighanna, previously a docile, almost goody-goody child, was answering back and refusing to do anything she was asked to do. Lauren's penchant for temper tantrums, a trait that surfaced when she was a few months old, was gaining in momentum, volume and frequency.

Sarah became very quiet when either one of them misbehaved, which of course made them carry on even longer. Leighanna would eventually stomp out of the room, sometimes even out of the house, and Lauren would go to her room and break things. Sarah found she did not feel inclined to get involved. So she did nothing and was relieved when they finally left her alone.

One evening, when Bill's mother had invited herself for dinner, Sarah overheard them talking in the family room as she was coming downstairs from refereeing the girls' bath-taking and pajama routine. "Bill, Sarah should discipline the children more. The girls are running wild, answering back. They even ignore me when I try to make them behave," Irene whined to her son.

Sarah stopped on the carpeted stairs to listen to Bill's reply, thinking, of course, Bill's mother would never suggest that perhaps Bill should in any way be at fault, or could be of any help in the matter. Sarah could hear from the rattling of the newspaper Bill was hiding behind, this wasn't a conversation he wanted to have with his mother or Sarah. He paid little attention to his children; as far as he was concerned that was women's work. "Ma, I haven't noticed anything and the girls are fine. All kids are a little rambunctious now and then."

Sarah had leaned against the stairway wall, her eyes closed, softly letting out a sigh of despair. The truth of the matter was Bill hadn't noticed anything at all these months. He had three meals put in front of him, his clothes were clean and baseball season was in full swing. Life, at least his life, was good. Pushing those thoughts out of her mind, she quickened her pace down the beach, nearing David.

David smiled as he recognized Sarah coming toward him. They had been meeting regularly and walking the beach, talking about anything and everything. After having a latte they would part, never planning to meet again, but they both knew they would. David found he really enjoyed her company. She was funny, feisty and sharp. His astute mother would say Sarah was street-smart. And after getting over the shock, she would accept and perhaps like Sarah. His sister Bradley would not be so accepting. Therein lay one of the problems with this situation; they came from two different worlds. And the other major problem was she was married, with two children. He shook his head as he hurried along; this is not good. I should not be thinking along these lines. He had hurt Sarah badly when they were young and at the time he could not have cared less. Now he sincerely cared for her and the honest truth of the matter was they had to stop seeing each other because she would only get hurt again. And he was not ready for thoughts of commitment, never mind a messy divorce and taking on children.

They stopped in front of each other and Sarah, looking at his face knew what he was thinking. And she could not help it. Big tears started to roll down her cheeks and her chin started to quiver. David looked stricken. He took a handkerchief out of his pocket, and gently pulling her to him, he wiped her tears and rested her head against his shoulder stroking her soft blonde hair.

"Oh, Sarah, Sarah, I...I..."

"It's all right; I know we have to stop meeting," she sobbed softly. "I ... I ... didn't want to face it. I was planning to say something flip and sarcastic like all the Point girls and tell you I'm going to be real busy from now on, so see ya! But I guess I can't even begin to pull it off and ... I ... I ... don't know what to do or say. I'm so miserable; it's my fault. I let this go on, living in a stupid dream world." She pushed away from him, smiling ruefully through her tears. "At least this time I can't blame it all on you."

David gave her his handkerchief and she wiped her eyes and blew her nose. " Well, you can blame a lot of it on me," he said sadly. " I didn't want to face reality either. I enjoy being with you so much; you are so funny and I must say, at times, so completely irreverent," he laughed.

He took her hand and said gently, "Let us walk down the beach and we can talk about this and figure out how to remain friends.

They walked silently, in turmoil, toward the huge stone barrier at the end of the public beach. Reaching it they turned and leaned against the fortress that nature had provided to guard the folk of Azimuth Point from the general populace. They listened to the sea gently slap against the mossy jagged pile of rocks peeking above the incoming tide, neither wanting to be the first to speak.

Sarah, taking a deep breath and fighting for control, laughed quietly. "Even God is on the side of you people."

"Whatever do you mean?" David asked.

"This damn thing he put here." Sarah motioned backwards with her thumb at the rocks. "Let's face it; all these weeks we have been pretending we are the same, just two people meeting on the beach. In fact, I think eagerly meeting on the beach. But we both know even if I wasn't married, there would be no way in hell I could successfully hurdle this friggin' ledge. Whoever said the rich are different than you and me was right. You are the rich guy from the Point and I'm the townie. I can't see your family having any tea parties in my honor," she spat out bitterly.

David closed his eyes, shaken by her honest outburst, hearing the pain and fright in her voice. Turning toward her he traced the grim set of her jaw with his finger and caressed her cheek. " Please forgive me for doing this to you. I have been very selfish. I ... I have enjoyed being with you so much these past weeks. You brought light into my life. I looked forward to being with you even though in the back of my mind a voice was saying to stop this right now. Don't go out on that beach. Leave that girl alone; she's married, she has a family." He rubbed his forehead with the palm of his hand, his voice choked with despair. He almost whispered. "I felt myself starting to care for you too much and I let it happen."

He reached for her clenched fists. " Sarah, again, forgive me, we both know we can't walk the beach together anymore, at least not on a regular basis. But if we see each other now and then, we will talk as friends. I really look forward to hearing how you'll whip that hospital board into shape."

Sarah having calmed down, realized that it wasn't too long ago David was in very poor emotional shape, and she had to get a grip on herself and lighten this up. She laughed and said, "Oh boy, that will be the day that group pays any attention to me. But believe me you'll be the first to know."

David swallowed hard and grinned at her. "You'll do it!" Not wanting to part on this note he asked, "May I treat you

155

to a latte, my fair lady, or is it warm enough for some iced mocha?"

"An iced mocha sounds just right for the start of summer. You're on," she said quietly starting down the beach. Then turning, she looked at him dolefully, reaching out her hand. "Come on, let's go."

****

Diana slowly picked at her salad and gazed out the window toward the beach, half listening to Sweets prattle on about her summer sailing plans.

"Sweets, speaking of summer plans, we have a new doctor ... unmarried doctor ... joining the staff at the end of the month. He mentioned looking forward to meeting people and going sailing. So I thought, why not have you both over for dinner. He is nice and very attractive and you're not going with anybody. Let me arrange something."

"No."

"No?"

"I'm actually seeing someone."

"You are? Who? Why haven't you told me?

"It's none of your business," she spat out.

Diana was shocked. "I didn't mean to ... well I don't know what I meant to ... I'm surprised. We used to tell each other everything."

"I'm not telling you about this and don't go any further with it." Sweets scowled and stabbed at her lunch.

Taken aback Diana shook her head and looked out the window again. She noticed David coming up the boardwalk stairs talking to a girl she could not see. Hmm, that's interesting, I wonder who she is? David said something to the girl, motioning toward the Coffee Bean. The girl sat down on a bench and smiled up at David. Diana was about to bring this to Sweets's attention when she realized the girl was Sarah James and the look on her upturned face told it all. OhmyGod, thought Diana, her mouth dropping open, how in the world did this come about? How do they even know each other? Sarah immediately put on dark glasses and a hat. Diana was relieved Sweets hadn't noticed a thing.

****

David returned to Sarah with two cups and sat down next to her, his thigh touching hers. He handed her the cup and searched for something to say.

"What are you doing this summer?" she inquired neutrally.

"I'm going to do some sailing. I haven't raced in years so I'll be doing the Nantucket Bucket and my parents want me to join them for the New York Yacht Club Cruise in Maine."

"Then you will be going back to Washington in the fall?"

"Well, no, not right away. I'm ... uh ... not sure when I will return to D.C. The house is rented until New Year's, some diplomat my mother found, and another family wants to rent it until next summer. The law firm gave me a leave of absence until Christmas. I have been doing some work for them ... what with e-mail and fax machines it's not so hard," he trailed off. "What will you be doing?"

Sarah stared out at the ocean, the prospect of a long hot summer filling her with dread. She knew she would make sure her children's activities would not include many trips to the beach. "My girls go to day camp and soccer camp and we always go to North Carolina. Bill's mother's family lives near the Outer Banks."

"Oh, my grandfather used to go to North Carolina to hunt. I never went because my mother dislikes hunting and would never let us go, even if we wanted to, which we didn't. I've never been to the Outer Banks."

"It's okay, but really hot. Actually, I am planning to go back to work," Sarah said brightly. She hadn't been planning that at all until it struck her that moment.

David looked at her strangely. The only work he remembered her doing was waitressing at the Ebb Tide Inn, which was how he met her that summer long ago.

Sarah smiled at him wickedly. "I did move on from the Inn, you know...."

"Er ... um ... I didn't...."

"Your face is such a giveaway," she laughed. " While at college I worked at the Bay Campus as a secretary, and after I graduated I worked full time as an assistant to one of the professors. I loved the work and was trying to figure out how I could pay for graduate school. My parents were against it and gave me a hard time. I was living at home. I never would have been able to support myself and go to school. They wanted me to get married. They thought Bill was a real catch ... and the next thing I knew I was married. The worst mistake of my life," she blurted out, her voice full of contempt.

David hadn't a clue what to say next. That was the first time Sarah mentioned anything about her marriage, or that she felt it had been a mistake.

"I might take some classes this winter and start in on that degree. So will you be here in the fall? Or are you off sailing?"

"Well you might not believe this, but I'm going to Positano, to cooking school, for a week and then to Sardinia to crew on a boat for a week."

Sarah almost fell off the bench. "Cooking school? You have to be kidding."

"I told you, you wouldn't believe it."

"How? Why?"

"Diana is going with me; it started as a joke."

"Diana Manning, the doctor?"

"You know her?" David asked.

"No, I don't really know her, but she's on the board of the hospital with me." Sarah was not about to let on that the reason she came to see David in the first place was because she overheard Diana and Sweets talking about him at the board meeting.

"Oh, I guess I forgot Diana was on the board. Anyway, when I came to the Point, Diana was great about having me over for dinner and also sending dinner over to me almost every other night. And she had Mildred teach me how to do some simple meals. Over cocktails one night, perhaps too many cocktails, we talked about going to cooking school. Since Diana, at this point, knows less about cooking than I do, when we sobered up we thought, why not? So she made the arrangements and we're going in September; once her twins go back to school."

Sarah shook her head, the situation was ludicrous; the two rich guys from the Point were going to cooking school as a lark, and she was going back to work to save her sanity. She wondered fleetingly if she would go to cooking school if she had the money. Oh well, I can't go there and I'd better get out of here.

"It's time," she announced as she stood up, "for all good friends to part."

David stood up too, and they looked at each other. "Let me walk you to your car."

"It's best you don't," she said softly.

He put his cheek on hers and then brushed her lips gently. She kissed him back longingly and then stepped back, her eyes full of tears. Turning abruptly she ran to the parking lot and got into her car.

David watched her go and then slowly walked down the boardwalk steps to the beach and Azimuth Point.

****

"Diana, what's the matter? You look like you have seen a ghost."

"I ... um ... want some dessert."

"What? You didn't eat much of your salad and now you want dessert? I thought your stomach was upset."

"Well, yes, perhaps custard would be good."

"Custard," Sweets said, in disgust.

"Yes, yes, here look at this menu." Diana shoved the dessert card under Sweets' nose.

Sweets scanned the card with a puckered up face. "You know I never eat dessert."

"Well you should eat dessert. You're too thin."

Sweets frowned at Diana. "I'm not too thin. I'm the way ... um ... the way I want to be. Just because you don't have to

159

watch your weight doesn't mean you can tell me what to do."

Diana glimpsed Sarah and David standing up, and quickly switched her attention to Sweets, who was asking her a question.

"Are you *sure* you want some custard?"

"Huh? Er ... um...." Diana forced herself not to look out the window.

The waitress appeared at the table and asked if they wanted anything else, and Sweets asked her if they had any custard. Diana looked out the window and saw David kiss Sarah so tenderly that she wanted to cry. She watched Sarah run to the parking lot, and David slowly walk down the boardwalk stairs to the beach. Diana turned back to the table in shock. She could not believe what she had just seen.

"I don't need any dessert," she blabbed. "Let's just get the check."

The waitress left to get the check and Sweets glared at Diana with a pained expression. "Have you thought about taking a vacation?" Sweets inquired sharply. "Or has your mind just taken one?"

"Well, I've had a lot on my mind lately and perhaps I'm not thinking too clearly."

"Perhaps," agreed Sweets tonelessly as the waitress returned with their slips. They paid for their lunches and got up to leave. Diana looked out the window and noticed with relief that David was way down the beach walking toward the Azimuth Point rock.

"It must be low tide," she said out loud.

"Yes. I guess it is," agreed Sweets, looking at the ocean, as they walked out onto the boardwalk. "What difference does that make?"

"Um, no difference ... I just noticed it." Diana hadn't meant to say anything out loud about the tide, she was just thinking that it must be low tide or David would not be able to walk around the rock to get back to the Point, a fact she was definitely not going to share with Sweets.

Diana felt queasier than she had before lunch. Finding David, maybe, in a situation as complicated as her own was upsetting, especially after what he had gone through after the death of Fiona and the baby. And Sweets's reaction was also upsetting. What was going on? Who was she seeing?

"It's a good thing I'm driving," intoned Sweets. "I think you are in a fog."

"Mmmm...." answered Diana vaguely.

"Maybe you had better go home and take a nap."

"I can't take a nap. I have to go to Marianne's recital."

"Ah, yes, the tuba prodigy. I do hope you're bringing a camera."

****

Sarah sat in her SUV watching David walk down the beach. She felt hollow and withered, like an old dead vine drooping on a fence in a spent field. She rested her head on her hands, gripping the steering wheel; her breath came in hot gulps, but no tears. She didn't have any tears left. Straightening up, she started the engine and backed out of the parking space. The radio was playing Phil Collins' *Another Day In Paradise*. How appropriate, she murmured as she drove home to her real life.

****

Robb walked through the Dutch door into the spacious hall of his weather-shingled summer home. He looked through the opposite Dutch door at the end of the hall and noticed that the wicker rocking chairs on the porch were moving slightly from the breeze blowing in from the ocean beyond the rolling lawn and beach. He breathed deeply. What a beautiful sight.

"What is that?"

Robb dropped the suitcases he was carrying with a thud, and turned toward the shriek in surprise. Equally surprised was a chipmunk, which had followed Robb into the house. The chipmunk had risen up on its haunches and was stock-still with fright.

"There, there beside you," shrilled Helene.

"Robb looked down and saw the chipmunk and laughed.

"It's a chipmunk. I'll get him back outside."

Robb pushed the suitcase toward the chipmunk hoping he would turn around and run back out the open door. But he didn't. As soon as Robb moved, the chipmunk ran into the living room. Helene yelled again. Robb didn't know what amazed him more, Helene making more noise than she had in all their years of marriage, or how fast a chipmunk could disappear in your own living room.

"Helene, really, it's okay. A chipmunk won't hurt you, they don't bite or anything."

"Are you sure?" she asked timidly.

"Yes, yes, now come on in here and help me get him back outside."

"How?"

"Hmm, well, I'm not sure. You go to the other end of the room and start making some noise, clap your hands or something. Let's see if we can find out where he is."

Helene clapped her hands and nothing happened. "Now what should we do?" she asked, flopping down on the sofa nearest her. The chipmunk shot out from under the sofa, ran right between Robb's legs and headed for the dining room. Helene and Robb laughed and ran after it. The three of them ran around the dining room table a few times and the chipmunk ran back into the hall.

"Thank God he's going toward the door!" Helene screamed.

At the sound of Helene's voice the chipmunk stopped and veered into the lavette.

Robb grabbed Helene's hand and ran in after the chipmunk and shut the door. Breathing heavily they looked around.

"Don't yell again," whispered Robb.

"Okay. Where could it hide in here?" she whispered back.

Just then the chipmunk ran from behind the pedestal sink to the back of the toilet. They both jumped and collided with each other laughing.

"This is ridiculous, we need some kind of plan," Robb said.

"Good idea," agreed Helene. "Why don't we plan to have me leave and you can figure out how to catch him?" She grinned.

Robb looked at Helene in wonder. He had never seen her so animated, much less trying to be funny. He grinned back. Maybe chipmunk chasing had been her hidden passion all along.

"Nice try, but if you open that door we'll lose him. Now look, I'm going to take this wastebasket and aim it toward him. You get on that side of the john and wave your hand or something to get him to come toward me."

Helene did and the chipmunk ran into the wastebasket and Robb up-righted it. He and Helene were so excited that they both tried to grab the plastic bag in the wastebasket and the chipmunk ran up the side of the basket and jumped into the sink. They looked at it in disbelief.

"How did he do that?" Helene gasped.

At the sound of her voice the chipmunk ran down the wall and hid behind the toilet again. "This is the dumbest thing I've done in my life." Robb laughed in exasperation. "Let's try this again, but if we get him in the basket, I'll hold it against the wall so the little son of a bitch can't escape."

Once more Helene motioned to the chipmunk on one side of the toilet and it ran into the basket. This time Robb slammed the basket against the wall before the chipmunk had time to turn around and run out. Robb sat on the toilet and slowly moved the basket up the wall. Helene stared at him, baffled.

"Now what?"

"Um, well, I need something to slide between the basket and the wall, so the little bastard won't get away again."

They looked around the tiny bathroom and then looked at each other.

Helene hunched her shoulders and opened her hands, perplexed. What can we use to do that?"

"The cookie sheet! That should do it. Is that old cookie sheet Betty uses to bake those wonderful chocolate chip cookies, still in the kitchen?"

"You like chocolate chip cookies?"

Robb mused to himself that he and Helene really did not know much about each other.

"I did when I was a kid. Could you please look in the kitch-en. No wait, it used to be in the pantry in one of those stand-up cupboards."

Helene opened the door and cool air filled the tiny room. "That certainly feels better. Can I leave it open?"

"For God's sake yes, and hurry up; my arms are going numb."

Robb lowered the basket a bit and rested it on his knees. Helene returned with the old cookie sheet.

"Close the door. I don't want to take the chance that he might run out of here and get loose in the house again. Kneel down next to me and put the cookie sheet against the wall."

Helene took a quick look at Robb, realizing this was closer than they had been in years. The same thing crossed Robb's mind and his shoulders began to shake with laughter. Soon they were both giggling at the absurdity of the situation.

"Okay, okay," wheezed Robb. "This is priceless, isn't it?" Helene nodded in agreement.

"All right, now we have to get out of here. Listen, just slide the cookie sheet up the wall and I will ease the basket on it. When the sheet covers the top of the basket I'll turn it over and you open the door, okay?"

Robb got the sheet on top of the basket and Helene opened the lavette door. "Shut the bottom of the Dutch door after I get out, so he won't try to come back in here," Robb called out as he ran out the door and onto the lawn.

Robb took the cookie sheet off the wastebasket and turned the basket upside down on the lawn. The chipmunk didn't come out. Robb looked in the basket and saw the terrified creature shaking at the bottom of the basket.

"Now you stay in the basket. Just my luck." Slowly Robb pulled the plastic liner out of the basket and shook it on the grass. The chipmunk fell out and quickly scurried away. Robb laughed all the way back to the house.

Entering the house Robb saw Helene leaning up against the hall wall, tears running down her face.

"Helene, don't cry. I didn't hurt him. I just dumped the little bugger on the ground and he ran away."

"It's not that," she sobbed.

"Then what's the matter?"

"I ... I ... It's everything. My life, our life. What I've done ... I've done something awful, and I don't know what to do. I feel terrified and like I am going to explode."

Robb took Helene in his arms and held her tight. " You haven't done anything awful."

"Yes, I have; you have no idea."

"Come on, let's go sit down and we'll talk this over," Robb murmured soothingly. He put his arm around Helene's shoulders as they walked into the living room. He rolled his eyes, wondering, how in the world do I handle this? Do I tell her I know, that I saw them? Will she be furious that I never said anything? And she has been in such agony all these months? Do I tell her about Diana?

Helene was sobbing so uncontrollably that Robb picked her up and carried her to he sofa.

"Please, please stop. It's not that bad; believe me, we can work this out. It's not as bad as you think."

"You don't know what I have done. I don't even ... oh, God ... please help me."

"Helene, stop this; listen to me."

He held her tightly in his arms, and said quietly. "Helene, it's okay, we can work this out. I know what happened."

She stiffened, awaiting the worst. " How do you know what happened?" she whispered.

"Because I was there that night, the night of the big snow-storm. I came home looking for some plans I had done two years ago to take to the meeting that night. I found them but I wanted to tell you that I would be home after all, so I went upstairs and found you with Selina."

Rigid with fear and embarrassment, Helene whispered," I ... I ... didn't see you."

"No, you didn't."

Helene sagged against Robb. The fact that Robb might have seen what she and Selina had done that night made her faint with shock, fright and misery. She felt sick to her stomach.

"What ... what ... ?" she whispered faintly, unable to finish the sentence.

"You were asleep, and quite honestly, I didn't have the faintest idea what to do or say, so I did nothing. I was astonished. It was the last thing I ever thought I would encounter in my life. But as I calmed down and thought about it, I realized why our relationship had never ... well ... never been a relationship," he finished lamely.

He was at a complete loss as to where to go from here. He couldn't tell Helene that since he had been having sex with Diana, he knew what had been missing all the years he had been married to her. While he was trying to figure out what to say and how to say it, great big tears rolled down Helene's face again. Robb wiped her face with his handkerchief. He opened his mouth to say something, anything, to get the conversation started, when Helene uttered in vague surprise. " You are seeing someone, aren't you?"

"Well ... um ... I ... er ... yes, as a matter of fact. How did you know?"

"I didn't, until this very minute. It all of a sudden dawned on me how you have been away from home a lot this last year, and you don't seem upset about this. I have been so wound up in my own problems that I never noticed, until now," she stated carefully. "This is unbelievable! I don't know whether I should laugh or cry. I guess playing the unsuspecting wife is a stretch. But I am a bit mad that I have been going through hell and you have been aware of the situation for months!"

"I didn't know how to bring it up! I mean it's not really something I could casually mention during dinner at the Hale Club with your parents, or any of our friends. Can you just imagine the reaction from them if I let fly with, 'Oh, by the by, I saw you in bed with that attractive woman from Trinity; is it serious? Or just a fling?'"

Helene looked up at Robb through her tears and started to grin. The thought of her parents hearing that bit of news was just too funny. They started to laugh until their sides hurt and they were out of breath.

Helene, still on Robb's lap, fell back on a pillow, resting

her head on the arm of the sofa. Folding her arms across her stomach she thought quietly for a moment. "Who is it?"

"Diana."

"Of course ... Diana. You have always loved her, haven't you?"

"Oh, Helene, don't do this ... I...."

"I'm not agonizing, if that's what you mean. We both know it was never right with us. You have been a good husband and a wonderful father. But there was nothing there. Honestly, until Selina, I didn't have a clue what should be there."

At this Robb looked slightly aghast and Helene felt her color rising. "Yes, well we certainly don't have to pursue that line of thought," Helene said. Robb nodded with an uncomfortable grin and Helene continued, "The question is...what do we do now?"

"What do you want to do?"

"I want to go to New York, to be with Selina and see if this is right for me. I know our life is not what I want anymore, but I'm not sure if that life is what I want either. I do know we are over ... we really never were. There's no going back now. I realize that. But we have a rather rough road ahead of us. How and what are we going to tell Miranda?"

Sitting up, Helene looked wildly at Robb; she swung her feet to the floor and stood up. She paced around the room, her speech becoming more frantic, one arm hugging her stomach while making sharp gestures in the air with the other. Then, hands on her hips, she turned to look at Robb. She paled and looked faint.

Robb jumped up and held her in his arms. "Calm down, Helene. At some point we will find a way to tell Miranda ... together. Now is not the time. We don't have to tell anybody anything. Right now this is just between us, and we will decide what to do." He looked out the window and saw it was twilight, and shook his head at how much time had passed. "One thing I know I'm going to do is make us a drink. Go sit on the porch. I'll bring you some sherry."

"Tonight I think I would like a scotch ... on the rocks."

"Coming right up, my dear." Robb, slightly surprised at

167

her request, gently hugged Helene and kissed her on her forehead. "I'll bring out a sweater with your drink. Do you want to go to the club for dinner?"

"No, the last thing I want to do is see anyone. Perhaps we could have dinner sent over and eat on the porch. Funny we've never done that," she mused.

"I guess you're right; we haven't. I'll get the drinks and be out in a minute." He gave her another hug and walked into the pantry to get the drinks.

Helene watched him for a few seconds and then walked down the hall and on to the porch. Settling in a chair, she slowly rocked, inhaling the salt air. Looking at the beach and rolling ocean beyond the sweeping green lawn, she wondered idly if she and Selina would ever be able to visit Azimuth Point. That's not something I have to think about now, she sighed. I certainly have enough to get straightened out without looking for problems.

****

The hospital conference room was hot and stuffy. Southern Rhode Island was experiencing an early heat wave, unusual for June, and the air conditioning had failed an hour before the start of the trustees meeting. Liam was on the house phone, speaking through clenched teeth to the head engineer about the situation. He gazed around the empty room, noting that the ice cubes in a bowl on the refreshment table were quickly turning to water, the platter of cheese and salami looked unappetizing and the cut-up-fruit and vegetables were wilted and curling up right before his eyes.

The engineer droned on in Liam's ear, cautioning against opening the windows and filling the room with the thick humid air wafting in from the ocean. The conference room was on the waterside of the hospital. The winter-chilled sea could be heard slapping against the rocks below the fog-shrouded ledge. Liam seethed, the sweat rolling down his back, ruining his fresh shirt. "This morning after it failed you told me that it was fixed."

"The operating rooms and floors are fine. Those are the first priority," the engineer announced loftily. He probably hoped to divert his ineptitude from Liam's line of thinking by quoting Liam's own dictums. Pulling at his collar, Liam wished desperately he had gotten a haircut that morning. His too-long thick black hair had spiraled into damp ringlets and sweat was dripping down his neck and temples. "This is the second time today the air conditioning has broken down in this wing. It has never broken down on the floors of the OR, at least not today," he hissed into the phone, and then, his voice rising, he ordered, "Fix it now."

Liam's secretary walked into the conference room, carrying a large bundle of papers and files. She stopped, reeling from the blast of smoggy heat that assailed her. Looking around in surprise, she listened to Liam's demeanor on the phone. Then, smelling the odor of over-ripe fruit and vegetables as she approached the conference table, she pondered what, if anything, she could do to help alleviate the situation.

"Liam, what can I do? Should I call down to the kitchen and get rid of this stuff?"

"Yes, and get them to send up drinks, bottled water and ice, lots of ice ... and in an ice bucket of some kind."

"How about some fans? Perhaps that would help."

"Yes, yes ... fans, that would be good."

"Why don't we open the windows? Wouldn't that help a bit?"

"No ... shit ... yes ... I guess it would. But the engineer keeps telling me that it will be fixed in a minute and not to open the windows."

"Er ... um ... okay ... whatever you say. Here, give me the phone so I can call the kitchen."

Liam handed his secretary the phone just as Whip walked into the room.

"My goodness, it's hot in here; what's wrong with the air conditioning?"

Liam gritted his teeth. Holding back a few obvious snappy retorts, he managed a tight smile, "A minor problem, Whip.

169

It'll be fixed in no time."

"A minor problem. Couldn't we open some windows?"

"The engineer feels it will be harder to cool down the room if we let in the foggy humid air."

"Oh, then I guess I'll get some water." Sidling uneasily up to the refreshment table he stared perplexed at the bowl of melting ice cubes. Returning with a bottle of tepid water, damp with condensation, and an equally warm glass, he sat down.

Sweets arrived just ahead of maintenance men carrying floor fans. Surprised by the smell and the heat she stopped short, and the maintenance men almost ran her down. With a lot of clunking and banging they managed to go around her and looked around the room for wall outlets.

"Wow! It's hot in here. Can't we open some windows?" she exclaimed. A chorus of No's, along with various garbled, short-tempered explanations greeted her; she sat down at the table in silence.

Liam's secretary walked around distributing papers, which had not been printed in time to be sent with the board packets. Liam was back on the phone again.

Sarah walked into the room in a short-sleeved pastel summer dress, undoubtedly the person most perfectly dressed for the heat of the room, and not knowing what to say about the situation, she quietly took a seat and studied the papers in front of her.

Kimberly and Louis came into the room, looking as only two people can when they sharing a little secret, not noticing, at first, the heat or the unpleasant odor. Then Kimberly drew up sharply and twisted her nose in dismay. " My God, what the hell is that smell?"

Louis scanned the room wondering the same thing, and noting the closed windows, turned to Liam, still on the phone and tapped him on the sleeve. "Liam, why don't I open some windows?" he asked quietly.

Diana hurried through the double doors and was overcome by the heat and odor of rancid salami, warm cheddar cheese and decaying vegetables. She swallowed hard and took a deep breath. It did no good; she felt the bile rising in her throat. Pivoting she ran out of the room. Dashing by Robb and Hunt on their way into the conference room, one hand over her mouth, the other waving them aside, she raced down the hall and burst into the ladies' room. Luckily it was empty and Diana was able to get rid of the problem in private. Sweets rushed by Robb and Hunt and also disappeared into the ladies' room.

"Hmm ... ," Hunt said, thoughtfully staring at Robb. "Did the kitchen send up something from one of the labs as a special, or do you think those two are just showing their true feelings for Brax?"

Robb, in a real quandary, worried about Diana, but knowing he couldn't go after her, laughed, shrugged his shoulders, and the two men continued to the conference room.

As they entered the room, the maintenance men, having plugged in the fans, turned them on. The blasts of wind from different directions immediately buffeted all the loose papers around the conference table and blew them into the air. The stacked clean glasses on the refreshment table fell over and shattered. The turbulence formed waves in the bowls of melted ice cubes and slopped water over the broken glass, platters of spoiled food and stale cookies. Papers swooped down, landing on the refreshment table, adding to the soggy mess. Most continued flying around the room, with some board members chasing them, and the rest were plastered against the walls and windows.

Liam, dripping with sweat and flushed beet red, could contain himself no more. Throwing the phone on the floor he turned and roared, "For Christsakes, shut off those fans and open the fucking windows."

Startled, no one moved; then a frenzy of activity followed. The fans were turned off, papers started to drift down to the floor, people stumbled into each other trying to get to the windows and then began arguing as to exactly how to open them.

Liam stood rooted to the spot, horrified he had lost control of the situation. His secretary hurried over, picked up the phone from the floor and hung it up.

John Lansdowe arrived and was astonished. He walked in slowly, looking around and wondering what in the world had happened to cause this mess. The room, now with the windows open, started to fill with wafts of damp fog as predicted.

Sadie Brockwell, impeccably dressed in a white, summer Chanel suit with navy blue trim, stood at the door and surveyed the room with amusement. "I must say, things really do fall apart when I'm not here."

Robb went over to welcome her. Laughing, he gave her a hug. "You're right, the meetings went right downhill after you left for Florida."

"I'll say."

Liam turned toward Sadie, one of his favorite trustees, searching for something to say that would explain the chaos. The rest of the people in the room, not knowing what to do, also looked at Sadie as she walked into the room with Robb. In the silence the phone shrilled. Liam's secretary answered, listened for a few seconds, and wide-eyed handed the phone to Liam. "It's Mr. Montgomery." Liam paled and took the phone with a wet hand. Everyone in the room started talking to the person next to them or picking up papers from the floor. Liam explained the situation to Brax, abruptly took the phone away from his ear and hung it up. He walked to the head of the table and announced that, under the circumstances, Mr. Montgomery had cancelled this month's meeting. The trustees would meet in July instead of skipping that summer month, as they usually did.

Sadie patted Robb's arm and said, "A saving grace if you ask me. Come to my home for a drink, won't you, my dear?"

"Sadie, I'd love to. Let me walk you to your car and I'll get my car and join you at the Point."

****

Brax Montgomery sat back and smirked with delight after telling his driver not to continue toward East Meridian but to take him to Providence. Phone still in hand, he congratulated himself that he didn't have to deal with that boring bunch of meddling idiots at East Meridian Hospital. Those sanctimonious bastards, Robb and Hunt, would want to start another commotion about building the atrium. Brax didn't want any more interference from those damn do–gooders. He'd fixed that lily-livered O'Connell's ass by threatening to fire him if he voiced his opinion about the atrium again. Brax's plans were falling into place; he knew what was best for that pitiable excuse for a hospital and what was best for the town. He felt powerful, in control and aroused. Grabbing the car phone he keyed in a number in Providence with his thumb and made arrangements for a girl to entertain him for the night.

****

"Dr. Manning."

"Diana, are you all right? What happened? Are you sick?"

"Oh, Robb, I don't know what's wrong. My Lyme Disease test came back negative, but of course sometimes it takes weeks to show up. I'll feel fine for a while and then I don't feel so fine. That ghastly smell and the heat in the conference room was more than I could take, but once I threw up I felt better. Where did you go? By the time Sweets and I got back into the room you had left."

"Sadie asked me to go back to her house to catch up and have a drink. I'm just leaving her house now. Where are you. At home, I hope?"

"No, I'm still at the hospital. I have to do an emergency appendectomy in an hour."

"Is it on a child?"

"Yes, a little girl, why?"

"Every time I hear about that kind of an operation I think of the Emily Wells story and how the hospital came about."

"That's right; she would have been your great-aunt, or cousin?"

"She would have been a great aunt, I think. Listen I have great news. Helene and I have talked. How it took place was pretty funny, although not quite as funny as your snake story."

"Wow, this should be good; what happened?"

173

"It's too long to go into now but the gist of it is that Helene is leaving for New York in a couple of days and we're making an appointment with our lawyer to sign the separation papers!"

"OhmyGod, you're kidding! You have to tell me what happened! I can't wait! Does anybody else know?"

"Nobody else knows. We're keeping it quiet until we get a chance to somehow tell Miranda. And what we're going to tell Miranda is a bridge we haven't crossed yet either. Anyway, can you come to the cabin tonight? Even for a little while?"

"Let me check in at home. I think all is under control for a while there. They know I'm on call tonight, so if I don't call you back I'll be there. I'll call you after the operation when I'm on the way. Oh, Robb, please pick up something to eat. I'm hungry now, so I'll be starved by then."

"Okay, sure; you must be feeling better. Do you want to check with Liam and see if there's any food left over from the meeting?"

"Oh, gag. Now I'm getting sick again. Don't remind me of that smell. Speaking of that, I couldn't believe the condition of that room when Sweets and I returned. What a fiasco."

"Was Sweets sick too?"

"No, she came to see if I was all right."

"Hunt suggested the two of you were reacting to Brax Montgomery's latest pronouncements."

"Mentally that's how I react to most things he does, but this time I was sick. I have to go and scrub, but I can't wait to hear all you have to tell me! Bye. Love you."

"Me too; bye."

****

Slumped in a chair, his shirt damp and soiled, tie and coat thrown in a heap on the floor in back of his desk, Liam O'Connell was not a happy man. The phone ringing intermittently went unanswered in the darkened office as he gazed absently out at the murky seascape. The gloom of the encroaching evening certainly fit his mood. Today had been a disaster;

in fact his whole life was a disaster. Shaking his head, he ran one hand over his face and through his damp hair. This hospital and the town of East Meridian, so ideal when he first looked at it, was anything but. Instead of being a place that could help heal his heart, it was a hornet's nest of petty ambitions. The doctors, a surly bunch, spent a lot of time defending their own fiefdoms and they were furious about this damned atrium, which they should be furious about. And the board, one of the most ineffectual Liam had ever come across, spent the meetings arguing with each other or giving the most inane reports Liam had ever heard. And that son of a bitch Brax, what was he up to? He seemed to have a goal but Liam couldn't figure out what it was, and Lansdowe; those financials he gave each month were unreadable. Every time Liam asked the financial office for numbers, they said Mr. Lansdowe was working on them and they would be ready for the meeting. And they were, but they made no sense. Liam sat listening to the bleat of the foghorn and wondered about his future.

****

Sarah James watched the fog drift in once more, obscuring the ocean. Glancing at the dashboard she realized she had been sitting in her car for over an hour. She didn't remember driving to the beach; she remembered that crazy scene at the hospital, and getting into her car, knowing she didn't have to be home for at least two hours. She wanted to be near David. Even though he might be off sailing somewhere, she needed to be near the memories of him. The foghorn sounded in the distance warning anyone on the water that they were near Point Judith, near danger. As was she, or she had been, during those months with David. Throwing herself back into her life, she pushed David out of her mind every time a yearning threatened to surface. She applied to school and was accepted. Bill, his mother and her parents were furious. They each had different reasons for not wanting her to go back to school. Right now she didn't know how she was going to pay for it, but she didn't tell them that. She just told them she was going. The fog lifted a bit and for a moment she could see the outline of the Azimuth Point ledge. Was he there? Had he made a fire? Was that awful dog sitting beside him begging for cookies? Was someone else with him? Well, if so, I hope that bitch of a dog bites her. Sarah laughed out loud. For some reason she felt better and decided to get a latte from the Coffee Bean before she drove home.

****

Louis and Kimberly's flight to New York was delayed because of the fog. They were not too worried because the airline assured them the whole east coast was fogged in and the flight to Italy would be delayed also. The question was ... should they wait in Rhode Island or rent a car and drive to New York? Kimberly didn't care. She was ecstatic. They were returning to Taormina and she knew Louis was going to ask her to marry him. He told her he had his lawyer draw up the divorce papers weeks ago and they had been served on Vi this afternoon. Louis walked down the concourse toward Kimberly, his cell phone to his ear. He was trying to get in touch with the driver who had dropped them off at the airport to see if he could drive them to New York, because there were no cars available for rent.

Kimberly perched on the pile of luggage, crossed her legs, put her elbows on her knees and dangled one spike-heeled shoe, daydreaming about Louis and Italy. Smiling, she watched Louis gesturing on the phone.

"Hey, Kim, you goin' on a big trip? Betcha not alone ... must be someone special, huh?"

Astounded at hearing a familiar voice from her past, Kim turned and looked toward the speaker, one Frankie "Da Skippa" Vincente, Louis's brother-in-law. She slowly rose from the luggage. "What the fuck is it to you, Skippa?"

Frankie, who earned his nickname not from his prowess on the sea but from his constant absence from the high school they had attended, laughed menacingly. Kimberly frowned; a shiver of fear went down her spine. She dared not look toward

176

Louis and hoped he had turned around and gone the other way.

"It's more like who you fuckin', is the question." he growled at her. "My sista's in that Womens' Hospital, real sick. And you and that prick of a husband of hers put her there."

Kimberly put her hand to her mouth and stared at Frankie, not uttering a word.

"Why is Vi in the hospital?" Louis asked quietly. Kimberly and Frankie both turned toward Louis. Kimberly, wide eyed, felt her whole world slip away. She shook her head at Louis, opening her mouth but words did not come out. Louis took a step toward Frankie and asked again, "You heard me; why is Vi in the hospital?"

Frankie, a typical bully, reverted to a more subservient demeanor when confronted by Louis. "Ah, she's in a bad way. When da guy with those papers you and your lawyer made up arrived, she got real upset, and then she fainted and fell against the desk in the office. Then she went into some kinda premature thing and Mama called the rescue squad and they took her to the hospital. Now da doctors are trying to save da babies, they're too young to be born, da doctors said. So Mama told me to find you and bring you to the hospital. Your office told me you were at the airport."

"Babies? What babies?" Louis whispered, white-faced.

"Dose twins you got her with before you left her," Frankie said self-righteously.

Louis, so shocked at this revelation, didn't bother to remind Frankie that Vi had left him. But Kimberly, quickly realizing she was in danger of losing everything she'd worked for these last months, stood in front of Louis facing Frankie, her arms folded across her chest and said with defiance, "Louis did not leave Vi; she left him."

Louis put his hands on Kimberly's shoulders and turned her around facing him. "No, Kim, not now. I have to go with Frankie; it's the right thing to do. I ... I'm sorry. My driver will be here in a few minutes. I'll tell him to take you home."

Kimberly looked wildly from Frankie to Louis and started to say something when Louis pulled her toward him and whis-

177

pered in her ear, "Don't, please don't ... I'll call you as soon as I can."

He turned and walked away with his brother-in-law. Kimberly stared at the two retreating figures and raised her fist at them. Shaking with anger, she started to kick the pile of luggage.

JULY

Selina Pitt, holding a bouquet of the calla lilies Helene loved, anxiously looked down the tracks awaiting the arrival of the train from Providence. She was thrilled and shocked when Helene called and told her she was coming to New York, and eventually it might be for good. She and Robb had separated formally. They told Miranda and her parents, not the whole situation, that would come later, but they started divorce proceedings and it would be final in the fall. Selina heard the engine approaching and signaled to the porter to follow her down to where the parlor cars would stop.

Helene saw Selina hurrying down the platform and her heart quickened. Last night she and Robb said their farewells. He was not there when she awoke. In the early morning light, hugging her years-old, soft blue robe around her, she went to the window and watched the sun come up over the ocean. In the kitchen she made herself a cup of coffee and walked around the house where she had spent so many summers.

Reaching out and touching pictures displayed on the tables, memories were kindled. Closing her eyes she inhaled the sea air, then, picking up and holding treasures Miranda had made over the years at The Beach Club Camp, she wept.

Later, dressed as any proper lady, she was picked up and driven to the station in Providence. Helene did not want to take the chance of meeting anyone she knew at the Kingston Station, and in the summer everyone she knew left Providence.

During the four-hour train trip Helene vacillated between extreme excitement and gut-wrenching dread. She had not seen or talked to Selina in six weeks, except for one short phone call saying she was coming to New York. Was she making the right decision? Helene did not know, but she did know even if it did not work out with Selina, her marriage was over.

Her parents, initially surprised at her announcement, were greatly relieved when they found out there was not going to be a messy divorce their friends would delight in talking about. Not having much interest in Helene, they were suddenly intrigued with her decision to move to New York. "Why New York?" her mother kept asking. Helene would just shrug her shoulders and say offhand it seemed like an exciting place to live, and she was thinking of taking up the piano again.

Helene inherited a large sum of money from her grandmother years ago and Robb managed it for her. She realized this money made her independent; she could do whatever she wanted ... thank you, Granny! Of course Granny might twirl in her grave a few times if she knew of the change in Helene's lifestyle, but then again maybe not; Granny had been rather independent and a forward thinker for her day.

Robb and Helene worked out a financial plan for both of them to contribute toward Miranda's education. They would share custody, even though she would live with Robb in Providence and at Azimuth Point. Robb turned over all of Helene's financial affairs to a money-manager they both agreed on, and would work out later the use of the Azimuth Point house which had been in Robb's family for years. It did cross Helene's mind that perhaps Robb would not be quite so amenable had Diana not been in the picture, but again who knew? Robb was a good person and eventually someone would have been in his future.

Miranda, in the beginning, was worried about exactly how her life would change. She was not close to her mother and the thought of moving to New York did not appeal to her at all. She was thrilled to find out she would be staying with her father, and not much would be different in her wealthy adolescent world. She assured her parents that half of her friends' parents were divorced and she was fine with it. Separately, both Robb and Helene were sure that Miranda's acceptance of the situation would not continue on such an even keel, once Diana and the twins entered the picture, but they did not mention it to each other.

The conductor helped Helene with her luggage, and Selina was there waiting. She enveloped Helene in a bear-hug, holding the flowers off to the side, stepped back to look at her, both of them jostled by the crowds on the platform. She gave the flowers to Helene and kissed her cheek. The porter piled luggage on his cart and headed toward the station. Turning to follow the porter, Selina put her arm through Helene's and tugged her toward the station, beaming at her.

"Welcome to New York and my ... our life."

"Oh, Selina, I can't believe I'm here. Thank you for the flowers; you know they are my favorite."

"You look wonderful. How was the trip?"

"It was fine ... um ... long, actually."

"Have you had lunch?"

"No, I ... I ... I was too nervous to think about eating."

Selina put her arm around Helene's waist and pulled her close, "Good. We'll have lunch at my apartment; we have much to talk about. I didn't hear from you for so long I didn't know what to think, but now you are here and I'm so glad."

Helene hesitated and looked at Selina apprehensively. The extent of what she had done stopped her cold. She had thrown away her former life and now she felt terrified.

Selina stopped in the rushing, bumping crowd. Turning Helene toward her, Selina put her hands protectively on Helene's shoulders. "Listen, my dear, you have been through a lot these last few weeks; don't be nervous. Everything will be fine. We have a whole new life in front of us, and we are not in a hurry. Don't be scared, or at least don't be too scared. I love you; I will never let you be unhappy again."

Helene gave Selina a feeble smile and sighed, "As my old granny used to say, I had a sinking spell." She laughed and hugging Selina back, she felt better. "Okay, let's get on with this new life!"

****

Louis Tedisco was a man in torment. Three weeks ago he had been on top of the world, a successful Providence businessman, in control of his destiny, ready to take on whatever the future held. With two words: "the babies," his world became a quagmire and he faced a future plummeting out of his control.

Standing in the foyer of his newly purchased summer mini-mansion, he eyed the crystal chandelier hanging above the marble floor and felt numb. The voices of his mother, Nonna and mother-in-law bustling around admiring this wonderful house, so much nicer than that drafty old thing Louie bought on the East Side, were like a death knell.

Louis felt cold, chilled to the bone, on this summer's day. He closed his eyes and clenched his fists, wishing himself anywhere but here. He opened his eyes and gazed past the pink damask-draped windows, to the ocean beyond the cliffs. He frowned at the ornate vase of mauve and pink silk flowers of funereal proportions plunked on an enormous white and gold piano in the center of the room. The velvet-and-satin-covered furniture lining every available inch of wall space in the circular hall around the piano made him shudder. Though the day was not overly warm, the house was shut up tight and the air conditioning was on full blast to keep out the salt air and sand.

A large headache thundered through Louis's head. Through the glass scrolled and filigreed double front doors, he glared at the relatives from both sides of the family, arriving in Cadillacs and huge SUVs.

This family gathering was to welcome Vi home from the hospital. For the rest of her pregnancy she had to stay in bed with round-the-clock nursing care. Vi's mother, Angie, moved in to help take care of Vi and was planning to stay after the babies were born. Louis's mother and Nonna would also be on hand to help.

The doctors told Louis and the family saving these babies meant keeping Vi very quiet. She needed complete bed rest and was not to be upset in any way. Vi, delighted at being the center of attention, made sure she got what she always wanted, a house at the beach with lots of marble, wall-to-wall carpeting, and silk and velvet covered furniture.

Her mother's cousin, Sal, the realtor, convinced the owners of a home in Ocean Crag they could really do well on the deal. Within days Louis was in the house and out a large sum of money.

Vi loved the video of the house, and ordered more furniture and new wallpaper for the rooms from her hospital bed. The only thing she didn't like was the driveway of ugly stones. She insisted upon replacing the gravel driveway with asphalt. Louis's father was only too glad to help; nothing was too good for the mother of his first grandchildren. He had his men and equipment in and out of there in a week. Vi was thrilled with the pictures he took of each day's progress, which he brought to the hospital for her approval. The new driveway was an overwhelming success.

The only thing Louis had liked about the house was the gracious curving gravel driveway and boxwood hedge that surrounded it. The life he aspired to and worked so hard towards, had been bulldozed, right along with the gravel. The new asphalt driveway could easily handle the clientele of a small supermarket. The house, which he had despised from the first minute he had seen it, looked like a bordello on steroids.

Outside, the assorted Tedisco and Vincente family cars slammed to a halt, as if entering a NASCAR pit stop. Louis's mother and Nonna rushed past him, out the grand entryway, to greet the family. With loud whoops and squeals, doors flew open, dispensing yelling children carrying buckets, toys and bathing suits. Wives, aunts and grandmothers emerged, greeting each other in high-pitched nasal tones, while juggling large foil-wrapped bowls filled with macaroni, meatballs and sauce, sausage and peppers, and lasagna. Victoriously the women trooped over to the pool area and entered Vi's immaculate new kitchen, approving of it, while eyeing each other's offerings.

The men, after faking jaw punches and whacking each other on the back, both actions accompanied with pithy comments, headed for the bar under the covered deck beyond the pool. Unwrapping cigars, they found beer and settled in for the day.

His mother-in-law watched Louis, enjoying his obvious discomfort. She walked over to him, both hands on her ample polyester flower-draped hips, leaned slightly forward and smirked. "Welcome home, Louie. You been away far too long. We're one big happy family again. Right, Louie? Got you by the short hairs now...." Laughing, she walked outside, slamming the door behind her.

The sound of her malicious glee echoed around the frigid foyer.

****

Diana, weak-kneed, didn't know whether to laugh or cry. She looked at herself in the mirror over her bathroom sink and giggled. I'm pregnant, that's what's the matter. I'm not sick. Looking again at the First Response test, she shook her head in wonder.

Earlier, on the way home from the hospital she remembered that Mildred was making chili for dinner, the kids' favorite. A wave of nausea engulfed her, and gagging, she thought, oh no! The smell of chili had made her sick when she was pregnant with the twins, years ago. Stunned, she almost ran off the road. Gripping the wheel, eyes wide open she grappled with the realization.

Changing lanes she got on to Route 1 and drove south to the Westerly Wal-Mart, where she hoped she wouldn't see anybody she knew, and bought a pregnancy test.

Arriving home she walked into the back hall and was immediately overcome by the aroma of chili wafting out from the kitchen. Dashing up the back stairs to her bathroom, she threw up.

Yes, two pink lines, it was positive. Well, this will change things a bit. I wonder how Robb will take this? I wonder how I will? How can I be pregnant? I'm on birth control pills. Then she remembered when she had the flu and a high fever. She went into the bedroom to phone Robb.

"Hi, it's me."

"I know. Are you feeling better?"

"Um, yes."

"What is the matter? Are you alright?"

"Yes, I'm fine," she laughed, "But I have to talk to you."

"Okay, I'll come over"

"Um ... no, I'll come to your house. See you in a few minutes."

Diana quickly changed her clothes, grabbed a sweater and went downstairs to tell Mildred she was going over to Robb's and not to wait dinner, inwardly gagging at the thought of chili. Walking the beach she hugged herself. A baby, she thought, I can't believe it. Talk about an unplanned event.

Arriving at Robb's she yoo-hooed through the opened top of the double door. "I'm here."

Robb came out of the living room, opened the door and hugged her. "You certainly look better. Do you feel better?"

"Well, yes and no," she grinned.

"What do you mean? Is it some kind of secret?"

"It was even from me."

Robb looked perplexed. Dianna reached up and softly holding Robb's chin with both hands she kissed him. "We're going to have a baby."

"Us, a baby?'

"Umhmm, can you believe it?"

"No, yes, I'm thrilled. Oh Diana, this is wonderful. A baby, how? We took all sorts of...."

"I know, but remember when I had the flu?"

"Yeah, I guess."

"I took antibiotics."

"So, what?"

"Sometimes they negate the pill. And this time they sure did."

Robb hugged her and twirled her around. "I'm so happy. We made a baby. Oh, maybe I shouldn't do that."

"Robb, I'm pregnant, not an invalid. I'm so happy, too. After all these years we are blessed."

"Let's drink some champagne. I want to celebrate."

"I want to celebrate too, but with ginger ale."

"I love you, Diana; I love you so much. This is wonderful. A baby. I can't believe it."

"Robb, this is not such a stretch. Actually, it's a rather normal occurrence."

"I know, I guess, but I never thought I would father another baby."

"You have, we have. And let's not think of the commotion this is going to cause."

The hugged each other and collapsed on the living room sofa in joyous laughter.

****

"For crissakes, Sarah, why don't you take the girls to the beach? It's all they keep whining about."

"Why don't you take them to the beach..."

"Me?"

"Yes, you."

"I don't do those things."

"Well, maybe it's time you thought about doing those things. Besides, what else do you have to do?"

"I have a baseball game. I would never get back here in time to shower and change with all the beach traffic, and besides it's too hot and the beach will be crowded on a weekend like this," he finished lamely, realizing he had just given perfect reasons for not going to the beach.

"I agree and that's why I think it would be a good idea to put in a pool."

"A pool, are you going to start that shit again? Dammit, I'm not going to have this yard dug up for some dumb-ass thing like a pool."

"Your mother would love it."

"Yeah, right. My mother's comfort has always been high on your list."

"We're making lists, are we? Okay, Bill, just exactly what is high on your list? Let's see, playing baseball every night, golfing with your buddies, watching dumb-ass sports endlessly, drinking beer and, yes, kissing John Lansdowe's behind. Mustn't forget that daily ritual."

"I don't kiss Lansdowe's behind, but if it wasn't for him you wouldn't have a house and yard to bitch about putting a pool in!"

"You're right. I'm the one who has to kiss his ass; it slipped my mind for a moment."

"Fuck off, Sarah, I'm going to the bowling alley, you do something with those kids."

"Ah, yes, more intellectual stimulation."

"Yeah, yeah. It's more stimulation than I get around here. The last time you got stimulated was New Year's Eve when you had a few of those fancy drinks."

"The drink is a Cosmopolitan, something you're definitely not! And a lot of good it did me. You couldn't get it up then and you haven't since."

Sarah glared at the slammed kitchen door, her fists clenched. She was shaking, furious, and frustrated, and at the same time, ashamed.

****

"Good evening, Mr. van Dorn."

"Good evening, Elwin. It's a fine evening, isn't it?"

187

"Yes, a real Azimuth Point evening."

"Are my parents here yet?"

"No, Sir. They haven't arrived, but I'll tell them you are here when they do. Where will you be, Sir?"

"On the veranda enjoying the sunset and some rum."

"Yes, Sir."

David smiled at the doorman and bounded up the wide, pillared steps and through the entrance of The Beach Club. He nodded to staff he had known for years while walking through the spacious lobby toward the bar.

The clubhouse, rebuilt in 1939 after the original club had been destroyed in the Hurricane of '38, did not reflect the thinking of its founders. It was three times as large as the original one-floor stucco building built in 1929. The ceiling in the lobby was two stories high, and the old-timers, who could remember the original club, referred to the enormous dining room as "that ridiculous shore dinner hall." The middle-aged members grumbled that you couldn't hear yourself talk when the room was full. And the high pitched yakking, echoing through the cavernous room during fund-raising luncheons, was guaranteed to give staff and members alike colossal headaches.

The younger members like David, having grown up with this club, didn't think much about the aesthetics. They knew it was their club and reveled in their God-given right to be there.

David walked through the bar, empty at this early hour, and continued outside. He sat at a table overlooking the long stretch of beach leading down past the rock to the village of Azimuth Point. Ordering a Mount Gay and lime from the comely waitress, who eyed him longingly, he sipped the amber liquid and watched the sun sink lower into the west.

He closed his eyes and there was Sarah. Where was she right now? Did she ever think of him? Was she happy at home with her children and her husband? Had she applied to the school? Had she been accepted? Did she think of him as much as he thought of her?

He let out a sigh of remorse, thinking of last weekend in Nantucket. The sailing had been great. Their boat won first place and they celebrated until almost sunrise. He was drunk for the first time in over a year and he had sex with a girl he had known in prep school. The next morning she kissed him goodbye and gave him her address in Boston. He had lain there, sorely hung over and in misery. Sarah's face flashed in his mind and he had pushed it away quickly.

Two arms went around his neck and a female voice whispered in his ear, "Buy a lady a drink, sailor?"

"Of course, Diana, what would you like? White wine or Mount Gay?"

"How did you know it was me?"

"After all these years I should know your voice, but it was your perfume. I knew it was you before you said a word."

David stood up and reached for Diana' hand, leading her around his chair and seating her next to him. "You look lovely tonight, even glowing, I might add. Mildred told me you thought you had Lyme disease. Not true, eh?"

"No. I ... um ... don't have Lyme. Actually, I'm fine." Diana decided quickly she didn't want to tell David about herself and Robb and the baby before she had told her parents. She wasn't even going to tell her parents about the baby until they had time to get used to the first news. "Are you staying for dinner or are you just enjoying a drink and the sunset?"

"I'm doing just that and also staying for dinner. Mom and Dad should be here any minute."

"I heard you did well in Nantucket. Got a first, right?"

"Yeah, we did."

"You don't seem too excited about it. You've never won the Bucket before, have you?"

"No. The sailing was great. It's ... well.... I got drunk and was ... um ... let's say indiscreet."

Diana gazed at David, not sure what to say. Could he possibly have been with Sarah? That seemed far-fetched; how could Sarah have gone off on a weekend sailing with him? She was married and had kids. Should Diana mention that she had seen them together? She decided not to, and went in a different direction. "Um, well, David, it's been almost a year ... and you are a healthy young man ... and...."

"It's more complicated, in a way. I mean I knew the person, we had gone to school together ... but it wasn't right. Well, that's not true. I mean it was all right, what I remember of it, and ... she knew it was just a thing. But ... ah, hmmm ... I'm not making much sense, am I?"

"Actually you're making a lot of sense, more than you know. When we find ourselves in situations where we don't want to get hurt and more importantly hurt other people, if we have any conscience at all, we agonize."

"You make it sound much better than what I was thinking. I like your version."

"Good," she said leaned over to give him a hug.

"My goodness, what are you children up to, hugging in public?" boomed David's mother Emily as she and her husband Weistma, appeared suddenly beside David and Diana. "Do you two have something to tell us?" Her weathered face broke into a big wrinkly smile.

Surprised, David and Diana let go of each other and stood up to greet David's parents. "We can't get enough of each other, Aunt Em," laughed Diana as she hugged Emily van Dorn.

"Are you here all alone, my dear?" inquired David's father, kindly taking Diana's hand in his own.

For generations the van Dorn family had named their children after various Dutch ancestors. David's father was named Hans Weistma van Dorn after his grandfather, who was still alive at the time of his birth, so the baby became H. Weistma van Dorn. Emily Parsons van Dorn found this naming tradition ridiculous, so when her children came along she insisted upon regular names. The fact that her daughter became Bradley instead of Mary, she didn't consider upsetting enough to cause a commotion about. David stayed David and that was enough for her. Emily van Dorn knew when to pick her battles.

"Will you join us, Diana?" Emily inquired.

"No, thank you, I'm waiting for my parents. They will be here any minute."

"Not any minute, we're here right now!" Lucia Manning exclaimed with fervor, giving air kisses to all and with a swirl, indicated that the party could now begin. "Emily, so wonderful to see you! It's been ages. Let's all sit together and catch up."

"My thoughts exactly, dearie. Weists, be a love and arrange the table change with Jorge." Weistma van Dorn went off toward the headwaiter and Diana's father headed toward the bar.

Diana and David shrugged their shoulders in resignation as the mothers chatted intently. Diana realized that tonight was not going to be the night she would tell her parents her news.

****

Robb Wells drove up the driveway to the East Meridian Hospital and parked his car and left the motor running, listening to Frank Sinatra sing "My Way." He continued to sing along loudly until he heard a knock on the window. He looked to his left and saw Diana standing there, laughing at him. Sheepishly he turned off the engine and opened the car door.

"Do you have any of Mr. Sinatra's vices too?"

"I can only hope so," Robb said, exiting the car.

She smiled at him as he stood up, her green eyes sparkling and her golden hair shining in the late afternoon sunlight. Then, remembering where they were, she stepped away and assumed a neutral expression. They both started to walk toward the door, neither sure if they should go in together.

"Well, if it isn't my favorite doctor and my very favorite young man. How are you both this lovely afternoon?'

"Sadie!" they both exclaimed with delight, turning toward her voice.

She gave both Robb and Diana a kiss and then, linking her arms through theirs they moved slowly toward the conference room entrance, talking animatedly.

Brax looked up scowling as Diana, Sadie and Robb entered the room. Hunt was already seated and Brax had hoped that Robb would not show up. Now, not only was he here but that old bat was with him and she was sure to cause trouble. His expression grim, Brax turned to Liam's secretary next to him and snarled at her to get him a Diet Coke. Infuriated, Liam frowned at Brax, as his secretary leaped up heading for the refreshment table. Flushed, Liam looked down at the papers in front of him.

Robb placed Sadie in the seat next to Hunt, who greeted her with enthusiasm. Then he went off to get them both a cold drink and Diana went around the table to the seat between Kim and Sarah. Diana nodded hello to both of them. Kim barely acknowledged her and Sarah gave her a wan smile. Diana noticed that Sarah's face was pale and she had dark circles under her eyes. She wondered if she should try to draw Sarah into conversation after the meeting, but she didn't want to cause more anxiety so she decided against it.

Over the talking and shuffling of papers Brax stridently questioned if the social hour could be cut short and the meeting begin. Robb looked over at Brax, lifted his drink in salute, smiled congenially, and with maddening slowness, walked back to his seat next to Sadie. Sadie put her hand in front of her mouth to hide her expression and looked down at her board papers. When Robb sat down Sadie patted his knee.

As Brax droned on through the agenda items Kim looked expectantly toward the door. Louis had not yet arrived for the meeting. She had not seen Louis since that terrible night he had left her at the airport. She knew he bought a house near Azimuth Point at Ocean Crag because he had called and told her, and because of Vi's problems with the pregnancy he couldn't possibly get away for a while. As soon as he straightened out the situation he would get together with Kimberly. She was annoyed that Louis was not there; she peeked at the door once more, tapping her long red nails on the conference table.

John, hearing the noise, glanced at her hand and up at her, his expression inscrutable. She gave him a wide melting smile. Never changing his expression he turned away when Brax called his name to give the financial report.

Liam's secretary finished handing out the financial reports to each trustee and returned to her seat. Sadie looked through the pages quickly; puzzled, she looked up and asked why these financials were just now being given to the board. Liam started to agree with Sadie when his secretary spoke up saying that Mr. Lansdowe had faxed her the financial statements that morning and that she didn't have them to send out with the board packets earlier in the week.

"John, why in heaven's name can't you get these numbers to us earlier?"

"It is more of an earthly reason, my dear Sadie."

"Do tell..."

"The hospital has neither the staff or the software to issue complete reports in time for the trustees meetings, so my staff ends up compiling the hospital monthly reports and they can only do it when they receive the numbers, which happened to be yesterday."

"How good of you, John, to give the services of your staff to the hospital..."

"Thank you, Sadie."

Sadie glared at John as he continued to give his financial report. She whispered to Robb, "I do believe we have the devil counting the woodpile."

John finished the financial report and Diana gave the medical staff report. Brax gathered his papers together and asked John to give the building committee's report.

"The schematic design for the future atrium has been completed and approved by Mr. Tedisco and the building committee. The design will encompass the entrance, roadways and traffic patterns, along with landscaping and signage. The ground-breaking will take place sometime in the early fall, probably Labor Day weekend."

John finished his report and looked toward Brax to end the meeting before any questions came up, when Liam, who had been silent during the whole meeting, spoke out.

"I must, as CEO of East Meridian Hospital, go on record saying I am very much against the building of this atrium. The hospital needs many things and an atrium is certainly not one of them. By doing this you are endangering the future growth of this organization. I feel that this whole situation should be addressed again."

Brax drew his mouth into a cruel grimace and sneered, "Mr. O'Connell, may I remind you that you sit at these meetings at the pleasure of the board. You do not have a vote, nor are you here to make policy. Your job is to run the place, at our direction."

"When I think your direction is wrong, I feel I must say so."

"Really…" Brax's demeanor was so frightening everyone was stunned into silence.

The only sound was the hum of the air conditioning.

Sadie was the first to speak up. "Braxton, I think Mr. O'Connell has every right to speak his mind. And I for one agree with him. I think…."

"Mrs. Brockman, I think you have little right to talk after not attending the last four meetings. This matter has been discussed ad nauseam, voted on by the board, voted on by the town council and we have all the permits. It will be built!"

Sadie's eyes opened wide and she stared at Brax dumbfounded. "Don't speak to me like that, young man!"

Brax gave Sadie a withering glance. "The meeting is over." Picking up his attaché case, he walked out of the room.

Robb and Hunt started yelling at Brax's retreating form that the matter should come up for discussion again. This atrium thing could be stopped right now. Sadie was shaking, she was so angry. Diana, alarmed at Sadie's shaking, jumped out of her seat and rushed over to her side.

"I'm all right, my dear, but I could kill that arrogant little bastard."

Liam also got up to go to Sadie. Assured that she was fine he walked out of the room. He took the elevator to the third floor, entered his office, shut the door, and reached for the phone. While waiting for the headhunter's office to answer the phone, he mentally wrote his letter of resignation to the Board of East Meridian Hospital.

John Lansdowe quietly headed for the door and was stopped by a small hand on his arm. Turning he saw Sweets looking at him plaintively. "John, why is everyone so upset about building this atrium?" Sweets, although in her thirties, still had the aura of an adolescent about her.

John found her innocence appealing. "Don't you worry about it, Rose Ellen. Sometimes when an idea comes along, especially one with a lot of money attached to it, the people who didn't come up with the idea are against it. And they think they should decide how to spend the money. What everybody loses sight of is what is best for the hospital, right, Honey?" Sweets nodded in baffled agreement.

She and John walked out the doors onto the parking lot, shimmering in the late afternoon sun. Sweets took off the beige linen jacket she had been wearing over her matching beige, silk, skinny tank top and skintight, black linen jeans. Her small rounded breasts and nipples were outlined against the filmy fabric. She flung the jacket over her shoulder and gave John a big dimpled smile. "Thanks for explaining it to me, John. The next time Diana and I get into an argument over this I will tell her what you told me. That ought to keep her quiet."

"Do you and Diana argue about this very much?"

"We did and she got angry at me. She said I was an idiot not to understand; an atrium was not doing the hospital any good. We didn't speak for a while. Then we decided not to talk about it again."

"Good, don't you worry your pretty little head about it anymore."

Sweets was about to continue the conversation when she noticed Mona O'Shay heading in their direction. Sweets didn't like the harridan and did not want to have to talk to her, so she thanked John again; and walked off to her car.

John slid into his car. The seat was hot. He swore and quickly turned on the engine to start the air conditioning. As Sweets sauntered away from him, he watched her round little rear end and pressed his legs together. A shadow fell on him. Startled, he looked up and saw Mona.

"I'll be able to get what you want into your hands soon."

"What? Oh, yes, yes, that's good. I've er ... umm ... been meaning to get up to see you."

"It wouldn't do you much good right now; my office is be-

195

ing painted, and it will be torn up for a week. Got any other ideas?" she inquired with a raised eyebrow.

John shook his head. Mona had a silent battle with herself over her rule not to let business interfere with her private life. She had never suggested John come to her condo. But now she might have to, because she wanted some things taken care of at the hospital and Liam was getting in her way.

"Okay, Big Boy, you're about to see how the other half lives. Meet me at The Sea View Condominiums, number 405, in an hour. Oh, yeah, park in the visitor's area and bring some red wine."

John watched Mona walk back into the hospital and felt his erection stiffen in anticipation.

****

Diana and Robb helped Sadie to her car. Graves was waiting for her at the front door of the hospital. She was still in a rage about the scene in the conference room.

"Who does that low-life think he is? How dare he talk to me like that? Poor Bitsy, now I have some idea of what has been going on!" Sadie stopped stock-still and looked from Diana to Robb. "He has been treating her like that for years, and she never said a thing. She looks awful. I wouldn't be surprised if he is hurting her. That bastard, he'll be sorry he decided to take me on!"

Diana and Robb looked at each other surprised. Neither one of them liked Brax but it never occurred to them he was abusing his wife, and they had never seen Sadie so mad.

Helping Sadie into her car Robb knelt down beside her. "Are you going to be okay? We could come stay with you for a while." Robb looked up at Diana and she nodded in agreement.

Sadie patted his hand and grinned, "Well, this is one way an old lady can get some attention. As a matter of fact I would be delighted to have both of you come to my house for drinks and dinner. Right now! What do you say?"

Robb said, "Sure, it's not a problem for me," and looked

at Diana.

"It's not a problem for me, either. Lisle has taken the children out for dinner and a movie because they didn't know when I would be home. But I'm on call so I'm afraid I'll have to forgo the drinks."

"Good. I mean I'm delighted that you both can join me, but I'm sorry that Diana can't have some wine." Sadie unclasped her purse and took out her cell phone and waved it toward Robb. "Aren't these things wonderful? I'll call Louisa and tell her we have company. A matter of fact, I have something I would like to discuss with you two...and it doesn't have a thing to do with the hospital." Sadie smiled sagely.

Robb blew Sadie a kiss and shut the car door, saying they would both be there shortly. "She can't possibly know about us, can she?"

Diana shook her head, "No, how could she? We have been so careful, it must be about something else."

"Yep, you're right."

****

Kimberly yanked open her refrigerator, and with her hands on her hips tried to decide whether to quench her raging thirst with lemonade or wine. She settled the dilemma by taking out both. After downing some of the ice-cold lemonade she opened the wine, found a glass and headed for her terrace. She left the French doors open; the air conditioning was not on and the night air not too warm. She drank a glass of wine quickly and poured another. She sat in misery, oblivious to her beautiful moonlit garden, not hearing the peepers clicking away with joy under the cover of darkness or the water softly cascading down the fountain. But she did hear the key turning in the lock of her side door. Her heart raced. It was Louis; he was the only person who had a key. She forced herself to stay seated. Let him find her.

"Kim? Kim, where are you?" Louis walked through the family room to the kitchen, opened the refrigerator and got a beer. Flipping the top off he called again, "Hey, Kim, where are you?"

Barely breathing, she listened as he walked from room to room calling her name. In the hall he noticed that the French doors were open; walking toward them he made out Kimberly sitting at the table. He walked out and sat on a chair opposite her. She stared straight ahead; he glanced at her, rolling the beer bottle between his hands.

"Kim ... I ... I don't know where to begin. This month has been a nightmare. Vi is back in the hospital. She went in this afternoon. That's why I wasn't at the hospital meeting. I was just leaving the house to go there and she started having pains, the nurse hooked up an I.V. and the rescue came ... we rushed to Womens and Infants. She's going to stay there until the babies are born. Kim, I ... it's ... We can't ... Oh God...." Slouching over, he put his head in his hands, rubbing the cold beer bottle against his forehead. Then, straightening up, he turned to face Kimberly. Putting his beer on the table he started to reach for her then drew back his hand.

"What we did ... I mean ... we were wrong. No, not wrong ... but ... I care for you and I shouldn't ... I can't. Kim, you and I are just not meant to be; it didn't work when we were younger and it can't work now. I have a duty to Vi. She is my wife. I have to stay with her."

Kimberly slowly turned and looked at him. Her dark hair framed her pale face in a cloud of curls, her eyes full of unshed tears. She looked beautiful and anguished. Her full red lips quivered slightly and she turned away.

"Goodbye, Kim."

The sound of her house key being put on the glass table resonated around the garden walls. She sat, rigid in the soft evening air, her hands, red nails gleaming in the dappled moonlight, clasped over her abdomen.

AUGUST

Slouched in her beach chair, Sarah James squinted at her daughters as they raced in and out of the waves. Earlier, she had plunked her chair at the water's edge to keep cool. By now, late afternoon, the incoming tide soaked her bottom with every wave. Hot, sandy, sunburned and cranky, she knew she should do something; move, put on a cover-up or even go home. But she didn't have the energy to argue with the girls to get them out of the water. She splashed water on herself as another wave swirled around her chair. Her sunburned shoulders puckered and stung when she reached up to take off her straw hat. Filling it with water, she plopped it back on her head, soaking her hair and the rest of her body that wasn't already wet.

All day she had willed herself not to look to the left, toward Azimuth Point. With steely determination she had kept David out of her thoughts all summer. She was sure he was enjoying the high life with somebody and didn't even remember that she, Sarah, existed. She slunk further down in the chair, stretching her legs out in front of her, the cool incoming tide covering her scorched knees. The reason she was at the beach, something she had resisted all summer, was to escape her mother Bernice.

Bernice, a pointy woman, tall and thin, had large hands and knobby fingers always aimed at someone or something. Her ungainly body was made more unattractive by the flowered or print dresses she favored, belted tightly at the only part of her that had any extra flesh, her waist. Once she was presentable (her phrase) in the morning, she never found anything else that *was,* including Sarah, whom she disliked from the moment she was born. Sarah was Al and Bernice O'Brien's first child and the reason that her parents had to marry. Two more followed: a boy, Al junior, and a girl, Marie, both equally unattractive replicas of their mother. Bernice doted on the last two. Sarah was the image of Al's beautiful, vivacious mother Elisabeth Munroe O'Brien.

Unfortunately this did not endear Sarah to her father either, as his mother Elisabeth, bored to death with Al's dreary father, had run off with a visiting Chinese professor lecturing at URI when Al was five years old. His mother and the professor moved to California, married, and had four children. Young Albert, thoroughly conditioned by his father and his horrified, racially intolerant relatives, soon lost all interest in his mother and his California siblings. Dull-witted and emotionally locked up, Al slunk through life in a loud-mouthed, drunken stupor. He ignored his children and his wife and lived for beer with his buddies and sports on TV. Many a night at The Dew Drop Inn, too much alcohol prompted ruminations about how Bernice Alchorrio had tricked him into marriage, and cost him a future in the NFL.

Sarah grew up at first trying to please her parents, which was never possible, and eventually despising them. Marriage to Bill and motherhood had not brought the happiness and contentment she thought it would, and now she was more miserable than ever. But she was determined to better her life by going to work, and no matter what anyone said, she was going to get a master's degree.

This morning her mother left a message on the answering machine that she was coming over to talk Sarah out of this foolishness. Sarah belonged at home, not off gallivanting, and Bernice was going to make sure that Bill's mother Irene would not babysit the girls either! That's when Sarah had piled the girls in the car and raced to the beach.

****

Robb hung up the phone after talking with Miranda. He thought the conversation had gone all right, but was not entirely sure. He had wanted to tell his daughter, over dinner, not over the phone, that he was getting married. But Miranda had been busy visiting friends in Europe, the Cape and the Hamptons; she hadn't been home for two days straight all summer. She seemed to take the news calmly enough and was very relieved to know that she and her father would not be moving out of their house on the Point. At least for now, Robb thought. He and Diana had not even discussed where they were going to live. Tonight he and Diana were going to tell her children about their marriage, at dinner. Robb hoped that all would go well. He knew the twins didn't really remember their father, but they might not exactly welcome a new man in their lives, never mind a new baby.

****

Kimberly lay back in the bed watching the silver reflections from the water in the harbor below dance across the ceiling. She raised her arms up and clasped her hands over her head to ease her tender swollen breasts. Despite the air conditioning, earlier she had opened the windows of the suite, and outside she could hear the sounds of Newport.

She heard the murmur of voices in the open-air restaurants, along with occasional shrieks of laughter as people enjoyed the languid summer evening. Sporadic horn tooting echoed around the room as cars moved slowly down the quaint, old, narrow streets. She heard the water slapping rhythmically against the moored yachts as launches passed by, and the night wind whistling through the rigging of the boats docked below her window.

She looked around the luxurious top floor suite with indifference. The weekend had cost him a fortune. Dinners at the White Horse Tavern and Clarke Cooke House, rather risky because someone might recognize them, golf at the Newport Country Club and an even more daring lunch today at the New York Yacht Club. She thought of her recent past and what had prompted her to spend these hot August nights in Newport. The memory of Taormina clutched at her heart. She drove it out. She only had one goal now ... what was best for Kimberly.

Lowering her eyes, her heart cold, her body numb, she watched Brax Montgomery grunt to a climax. Rutting into her, ramming Louis's baby.

****

"Are you going to be my Daddy?" Jamie asked wide-eyed.

"No, your daddy will always be your daddy."

"Then what will you be?" he inquired.

"I will always be there for you and Marianne and your mommy."

"Always?"

"Yes, I promise."

Jamie smiled in relief, and went on to more pressing subjects. "I have lots of cars and trucks. Do you want to see them? Do you like to sail? I would really like to go sailing. Uncle David said he would take me sailing but he hasn't had time yet. Wouldya?"

Robb took the little boy's hands in his and promised to do both things. Diana put her hand in front of her mouth and smiled.

Marianne was not so easily satisfied; she looked at Robb with a hint of defiance. "Do you have any children?"

"Yes, I have a daughter; her name is Miranda."

"How old is she?"

"She's thirteen."

This was a surprise to Marianne. She was instantly alarmed. "Will she have to sleep in my room?"

"No, she has her own room."

"She has her own room here?"

"No, at my house."

"I'm not moving to your house. It's too big. Mommy took us by there yesterday and I didn't like it."

Diana sat up on the sofa to reprimand her daughter. Robb shook his head at her, and answered the scared, little girl. "Marianne, your mother and I want all of our children to feel safe and loved. We wouldn't move you out of your room or your house. Miranda doesn't want to move out of her room either. We will keep both houses open; you'll see, it will all work out very nicely," Robb said, with hope in his heart.

Marianne, being a tenacious child, was not about to give up graciously. "Is her mother dead like my father?"

"No, her mother lives in New York."

"Why doesn't Miranda live in New York?" Marianne asked, elated that she had stumbled upon an excellent way to perhaps get the mysterious Miranda completely out of the picture. Then she put her hands on her hips, put her face right in front of Robb's and added ominously, "I thought all children were better off with their mother..."

Robb had difficulty keeping his face straight. Diana restrained herself from throttling her sassy child, and Jamie, sensing something untold in the air, stopped playing and looked up at his twin. Mildred, coming into the room to announce dinner was ready, broke the silence. But Marianne kept looking at Robb, waiting for an answer. He smiled at her and said gently, "Miranda doesn't want to leave her house any more than you do, Marianne. And most of all, your mother and I don't want to make anyone sad, and we will work very hard to make sure everyone is happy with the arrangement. Now, may I escort you into dinner, Miss Marianne?"

"Okay." Marianne took Robb's hand and started to skip beside him. Looking up she asked, "Will you be sleeping in my mother's room?"

"Only after we are married," Robb answered in a deeply

serious tone, looking back at Diana and rolling his eyes.

After dinner Lisle took the twins up for their bath. Mildred congratulated Robb and Diana on their up-coming marriage and went to her room to watch TV. Diana curled up beside Robb on the sofa and rested her head on his shoulder. "Whew! I'm more exhausted than if I had just spent six hours in the OR. But all in all it was a great success. Jamie is relieved to have a man around. He told me quite seriously not so long ago that all these women drive him to distraction."

"That's a big word for a six-year-old, isn't it?"

"My mother is always saying that something is driving her to distraction; he picked it up from her. You handled Marianne very well. I was ready to wash her mouth out with soap."

Robb chuckled. "She's a pistol and doesn't miss a trick. I imagine it's hard to keep one step ahead of her. Miranda isn't like that at all, she is ... well ... ummm...a distant child is the only way I can think of it. The three of us were not close, like you are with your children, with your whole family in fact, as well as Lisle and Mildred. This house is bursting with life and noise. Our house was always very quiet. We rarely saw Helene's parents, and my parents died in that terrible accident. Miranda was always at some other child's house ... like she is now."

"How did she take the news of our marriage?"

"She seemed fine with it. And she also wanted to know if all of you are going to be living with us. Obviously those two girls don't want to lose control over their territory," Robb laughed.

"I hope that the children get along with each other ... it might be difficult ... there's a big age difference. When will I meet Miranda?"

"She'll be home at the end of the month for a couple of weeks before she has to return to school."

"Okay, we'll start slowly. Lunch or dinner with just the three of us; I don't want to subject her to Marianne right off the bat," Diana laughed.

"That will work itself out ... but ... I dunno ... well ... I had a thought the other night that perhaps we should think about maybe starting our lives together in a new place. One that would be just ours."

Diana sat up and looked at Robb in surprise. "You mean someplace outside of Rhode Island? The only other place I can practice is New York. I surely don't want to move back to that city. Why do you want to do this? You just assured both girls they could stay in their rooms in their houses."

"Don't get upset, I...."

"I feel like you've blind-sided me. Where did this come from?"

The thought ran through Robb's mind that Diana's quick teenage temper was surfacing after all these years. He realized that he had not managed this great idea, his great idea, very well. They should discuss together what to do with their lives. With a sinking feeling he remembered all those years ago when he had what he thought was a great idea. He had blasted her with it, and she walked out.

He took her hands saying, "I'm sorry I didn't handle this very well. Please let me explain."

Diana looked at him warily, "Yes, go on...."

"Last week I found out that Louis Tedisco is putting that wonderful house he restored on Congdon Street up for sale. And I just wondered if we should look at it and perhaps think about living, for the winter anyway, in Providence. That way we would be on neutral ground. I never meant we would leave Azimuth Point. We'll keep the family houses here and come back for the summer. You could practice at Providence Bay Hospital; you're always getting offers from other doctors to join them. And we both know that Brax Montgomery will ruin East Meridian Hospital and I don't think there is a thing you or I or even Sadie can do about it."

Diana looked away, and deep in thought, held Robb's hand, gently caressing the tops of his fingers. "You have a good point about neutral ground, maybe Providence in the winter would work out. Quite honestly, I've been thinking about where the twins should go to school now that they'll be in first grade, or at the latest what I should do about second grade. I was mostly concerned because Marianne shouldn't be in the same class as Jamie, and down here they would, like they were in kindergarten. But I'm not sure about Providence Bay; the reason I decided to move here was that I didn't want a big hospital. Let's get through this year and let all of us get used to each other. Is this our Louis Tedisco, from the hospital board? Why is he selling his house?"

"I understand he bought a house in Ocean Crag."

"Ocean Crag? Good heavens, that's a lot different from anything on the East Side. Well, I wish he would stick that damn atrium on his Ocean Crag house instead of the hospital."

"I agree. Sadie is having her lawyer look into the hospital by-laws to see how we can get rid of Brax, or at least stop this atrium nonsense. She said she hopes to have something before tomorrow's board meeting. To tell you the truth, I'm so disgusted with Brax and John I would like to resign and walk away from the whole mess. So when I heard that the Tedisco house was going to go on the market, I thought you and I could look at it and if we liked it, buy it and be done with East Meridian Hospital."

"Oh, Robb, I can't even think about moving at this point. We have to get through your divorce, get married and the baby. I still can't believe about the baby. I always used to laugh at pregnant brides and now I am one. And I will be a very obvious one; we should get married the day after your papers arrive. The Point will have a field day over this. Wait until my mother finds out about the baby."

"Your parents took the news of our marriage pretty well. They seemed more surprised than anything."

"I guess we did cover our tracks rather well. Everybody was surprised at first, because so few people even know that you are divorced ... or getting a divorce. Oh well, this is a happy time for us and I'm not going to let anyone spoil it."

"You're right. Give me a hug and I'd better be on my way or I won't be able to keep my promise to Marianne."

"What promise to Marianne?"

"That I won't be sleeping in your room until after we are married."

"I didn't realize that was a promise."

"Yes ... but only for this house."

"I see...."

****

Sadie Brockman's step faltered as she walked from the hot outside deck into the cool empty lobby of the Azimuth Point Beach Club. She put her hand on the back of a chair to steady herself, thinking, I must have stayed in the sun a bit too long during lunch. She looked through the lobby to the front door, and realizing Graves had not arrived to take her home, she decided to sit and wait for him in the wing chair she was leaning on.

She settled herself when she heard voices behind her belonging to two men coming out of the bar. She instantly recognized Brax Montgomery and John Lansdowe speaking in conspiratorial tones. Sadie listened intently, wondering what those two were up to now.

"Brax, we need those deeds to the land on Route 1. I want to get this project going with PuisSantMeritor. They're getting impatient and worried."

"What are they worried about? We know we can convince the board to sell, once we show the hospital is so in debt that we need to merge with a rich company for the hospital's so-called future. The hospital's losses are ample enough, at this point, to undermine the whole system."

Sadie's eyes opened wide at the revelation and she put her hand to her mouth.

"Neither they nor I am worried about that. What I'm worried about is that woman with the Volunteer Foundation. She is traveling all over the United States speaking before legislatures to convince them that the states' attorney generals should have regulatory authority over charitable assets of private not-for-profit institutions. Another company, like PuisSant, Columbia HCA, has bought up many not-for-profit hospitals all over the country, taken their endowments and then closed the unprofitable hospitals, a great business move. Now this woman is convincing many states' legislatures to stop this and she's due to come to Rhode Island next spring."

"Christ Almighty! Just what we need! Another do-gooder. How do we stop her?"

"That's just it, we can't stop her. We have to get the board to agree to sell out to PuisSantMeritor before this woman gets to our legislature. East Meridian doesn't have a large endowment, just the small one Edward Brockman left for the ER, and PuisSantMeritor isn't after that, but they do want the permits the hospital has, to transfer to the new modern facility they're going to build in the shopping center. We have to get them signed and announced to the board and the community as a done deal. Can you imagine if this woman and some politicians get in the middle of this and start yapping about the public good? We'll be in a terrible mess."

"Okay, okay, I'll get the deeds signed over as soon as possible." That old fart of a family lawyer is impossible to deal with, Brax thought. I could wring Bitsy's neck for holding this up. He then continued, "We should bring this to the board after we have finished the atrium, say February."

"Good, we'll convince them that it's in the hospital's best interest to do this. After everything is signed and sealed, there won't be a thing they can do about it. We know that PuisSant-Meritor will decide to close the hospital, get rid of the free care and move only the profitable operations up to the new facility in the shopping center, but the board doesn't have to know that."

"Well, the board won't know that, and the biggest coup of all is getting Tedisco to pay for the new atrium. It will make a handsome entrance for the condos we'll build in the old hospital building once we buy it back, for a song, from PuisSant-Meritor. After all it's the best thing for us to do for the community, right, John?" Brax intoned with a smug smile.

"We'll take that old eyesore, sitting on acres of prime waterfront property, and make it into something nice."

They both chuckled as they walked away.

Sadie was in shock. She sat quietly until John and Brax walked out the front door of the club. She watched as they chatted waiting for their cars. The valets brought them and the men, with knowing salutes to each other, got in their cars and roared away into the afternoon.

Shaking with anger, Sadie reached in her purse for her cell phone to call Robb. Her mind was a jumble with what she heard, and she was furious. Instantly she put her cell phone back realizing anyone coming by would overhear her like she overheard Brax and John. Instead she would use the house phone in the private booth across from the reception desk.

Sadie stomped across the lobby, gritting her teeth, "The audacity of those scumbags," she seethed under her breath. "I'm going to stop those two right in their tracks and have a lot of fun doing it."

She pulled open the phone booth door, sat down, reached for the phone and gave the club operator Robb's private number. She was so mad, the mirror above the shelf that held the phone was swimming before her eyes. Robb answered the phone. Thank God he's there, she thought and started to tell him about John and Brax. But the words wouldn't come out. She felt a terrible pain in her head; her image was fading from the mirror.

Robb said hello, and then hello again and looking at the phone in frustration, hung up.

****

Later that afternoon in the boardroom Robb wondered where Diana was; he had talked with her an hour or so before the meeting. Sadie and Kimberly were not here either. He listened to Brax drone on, and then a pager went off. Liam started in surprise, and went to the house phone. After a terse conversation he went over to Robb and said Dr. Manning asked him to come to the ER immediately. Robb's face turned white. He hurried out of the room, leaving board members wondering what happened. Brax had little interest in what happened and was glad Robb left, and wished Hunt would have gone with him.

Robb rushed down the hall and frantically punched the

elevator buttons to take him down to the ER. Tearing through the doors as they opened he ran up to the admitting desk and asked for Dr. Manning. A nurse directed him to Trauma Room 5. He slid the door open and saw Diana sitting beside a bed, holding Sadie's hand in hers. Diana turned and looked up at Robb, her eyes spilling with tears. "Oh, Robb, I can't ... I can't do anything ... she's in a coma ... she's had a stroke. Could you please call Bertie and tell him to get up here right now."

****

Louis Tedisco opened the door of his beach house and let out a sigh of relief. Not because he was home; he hated the beach house more than ever. He was relieved to be out of the boring hospital board meeting, and he was thankful Kimberly had not been at the meeting.

He knew if she had been there, she would have ignored him, but being in the same room with her would have been difficult. He missed her and thought of her all the time. He suffered over his decision. What he wanted, more than anything, was to be with Kimberly. But he was a father now and he had responsibilities to his wife and newborn twin girls.

Many nights this summer he had woken up (not next to Vi, she slept in another room), feeling so trapped in this hermetically sealed house, he needed to open the bedroom windows to smell the salt air. He would lean against the window frame and greedily gulp in the damp air, trying to cleanse his lungs and his heart. The pain and longing refused to go away.

Rubbing his forehead he pushed thoughts of Kimberly out of his mind and walked over to the pile of mail on the hall table. He leafed through the envelopes, ripping open some, piling up others to take to the office. And then he noticed one addressed to him in Kimberly's handwriting. Guiltily he glanced through the dining room at the kitchen door where his mother and mother-in-law were preparing dinner; they didn't know he was home.

He opened the envelope and stared at the paper. He looked, in horror, at the copy of a bill and medical report of an abortion of a three-months-old male fetus, done on Kimberly MacComber. Pale and shaken, Louis crumpled the papers in his fist and strode out of the house. He walked the beach for hours, devastated.

****

Sarah James hesitated as she got out of her car. With apprehension she looked at St. Peter's of the Dunes Church, marveling at the red shingle-clad building that had ridden out many storms and hurricane surges, especially the devastating one of '38. The church was not on Azimuth Point, but outside the entrance to the Point on Route 1A. It was on a knoll next to the dunes, bordered on the far side by sea grass at the edge of Ashwam Pond. Azimuth Point families had worshiped here for generations. To this day many arrived for services by boat, rowing or under sail to tie up at the church dock. Sarah had never been in the church before; her family and Bill's had attended the Methodist Church in East Meridian.

Adjusting her eyes to the dim interior as she entered, she shivered slightly from nerves and walked over to sign the book. Seating herself toward the back, she knelt down and said a prayer. She felt a catch in her throat and tears filled her eyes. Sadie had been kind to Sarah when she joined the hospital board. She was the first to greet Sarah and introduce her to other members. At meetings Sadie always made an effort to include Sarah and put her on some of the committees that Sadie was chairing.

Sarah sat back and reached into her straw summer purse to get a handkerchief and blew her nose. She was going to miss Sadie, and judging from the crowds filing into the church a lot of other people felt the same way.

As the service began, Sadie's son Bertie, his wife and three children came in the side door. Sarah looked at them with interest. Bertie was tall, handsome and blonde. He and the youngest daughter resembled Sadie. Bertie's wife was very attractive and resembled the perfectly appointed Azimuth Point women in the church. The other two children looked like their mother. The little girl, the one who looked like Sadie, started to cry and her father picked her up and wiped her eyes with his handkerchief. Sarah wondered if she was scared of the music and the crowd, or if she missed her grandmother.

Some people came into her pew. Sarah didn't look at them. She was too interested in looking around at the crowd, so she moved over without giving them a thought. She noticed Diana with Robb Wells and another older couple. She heard, at the hospital, that Diana and Robb were going to be married. The couple with them, she was pretty sure, were Diana's parents.

The church was decorated with blue, yellow and white flowers. Sarah knew the white ones were daisies, but had no idea what the other flowers were. These flower arrangements were soft and pretty, not the formal swags she usually saw at funerals in East Meridian. Gazing around the church Sarah recognized other board members sitting throughout the congregation.

The choir started to sing a rousing hymn and Sarah tensed, remembering the fight with Bill about staying for the funeral. Bill said there was no need for Sarah to go to Sadie Brockman's funeral. Sarah, dreading two weeks in the South with Bill's family, stood her ground. Bill, his mother and the children had left for North Carolina two days before the funeral. Sarah was to fly down later; she hadn't yet told Bill she had not even called the airline for a reservation. Giving her head a slight shake, she realized with relief she had a few days off before facing his relatives and the heat.

The minister finished the eulogy and the congregation stood up to sing a hymn. Sarah reached for the hymnal just as the person to her left reached for the same book. The hand in front of her looked familiar. She looked up at David van Dorn.

He smiled and graciously handed her the book. Wordlessly she took it and unbelievably opened to the right page. David moved close to her and held the other side of the hymnal and started to sing. It registered on her paralyzed brain that he had a nice voice. Sarah felt her throat constrict. The intense emotion running through her body had left her voiceless. She inched back a bit to look at the couple next to David. Were they his parents?

For the rest of the service she was in a terrifying fog. Her knees were shaking and she gripped the back of the pew in front of her to stop trembling. If David was aware of her turmoil he did not show it. At the end of the service the minister invited the congregation to go to Sadie's house for a reception and led the family out of the church.

David turned to Sarah, "Hi, I'm so glad to see you. You look so nice, and you're very tan."

Sarah, remembering her sunburn and the agonizing that went into her decision of what to wear, smiled. Should she be summery or conservative? The conservative navy blue linen had won.

"Thank you ... I ... um.... how have you been?" she faltered.

The church was emptying out and David left the pew and waited for Sarah to walk with him.

"I ... well, it's been an interesting summer. Could I ask you a favor?" he said, taking her elbow and steering her up the aisle.

"Uh ... sure."

"My car is in the shop; I took a cab here. So perhaps you could give me a lift to Sadie's? It's right across the street from my house, um ... as ... you know."

Sarah, who had no idea which house was Sadie's and no thought of going to the reception when she entered the church, nodded in agreement. David kept up the conversation as they left and headed for her car. Sarah, dumbstruck by this encounter, could not think of a thing to say.

They got into her car and David asked lots of questions about her summer, to which she mumbled replies. Stopping at the Azimuth Point gatehouse, David motioned to her to let the driver's side window down.

"Hey, Lionel, this is a friend of mine, we're going to the reception for Mrs. Brockman's funeral."

"Okay, Mr. van Dorn. So sorry about Miz Sadie, a lovely lady. I will miss her."

"We all will, Lionel."

Sarah drove, for the first time, down Azimuth Point's main

road. This day was in no way resembling the one she expected. She turned into David's driveway.

"Where do you want me to park?" she asked.

"Huh? Oh, it doesn't matter. Just leave your keys in the car. When they deliver my car they'll put it in the garage, then move your car around."

Sarah smiled to herself; Azimuth Point people expected people to cater to them, delivering this and that and also putting them where they belonged.

Getting out of the car, Sarah felt a shiver of apprehension. All her life she had waited for this moment. And now she was here and did not have the faintest idea what she should do. She felt as if she had landed on Mars without a space suit.

David smiled and motioned across the street. "Shall we go?"

Sarah nodded in agreement, took a deep breath, squared her shoulders and started toward Sadie's house. Many cars were parked on the grass on either side of the road. Sarah and David walked silently up the road past the tall hedges that hid of the Point homes from view.

Sarah felt nervous. Her usual aplomb had left her. All her witty, sarcastic judgments about people on the Point swirled around in her mind. She was beginning to panic, realizing she was going to be surrounded by those very people.

David's thoughts were far afield from Sarah's. He was undone by the feelings that Sarah's presence aroused in him. He realized that although he had pushed thoughts of her out of his mind all summer, she still had been uppermost in his subconscious.

Cars were turning into an opening in the hedge marked by a sign low to the ground saying *Seaside*. David, deep in thought, stepped around the sign and turned right into the gravel driveway.

At the same time another car turned into the driveway and David had to jump backwards onto the grass, and Sarah, locked in her own torment and not watching where she was going, collided with David. They both fell down, into the bushes. The car stopped and Diana jumped out of the passenger side. "Are you all right? What happened?" She called as she ran over to them. Helping Sarah up, she looked at David sprawled in the bushes and started to laugh. "Usually, van Dorn, you look like the Great Gatsby, but right now you look like the Great Flatsby!"

"Thanks so much, Diana, I always knew I could count on you as a friend," David, groaned peevishly.

Laughing, Diana reached down to help David up, and gave him a hug "No broken bones I hope?"

"Nope, just a bruised ego."

Diana, glancing from David to Sarah and having seen the look of confusion and mortification on Sarah's face but not sure what brought these two together again, decided some quick action was in order. She made an attempt to brush off David's backside and gave him a whack. Reaching out she took Sarah's hand in hers, and turning she waved to her parents and Robb, calling out, "Go on up to the house. We're all right here. I'll walk up with them."

Robb shrugged his shoulders, waved Diana a kiss, and quickly accelerated, throwing his soon to be in-laws against the backs of their seats with a thump.

Sarah glanced furtively at David and dropped her eyes. David looked at Diana in dismay, as if he had, for the first time, realized the implications of asking Sarah to bring him home and accompanying him to the reception.

Diana put her arm around Sarah and gave her a warm hug. "We're all going to miss Sadie very much, aren't we?"

"Yes, she was so nice to me."

Diana made conversation as they walked toward the house. She talked about the service, the beautiful weather and anything else she could think of. "Sadie must have ordered this day, there's absolutely no humidity. She hated humid weather."

They climbed the wide front steps and David opened the screen door, saying, "From the sound of things everybody's on the porch."

They walked through the hall. The house was different from anything Sarah had seen before. On the left was a handsome library, with a man's portrait over the fireplace. She wondered if that was Mr. Brockman. The hall was light and cheerful with a flower-filled table in the center. Sarah glimpsed a formal dining room after the library and to the right, a living room that went the length of the house. There were groupings of sofas, with straight chairs at either end, around oblong coffee tables, and big footstools on the other side of the tables. The whole effect was of soft floral designs and prints that did not exactly match but went together beautifully. On each of the tables were small bouquets of white flowers and on the tables against the walls were large sprays of salmon gladiolas in silver vases. Sarah stood in awe, staring into the living room.

"It is beautiful, isn't it?" Diana murmured, standing with Sarah.

Sarah nodded, "The room reminds me so much of Sadie, even of her perfume."

"Sadie had beautiful taste and it is her perfume. Those small white flowers are tuberoses. She always wore Mary Chess Tuberose perfume. Years ago, when Sadie first came to the Point, Edward brought the flowers with him, every weekend, on the train from New York. He knew how much she loved those flowers; you couldn't get them in East Meridian then. The ladies of the Point were very jealous of Sadie and her flowers. Not that they would ever let on, but that's another story," Diana grinned.

David had started out the porch door, realized that Diana and Sarah had stopped at the entrance to the living room, and went back to join them. "We had lots of parties in this room, didn't we?"

"We sure did. I so loved Edward, as did Sadie. He was a hard act to follow. I'm sure that was the reason she never married again."

While Diana was talking, David glanced at Sarah. He was so aware of her it almost hurt to breathe. Sarah was so impressed with the serenity and beauty of the room she momentarily forgot her turmoil.

"Do you know Bertie?" Diana asked her.

Sarah turned and said with an amused smile, "No, can't

say that we ever met. I don't think he ever came to the Inn for dinner on my shift."

Diana looked confused.

"The Ebb Tide Inn, I worked my way through college there ... as a waitress ... I ... um ... don't remember ever seeing him."

"Oh." Diana digested that bit of news without glancing at David. Now I get it ... David used to hang around the Inn a lot during his wild teenage years. Obviously these two had a past, she thought, intrigued. "Well let's find Bertie ... this is always the hard part. In my heart I don't want to believe that Sadie has gone." Diana started toward the porch door with tears in her eyes.

David moved forward to open the screen door for both of them. Diana went out onto the porch and David touched Sarah's arm as she started past him. She stopped in the doorway and they looked at each other for a few seconds longer than they had to.

Then a tear-choked voice behind them made them jump apart. "Oh, Mr. David," David turned and found Louisa, Sadie's housekeeper, standing there holding a tray of sandwiches, tears running down her cheeks.

He took the tray from her, put it on a table, and he hugged Louisa while getting his handkerchief out of his back pocket to give to her. He spoke soothingly to Louisa as she wept. Sarah was touched and surprised at this side of David, so different than the uncaring youth she had known so long ago.

"Mr. David, I miss her so much. I can't believe she has gone."

"I know. We all feel the same way."

"I just keep falling apart ... and there is so much to do ... I ... I."

"I'm sure Bertie would understand if...."

She brightened at his mention of Bertie, and smiling at David, she wiped away her tears. "Mr. Bertie and his family are staying for the rest of the summer. And you know Miss Sadie would be very upset if I didn't do right by them. She always loved having them here. I'm better now. I'll give this a wash and get it back to you soon." She motioned with the damp handkerchief, put it in her pocket and picked up the tray. Then with her head held high she marched through the porch door that David held open for her. Sarah watched with admiration and gave David a wide smile.

"Hey, I never realized you have a dimple," he said touching her cheek.

"I forgot it myself to tell you the truth," she laughed as she walked by him onto the porch.

Sarah froze, confronted with a porch full of people she did not know. David put his hand on her elbow and guided her to the group of people surrounding Diana. As they joined the group, Diana introduced Sarah to her parents and some of Sadie's relatives, including Bertie and his family. Bertie accepted her condolences and surprised Sarah by saying that his mother had mentioned Sarah to him when she talked about the board at the hospital. She was so conscious of David's presence she did not dare look at him, even though she knew he kept looking at her. The sexual tension between the two of them became almost unbearable. The crowd mingled and split until Sarah found herself at one end of the porch and David at the other. She wanted to be with David, and if the way he looked at her meant anything, he felt the same way.

The sky to the north darkened and Sarah realized the incoming squall was the excuse she needed to say she must leave. Staying so close to David was too dangerous. She wanted him so much and it was not right: she was married. After saying goodbye to Diana and Bertie she slipped away quietly and walked along the garden path to the driveway at the opposite end of the house.

David looked across the porch, and realizing Sarah was nowhere to be seen, went into the house to look for her. He got to the front door and saw her walking through the hedge opening towards her car. He opened the door and started to run up the driveway as the breeze picked up and the sky darkened.

Sarah was opening her car door when she heard footsteps behind her on the gravel drive. She turned as David skidded to a stop. They looked at each other. He took her face in his hands.

"Sarah, Sarah, I can't get you out of my mind ... I ... I don't want to ever hurt you again, and yet I don't know what to do ... I...."

Her heart was beating loudly, so loudly she wondered if David could hear it. She put her hands around David's waist and brushed her lips softly on his. "You won't hurt me this time, I ... we...." She started to answer when a bolt of lightening shot across the sky and thunder filled the air.

They both jumped, and heavy raindrops splashed on them as they fell into each other. David pulled her toward him, his mouth was open when he found hers and she shuddered, leaning against him. He kissed her hungrily; she felt his hardness as he ground into her. She pulled his wet shirt out of his pants and ran her hands over his back. The warm rain soaked them and they heard people running for cover and car doors slamming on the other side of the hedge.

He pulled back from her, gasping, "Sarah, Sarah are you sure?" She nodded and ran her tongue around her lips. Realizing that half the neighborhood was only a few feet away, he grabbed her hand and they ran toward his house.

He opened the door and they stumbled into the living room. Still kissing her, David led her to the bedroom. He unzipped her sodden linen dress and it dropped to the floor.

Against the violent flashes of lightening and the crashing thunder they devoured each other. He undid his shirt and she undid his belt. He unhooked her bra and she unzipped his pants, pulling them down. He pulled her panties down, kissing her until she moaned and pulled him toward her, wanting more. The mounting sensations made her weak and she fell against the bed. She lay there wanting him desperately; he could see it in her eyes as he lay down next to her running his hands over her sensual body. She responded by touching and teasing him until he started to tremble. No woman had ever made him tremble before. She caressed him and he groaned. Lost in unbridled desire, a desire that had smoldered in both of them over the summer, he entered her rock hard, and quivering she rose to meet him. They moved together, rolling over until she was on top. She stopped and sat up, feeling him pulsing beneath her. She ran her hands up her body to her breasts, cupping them as an offering to him. He held back, savoring the vision of her above him hot with desire, wanting him as much as he wanted her. Slowly she started to move, tantalizing him, bringing him to the edge, until they could not stop. She sank down on him, climaxes roaring through her. They rolled over and came together, crying out, as the storm raged and rain beat down on the roof.

****

Diana and Robb, wrapped in blankets, sat on her porch, watching lightening zigzag over the ocean and listening to the storm. She asked, "Do you think Sadie brought this storm on because she really didn't want to leave?"

Robb shook his head, "I don't know. She always made an entrance, so perhaps this is a fitting exit."

"I have the oddest feeling she is trying to tell us something"

"What, like it's wet outside?"

"That ... is rather obvious. No, well ... I don't know what I mean. Just a weird feeling I have."

"Pregnant women always have weird feelings."

"You're right about that. And I'm going to have to tell my mother soon. My clothes are getting tight and she is sure to notice. Oh God, then the you-know-what will hit the fan."

"She'll get over it."

"I suppose ... I'm tired. I wish you could spend the night."

"So do I, but then we would have the explanations in the morning. I'm not sure I could out-talk Marianne," Robb chuckled. "Come on, let me get you into bed and I'll lock up and go home."

"First of all, if I let that happen you would never leave, and second, I have to let the dog out."

"I'll let the dog out."

"He won't go for you."

"Oh, good Lord, we'll both let the dog out."

"Okay."

They huddled under the umbrella, waiting for the dog. "Do you think there is anything going on between David and Sarah James?" asked Diana.

"How would they have even known each other?"

"Well ... I ... um ... they didn't seem strange to you?"

"Strange ... no ... I didn't think so. She is a very pretty girl. But what makes you think there's anything going on?"

"Um ... oh ... well, nothing...you're probably right." Diana kept to herself that she had seen them on the beach and she had also seen David run after Sarah when she left Sadie's house.

****

Sarah woke up to a grey morning. Hearing the rain dripping off the eaves, she wondered for a moment where she was. Then remembering the night, she blushed. Sex with Bill had been a quick ho-hum duty, not unpleasant but certainly never like this. She and David had made love two more times in the night, slowly bringing each other to new heights of sensation. It wasn't until just before dawn, wrapped in each other's arms, exhausted, that she wondered about the dog and was relieved to hear it was at the vet's with a broken paw.

David slept beside her, his arm thrown over her waist. She snuggled closer to him savoring the moment. She had no idea what was going to happen next, nor did she care. It was as if a huge dam had broken inside her and the terrible past had been washed away. How it was going to play out she didn't have a clue. But for the next ten days she would live her dream and then get on with her new life.

****

Bitsy Montgomery looked out the window of the private plane Uncle Rutherford had chartered and watched Green Airport disappear as they flew into the clouds. After Sadie's funeral, which Brax did not attend, Rutherford and his wife Kitty noticed bruises on Bitsy's arms. Bitsy, so emotionally fragile, could no longer put up a good front, and collapsed in her Aunt Kitty's arms. Crying, she blurted out the story of her horrible marriage, the abuse and her fear for Ben.

That summer Brax had threatened Ben that if he didn't work for free in Brax's office in New York, he would not pay his tuition at Yale. So Ben had no choice but to stay in New York and be ridiculed daily, in front of the other staff, by his father. Rutherford and Kitty were horrified. Kitty had known the marriage was not one of the best but she never thought of Bitsy being physically hurt, and to abuse one's own son was beyond her comprehension.

Rutherford was so appalled he could hardly grasp what Bitsy had been through these past years. He was infuriated that Brax was holding the tuition money over Ben's head. "Why," he blurted out, "Ben's tuition is paid for by me! It comes out of the trust money; Brax doesn't have anything to do with it. That bastard, that bastard..!"

For once Kitty didn't utter a word of reprimand at Rutherford's oath, because she agreed with him. Rutherford got on the phone immediately and sent a car for Ben in New York. Brax was out of town so Rutherford did not have to deal with him. He told Ben his mother was not well and he must come to Azimuth Point.

When Ben arrived they sat down and more of the story came out. Rutherford arranged for Ben to take a semester off from Yale, and rented a house for Bitsy and Ben near his and Kitty's vacation home in Montana. Kitty was flying with them. Rutherford stayed behind to secretly arrange divorce proceedings and lock up the deeds and trusts so Brax couldn't get at them.

Rutherford told Brax that Bitsy was not well and he had asked Ben to come up to Rhode Island to be with her. Brax had no interest in how or where Bitsy was, but he was pissed off he couldn't torment his son, the son he was so jealous of because of his good looks, innate charm and quick mind.

Rutherford was very pleased that he could quietly make arrangements to throw Brax out of Bitsy's life, hopefully without a cent of her money.

SEPTEMBER

L iam, furious and fed up, glared at Brax Montgomery. "Brax, you are ruining this hospital. I cannot imagine why you're intent upon doing this, but I do know I don't want any part of it. There's no use of me staying around here while you get another CEO because in a few months this hospital won't even be in existence. All you will have is an empty building with a ridiculous atrium stuck on the front, which seems to be what you and Lansdowe are hell-bent on doing! My office is cleaned out and I wouldn't be surprised if you put yourself behind that desk," raged Liam O'Connell as he threw his letter of resignation on the desk, picked up his briefcase and walked out of East Meridian Hospital for the last time.

Brax Montgomery watched Liam leave, thinking, yes, that's exactly what I'm going to do. He picked up the letter, delighted that O'Connell had played right into his hands. Now that Liam was out of the way, Mona could run the hospital, which she had been doing anyway. Only now she would really be unbearable and cause even more trouble than she had before, behind Liam's back. But little did she know that O'Connell was right, and within months she would be out of a job. Soon the hospital would be an empty building and the marvelous new (paid for) atrium would make a fine entrance for the luxury water-front condominiums Brax and John would make out of the old building and sell for a couple million apiece.

Brax barked at Liam's secretary, now his secretary, on the intercom, "Get John Lansdowe on the phone! And tell Mona O'Shay to come to my office." Rubbing his hands together, a satisfied smirk on his face, Brax couldn't wait to tell John that Liam had walked out, and to arrange for a groundbreaking quietly this weekend, before any of the other trustees found out.

****

A grim Bill James accosted Sarah early in the morning in the kitchen, the night after he returned home with his mother and children from North Carolina, with, "What are you doin' sleeping in the guestroom? And where the hell were you for ten days?"

"I was on vacation."

"Vacation! Vacation my ass. The vacation was with me and the kids in North Carolina."

"I decided that I needed some time to think things out."

"What the hell was there to think about, that you couldn't do down there?"

"We've been going to North Carolina for vacation every year since we've been married. And I HATE North Carolina!"

"Yeah, well you better get used to it, and you can forget this back to school shit. As of next month you'll be living in North Carolina."

"What...what are you talking about?"

"I'm going to be the general manager of Uncle Ed's swimming pool company."

"Swimming pools ... swimming pools....You hate swimming pools. You even refused to put one in your own yard."

"We didn't need one here, but everybody needs one in the South, and we have a house next door to Mom's other sister Ida. Mom's thrilled."

"What do you mean, your mother is thrilled. She's moving too? Bill, have you lost your mind? You can't make all these dumb-ass decisions without saying a word to me."

"Maybe if you hadn't been on your little vacation to think things out, you might have had something to say about it," he sneered.

"You are out of your mind. You have a job here, and the children start school next Tuesday, right after Labor Day. What the hell happened down there? Were you kidnapped by aliens? Or did all that barbecue, beer and biscuits turn your small brain into cement?"

Bill grabbed her arm and shaking her, yelled in her face, "I've had enough of you lording it over me. I'm gonna run our life from now on. I told the school that the kids would be transferring in October. I called Lansdowe from North Carolina and gave notice; I'll be out of there in two weeks. And you better get this house cleaned up, 'cause as of yesterday it's up for sale," and he threw Sarah into the chair next to the kitchen table and stomped out of the house.

Sarah started to shake uncontrollably. This was the last thing she had anticipated. After a magical ten days with David on his boat visiting places like Cuttyhunk, Edgartown and Martha's Vineyard, eating scrumptious seafood, and enjoying every moment of each day and night being with David, she knew it would have to come to an end. She was prepared for ending the dream and changing her life, but she never had anticipated that Bill would beat her to it, planning to move to North Carolina.

Panic set in. She had to get breakfast for her children, and at the same time keep in control and try to figure out what to do. She was going to school, and she was not moving to North Carolina.

****

225

Robb's phone rang at 6 a.m., waking him up. His heart was thudding; no one ever called him this early unless something awful had happened.

"Have you seen the paper?"

"Hunt, is that you?" Robb croaked, looking at the clock. "It's six in the morning. No, what paper?"

"The local paper. There's a picture of Brax and John at the groundbreaking for the new addition at the hospital."

"What groundbreaking?"

"My question exactly. Robb, this is unbelievable. Those two bastards, along with Mona O'Shay, are holding shovels and standing with a couple of very happy-looking town officials."

"When did this happen?"

Hunt rattled the paper, looking for the date of the groundbreaking, and exclaimed, "Saturday afternoon. And the news story doesn't say what the addition is, just that it is an addition. That son-of-a-bitch staged this over the weekend so none of us would get wind of it until too late."

"Well, he'll hear about it from us at the board meeting this afternoon. "

"Robb, are there enough of us left to make a difference?"

"I dunno, let me shower and get some coffee and I'll call you back."

****

"Brax, it's John. I just saw the pictures. We sure look like a happy group."

"That's because we are a happy group, John."

"How did you get those two town officials to show up at such short notice?"

"Mona met one of them at Happy Hour last summer at the Surf House in Scarborough. By the end of the evening she found out that he was very bitter about the hospital. Seems he had been let go years ago and vowed to get back at the hospital."

"Oh, I forgot; he was the guy that slid the permits through so fast because he knew that the hospital would never be able to put on another addition without going through the hassle of trying to change the town's comprehensive plan."

"You're right, nothing like a guy who wants revenge; they are so useful. We didn't even have to pay him off. I don't think Mona let him in her pants either, the guy was so pissed."

John Lansdowe frowned; he hadn't contemplated the thought that Mona was putting out for guys in bars. "Well, this board meeting should be loud."

"Who give's a rat's ass? We still have enough votes on our side."

"What about Kimberly? She wasn't there last month."

Brax smiled, remembering his weekend with Kimberly. "She'll be there."

"Good, see you this afternoon."

****

"David, it's Sarah."

"Yes, I know; what's wrong? You sound funny."

"I need your advice. I have to do something fast and I don't have a clue what to do. May I meet with you this morning?"

"Of course, come over right now."

"In an hour. My sitter can't come for a while. How do I...."

"I'll leave your name at the gate."

"Use my maiden name."

"Um ... okay ... O'Brien, right?'

She smiled, "That's right, tell 'um it's Ms. O'Brien."

"See you in an hour, Ms. O'Brien ... Sarah...."

"What?"

"I've missed you."

"I've missed you, too. Bye."

****

Robb got out of the shower and swore, hearing the phone

227

ringing in the bedroom; clutching a towel around himself he dashed in to answer it.

"It's Diana, Robb; Liam has left and there is a picture of...."

"I know, Hunt woke me up with that information at six a.m. Liam has what? Where are you?"

"I'm doing rounds and the whole hospital is buzzing about it. And it isn't a happy buzz. Everyone is wondering what's going to happen and Mona hasn't been around either. Nobody is sure that she hasn't left too."

"Liam has really left? Are you sure?"

"Yes, his office is empty."

"I'm going to talk with Hunt and I'll call you back."

"Okay, use my pager. Bye."

****

"Mom, I'm glad you could come over for lunch. I..."

"Well, Diana, I don't understand why you wanted me to come to your house. Mildred isn't here to serve lunch, and we could have a perfectly nice lunch at the club."

"Mildred has already made lunch. It's one of your favorites: cold salmon with lemon and capers and chocolate mousse for dessert," Diana said with a smile. She inwardly prayed her stomach could tolerate the meal; she really wanted crackers and ginger ale.

"So ... the reason I wanted to talk with you is...."

"Cold salmon? That's nice, dear, but I had that yesterday. I know Mildred's is better though. You should have told me, then I wouldn't be having the same thing twice in a row."

"Yes, um ... I never thought you might have eaten the same thing yesterday," Diana lamented, as she fought to bring the conversation back to why she wanted to have lunch with her mother. "Mom, I came home from the hospital this noontime to talk to you because...."

"I'm glad we have this chance to talk too. In fact, I've brought with me the guest list for the wedding," gushed Mrs. Manning pulling papers out of her purse. "It's really small, only two hundred and fifty. You know I never got a chance to give you a lovely Azimuth Point wedding because you and Steven eloped, and then you lived in the Mediterranean for so long. And when you came back to New York you were pregnant with the twins, so it seemed foolish to have a reception. At that point you were hardly a blushing bride. So here's the list and I've already been in touch with Dennis to bartend. It wouldn't be a Point wedding without Dennis, would it? Now, I've checked with the caterers and if we want Christmas week we have to get a date set today. So...."

"Mom, the wedding will be in October; that's when Robb's divorce will be final. And it will be only family and a few friends."

"Well, why in the world do you want to do that?"

"Because ... what I've been trying to tell you is, I'm pregnant ... that's why!"

"Oh ... I see ... do you have any wine to go with salmon?"

****

Anna Morgan drove down Route 1 with a light heart. Her cancer was in remission, her hair had grown in soft and curly after the chemotherapy, and the cataract operation had taken away her need for glasses. She truly looked like another woman. The owner of the apartment she rented in Providence had returned and Anna's Canton Avenue house was sold so she rented a small house in Azimuth Point Village for the winter. And tonight Hank Lombardi was taking her out for dinner at The Ebb Tide Inn.

She hadn't been out with a man in years. Dinners with Jeremiah were always in the hotel room so no one would see them together. This was exciting, and Hank had been so wonderful to her over the months she was sick. As a doctor he understood her illness and explained the therapies to her, and as a widower whose own wife died of cancer he understood her fears.

For the first time in her life she had true women friends from her cancer support group, and a man who liked her company, in public. Traffic stopped because someone in her lane wanted to make a left turn into Azimuth Point. Looking over at the entrance, Anna noticed Sarah James coming out of the Azimuth Point exit in her SUV. That's odd, she thought, I wonder whom Sarah knows in the Point?

****

Diana entered the conference room and looked around to see what board members had already arrived. With a sigh of relief that Robb was there she hurried over to join him. "Hi, what a day this has been," she whispered.

"Why, what else has happened?"

"Don't you remember that today I was having lunch with Mother to tell her why we had to get married in October instead of at Christmas?"

"To tell you the truth I forgot completely. Was she upset?"

"No, astounded was more like it. She drank almost a whole bottle of white wine at lunch. I think she was fortifying herself to tell Daddy tonight."

"So she agreed to a smaller gathering?"

"Yes, she even called the caterer and Dennis after lunch and said there would be some new arrangements."

"Good, at least one less thing to be worried about."

"What are you two whispering about?" boomed Hunt, sliding into the seat next to Robb.

"We are contemplating getting married in Tibet," announced Robb.

"You will come, won't you?" chimed in Diana.

"Wouldn't miss it for the world. You're paying the airfare for all of us, right?" Hunt inquired seriously of them both.

"Naturally, in fact we've hired the Tibet Hilton for a week," announced Robb. Diana nodded in agreement.

"Great, now, have either of you heard anything more about why Liam left?"

Diana and Robb shook their heads no.

"Do we have any recourse against this jackass Brax? I've been trying to get him on the phone all day," said Hunt.

"Me too, he never returns a phone call. Let's see who

shows up and if we can muster enough votes to at least stop this atrium for a while."

Sarah James arrived and took a seat at the far side of the table. Brax came into the room with Mona O'Shay and John Lansdowe. They sat down at the head of the table. What is Mona doing here, Sarah wondered, and where is Liam; he's not usually late.

Sweets came in and after getting some bottled water sat next to Diana. Gee, everybody looks rather grim, she thought, and what's that witch Mona doing here?

Whip and Kimberly arrived together and sat near Sarah. Hunt, Robb and Diana looked up and glared at Brax defiantly. Brax ignored them.

Brax cleared his throat importantly. "Ladies and gentlemen, I have a sad announcement to make. Liam O'Connell, our fine CEO, has left to pursue his career elsewhere. While we will miss him and wish him well, we need someone to run this hospital, so I have appointed Ms. O'Shay as interim CEO, while the committee does a search."

There were gasps around the room as trustees, who didn't know Liam had left, digested the news, and were incredulous that Mona was to be the interim CEO.

Robb lashed out, "I'll bet you're going to miss him. And who is the head of your so called search committee?"

"Why, Robb, I have been trying to get you on the phone all day to ask you to head that committee," Brax said graciously.

At this John raised his eyebrow inquiringly at Brax, and Mona's head snapped up in surprise from reading the board report she was about to give.

Robb just about yelled, "Like hell you've been trying to get me on the phone, you wouldn't take one of my calls all day!"

"My secretary must not have been able to find me. Now does that mean you'll accept the challenge and head this search committee?"

"I will, and I will also appoint the committee members myself," Robb growled as Hunt and Diana looked at Robb, surprised at this turn of events. John Lansdowe, knowing full well that by the time Robb found a new CEO, East Meridian

Hospital would cease to exist, smirked, thinking, Brax, you sly bastard.

"Good. Ms. O'Shay has a list of firms that headhunt CEO's, if you wish to make use of them. I look forward to your report at the next meeting."

"Now, Dr. Manning, would you please give the medical report?"

Diana, perplexed, dragged her gaze away from Robb and looked at Brax, speechless.

"Er ... Dr. Manning?"

"Wait just a minute," yelled Robb. "Not so fast. What about this groundbreaking ceremony you cooked up without notifying us?"

"Yes, that's right," chimed in Hunt.

"Yes, it worked out well, didn't it? The town council was available for a picture. Great publicity for the hospital, don't you think?"

"I don't think great publicity is quite the right phrase," barked Hunt. "From the phone calls I've been getting all day, the phrase should be more like, 'what the hell is going on at the hospital?'"

"We thought about that, Hunt, and a publicity release went out explaining the wonderful gift Louis has given the hospital."

"This is ridiculous," Robb cried out, slamming his hand on the conference table. "Brax, you know most of us don't want that damn atrium and..."

"And nobody on the medical staff wants it either!" Diana interrupted in anger.

"Is that so, Dr. Manning? And most of you trustees, too, really? Well, why don't we take a little vote here, right now," beamed Brax, looking around the room figuring he had seven votes, Sweets being the only wild card, and Robb only having four votes.

"I certainly vote for the atrium," Brax continued unperturbed. "Now, I know Mona is in favor of the atrium, but of course she can't vote, so, John, what's your vote?"

"I vote, yes, it will be a marvelous addition to the hospital."

"Kim, how do you vote?"

"I vote yes," she murmured not looking at anyone in particular.

"Whip, what is your feeling on this matter?"

"Oh, I vote yes...we really need this.

"Now, Sarah, how do you wish to vote on this?"

"I think it's the most dumb-ass project I've ever heard of, and I vote no." All heads swiveled in Sarah's direction, stunned, as Sarah continued. "I've sat here over the months and listened to you two talking heads," she indicated with a nod toward Brax and John, "run roughshod over this board and force this ridiculous monstrosity on us, for no apparent sane reason. So I vote no; it's a stupid thing to do."

John Lansdowe was purple with fury. "Sarah, are you sure you don't want to rethink this decision of yours?"

"No, I don't think so, John. I vote no."

John Lansdowe glared at Sarah. He was livid, and there was nothing he could do. Her husband was leaving John's company next week, which meant John had no hold over how Sarah voted.

Sarah smiled sweetly at him, mentally thumbing her nose at the son-of-a-bitch. Hearing a snort of laughter across the table, she looked over at Diana, Robb and Hunt who were smiling and nodding at her.

Brax was not happy at all with this turn of events. He glared at John, who threw his hands up in the air. Oh, great, thought Brax, Sweets is the swing vote; this could be dicey. Clearing his throat he continued,

"And Hunt, your vote?"

"I vote no."

"Yes ... um ... Robb?"

"Of course I vote no on this stupid atrium."

Brax frowned at him and turned to Diana. "Dr. Manning?"

"I vote no."

Looking at Sweets, Brax smiled encouragingly, inwardly seething that this idea of his had gotten so out of hand. "Rose Ellen, I don't want to make you nervous, but the success of this project rests in your hands. How do you vote?"

Sweets paled and glanced at John, who smiled back intently. Diana reached over under the table and gave Sweets' hand an encouraging pat. Sweets jumped at her touch. Her eyes got very big and she gulped, "I ... I ... um ... I vote yes."

Brax sighed in relief, saying, "Thank you, my de..."

Diana, interrupting Brax, turned to her childhood friend and exclaimed, "What do you mean you vote yes? This damn thing is a travesty, and the last thing the hospital needs. We need equipment and modernization, not some phallic symbol stuck on the front of the building in honor of a creep from out of town!"

Sweets shrank back in her chair, away from Diana. "I ... I ... think it will look nice, and ... and...." Very flustered, Sweets looked at John in desperation.

"Look nice!" Diana yelled. "Do you realize this look nice thing means the hospital will never be able to put on another addition to expand for medical reasons without getting the town comprehensive plan changed? Which will be about impossible."

Sweets' chin began to quiver. "No, I don't believe you; it's not true," and she looked wildly at John. He smiled back encouragingly, not saying a word. Sweets slowly stood up and backed away from the table, her hand in front of her mouth. Then her face contorted and she sneered, "You always have to be right, don't you, Diana? You always got the prizes, you got to be the doctor, and now you've stolen somebody else's husband and you still think you're right and have all the answers. Well, this time I have the answer!" and she ran out of the room.

Diana, white with shock, turned to Robb speechless. She swayed and looked as if she was going to faint. She fell into Robb's arms as Sarah and Mona both got up and rushed to her side. Mona pushed Diana's head down between her knees, broke open some smelling salts and gave them to Sarah saying, "I think she has only fainted. Sarah, put these under her nose and Robb, hold on to her. I'll get a gurney up here from the ER, we'll check her out just to make sure." Mona went to the house phone and quietly issued orders.

234

The rest of the board looked on, not knowing what to do. Sweets's outburst and Diana's collapse were so unexpected that even Kimberly was shaken out of her depression. The conference room doors flew open and the orderlies headed for Mona and Diana; together they lifted her onto the gurney. Mona looked at Robb. "You better come with us."

Robb nodded, and stood up to walk beside the gurney. Sarah, looking around the room, realized she certainly didn't want to stay for the rest of the meeting, so she blurted out, "Uh, I'm coming, too," and she hurried after the group and helped close the conference room doors.

Brax broke the silence by asking that the meeting be continued at a later time. Everyone agreed.

John asked the secretary if she had recorded the vote in her notes and she nodded yes. Satisfied that the meeting had turned out far better than he had thought it would have a few minutes ago, he picked up his briefcase, gave Brax a salute and left. The others, one by one, picked up their papers and filed out of the conference room.

"Mr. James."

Bill James, busy cleaning out his office, was annoyed by his secretary's interruption.

"What do you want?"

"There is someone here to see you."

"Who is it?"

"A Mr. Mallone. He says he needs a minute of your time."

Exasperated, Bill moaned, "Okay, send him in."

A burly man, in an ill-fitting suit, came through the office door, he asked, "You, William James?"

"Yes, what do you want?"

"I'm serving these divorce papers on you." Handing the envelope to a dumbfounded Bill James, Mr. Mallone turned and walked out, shutting the door behind him.

****

"Good Lord, Sarah, what a day you've had," David uttered shaking his head as he threw another log on the fire. "Are you sure Diana is okay?"

"Yes, it seems that she hadn't eaten much all day and the scene with Sweets was so unnerving she passed out cold. When she came to in the ER she was embarrassed to death. She caused a big commotion and insisted that she was fine and wanted to go home. Robb finally convinced her to let him drive her home in his car and he would arrange with someone to go back and get hers."

"That sounds like Diana," David laughed.

"David...."

"Ummm...."

"I can't thank you enough for helping me. I never would have been able to find a lawyer and get those papers served today, and the man at the bank ... he said there wouldn't be a problem with a student loan. And I'm having an interview at the school for a 'mother's hours' job tomorrow. It's really too good to be true. Between all that and the scene at the hospital, I'm exhausted, but exhilarated at the same time."

David put his arms around her and softly kissed her fore-head. "I'm so glad I could help. I really want only the best for you; you deserve it."

"I ... I ... um ... David, please understand that I'm not holding you to any commitment of any kind. I'm a big person now, and even though I need some help at the moment, I don't want you to think that ... I mean I have a mess to get myself out of and I have children and...."

David sat up and looked at Sarah. "I care for you very much, and I want to be there for you. But I, too, know we have to go slowly ... or ... um a bit more slowly than we did those past ten days." He grinned and Sarah blushed. "We'll take one event at a time, okay?"

Sarah nodded her head and reached over and kissed David deeply. He moved toward her, caressing her and she pulled away. "Whoops, this might be a mistake," she laughed. "I might not be able to leave for another ten days." At this the dog growled. "How did that animal understand what I said?"

"She still hasn't forgiven us for leaving her at the kennel while we went sailing."

"That might be true, but I don't think she'll ever forgive me for arriving in your life."

David agreed, shaking his head. "You're probably right, but maybe you could bribe her."

"I don't think so; the only thing that would make her happy is if I told her I had a one-way ticket to Sudan. Speaking of that, I'd best leave and get ready to face the music at home. It's going to be quite a scene, now that Bill has been served papers. Thank heavens the girls are spending the night with friends."

David looked concerned, "Are you going to be all right alone with him?"

"I'm not afraid. Bill has never, in all our years of marriage, hurt me. If I can, I will call you later, but don't wait up."

David walked Sarah to the door and kissed her goodbye. "I'll be with you, remember that."

"I will, thank you so much," she whispered, as she kissed him again.

David stood in the door and waved to Sarah as she drove out of his driveway. If she ever finds out the reason she got in to see the best divorce lawyer in Rhode Island and also got a student loan was because I made some phone calls and backed up her loan, she will be furious. But there is no reason for her to find out, and I so want her to succeed in getting her master's degree, and also be able to keep her house.

Whatever happens with us, who knows, but I feel better than I've felt in years. He shut the door and went back to his chair by the fire. Scratching the dog's ears, he said,

"You know, Cynthia, you have to be nicer to Sarah." The dog lifted her lip, stood up, turned around in her bed and settled herself away from David. David looked at her. How can that dog possibly understand what I'm saying?

****

"Mommy."

237

"Yes, what, Jamie?"

"How come my last name is Etheridge and your last name is Manning? Didn't Daddy marry you?"

Diana laughed, "Of course Daddy and I were married. And the reason my name is different than yours is because I was already a doctor when your Daddy and I got married; so instead of changing my name on all the papers and stuff we decided that I would keep my professional name as Manning. Does that clear things up for you?"

"I guess so. What about the baby?"

"What baby?" Diana asked weakly.

"A boy in my school said when two people got married they have a baby. So what will the baby's last name be?"

Diana, relieved Jamie was only thinking about a hypothetical baby, patted her son on the head and pulled him to her in a hug. "Jamie, my wonderful son, if Robb and I have a baby its last name will be Wells."

"Oh, good; I thought it might have to have my last name. Can I go swimming?"

"Swimming ... Jamie, it's September, it's too cold to go swimming."

"I know. Lisle already told me that, but I thought you might let me go," he grinned.

****

"Mona, it's John.'

"Yes, I know."

"Quite a scene in the boardroom today."

"Yes, that Rose Ellen, what is the ridiculous nickname she has?"

"Er...Sweets."

"God, all you Point people, you either have last names for first names or some Biff or Popsey nickname. Anyway, is Sweets whacked or something? She seems wound a bit tight, and she sure doesn't like Diana."

"Umm ... anyway, I'm leaving next week, er ... do you think the stuff I asked you for will be ready?"

"Of course, I told you it would be in the top middle drawer of my desk. Come in late next Thursday night; it will be in a plain envelope."

"Mona ... um ... I really appreciate this."

"Yeah, I suppose you do."

****

Sarah arrived home and saw cars belonging to her parents and mother-in-law and someone else in the driveway. She let herself in the back door thinking, this should be interesting. She walked quietly through the house and stood in the living room doorway and stared at Bill, their lawyer, Joe Thurston, Bill's mother and her parents. "I should have known, Bill, you would be unable to handle this situation by yourself," she said tartly.

Bill stood up and crossed the room shaking his fist at Sarah. "I'm not taking anymore sass from you, you ... you bitch."

Sarah's mother smirked; now that uppity daughter of hers would get her comeuppance. Sarah's father looked at her through an alcoholic haze. Bill's mother jutted out her jaw, exposing her huge yellow bottom teeth in a grimace of hate. Bill was standing in front of Sarah, yelling and still shaking his fist.

Sarah looked at Bill in disgust, not saying a word, as Joe Thurston hurried over to Bill saying, "Whoa there, wait a minute, Bill. You asked me here to help you settle this matter. I strongly suggest this is not the way to do it." He took Bill by the arm and led him back to the sofa. Sarah continued standing in the doorway; her mother and mother-in-law looked disappointed Bill had not pummeled her.

Joe, still standing, looked at Sarah. "I understand that you had divorce papers served on Bill today."

"Yes."

"Sarah, can we sit down and talk about this?"

"No."

"Sarah, have you considered counseling? After all, getting a divorce because you don't want to move to North Carolina is a bit drastic. I'm sure we can work this out ... and...."

"Say, Joe, how would you like to move to North Carolina?"

"Well ... er ... my life is here and...." too late he realized he had talked himself into a trap. "What I mean is..."

"Exactly," smiled Sarah. "Now, Joe, did Bill suggest counseling?"

"Umm ... no."

"I though not. Now, I think it would be a good idea for all of you to leave. This is between Bill and me. And Joe, you know you can't represent Bill, because you have represented both of us in other matters."

Bill turned to Joe, "Is that true?"

"Well ... um ... yes, she's right."

"Why didn't you tell me that?"

"Bill, you asked me to come over to...."

Sarah interrupted, saying, "Bill asked you all to come over tonight to browbeat me into submission. Well, it won't work. I'm getting this divorce; I'm staying in this house; the children will stay in school here and I'm getting my master's degree." Reaching into her purse she got out a card and handed it to Bill. "Here is the name of my lawyer. When you and your bumbling friend come to grips with the situation, and you get another lawyer, we will talk through them. Now, may I remind you, you have until tomorrow to leave this house. Goodnight." Sarah walked out of the room and up the stairs. She heard Bill ask Joe if he had ever heard of her lawyer. He must have glanced at the card because she heard him say, "Yes, he is the best divorce lawyer in the state."

"Shit."

Sarah grinned as she closed, and locked, the guest room door.

****

Brax Montgomery swore under his breath as he tore apart his wife's desk looking for the deeds he needed to be able to sell the property to Tedisco. "That bastard," he uttered. "Tedisco is holding up the final check until I have the sales agreement in my hands. And I need that money to start the excavation next week. He pulled things out of the desk, including Bitsy's checkbook, which he threw on the floor. Then he had an idea, and picked up the checkbook. Looking over her neat entries he realized he didn't need the deeds. He could get copies from the Town Hall and all he had to do was make up a sales agreement and forge Bitsy's name, something he had done for years when he needed money, or wanted to pull off a deal that he didn't want her to know about. This would enable him to start the atrium next Monday. Thrilled, he fairly danced out of the room, leaving the mess for the housekeeper to clean up, without giving it a thought.

****

"Diana, have you talked with Sweets?"

"No, it took me a while to calm down, and when I did I still couldn't believe what happened. I always thought of her as my best friend; I never realized she ... she ... had those thoughts about me."

Robb rubbed his forehead wondering how to phrase his thoughts. "Um ... er ... have you ever wondered why Sweets never seemed to have a real boyfriend? I mean, well, I don't know ... she never went out with a boy for any length of time that I can remember."

"No, she was always part of the group when we went to dances at the club, and sailing, but you're right, she never really had a serious boyfriend. But to tell you the truth I never gave it much thought."

"Well, I never gave it much thought either, but if you take a good look at her family you get a clue as to why she might be a bit odd. Those over-chromosomed brothers of hers, always playing inane sports in all types of weather and traveling to dark continents to shoot endangered species of animals, and that dumb ass of a father of hers, always pontificating about everything, never making a bit of sense."

Diana shook her head, "I always wondered why she stayed so thin; she hardly eats a thing, and if you say anything to her about her appetite she gets furious."

"Do you think she has one of those eating disorders? And I've even wondered if she's ... um ... gay."

"You're right, as a doctor I've wondered if she might have an eating disorder, but I know she is not gay."

"How do you know that?"

"A couple of weeks ago we were having lunch and I mentioned that a new young doctor was joining the staff ... an unmarried doctor and he wanted to meet people and he also liked to sail. Well, Sweets lit into me; she was seeing somebody and no, she did not want to meet this guy. I asked who she was seeing and she got nasty."

"Wow, it is hard to imagine Sweets being nasty."

Diana's eyes widened. "I never thought of this, but maybe it is a woman and that's why she got nasty. She never said who it was."

"Is there a side to her nobody knows about?"

"I guess so. Anyway I still haven't gotten over that scene in the boardroom. I've called her many times, but I'm always told that she's not home."

"I guess there's not much more you can do."

"No, but my heart still hurts."

****

"Sarah, I'm afraid we have a problem. I want you to understand that the fact your children have decided to live with your husband, and are living with him and his mother now, has put a different light on your situation." The lawyer, Richard Brisbane, stared at her intently as he spoke.

Sarah's eyes filled. She turned, looking out of the window at the traffic on the city street below, blinking back the tears, fighting for control. Giving up, she reached in her bag for a tissue. Blowing her nose and wiping her eyes, she remembered her children confronting her three days ago, stating they were going to live with their father. It was an awful memory: her daughters, looking at her defiantly as they stood next to the kitchen door, their backpacks strapped on without her help, two huge duffle bags beside them on the floor, packed without her help.

They had called Bill to come pick them up, and he was on his way. Leighanna, dressed in clothes far too skimpy and sophisticated for her age, announced to Sarah that they didn't like her very much and they weren't going to live with her. They were going to North Carolina with Nana and Daddy.

Her baby, Lauren, white-faced, her lower lip quivering and clutching her favorite doll moved closer to her older sister and nodded in agreement. Sarah couldn't speak, she was so shocked. It never occurred to her that her daughters would have the slightest interest in leaving their home and friends and school to go live in North Carolina.

She tried to reason with them: this was their home and the schools were much better here than down there. "That's not true," Leighanna had shot back at her. "We will be going to a very good school. We're already registered there. And we have lots of cousins that are a lot nicer than any friends we have here. And what's more, our new house has a swimming pool!"

At that point Bill arrived and the girls greeted him with whoops of joy. He told Leighanna how cute she looked and told them to get into his car. Out they rushed, never even saying goodbye to their mother. Picking up the duffle bags, Bill gave Sarah a look of smug satisfaction, saying, "See ya in court."

Sarah leaned against the doorjamb and watched her family leave. Leighanna parked herself in the front seat buckling on the seat belt, even though by law she should be in the back seat, and threw Sarah a look of triumph. As the car moved away, Lauren turned and looked back at Sarah and put her little hand up as if starting to wave, then quickly, glancing at her father, put her hand down and turned away.

Sarah stared at the empty driveway for a long time, numb with the realization that no matter how bad her marriage had been, by ignoring her daughters and being totally obsessed all these months with thoughts of David, she had brought this about, all by herself.

"Sarah, are you all right?"

"Um, yes, Richard, I ... I ... just needed a moment."

"So, I feel as your lawyer, that I must recommend we try to settle this without going to court. The only asset you and Bill have is the house, and a small savings account. Luckily you saved the paperwork showing you had contributed more than half the down payment from your own savings."

Sarah nodded, not saying anything. Richard continued, "My advice is to sell the house, split the proceeds and split the savings account of six thousand dollars. We will ask for a large amount of alimony, your tuition payments for your master's degree so that you will be able to be self-supporting in the future, and obviously, you will not be getting child support. Do you have a job?"

"Yes, it doesn't pay much, and at the moment I'm only working mother's hours. I suppose I could ask for more hours now ... now ... that I don't have to be home right after school gets out."

"No, stay with the hours you have. I don't want you making more money."

Sarah nodded yes, fearing if she spoke, she might start to cry again.

"Okay, good. I will contact Bill's attorney and call you as soon as I have anything to report."

OCTOBER

John Lansdowe sat alone on the terrace, in the dark moonless Bahama evening, sipping an after-dinner drink of Johnny Walker Red. His wife Neena had gone to bed an hour ago. He said goodnight to the Bahamian couple who had worked for them for years. After the lights of their car disappeared down the road he finished the drink and stood up. He went around the house shutting and locking the doors and windows, and then turned the air-conditioning on to its coldest setting.

Walking down the hall he entered his bedroom, shut and locked the sliding glass doors and drew the curtains. He went to the closet, and pushing his clothes to one side, he pressed a piece of paneling, which slid over to expose a safe. Deftly spinning the combination lock he opened the door and took out the package from Mona's desk. Shutting the safe and arranging the hangers back where they had been he closed the closet door.

He went into the bathroom and opened the package, and

placing the contents on the counter between the double sinks. After putting on latex gloves he took out the syringe, filled it and held it up, gently pushing out the air. Satisfied, he smiled. Capping it he turned and walked out and through the bedroom and down the hall to his wife's room.

He stood for a moment in the doorway looking at her, making sure the sleeping pill he had crushed and slipped into her after-dinner coffee had put her into a deep sleep. She lay on her back, lightly snoring.

He walked into the room, and holding the syringe against his right thigh, went over to the sliding glass doors, closed and locked them and drew the curtains. Turning he went over to the bed. He uncapped the syringe. Goodbye, Neena, you miserable bitch. He plunged the bolus of potassium chloride right in the middle of a freckle in her skinny, wrinkled upper arm. She stopped snoring forever. He took the bedcovers off her, and the phone rang. Startled, he stopped short. Turning quickly to check that he had indeed pulled the curtains over the sliding glass doors, his eyes locked back on the phone. Sweat gathered on his upper lip as the ringing pierced the silent room. Slowly he walked over to the table and reached for the phone. Answering it he heard a native voice ask for someone he had never heard of. "No, no, you have the wrong number," he told the caller. Hanging up the phone he let out a ragged sigh of relief. He walked out of the room, turning off the lights before he shut the door.

He walked back down the hall to his bedroom and went into the bathroom and took apart the syringe, and smashed the container that held the potassium chloride, cut up the gloves and flushed everything separately down the toilet. He reached under one of the sinks, and taking out a container of bleach wipes, he cleaned the area and ripped the wipes into tiny pieces and flushed them down the toilet.

After washing and drying his hands he went to the living room, picked up his empty glass and went over to the bar to refill it. Taking the drink with him he turned out the lights and returned to his bedroom, put on his pajamas and a heavy sweater, set the alarm for 5:30 a.m., got into bed and turned on the television hoping to find a good movie on one of the cable channels.

John woke up before the alarm went off, immediately got up and took off the sweater and put it away. He went around the house, opening the windows and turning off the air-conditioning. He didn't unlock the doors because the native couple had a key to let themselves in. He opened all the sliding glass doors to let in the warm morning air and then went into his wife's room, and keeping her sliding glass doors closed, he pulled the bedcovers up over her cold, motionless body.

At quarter of six John went around shutting the house up again, so that the native couple's usual routine would not be different. Back in his own room he took off his pajamas and went into the bathroom to shower. Emerging, he could smell coffee and bacon being prepared in the kitchen. He dried off and dressed for his early morning golf date went into the kitchen to say hello and say he would like scrambled eggs this morning and went into the dining room to read the paper beside his placemat.

After breakfast he left for his golf date through the kitchen, saying goodbye to the native couple after telling them that he was lunching at the club today. As he passed by the granite-topped kitchen island, on his way to the garage, he noticed his wife's breakfast tray of tea, orange juice and a pineapple slice awaiting the toast, which was in the toaster. She was fussy about the toast. She wanted it hot. He hurried out and got into his car, thinking, she won't care if the toast is hot or cold this morning. When he got to the golf club there was an urgent message for him to return home.

Over the next few days John was suitably bereaved. He notified Helene, telling her not to bother coming down, much to her relief, and would she arrange a memorial service at Azimuth Point, which of course she would do.

John readily agreed with the Bahamian coroner to have his wife's body autopsied before it was cremated. The coroner phoned John later saying that their small hospital would be unable to do the autopsy for two weeks. But he was sure that Mrs. Lansdowe had died of a heart attack sometime in the early morning, probably just before the housekeeper had brought in her breakfast tray. He would release the body to the funeral home for cremation. John, even though he was sure the potassium chloride would never be detected, was relieved. And by keeping his wife's body cold through the night, he made her time of death seem to be around 6 or 7 in the morning, when other people were in the house with him, perhaps when he was having breakfast or as late as driving to the golf club.

Two days later he flew to the States with Neena in a package in the hold, and was met at the Providence airport by the undertaker with whom Helene had made arrangements. He assured John he would take care of everything, and the service was to be next Tuesday at 11 a.m. Before John went to find his driver who would take him to Azimuth Point, he made a private cell phone call to New York.

****

"Robb, I just got out of the OR and the whole hospital is in turmoil..."

"Diana, that place is always in turmoil; anyway, Helene just called me, her...."

"Well, it's in more turmoil than ever, they started excavating for the atrium at 8 a.m. No one in the hospital, except Mona, of course, had any idea that the digging was to start today. We all come in the back doors so we didn't see that the front parking area had been cordoned off and there is a huge pile of asphalt and the damn hole is getting bigger every minute. Uh ... Helene called you?"

"Yes, her mother died in the Bahamas last Monday."

"Was she sick?"

"Well, obviously I haven't been up with the family gossip, but no, I don't think so.

Helene said she had a heart attack in her sleep. The housekeeper found her when she took in her breakfast."

"John didn't realize she was rather unresponsive when he woke up?"

Robb laughed, "I don't think they've slept together in

years. Even when Helene and I were first married they slept in separate rooms."

"When is the funeral?"

"Next Tuesday at 11."

"Does Miranda know?"

"Both Helene and I have talked with her. She will be here later today. As I've told you before, none of us were close to the Lansdowes. I don't think she had seen her grandmother all summer."

"Oh ... um ... do you want to come over and see this monstrous hole and the boarded-up front entrance? It's bedlam trying to find a place to park in the back and when visiting hours start it will really be fun. The ambulances are using the lawn to get to the ER."

"No, I don't want to come over; in fact I hope I never see the place again."

"Are you still coming for dinner?"

"Yes, but I'll be a little late. Helene wants to see me, probably about the funeral."

"Okay, uh, Robb, since Miranda's going to be home this weekend, could she come over for dinner or lunch or something, instead of two weeks from now as we planned? At least that will give us a couple of visits before the wedding. I still feel so badly we didn't meet this summer."

"I'm sure we can work it out. Don't worry; Miranda is fine with our marriage."

"Good, love you, I have to go."

"Bye."

****

Brax Montgomery was alone in the elevator whisking him up to Louis Tedisco's office. After they signed the sales agreement to the land on Route 1 for the shopping center Louis would give Brax the final payment. John Lansdowe was supposed to be in touch with PuisSantMeritor to start getting the papers ready to submit to the hospital board. The death of his wife had held that up. John must be relieved, Brax thought, to get rid of that wretched woman. He heard he married her for her money and her father's business. Hmm ... I did the same thing, he thought, but Bitsy had been easy to control and ignore. Neena Lansdowe had been anything but; anyway, she wasn't a problem anymore. Neither was Bitsy, and he hoped she stayed wherever she was until next year.

He got off at Louis's floor and looked around at the tasteful décor, thinking, this sure looks different than the reports I've heard about the showy house he bought in Ocean Crag.

Brax gave his name to Louis's secretary and was ushered right into his office. Louis got up from his desk and walked around to shake hands and showed him to the table in the corner next to floor-to-ceiling glass walls that looked over the city streets and up to College Hill. "Brax, glad we could get going on this."

Brax sat down at the table, which was round, thereby assuring nobody could sit at the head. "Nice office."

"Thanks, I built this building two years ago. The next one is going up over there," he indicated with a sweep of his arm toward the window overlooking downtown.

Brax looked out the window, impressed by the scene below, then turning back, he said, "Would you like to look over the agreement?"

Louis nodded and sat down reaching for the papers. Half an hour after the lawyers had arrived the deal was complete. Brax left Louis's office gloating. Once he was on the street he left a message on John Lansdowe's cell phone with the news.

****

Robb parked in front of the Lansdowe house, and walked up the stairs to the front door, thinking, I can't figure out why this house always seemed different than the other Point houses. He rang the bell and Helene opened the door immediately, as if she had been waiting for him in the hall.

"Robb, thank you so much for coming over."

"Sure." He leaned over and gave Helene a kiss on the check.

She looked surprised and seemed nervous. "Robb, I ... I ... um just talked with Miranda again and she wants to know if she can stay with you, instead of here. She ... she likes her own room."

"Of course she can, it's her house. And you know it's part of our agreement that you can have the house for a month each summer. I know you have this house, but..."

"Actually that's what I wanted to talk to you about."

Robb looked confused, and wondered why Helene didn't take him into the living room to sit down. Shrugging his shoulders he said, "Okay, is there some problem?"

"Er ... well ... is my car still in the garage?"

"Yes, I drove it now and then to make sure the battery didn't go dead. Do you want to come to the house to get it?"

"Yes, yes, I would ... and if you don't mind, I mean if it wouldn't be too upsetting, could I stay at the house, too?"

Robb stared at her. Then he noticed two suitcases were on the floor beside her. "Helene, when did you get here?"

"A couple of hours ago. I took a cab from the train station."

"I thought you made the funeral arrangements."

"I did, on the phone from New York."

"Is your father here?"

"No, I mean yes, he's probably at the airport now. He flew in from the Bahamas with um ... er ... and the undertaker is meeting him to take care of things and he has a driver to get him here."

"Helene, I'm sorry about your mother. I should have said so earlier."

Helene looked at him strangely and in a far off voice said, "I'm not sure how I feel about it all."

Robb shook his head, not sure what to say, and it was obvious she didn't want to stay in her family's house. "Look, if you want to stay with Miranda and me, that's fine."

Helene smiled, and quickly reached down to get her suitcases, asking, "Are you sure Diana won't be upset. I mean she might wonder why ... or something."

"No, of course not," Robb assured her, reaching for her suitcases, wondering what Diana would make of this turn of events. Helene locked the door behind them and hurried after Robb to the car.

Settled in the passenger seat, Helene visibly relaxed as they drove away from the house. "The Point is pretty in the fall, isn't it? I was always sorry when we had to leave for Providence. So many times I wished we could have stayed until Christmas."

"I had no idea you wanted to stay in the fall, you never mentioned a word about staying."

"No, I never did, did I," she mused. "Maybe Selina and I should take the house in the fall, if she can get away."

That ought to set the Point on its ear, Robb thought, trying not to react. "Anytime you want to come is fine with me, we can work it out."

"Robb, Miranda wants to come to New York for a weekend and stay with me. Do you think that is a good idea?"

"I ... er ... well, I guess it would be fine ... if ... um ... it's handled ... you know ... well," Good God, he thought, is Helene really this naïve, or is she just giving me a hard time?

"Oh, I forgot to tell you; I've rented the apartment next to Selina's. Her apartment was too small for my grand piano, and as you know I like to practice alone. My apartment has two bedrooms and I love it. I've never had a place of my own and I'm slowly learning my way around New York, too." Helene beamed at him.

She is still naïve, but not that naïve, he thought. "I think that sounds great; Miranda would enjoy it, I'm sure."

Robb drove into his garage and they both got out, and taking the suitcases, went into the house through the kitchen. Betty, the Wells' housekeeper, looked up in surprise as Robb walked in with Helene. "Miz Wells?"

"Yes, Betty, it's nice to see you. I'm only here for a couple of days, until after the funeral service."

"Of course, yes, of course. I'm sorry about your mother."

"Thank you, it was a shock, but at least she never suffered."

Robb glanced at Helene, marveling that she seemed so in control after her strange behavior at her father's house.

"Mr. Wells ... I ... didn't make dinner ... um ... because you said you would be out for dinner ... and ... if you all are staying in I can...."

"Betty," laughed Helene, "you are a dear, as always. I'm picking up Miranda at the station in two hours and we're having dinner at the club; don't worry about us. We'll be fine, and we'll see you in the morning. Please go on home. I'm sorry if I caused any fuss."

"No, no ... I um ... well ... you see...."

"Goodbye, Betty, everything is okay," Robb said, smiling at her.

"Right, see you tomorrow, Mr. Wells," uttered Betty, practically running out the back door, throwing on her sweater and grabbing her purse.

Robb and Helene looked at each other for a couple of seconds, and started to laugh. Helene hugged herself, grinning, "I never thought anyone would find anything I did much of a problem."

Robb grinned back, "My, dear, the fun has only just begun."

****

Sarah James's mind wandered as she waited for Ruth, the real estate agent, to find the right key to unlock the front door of the small Azimuth Point Village cottage available for rent in the winter. Because she had only recently started her job she didn't ask for time off to go to Neena Lansdowe's funeral that morning, not that she would have gone anyway. She had never met Neena, and John Lansdowe was certainly not one of her favorite people. As of the last trustees meeting, she was sure John was not too crazy about her either. David was going with his parents, who had returned from a summer of sailing. And this was not a time for her to meet them, not that there were any plans for Sarah to meet David's family anyway.

The realtor found the key, and opening the door, called to Sarah, shaking her out of her reverie. She walked into the small, light-filled, well-appointed cottage and smiled with delight, "This is lovely. I hope I can afford the rent."

"You can, for the winter. You don't have any animals, do you?"

"Uh, no, the cat, birds, fish and gerbils went to North Carolina," Sarah offered, thinking maliciously that her bitch of a mother-in-law must have loved sitting in the car with all the livestock for three days. "When is this available?"

"Right now."

"Does the same person own all three of these cottages?"

"Yes, he's an artist and he lives in the one on the left. He's very particular about the renters. No students, no animals, no children and he prefers quiet professional people or retired old people who don't give parties. And he is more favorable toward women, but only as renters, if you get my drift."

Sarah laughed. "Tell him none of my friends or family will even speak to me, so no loud parties are in my future."

"I told him you are getting divorced, you are alone and that your house will be sold probably within the day. I didn't tell him there is a bidding war going on, for fear he might raise the rent."

Sarah smiled gratefully at the agent. "Thanks, Ruth, I need all the help I can get in the finance department. I owe the bank so much money I can't sleep nights."

"Well, it looks like you might get at least ten thousand or maybe fifteen thousand more for the house than you're asking."

"I know; that is really almost too good to be true. Even if I only get half of it, every cent counts. I have to be out in ten days, so if this were available, I'd love to have it. What is the rent?"

"Twenty-five hundred a month, but that includes heat. It's really a good deal, and the area is nice, safe and you can walk into the village and to the beach."

"Wow, that's a lot! But it is nice. What does he get for the summer?"

"Ten thousand a month, or twenty-five thousand if one family takes it for June, July and August. That includes air-conditioning and maid service. Even at that high price he's still fussy about his renters."

"People pay that much?"

"Sarah, there's a whole other world out there."

Sarah, thinking of David and Azimuth Point, nodded. "I guess there is." She added, "I'll take it, and the furnishings are lovely," thinking, thank heavens, because she didn't have any furniture. Bill had taken all the furniture with him to North Carolina, with her blessing. She wanted the girls to be surrounded with things that were familiar to them. She had been sleeping on the only thing she owned, besides her clothes: an air mattress that she deflated and hid in her closet every morning, before the realtor showed the house.

****

Robb entered St. Peter's of the Dunes Church after the service for Neena Lansdowe had begun, and slipped quietly into the last pew in the back of the church. When he walked in after signing the book, he looked down the aisle at John Lansdowe and Helene in the front pew, noticing Miranda was sitting between them. Neena's brother, his wife and two children filled out the row, and in the pew behind them were two of Neena's distant cousins. Looking around he realized the church was not even half full; quite a contrast to Sadie's service, he thought.

Not surprising, Neena Lansdowe hadn't been very popular, and neither was John. A small group of people sat together on the left side; these people must be from John's office, Robb mused.

He recognized people from the Point Bridge Group, including the van Dorns and surprisingly, David, too. He was curious as to why David was here, and then realized David was the only person, beside himself, who was anywhere near Helene's age. It came to him, with a jolt: Helene didn't have any friends. Searching his mind he recalled as a couple they always were included in cocktail parties and had gone to many of the summer dances at the club, but it was always his friends' wives who called about making up a table.

A wave of guilt washed over him; during their married

life he had ignored Helene. She was so quiet and never complained; he never once took the time to wonder anything about her. He led his own full life, made all the decisions about their life and knew she would go along with it. He couldn't remember anything he had given her for any of her birthdays. He and Helene were strangers who had lived together for years. How did this happen? How could I have been so unfeeling? He felt wretched.

He wondered if Diana and Selina had not come along, would his and Helene's marriage have gone limping along for the rest of their lives? Many marriages do go on forever, he thought, and we probably would have too; look at my almost ex-in-laws' dreary marriage.

Well, I'm glad Diana came back into my life. Thinking of Diana, he had been relieved that she decided there was no reason for her to go to the funeral service. And she didn't seem bothered at all that Helene was staying at his house. Her reasoning was it had been Helene's house too, and who would want to stay with that father of Helene's, anyway? The service was ending, and since Robb was not going to the reception, he got up and left the church early.

****

Ed Jacobson, the Vista Construction foreman, approached Brax a week after the construction had started. "Mr. Montgomery, we have just broken through the original basement wall. They really built them in the old days. It took us a day and a half to move those big rocks and cement. And I need to talk to you about something we found."

"What's that, Ed?"

"This was originally the Canton mansion, right?"

"Yes, way back."

"We found some lead pipes in the cellar under the original part of the building, and from the configuration I think they were for gas, not water."

"So?"

"Back in the early 1850s gas was the modern thing for rich

people's houses. You know, gas lights, remember them?"

"No, not really, I'm not quite that old."

"I didn't mean you personally, I meant you must have heard of them."

"Yes, I have heard of them, but what does that have to do with anything?" Brax asked, getting exasperated.

"East Meridian never had gas lights, so I'm wondering why there are pipes all through this area in the old cellar, and some of them go up as if they went to the upper floors."

"What difference can all this make? Cut them off and cement over them."

"Mr. Montgomery, I think I should go to Town Hall and see if there are any plans for the old house. The Cantons might have had gas piped in here somehow, and if that's the case, we should have somebody who knows what they are doing, take these pipes out of here."

"Ed, pipes are pipes. I'm sure this isn't a problem. But since you're concerned I'll check with Town Hall to see if there is any information about the original Canton mansion. For the time being, saw off any pipes blocking the opening, and when I come back this afternoon I'll let you know if I find any information on the house."

"Good; I've never come across anything like this before." Relieved, Ed walked back to the construction site.

Brax, correctly perceiving these pipes could be a potential hold-up in the construction, had no intention of checking anything. He called Ed a few hours later saying there hadn't been any gas in the house, as noted in the Town Hall, so cut the pipes.

****

Sweets turned left and right, looking at herself in the mirror. "Rose Ellen Brown, you've been waiting for this moment for years," she laughed gaily.

Picking up the brightly colored bouquet of asters, sunflowers and multi-hued hydrangeas held together with ivy from the table in front of the mirror, she twirled around. Stopping, she danced a few steps in her ballet slippers and holding her bouquet to one side she curtseyed with a majestic flourish to her imaginary partner. Holding her arms out as if in his arms, she danced around the interior of the summerhouse.

The afternoon sun filtered through the broken shutters on the windows, highlighting the delicate fabric of the ankle-length gown billowing around her as she waltzed in happy abandon. Turning to and fro she relived years of memories in this, their hidden place.

As a lonely, shy, slim girl of twelve, she had been thrilled when he had asked her to show him the gardens her mother had so loved. When they came to the summerhouse they sat on the steps and talked for a long time. She explained to him her father ordered it closed up right after her mother died. This made her very unhappy, because she knew her mother loved the summerhouse. It never occurred to Sweets's father that she would think of going to the summerhouse after he boarded it up. And she didn't, until she was asked to show it to this man she grew to adore. Sitting on his lap she told him all her secrets, so happy somebody was paying attention to her. He would put his hand under her cotton stripped tee shirt and rub her skinny little back and pat her on her knees as she prattled away. The summer she was fifteen she had such a crush on him she actually thought she seduced him, not the other way around.

Over the years she had trained herself to eat small amounts of food and exercise for hours to keep her figure tight and hard and young, because that was what he so admired. And now all her dreams were going to come true. She was so excited; she started to sing as she danced around the shadowy room.

"Sweets, what in the world are you doing?"

She looked toward the man, backlit in the doorway, and smiling with joy she twirled to a stop in front of him. Throwing her arms around him, she said "I'm dressed in my bridal gown, silly. I know you aren't supposed to see it until our wedding day, but I had to show it to you. We are free! We are free! I've waited years for this day."

He moved into the room, slowly shutting the door and

stood watching her pivot around him in her white gown.

"I know we can't get married right away, but we could in a few months. How about in the islands at Christmas? It will be so wonderful to be together, oh, how I have dreamed..."

"Rose Ellen, we are not getting married."

She looked at him, color draining out of her face. "What ... what do you mean? Why wouldn't we get married?"

"I don't want to marry you."

"But you love me, you've told me you've loved me for years."

"No, Sweets, what I told you, for years, is I love what you do, what we did together."

"But ... but ... you've ... we've ... all these years, I've kept myself just for you, and waited and waited for you."

"Sweets, we had fun over the years. You have to admit we both enjoyed it, but I know I never said anything that would give you the remotest idea I was going to marry you."

"I've lived for you," she shrieked, throwing the bouquet on the floor. The ivy came unbound as the flowers hit the floor, the petals broke apart at her feet.

"I never gave you reason to think I wanted to marry you ... you know that, Sweets. You're a child."

"A child you've fucked for fifteen years!" she screamed, running toward him and beating him on his chest in fury.

He grabbed her shoulders and roughly shoved her away from him. He growled, "Don't you touch me, or I'll hurt you, and I don't want to do that, Sweets. You and I would never be anything more than what we were. We could've continued on, if you wished. But obviously that's not going to happen. It was a dalliance we both enjoyed over the years, but you must have realized I never had any serious interest in you. In fact in an hour I'm meeting Harriet Langton, an old friend I dated in college. We've kept up over the years and we'll be going to Europe next week for a month or so."

Sweets looked at him speechless, white and shaking.

He looked at his watch and then looked back at Sweets. "I've got to get going. I'm picking up Harriet and we're meet-ing Brax at the hospital to check on the construction before dinner at the club. And I don't want to be late." Giving Sweets a salute, he smiled, turned and left.

Sweets watched John Lansdowe walk away, her body numb and her mind fixed on one thing. After a few minutes she went out of the summerhouse and down the steps in a trance. She walked unseeing through her mother's neglected gardens, and reaching the four-car garage, she hesitated for a minute when she heard a voice calling to her across the lawn, from the house. Ignoring it, she got into her car and drove away. One of Sweets's brothers had yelled, "Where are you going dressed up like the Queen of the May?"

****

John Lansdowe, never giving Sweets another thought, greeted Harriet Langton with delight, and discussed plans for their trip as they drove to East Meriden Hospital.

Arriving, they saw Brax talking to the foreman, Ed Jacobson. John and Harriet joined them. "Brax, this has really progressed. It looks great. I'd like you to meet Harriet."

Brax shook hands and recognized her as the woman John was with in St. Croix last winter. If Harriet recognized Brax she gave no indication of it.

The Vista Construction workmen were putting up fencing to keep people away from the construction site during the night. Brax turned back to Ed. John and Harriet went over to look at the newly dug foundation.

"Ed, are those pipes cemented over yet?"

"No, Mr. Montgomery, I'm not sure that's the right thing to do. Those pipes worry me."

"Well they don't worry me. Get the damn pipes cemented and move on."

A car appeared at the entrance of the parking lot. The night watchman, just coming on duty, waved the vehicle, driven by a young woman in a white dress, over to the parking area on the right. The car stopped for a moment as Sweets looked around. She spotted John, and a woman she guessed was Harriet, standing to the right of the boarded-up old main entrance at the edge of the excavation. She pushed the gas pedal to the floor. The car leapt forward, leaving tire marks on the pavement, until it gained momentum and roared toward the two unsuspecting people. The night watchman, realizing what the driver was going to do, yelled at the couple by the excavation to run. They couldn't hear over the noise of the fencing being put up and the roar of the oncoming car. A couple of workmen nearest the car looked up, and horrified, started screaming and ran in different directions. John and Harriet, oblivious to the noise around them, continued talking.

Sweets clutched the wheel and watched through narrowed eyes as she raced toward John Lansdowe. Her hand blasted the horn; she wanted to make sure he knew what was going to happen to him. John turned around at the sound, and his face contorted in fear as he gaped at Sweets behind the wheel. She was the last thing he saw.

The car slammed into John and Harriet, killing them instantly. The force of the impact flung them up against the boarded-up hospital entrance. Sliding off, they landed with resounding thuds on the stone steps. Sweets witnessed it all before she joined John Lansdowe in the hereafter. Her car teetered on the edge of the foundation and in almost slow motion fell in and burst into flames.

Brax and Ed turned toward the noise. Ed grabbed Brax and yelled, "Run!"

Within seconds, gas seeping out of the pipes turned into a fireball. The front of the building exploded. The first- floor offices and second- floor surgical wing disintegrated as if a bomb had been dropped on them.

****

On Azimuth Point, Diana's dog, Inky, howled and scratched at the door. Mildred, making dinner, opened it and shooed him out, saying, "Stop all that noise."

Robb, on his way home from work, was a couple of miles away from Azimuth Point when the bulletin about the disaster at the hospital came over the radio. He continued past the entrance to the Point and sped up towards the hospital. In the middle of Azimuth Village he saw a black lab trying to cross the street. That's Diana's Inky, he thought. She never lets him out alone, never mind off the Point. What in the world is he doing here?

Robb stopped in the middle of the traffic and pulled Inky into the car, amid much yelling and horn-blowing. Inky sat in the passenger seat and looked at Robb with sorrowful eyes. "You look as worried as I am, fella," Robb said.

It was impossible to get near the hospital because police were keeping the streets open for the ambulances. Robb abandoned his car on someone's lawn, and taking the dog with him, ran down the road to the hospital.

When he got there, he could not believe the scene in front of him. The devastation was overwhelming; it looked like a war zone. Police and rescue workers were triaging dazed and bloody people sitting or lying all over the grass and parking lot. Flames licked out of a car upturned in the excavation site. The ripped-apart, blackened entrance walls, sagging at different angles, gaped eerily over the horrific scene. Trees were smoldering skeletons.

With a sinking heart Robb realized one of the reasons he was able to go through the barriers right to the scene was because he had Inky with him. In the confusion he must have been mistaken for an out-of-uniform policeman and Inky, his search dog.

He went up to a rescue worker. "What happened?"

"A car driven by a girl came roaring in and drove straight into a man and woman killing them; the car fell into the new foundation and caught fire and there was a terrible explosion. Nobody knows who she was or what caused the explosion."

Robb started to shake. He knew Diana had two operations scheduled and the operating rooms were toward the front on the second floor. The front of the building was gone. "Do you know Dr. Manning? Have you seen her?"

"I know her, but no. There are a lot of docs here, but I haven't seen her."

Inky stayed, as if glued, next to Robb. Heavy equipment

had arrived but was not yet in use, as searchers looked through rubble for survivors. Robb's cell phone rang. He yelled into it, "Diana! Diana, is that you?" Robb heard a sob on the other end of the phone and recognized Diana's mother's voice. "No, Robb, it's Lucia. We are about a mile away from the hospital; the police won't let us go further. Where are you? How bad is it? What happened? Is Diana there?"

"I'm at the hospital. There was an explosion of some kind. I got through because of Inky; they thought I was a search person. I'm looking for Diana."

"You have Inky? Thank God, the twins have been frantic about him."

"Yes, please tell Mildred I have the dog, okay? The twins ... do they know what happened?"

"No, Mildred and Lisle have them watching a video. Robb, please call my cell phone every once and a while; we'll stay in the car out here."

"Yes, of course." Robb put the phone away. It was getting dark. A volunteer gave Robb a cup of hot coffee, which he swallowed without tasting. He searched the site asking everybody if they had seen Diana. No one remembered seeing her. With Inky by his side he went around the building and walked down to the edge of the lawn. Waves crashing against the rocks drowned out the noise of the sirens. The dog sat down and leaned against Robb's leg. The distant fog was thick. Robb heard the bleat of the horn at Point Judith lighthouse. He recalled Diana saying she would always remember him when she heard a foghorn. He sank to the damp ground, buried his face in Inky's warm fur and wept.

A tap on the shoulder startled him. He looked up to see a uniformed policeman.

"Dr. Manning has been found."

"Where? Where? Is she alright?"

"I'm not sure ... umm ... all they told me on the radio was to bring the man with the dog to the garage."

Robb grabbed the man by the shoulders, "The garage?"

"It's being used as a morgue."

"Oh, no."

Holding back tears, Robb braced himself. The two men and the dog walked silently across the wet grass. At the entrance Robb could go no further. Florescent lights cast an eerie glow on the sheet-covered bodies lying on the cold cement floor. Inky's ears went up; he turned and took off in the drifting fog toward a rescue wagon. Robb ran after him.

A woman in a blood spattered white coat crouched down to hold Inky who was wiggling and wagging his tail furiously.

"Diana, Diana, ohmyGod, you're alright." He crushed her to him. "I was terrified. I couldn't find you."

"I was in the ER when it happened. In all the horror and trying to help people I couldn't call because I'd left my cell phone in my office. A rescue worker told me you were here and I asked him to find an officer to look for you. We're waiting for the helicopter to transport this patient."

"What can I do?"

"Robb, I'm staying here. I have to help. Please go to my house and be with the children."

"I can't leave. I just found you. I didn't know what happened. I ... I...."

"Robb, I love you. I'm all right. I have a job to do here. The best thing you can do is comfort my parents and children. Give me your cell phone. I'll call everyone and assure them I'm fine and that you are on your way with Inky. Give me a kiss and off you go."

****

Two days later Robb and Hunt walked down the corridor to the small conference room next to Liam's old, and now Brax's new, office. Outside, muffled noise from machines clearing away the damaged front of the building could be heard.

"The only good thing about this dreadful situation is insurance will pay for rebuilding and the town has to go along with it," Hunt said.

"Yeah," replied Robb. "Now let's vote out that bastard Brax. The gall of him sending out a news release saying the damn Tedisco Atrium will be built as planned. Even if Whip won't go along with us we'll still get rid of him."

"Tedisco will vote with him."

"Four votes to three."

They entered the room and sat down next to Diana. Sarah James sat a few seats away. Diana glanced at her, wondering what, if anything, was going on between Sarah and David. Her mother mentioned seeing David get off his boat a few weeks ago, in fact the week after Sadie's funeral, with a pretty blonde girl and did Diana know who she might be? Remembering the vibes going on at the reception after the church service she felt the girl might be Sarah. But she was perplexed, how could Sarah do this with a husband and children?

Mona O'Shay came in with a stack of papers and sat down next to Brax's hospital secretary. Mona was positively gleeful. Brax had asked her to take over as CEO and hire someone for the Head Nurse position. Mona, shocked as everyone was about the damage to the hospital, had been concerned about losing John Lansdowe. Not that she cared about him, she didn't want to lose her power, and now she *was* the power. Satisfied she had the situation under control she darted a glance at Diana and smirked.

Whip arrived in his usual flurry, yanking at his bow tie. He looked around for Kimberly and was disappointed she was not there. He sat down next to Mona, who looked at him with distain. He gave her a weak smile.

The room was quiet except for the rustling of papers. The group eyed each other as they waited for Brax, Louis and Kimberly.

Brax stormed in and stopped, surprised at the small group, as if the realization of losing John just dawned on him. "Good afternoon." He seated himself and nodded to his secretary who stood up and handed out papers. "The papers here are for the initial game plan to continue the atrium construction as well as rebuilding of the damage done to the hospital. I have..."

"You have no right to make any decisions or order any construction to begin without a vote from the board," Robb said.

"Robb, someone had to take over. After all, Ed Jacobson is still in a coma and work has to move forward." Brax was greatly relieved that Ed, who had saved Brax's life, was in a coma and hoped he would never wake up to reveal that Brax told him there was no gas in the pipes.

"No, Brax, we are going to discuss this and take votes. And we are hiring a hospital architect to design the new addition and there will be no atrium. A front door will suffice."

"And I suppose you are to be the architect."

"No, we need a professional who only designs hospitals."

"We'll see about that. There will be no votes until Louis and Kimberly get here. Now I've decided that Mona O'Shay will be CEO and we are looking at resumes for a Head Nurse."

Diana frowned; she knew how people in the hospital felt about Mona. This was not a good move. "Brax, not casting aspersions on Miss O'Shay, but I do feel this should be a board decision. In the past we have always formed a search committee to hire a CEO."

Mona stiffened in surprise, looked at Brax and turned to glare at Diana.

"Really, Dr. Manning, in this emergency situation I will be making the decisions," Brax stated.

"No you won't," retorted Diana, Robb and Hunt in unison.

Brax narrowed his eyes and snarled, "You trouble makers will have nothing to do with this. My mind is made up."

Sarah James laughed out loud, "I've had enough of you running the show. We board members will decide how to handle this."

Brax sneered at her. The other board members looked at her, stunned.

The conference room door opened. Louis walked in, stopped in the doorway and glanced around quickly, looking for Kimberly. Brax was relieved to see him. "Louis, I'm glad you are here. We have some decisions to make and...."

Louis moved aside, not speaking. Two men, in suits, both with an imposing bearing, entered the conference room behind him.

"Are you Braxton Montgomery?"

"Um, yes, why?"

"Braxton Montgomery, Chairman of the Board of Trustees of East Meridian Hospital?"

Brax glanced nervously at Louis whose expression was guarded. Brax looked back at the man questioning him. "Yeah. Who are you?"

Both men held up badges. "The FBI."

"What are you doing here? I had nothing to do with the gas explosion." Brax feared Ed had come out of the coma and implicated him.

The men strode over to Brax, roughly turned him around, and snapped on handcuffs.

"You are under arrest for forgery."

He paled. "Forgery of what?" Then he turned purple with fury. "Get away from me. Take these damn things off. Nobody treats me like this."

Reading him his Miranda Rights, the men dragged Brax out the door and down the corridor. Brax stumbled trying to wrench away and yelled, "You bastards, release me. Do you know who I am? Let go of me. I'll get you for this ... I want my lawyer!" was the last thing the trustees heard.

Robb looked around the speechless group. "I guess he will need his lawyer." He and Hunt started to laugh uproariously. Hunt, gasping, said, "We're rid of the son of a bitch."

Everybody started to talk at once, except Mona. Her power snatched from her once again, first due to Lansdowe's exit and now Brax's. She wasn't going to let it happen. Standing up she spoke above the din, "Excuse me, ladies and gentlemen."

Surprised, they looked at her: the last person anyone thought would take the helm. "I'm as shocked as all of you, but the immediate problem is running the hospital. And I..."

Robb interrupted, "Mona is right. We should get control of this right away. But first I want to ask Louis if he wants to stay on this board, which will be moving in a very different direction. We need a new chairman and I feel this person should not come from the present board. We need an outsider, with a fresh outlook."

Diana said, "I know just the person."

****

Marianne and Jamie sat on the piano bench giggling and devouring slices of the lemon mousse wedding cake. The fall afternoon sun was waning. The trio had swung into dance music on the Manning's enclosed sun porch. Lucia Manning's turquoise chiffon dress swirled about her knees as she danced with her new son-in law.

"Welcome to our family."

"Lucia, I'm so happy to be married to your lovely daughter and part of your family."

Diana and her father danced by; Diana blew Robb kisses.

"Daddy, this is one of the happiest days of my life."

"My dear, it is a special day for me too. It does my heart good to know you have a wonderful husband and umm ... er ... additions to the family."

"Well ... yes ... not exactly planned, but we are excited. Now let's get the rest of the family out here dancing."

Lisle, realizing Marianne was about to start a cake fight with her unsuspecting brother, joined them on the piano bench. "Marianne, why don't you ask your cousin Wills to dance with you? I will hold your cake plate until you come back."

Marianne scrambled off the bench and headed toward Wills. Lisle breathed a sigh of relief, two more minutes and Marianne's teal velvet dress along with Jamie's suit would have been adorned with blobs of wedding confection.

Robb took a glass of champagne off a silver-serving tray and searched the crowd for Diana. He saw Miranda dancing with a boy her age. He was happy to see her smiling and seemingly enjoying herself. Finding Diana speaking to her mother, he paused for a minute; she was glowing and looked beautiful.

"Lucia, may I steal my bride away for a few minutes?"

"Of course, I'm going to find Weits and dance."

They went outside; the sun was setting.

"Oh, Robb, what a beautiful day. I'm so happy."

"Dr. Manning, I'm very happy too. Here's to us," and he held up the glass of champagne. "I know you can't have any so I'll take a sip and give you a champagne kiss." Holding her, he confessed once more, "I love you so much. It was terrible when I was afraid I'd lost you."

"You will never lose me. I'm finally here to stay."

ROCKS AND SHOALS

Book Two in Azimuth Point Series

By Carroll Kenyon

PROLOGUE

Azimuth Point is nestled like a lover's secret in the heart of the Rhode Island coast. A small sign marks the entrance. Beach roses flank the driveway on either side. Pink blossoms peek out from clusters of waxy, orange rose hips, growing in a jumble up to the weathered six-foot high cedar fences. Behind the fences are evergreens gnarled by time and sheared by the prevailing winds. The narrow paved road leads to a gatehouse.

For Azimuth Point residents, young and old, summer didn't begin until they came through the gate. It was a ritual. First eyes would close, for a second, and then a deep breath of salt air was inhaled. Bodies relaxed as the sound of breaking waves soothed away the buildup of winter's prickly frets and irritations.

Children pressed their noses to the car windows wondering if Mr. Thompson would be around to wave that important welcoming hello. Elwin Thompson was one of the two most

271

important people on the Point. The other was Jack Brent. The difference between the two men was as great as the color of their skin and as little. Jack Brent ran Azimuth Point. Elwin Thompson kept Azimuth Point running. A white man worth millions and a black man who made the best of circumstances life had presented. They respected each other.

Elwin greeted the members by name, making them feel more welcomed than their relatives did at Christmas. He kept to himself the heartbroken woe of the young, and listened with patience to many a long-winded tale from the old timers.

Youngsters would scamper to him and cry, "Hey, Mr. Thompson!"

A smile would spread across his face; his brown eyes would twinkle. "Are you here for the weekend, or just for the day?"

The children would jump up and down laughing. "No, the whole summer!"

JUNE 2001

Shadows from the waning sun turned the sand shades of blue. The incoming tide slowly lapped up the beach. A lone fisherman cast into the sea. Bradley Blakesly looked down from the porch of the beach club watching her brother David and his girlfriend Sarah, laughing and talking as they sauntered along.

"Bradley, you may be silent, but your fangs are showing," laughed her friend Mallory.

"I can't stand it; there he is on our beach with that waitress."

"What are you talking about? She works at the university. And she is getting a master's in oceanography."

"He picked her up at The Ebb Tide Inn; she's a waitress."

"That was years ago; she was working her way through school. Which, my dear, is more than you ever did, and I don't recall you getting a master's degree...." declared Bradley's mother, coming onto the porch.

Bradley whirled and stared at her mother. "How can you

defend her?"

"I'm not defending Sarah. I stated a fact."

"You won't be so happily stating facts when she moves in, or even worse if he marries her."

"Bradley your venomous nature always astounds me. I should have named you Maude after Weitsma's cantankerous cousin. She was of similar ilk. Your brother's wife was killed two years ago. He has found happiness with Sarah. What will come of it, who knows?"

Bradley turned back toward the beach, sulking. Mallory threw her hands up and rolled her eyes. Emily van Dorn sighed, looked down at the couple and wondered, what *would* come of it?

****

Sarah, holding her sandals, chased the waves. "Isn't this a lovely time of the day?" she said, dancing lightly back to David while keeping her eye on his dog. That dog has the same attitude as many people on the Point, Sarah thought. Especially Bradley: they are both bitches. She laughed to herself.

"It is a lovely time of the day. I wish you would stay, enjoy the sunset and join me in a glass of wine," David said.

"Too dangerous, we have already gone down that road. I walked here so I wouldn't be tempted ... once in your house we throw caution to the winds. This way I have to be around the rocks before the tide comes in," grinned Sarah.

"We could go to the beach club, no temptation there." Sarah's face clouded. Too late David realized he had spoken without thinking. Last time they were at the club, Bradley pointedly made Sarah feel uncomfortable with references to her background. David had gotten angry, and told her to shut up.

David took Sarah in his arms, the dog started to zip around barking. "I'm sorry; I forgot. I'm trying to convince you to stay, because I like being with you."

She smiled. "I know. I like being with you, too. But I have a full day at work tomorrow and I have to study."

They clasped hands and walked toward the ledge which

separated Azimuth Point from the Village Public Beach. The tide was higher. At the rocks Sarah put her arms around David's neck and kissed him deeply. The dog ran in circles. "I'll call you tonight."

"Why don't I go with you and we can get a latte?"

"Nice try. The tide would be in and I would have to drive you home ... I don't think so." She kissed him again.

Diana and Robb came around the other side of the ledge, practically colliding with David and Sarah. "Aha, love at the beach," laughed Diana. The twins Marianne and Jamie followed, holding dripping ice cream cones. David's dog assailed Inky, Diana's Lab. Jamie dropped his cone in the sand and howled at his loss. The dogs dived for it. Lisle, the governess, came around the rocks into the middle of the confusion wheeling baby Hunter in a stroller.

"I'm leaving while I still can; the tide is really coming in." Sarah waved to everybody and splashed through the water and disappeared around the rocks.

Lisle sorted the children and dogs out and started back down the beach towards their home.

"How are things going with you and Sarah?" Diana asked David as the three walked up the beach together.

"Her divorce is finally over. She doesn't say too much about it, but it seems it was a mess. She wanted her girls to come visit this summer and they refused."

"Oh, dear. Are they teenagers?"

"The older one is twelve, I think."

"The perfect age to sock it to Mommy."

"I don't think Bradley ever grew out of it. She takes every opportunity to be hateful, to Sarah, that is."

Diana glanced at Robb; they had been in the bar the night Bradley started on Sarah. David ran his hand through his hair and grinned. "No one said it was going to be easy."

****

Anna Morgan sat on her back porch, facing the ocean, waiting for Hank Lombardi to arrive for their dinner date.

275

Anna was a changed woman. Her cancer was gone, her glasses, thanks to the cataract operations, were also gone and her hair softly styled. She smiled; she had a male friend. Not like in the past, when she had an affair with a married man and they could not be seen in public. And she owned these three wonderful cottages on the beach in Azimuth Point Village. The previous owner was offered a job in LA. He and his partner wanted to leave immediately so he named a price and Anna, who sold her house in East Meridian, could easily afford it. She came out of her reverie, hearing her tenant Sarah James drive into her garage. She and Sarah, despite their past thorny relationship on the East Meridian Hospital's board, had become friends over the winter.

****

Peter Hanson, the new CEO of East Meridian Hospital, having compiled all the information he needed for the upcoming board meeting, stood and walked to the window. A smile came over his handsome face. The setting sun's reflection rippled on the ocean in the distance. He was excited about the opportunity to put East Meridian Hospital on the right path. The search committee leveled with him on the state of the hospital's finances and past Chairman Brax Montgomery's incarceration for forgery. They couldn't tell him why Rose Ellen (Sweets) drove her car into John Lansdowe and his girlfriend while they were looking at the newly dug atrium foundation. The answer died with Sweets when her car fell into the foundation, caught fire and blew up the front half of the hospital. The designs for its repair were completed and construction began this month; it was on schedule to be finished in a year. Now, thought Peter, if only my family was as excited about moving here as I am. They didn't want to leave New Mexico. It would all work out, he was sure.

****

Sarah, yawned, took off her reading glasses and stretched.

Weary from studying, she stood up; she should eat dinner. Through a living room window she noticed a man standing at the edge of the sidewalk looking at a paper and the empty cottage next to her. He spoke to someone on his cell phone. Sarah called out from her screen door, "May I help you?"

The stranger looked around for the voice, seeing Sarah, he smiled. "Are you Anna Morgan?"

"No, Anna's house is over there," she said pointing to her left. "Why do you ask?" She wasn't sure she wanted him to know her name or that Anna was not home.

"Hi, I'm Ed Fielding. Ruth Belknap, my realtor, said I could come take a look at the cottage and that she would call Miss Morgan. Now she tells me there is no answer." He held up the cell phone.

Sarah felt more at ease since Ruth was the realtor she had used. "Ruth can arrange that for you tomorrow. I'll tell Anna you were here."

"Good. This cottage looks perfect. I would hate to lose it. Have you lived here long?"

"About a year. It is lovely to be right on the beach. That is if you like the sound of the waves. The other renter moved out when the lease was up; she couldn't stand the sound of waves breaking."

"You're kidding," he laughed.

"No, it's true."

"Well, I'll be going. Thanks for mentioning to Miss Morgan I was here." He turned, walked to a sports car and drove off in the gathering dusk.

Sarah closed the wooden door and started for the kitchen to make a sandwich, thinking, Anna won't rent to him if he has kids or animals. I guess such a small expensive sports car means no kids, but maybe a wife.

****

Louis Tedisco sat on his terrace sipping a martini as the sun neared the horizon. He didn't want to go in the house. This house, the one his wife and relatives all loved, he hated.

He yearned for his home, now sold, on the East Side of Providence. Times like this, when it was quiet, his guard slipped and he thought of Kimberly and the baby boy that was no more. Where is she? Does she ever think of me? He felt despair and tried to drink it away. Most of the time he buried himself in work. When he did come home it was late and he left early. But tonight he was home for the birthday celebration for his year-old twin daughters named after their grandmothers. He loved his children and hated his life.

Vi, his pretty blonde wife, yanked open the French doors. "Louie..."

"Yes."

"Stop sitting out there. It's getting dark. The family is arriving right now"

"It's called watching the sunset."

"Huh? Why bother?"

"Right."

"Get in here. The photographer is here. I want a picture for our Christmas card."

Louis sighed, yes, the happy family Christmas card. He walked in almost colliding with his mother in-law Angie, who was holding Angela dressed the same way as her twin Mary Beth, in a white frilly dress adorned with pink ribbons. The baby held her arms out to her father. Louis's face softened as he took his daughter in his arms.

"Hey, Louie, some day, huh? A full year of happiness in your beautiful new home."

Louis glared at Angie. Hands on ample hips she smirked back, enjoying his misery. The scrolled glass front doors crashed open admitting a bejeweled crowd adorned in silks and satins. The men in suits, black shirts, neck chains and patent leather shoes; children clad in their best, skipping, jumping and chirping. Streaming in like the opening of a Broadway show, the noise level rose and bounced around the marble hallway.

****

Mallory Woodward took a sip of wine and slowly swirled her glass gazing at the purple shadows deepening along the Azimuth Point beach. Behind her on the Wells "drinks porch," as they called it, she could hear David, Hunt, Robb and Diana, discussing the upcoming hospital meeting. Mallory went on the board to replace Kimberly MacComber, who had resigned. When David, now chairman of the board, asked her, she replied, "You need another female banker?" He laughed, replying, "It doesn't hurt."

Hunt Latimer, whose family had been founding members of the hospital, sat in a tilted chair resting on the porch rail. Folding his hands around a scotch on the rocks, a frown crossed his rubbery face. "Jack Morgan was pissed he wasn't asked to be chairman."

Diana, Robb and David nodded. Robb spoke up, "We all agreed to start fresh with somebody younger. I know it might be a problem. Jack has been very generous to the hospital. But if he was chairman we all might as well resign. It's Jack's way or the highway."

"I'd rather put Elwin Thompson on the board; he understands how the real world works," said David.

Mallory came back into the conversation. "What a perfect idea."

"Put Elwin on the board?" they all asked. The unspoken word "black" resounded.

"No, if only because he is too old, same age as Jack. But Elwin's son Michael is a lawyer in Providence and lives in East Meridian."

Hunt snapped his chair back on the porch floor. "I know him; our kids are on the same local soccer team. Mallory, I never would have thought of him..."

"You mean living in our white cocoon here?" laughed Diana.

Hunt threw her a marked glance. "As soon as I take the knife out I will answer you ... it is a great idea. We should have thought of having a black on the board before this anyway."

"This will set the Point on its rear," murmured Diana.

"At least the gossips will move on from my ex-wife tearing

down the Lansdowe house," said Robb. The uproar when she presented the plans for an ultra-modern glass house could be heard for miles.

"The ironic thing is these two, shall we say, ladies dedicated to each other, have Bert Long's construction company building the house. And Bert is definitely 'eye candy,' so good looking and unmarried," said Mallory.

"Well, back to Jack Brent. How do we handle this?" asked Robb.

"I've known him the longest. I'll talk to him," said Hunt. "Something along the line of, 'you have so much responsibility as it is: the Point board, all the corporation boards and you have to spend six months of the year out of Rhode Island.' And at the same time, I'll hope he continues to give generously."

ABOUT THE AUTHOR

Carroll Kenyon was born and raised in Rhode Island. Seventh generation on one side (here since they brought the rocks in) and second generation on the other (just off the turnip truck). She lived in Austria for three of her formative years and traveled around Europe in an ancient Volkswagen staying in youth hostels.

At the opposite end of the spectrum donning a white gown and white gloves she made her debut at the Philharmonic Ball in Vienna. Landing back in the USA, a real reality bump, she was part owner, photographer, and reporter of a small newspaper. She has three children and three stepchildren and resides in Rhode Island with her husband and a herd of deer.

Made in the USA
Charleston, SC
03 January 2013